Savannah's chest tightened. She wanted to dance with
Dash, but she knew damn well it was a big mistake. And
rig   e oil
an   em-
ist   her
wa

ou   heat
of   oap
sm   the
da

Re   the
he   ced
the   by
an   ing,
on   ight
qu   for
sile   the

Praise for Hope Ramsay's
Heartwarming Series

Last Chance Christmas

"4 stars! Ramsay's romance packs just enough heat in this holiday-inspired story, with lead characters who will induce both belly laughs and smiles. Her hero and heroine are in for rough times, but their heartache and longing had me longing right along with them."

— *RT Book Reviews*

"A captivating tale." —RomRevToday.com

"Amazing...These lovely folks filled with Southern charm [and] gossip were such fun to get to know...This story spoke to me on so many levels about faith, strength, courage, and choices...If you're looking for a good Christmas story with a few angels, then *Last Chance Christmas* is a must read. For fans of Susan Wiggs."

—TheSeasonforRomance.com

"Visiting Last Chance is always a joy, but Hope Ramsay has outdone herself this time. She took a difficult hero, a wounded heroine, familiar characters, added a little Christmas magic, and—Voila!—gave us a story sure to touch the Scroogiest of hearts...It draws us back to a painful time when tensions—and prejudices—ran deep, compels us to remember and forgive, and reminds us that healing, redemption, and love are the true gifts of Christmas." —RubySlipperedSisterhood.com

Last Chance Beauty Queen

"4 ½ stars! Get ready for a story to remember when Ramsay spins this spirited contemporary tale. If the ya'lls don't enchant you, the fast-paced, easy read will. The third installment in the Last Chance series is filled with characters that define eccentric, off the wall, and bonkers, but most of all they're enchantingly funny and heartwarmingly charming."

—*RT Book Reviews*

"Hope Ramsay has penned an irresistible tale in *Last Chance Beauty Queen* with its unforgettable characters and laugh out loud scenes…Watch how an opposites-attract couple find their way to each other…and a possible future. Grab this today and get ready for a rollicking read."

—RomRevToday.com

"Hope Ramsay has outdone herself…A feel-good read that will make you cry, laugh, and maybe even cheer. This tale could make the most skeptical believe all things are possible. Highly recommended."

—GoodReads.com

"A little Bridget Jones meets Sweet Home Alabama."

—GrafWV.com

Home at Last Chance

"4 stars! Nicely told."   —*RT Book Reviews*

"A sweet confection...This first of a projected series about the Rhodes brothers offers up Southern hospitality with a bit of grit. Romance readers will be delighted."

—*Library Journal*

"Hope Ramsay delivers with this sweet and sassy story of small-town love, friendship, and the ties that bind."

—Lisa Dale, author of *Simple Wishes*

"Ramsay has created a great new series...Not only are the two main characters compelling and fun, but as you read, the entire town of kooky but very real people become part of your life...I can hardly wait until I visit Last Chance again." —FreshFiction.com

"Touching...funny...Ramsay's characters were endearing and lovable, and I eagerly look forward to the rest of [the series]." —NovelReaction.com

"A sweet romance...sassy and fun characters."

—Book Hounds (maryinhb.blogspot.com)

"Captivating...great characterization, amusing dialogue... I am glad that the universe sent *Welcome to Last Chance* my way, and I am going to make sure that it does the same with Hope Ramsay's future books."

—LikesBooks.com

Also by Hope Ramsay

Welcome to Last Chance
Home at Last Chance
Small Town Christmas (anthology)
Last Chance Beauty Queen
Last Chance Bride (short story)
Last Chance Christmas

~LAST~ CHANCE
Book Club

HOPE RAMSAY

FOREVER

NEW YORK   BOSTON

Forever
Hachette Book Group
237 Park Avenue
New York, NY 10017

www.HachetteBookGroup.com

Printed in the United States of America

First Edition: March 2013

10 9 8 7 6 5 4 3 2 1

OPM

Forever is an imprint of Grand Central Publishing.
The Forever name and logo are trademarks of Hachette Book Group, Inc.

The Hachette Speakers Bureau provides a wide range of authors for speaking events. To find out more, go to www.hachettespeakersbureau.com or call (866) 376-6591.

The publisher is not responsible for websites (or their content) that are not owned by the publisher.

For Bryan, my very own good ol' boy

Acknowledgments

Every author has a few people who are always there for them. I would like to give my deepest thanks to my critique partners, Carla Kempert, Robin Kaye, and Lavinia Kent. You guys rock. I would like to thank the wonderfully talented Grace Burrowes, whose knowledge of horses helped me get through the de-tacking scene. Many thanks to Lillian Amundson for letting me write her adorable dog, Champ, into this book. And of course, thanks to my posse at the Ruby Slippered Sisterhood for coming up with so many funny and naughty things for Todd to do while his momma was being courted by a minister. As always, I could not get through writing a book without my dear husband, Bryan, my steady agent, Elaine English, and my talented editor, Alex Logan.

~LAST~
CHANCE
Book Club

CHAPTER
1

Savannah White pulled her twelve-year-old Honda into Aunt Miriam's driveway. She set the parking brake and studied the old Victorian house through the windshield. It had seen better days. Mauve and gold paint peeled from the shingles and bric-a-brac, the porch steps sagged, and the azaleas along the front porch were overgrown.

She studied the garden for a long moment. Clumps of daffodils sprouted in the side yard, shooting up through the pine needle ground cover. She had never realized that there were daffodils in the side yard. Savannah had only visited Aunt Miriam in the summertime, well past daffodil time. The whimsical yellow flowers were a reminder that she was taking a huge risk. Savannah had no idea if she would even like living in Last Chance year-round.

Of course, no one knew yet that she planned to stay. If she had announced her plans, her ex-mother-in-law would have done everything in her power to stop Savannah from leaving Baltimore. Claire White wanted complete control over the education of her grandson, Todd. But Savannah hoped that moving here might shake up Todd's father, Greg, who had canceled every weekend visitation for almost a year and who was behind on his support payments. Greg couldn't have cared less about Todd.

And that left Savannah to wage a never-ending battle with Greg's mother, who seemed more than happy to spend money on the boy and make up for the support Greg never sent. But there was a huge price tag associated with taking Claire White's assistance.

Savannah was tired of always being beholden. And she was tired of living close to her own mother, who never stopped adding up all of her faults and failures. When her last relationship, with Jeremy, had fizzled, Savannah decided to make a change in her life. She started planning a great escape back to her roots. She'd held tag sales to reduce the clutter. She'd put stuff in storage. Her lease was up. She was all ready to go when Uncle Harry died. God bless him, he'd provided the perfect cover for a clean getaway.

Guilt slammed into her chest for allowing herself to think such a thing, even if it was true. She was sorry that she wouldn't see her gruff old uncle again. Aunt Miriam was going to be lost without him. But Claire White hadn't even batted an eye when Savannah announced that she was taking Todd out of school for a few days to attend Harry's funeral. And of course, Todd didn't know the truth either.

She turned toward her twelve-year-old son. He sat in the passenger's seat completely engrossed in a video game. His brown hair curled over his forehead, and the tip of his tongue showed at the corner of his mouth as he concentrated. His eyelashes were amazingly long for a boy, but his skin was so pale he looked like one of those teen vampires from *Twilight*, albeit a slightly chubby one.

"It's time to put the game away," Savannah said.

Todd didn't acknowledge her request. Tuning her out had become a pattern.

"We have to go now. It's time to meet Aunt Miriam."

No response.

She reached over and took the game from his hands.

"Mom," he whined, "I was just about to win that level."

Savannah turned the damn thing off and tucked it into her oversized purse. "Sorry, kiddo, we're here. It's time to join the real world."

He rolled his pretty brown eyes. "Aw, couldn't I just stay in the car?"

"No."

"But I didn't even know Uncle Harry, and I'm sure Aunt Miriam is just some dumb old lady."

Savannah ground her teeth. "You will show respect to Aunt Miriam, is that clear?"

"Yes, but I hate it here."

"You've been here for five minutes, during which time you've done nothing but zap zombies."

He rolled his eyes. "Mom, *Semper Fi* doesn't have any zombies. I was shooting members of the Imperial Japanese forces occupying Iwo Jima."

Savannah stared at her son. "You do realize that World War Two is over, and the Japanese are our allies now, right?"

Todd crossed his arms over his chest and sank back into the seat. "I'm not going to some dumb old funeral."

"The funeral isn't until tomorrow. And you will

get your butt out of this car and go be nice to your aunt Miriam or I will put your PSP in a microwave and nuke it."

"You wouldn't. That would blow up the apartment and kill the microwave."

"Don't bet on it, kiddo."

"If you did that, Dad would buy me another one, and Grandmother would yell at you."

And that was the problem, right there.

She drew herself up into full-out mommy mode. "I don't care what your father or grandmother might do. You are with me right now, and you will get out of this car. Is that understood?"

He gave her a sulky look and then opened the car door.

She did the same and stepped out into a balmy March day.

"I've never seen a house painted puke green and purple before," he said.

"It's not that bad."

The boy wrinkled his nose in disgust. "It's mad warm here. Are we gonna stand around looking at the dumb old house all day?"

The muscles along Savannah's shoulders knotted, and the headache she'd been fighting since they crossed the South Carolina border was beginning to actually throb.

Just then the front door opened with a bang, and a white-haired lady wearing a blue polyester pantsuit and a pair of red Keds appeared on the porch. Dark, almost black, eyes peered at Savannah through a pair of 1960s-style spectacles festooned with rhinestones. "Well, look who just turned up pretty as a daisy. C'mon up here, sugar," Aunt Miriam said, opening her arms.

Savannah took the rickety porch steps in two long strides and gave her aunt a bear hug.

"Oh, I'm so glad you came," Aunt Miriam said.

Savannah pulled away and looked down at her great-aunt, noting the changes recorded in her face. Her apple cheeks now drooped a little along her jawline. Her skin looked pale and papery. Even the ever-present twinkle in her eyes was dimmed by time and sorrow. Savannah felt a sharp pang of regret that she had allowed so much time to elapse between visits. Aunt Miriam was getting old. Savannah wished with all her might that she could turn back the clock.

"I'm so sorry about Uncle Harry," Savannah said.

Miriam nodded. "He was old as dirt. And sick these last few years. I know at the end he just wanted to lay his burden down and go on home." Her voice wavered.

Savannah gave Miriam another big hug and whispered, "I'm sure he did. But I know you would have liked him to stay awhile longer."

Miriam pushed back and wiped a few tears from her cheeks. "Enough of this maudlin stuff. Let me see that boy of yours. Last time I saw him, he was no bigger than a minute."

Miriam turned her gaze toward the yard where Todd slouched. Savannah's son had assumed the preteen position—arms crossed and disinterest plastered all over his face.

"Hmm," Aunt Miriam said, "he's a big boy, isn't he?"

"Yes, he is."

"Too bad he doesn't live around here. I'm sure Red Canaday would be all over you recruiting him for Pop Warner football."

"Really? His father played football for the University of Maryland."

"Well, it looks like your boy may have inherited his genes. I think Todd would make an excellent center."

Savannah filed that information away. Todd probably had no interest in playing football. But Savannah was determined to get her son off the couch and out into the fresh air. Last Chance had lots and lots of fresh air.

"Well, son," Miriam said with a wave, "c'mon up here and meet your old Aunt Mim. I know you don't remember me."

The boy walked slowly up the stairs and stoically allowed himself to be hugged.

"Y'all come on in," Aunt Miriam said once she let Todd go. "I've got cookies and pie and enough food to choke a horse. The casserole brigade has been doing overtime these last few days. To be honest, I got so tired of Lillian Bray trying to take charge of my kitchen that I shooed them all away this noontime. They mean well, I suppose, but a morning with Lillian is enough to try even the most patient of souls."

She turned toward Todd. "I'm sure you're hungry, son."

Todd nodded. Todd was always hungry.

"Well, come on then. I'll show you the way to the kitchen."

A burst of cool air greeted them in the hallway. It took a moment for Savannah's eyes to adjust to the dark interior. The house had changed little in the eight years since her last visit. To the right stood the formal dining room with its gleaming mahogany table and chairs upholstered in light green moiré. The china closet filled with blue willowware still dominated the far wall. She could practically smell the ham and butter beans that Granny had served on those dishes all those years ago.

She turned her gaze to the left. The front parlor still contained Victorian settees upholstered in red velvet and striped damask silk. The baby grand piano, where she'd practiced endless scales and learned Beethoven's "Moonlight Sonata," still stood in the corner between the bay window and the pink marble fireplace.

She closed her eyes and breathed in the scents of lemon oil, beeswax, and memory. This house had once belonged to her grandfather, Aunt Miriam's older brother. Savannah had spent many happy summers here.

Miriam came to a stop beside the oak stairway. "Oh, there you are. I called you to come down five minutes ago," she said as a dark-headed man of about thirty-five sauntered down to the landing and leaned into the newel post.

He hooked his thumbs through the loops of his Wranglers, lazily crossed one cowboy-booted heel over the other, and assumed the traditional Western pose. Too hard and rangy to belong to the house with its 1940s cabbage rose wallpaper, lace doilies, and china figurines, he looked like he'd just stepped out of a grade-B western.

He gazed at Savannah with a pair of sexy eyes as blue as Bradley Cooper's, and the corner of his mouth tipped up in a craggy smile. "It's been a long time," he said in a twangy drawl.

She blinked a few times, taken by her visceral reaction to his accent. Recognition flashed through her like the Roman candles Granddaddy used to set off on the Fourth of July.

"Cousin Dash," she said. "You still sound like a Texan."

Dash's gaze did a slow circuit of her body, and she felt naked as a jaybird under his intense inspection. "And you've grown up some since I saw you last, princess."

"Don't call me that," she said through gritted teeth. "I'm not ten years old anymore." Granddaddy had called Savannah princess until the day he died, but in Dash's mouth the word came out as a twisted insult.

"No, I guess not." His eyes flashed to Todd and back. "And I see you've become a momma."

She turned toward her son. "Todd, this is Cousin Dash. When he was twelve, he put a snake in my bed and blew up my favorite Barbie doll with a cherry bomb. I'm sure he is very sorry for what he did. And I am very—"

"Did the Barbie doll melt?" Todd asked.

Dash chuckled. "As I recall, it blew apart in about a dozen flaming pieces. But yeah, it melted."

"It was my favorite, Twirly Curls Barbie. And—"

"Cool. What kind of snake did you put in the bed?" Todd asked.

"A garter snake, entirely harmless. Scared your momma to pieces, though. You should have seen her running through the hallway in her baby-doll nightie. It was the—"

"Dash, I really don't think we have to rerun our entire history for Todd's benefit, do we?" Savannah said.

"If we're talking about the past, princess, it's because you raised the issue."

Aunt Miriam entered the fray. "I declare you two sound just like you did when you were children. Now both of y'all act like the adults you are and c'mon back to the kitchen and have some dinner. I've got one of Jenny Carpenter's pies. A cherry one, I believe."

Dash flashed a bright smile in Miriam's direction. "Yes, ma'am, I will try to behave. But no thank you, ma'am, to the dinner and pie. I have errands to run up at the stable. Aunt Mim, will you be all right if I leave you with Savannah for a little bit?"

"You go on, Dash. I'm fine," Miriam said.

He nodded to Savannah. "Welcome back," he said without much enthusiasm. Then he strode toward the front door, his cowboy boots scraping across the oak floor. He stopped at the rack by the door and snagged an old, sweat-stained baseball hat bearing the logo of the Houston Astros. He slapped it down on his head and turned toward Miriam. "Don't wait up. I'll probably be late," he said, then turned toward Savannah. "Princess." He tipped his hat and headed through the open door.

"Dash, don't slam—" Miriam's admonishment was cut off by the loud bang of the front door slamming.

Todd spoke into the silence that followed. "He's really tight."

Oh, great. Dash Randall was the last person on earth that Savannah wanted as a role model for her problem child.

"Boy, *that* was a big mistake," Dash muttered as he watched the television above the bar. The Atlanta Braves' pitcher had just served up a meatball, and the batter had clocked it 435 feet.

"Uh-huh. Dash, honey, you want another Coke? You've been nursing that one for the better part of an hour now, and it's mostly water," said Dottie Cox, the proprietor of Dot's Spot, Last Chance's main watering hole.

Dash pulled his gaze away from the spring training

game on the television above the bar and looked into Dottie's over-made-up eyes. Dottie had to be pushing sixty hard, but she was outfitted in a neon green tank top and too-tight blue jeans. She might be trashy, but she had a heart of gold.

"Honey, you want another Coke?" Dot asked again.

Dash took a deep breath. "I guess I'll have to settle. Especially since I can't have you."

Dottie leaned over the bar and gave him the kind of wise look only a bartender could manage. "Dash, if you want to flirt, go find someone your own age. In fact, I have a suggestion—why don't you find your courage and do something about Hettie Marshall."

He squinted back up at the television. "They're putting in Ramirez. Good move," he muttered.

"I declare, Dash, you're a chicken. And I don't mean one of them chickens they process out at the plant. Hettie is a single woman now, and near as I can tell you've done nothing about it."

"She just lost her husband. She's in mourning."

Dottie leaned an elbow on the bar. It was a slow night at The Spot. The house band didn't play on Mondays, so the regular patrons were feeding their pocket change to the jukebox. And since the regulars drank too much, the jukebox was pumping out mostly drinking and cheating songs.

"Honey, you're afraid Hettie's going to say no."

He snorted. "Of course I am. She's been saying no for decades."

"My point exactly. You're so afraid of being alone that you don't even try. Which, of course, means you're destined to be alone."

He frowned. "Dottie, have you been sampling the liquor?"

"No, I haven't. And you know I'm right about this."

He tamped down his annoyance. He needed Dottie pointing out his fears and failures like he needed a hole in the head.

"Dottie, the truth is that I love Hettie, but she doesn't love me." He looked down at his soda pop and ran his finger through the condensation on the outside of the glass. Hettie was a sore spot.

He'd been carrying a torch for that woman since he was a teenager. They'd had a pretty hot thing going his senior year in high school, and then she up and dumped Dash on the same day he signed his first major-league contract. He was suddenly a rich man, but Hettie broke his heart by walking away from him. She'd left him for Jimmy Marshall.

But now Jimmy was dead. And everything had changed. Dash wasn't the big man with the major-league contract anymore. He was a recovering alcoholic with a busted-up knee.

He hated to admit it, but Dottie was right. Hettie wanted a different kind of man. And he'd have to change if he wanted to win her love. What if he put himself on the line, and she still said no? What if he let himself fall hard for her, and she walked away like she had all those years ago?

This was why AA suggested that people like him stay away from relationships. Dash had had a few in his twenties. But every time a woman turned heel and walked out, he crashed, hard. And then he'd go looking for a drink.

Shoot, his life was exactly like those stupid drinking and cheating songs on Dottie's jukebox. It was pitiful.

He straightened his shoulders and turned toward the jukebox, where Willie Nelson was singing "Blue Eyes Crying in the Rain." "It's a damn good thing I don't have a shotgun because I might be tempted to murder that thing. Don't you have any happy songs in there?"

Dottie laughed. "No, honey, I don't."

"Don't you believe in happiness?"

"Sure I do, but on the nights when the Wild Horses don't play I get patrons who just want to drink and listen to sad music. Ain't that right, Roy?" She turned toward Roy Burdett, who was, as usual, drunker than a skunk.

"Yeah."

"Well, *I* come here most Mondays and I'm tired of it." Dash pushed himself up from the bar stool and headed over to the jukebox. He didn't have a shotgun, but he was fully capable of disabling that infernal machine. He searched out the wall socket and pulled the power cord from the wall. Dot's Spot went quiet.

Half a dozen good ol' boys looked up from their beers and bourbons.

"Hey, why'd you do that?" Roy staggered to his feet and came toward Dash. "I like that song. You plug it back in."

"No, Roy, I won't. And besides, you're wasted. You should get on home to Laura-Beth. Have you ever thought what she must think of you coming down here every night and drinking yourself numb? Maybe you should think about joining AA. I've got the number of the folks at the Allenberg County chapter and—"

"Now, Dash," Dottie said, "don't you be trying to

sign folks up for AA. That's bad for business. Why don't you just go on home to Miriam? You should be with her tonight, anyway. The fact is, you don't belong here anymore. You know that, don't you?"

"Don't belong?" Dash's pulse kicked up. Folks were always telling him he didn't belong.

Dottie continued in her sweet voice. "Dash, honey, you're a recovering alcoholic. A bar is a strange place for a person like you. I think you've proved to everyone's satisfaction that you're tough enough to sit here surrounded by booze and not give in to temptation. So maybe you should start thinking about moving on. I'm sure Hettie would approve if you moved on."

"Yeah," Roy said, staggering forward. "And I really don't like your taste in music."

"Well, that's okay, Roy, because I don't like yours either. In my opinion, Willie Nelson sucks."

"He does not." And Roy Burdett, who had once been a member of the Davis High Rebel defensive line, rushed Dash like he was an opposing quarterback.

Dash might have been sober, but he was hampered by a bum knee—the injury that had ended his baseball career. And Roy was still surprisingly fast, even for a drunk.

Dash didn't see stars when Roy tackled him. In fact, Dash didn't even remember hitting the floor.

Savannah rested her head on the back of the rocking chair and cuddled a little deeper into her old cashmere sweater. It was almost too cold to be out here on the porch, but she held her ground hoping her summer memories might warm her up. Darn it, South Carolina had always been hot and humid when she came to visit. And that's the way she wanted it now. Like her most treasured memories.

Still, she wasn't about to let the late hour or the cold drive her inside. She wanted to sit here and remember Granddaddy.

But instead of finding the happy memories of her childhood, she ended up obsessing over the enormous thing she had done today. She had actually gotten off her fanny and taken Todd across several state lines. If she decided to stay here, there wasn't much Claire could do about it.

Of course, if Greg decided he was unhappy about the situation, he could cause trouble. Savannah was surprisingly ambivalent about that. In some corner of her heart, she almost hoped that Greg cared enough to cause trouble. But in her head, she knew that wasn't ever going to happen. Greg was a lot like her own father, who had walked out on her and Mom when Savannah was three.

So Savannah had faced the unhappy truth. And surprisingly, facing it only lent more urgency to her escape plans. Coming here to Last Chance might be her last chance to really take charge of her life.

She could also follow her dream of finally *doing* something about The Kismet, the movie theater Granddaddy had left to her. She wanted to renovate The Kismet and bring it back to life.

Accomplishing that dream would take a miracle, of course. Nothing had changed since the big chain theaters had driven Granddaddy out of business. A person like Savannah, with no financing and no business experience, had zero chance of succeeding where Granddaddy had failed.

She squeezed her eyes shut and tried to silence the negative voice inside her head. She wasn't much for praying, but she winged a little prayer skyward anyway. *Help me find the courage.*

Just then the sound of crunching gravel alerted her to the arrival of someone in the driveway. She opened her eyes to the glare of headlights. A moment later two back-lit silhouettes emerged from the brightness.

"Ma'am," a voice called out. "Is that you, Miz Miriam?"

"No, it's Savannah White. I'm Miriam's niece."

"That's the princess I been tellin' you 'bout, Damian." Savannah recognized that deep drawl.

An athletic-looking African-American dressed in the buff uniform of the Last Chance Police Department stepped up onto the front porch, followed by Dash, who was pressing an ice pack to his lip. The front of Dash's shirt was covered in blood.

The officer brushed his fingers along the side of his Stetson. "Ma'am, I'm Chief Damian Easley. Miz Dottie gave me a call about an hour and a half ago. I'm afraid Dash ran into a little bit of trouble with Roy Burdett down at The Spot."

Savannah stared at her unruly cousin. "You got into a bar fight on the night before Uncle Harry's funeral?"

Dash said not a word. Possibly because his lip was injured, but probably because he had nothing to say in his own defense.

Chief Easley grinned like he thought it was a joke or something. "Well, that's not all that unusual when you consider Roy Burdett. I took Dash over to the clinic, and Doc Cooper put a couple of stitches in his lip. The good news is that, even though Roy knocked the crap out of him, Dash doesn't appear to have a concussion. Otherwise Doc would have probably kept him under observation all night."

"I need to get my car." Dash's voice sounded muffled and slurred.

"I'll see about having someone drive it over in the morning. You probably shouldn't drive."

Well, of course not. Dash was obviously three sheets to the wind. Savannah watched as her cousin made his way up the porch steps. He leaned a little unsteadily against the porch railing and turned back toward the policeman. "Thanks, Damian."

Officer Easley tipped his hat a second time. "Good night, y'all. I'm sorry about your loss." A moment later the cruiser's headlights swung in a wide arc, and the night returned to darkness.

Dash turned toward Savannah. "Don't look at me like that. Roy tackled me because of Dottie's jukebox. Everyone's a music critic these days."

His words were hard to understand through the swelling and the ice pack.

"Do you need help getting to bed?" she asked.

"Are you volunteering to tuck me in?"

Was that a put-down? Or was it a come-on? *Ew.*

And just like that, a little unwanted vibration of awareness shot through her, underscoring the nonexistent status of her current social life. Dash had grown into an amazingly handsome man—all craggy-faced in a Harrison Ford kind of way. Even with a bloody shirt and a swollen lip, he looked like some larger-than-life movie cowboy. But still. This was Dash she was looking at. Her cousin.

Okay, so he wasn't really her cousin exactly, but they were still related.

And he was a total screwup. And a drunk. And he was trying to mess with her mind like he always did.

She gave him her Uma-Thurman-as-Beatrix-Kiddo squint that still put the fear of God into Todd. "Honestly, I should ground you or something. You're acting like an out-of-control teenager."

He didn't seem all that affected by the squint. He pushed off the porch railing and walked slowly toward the front door. He moved carefully like a drunk who didn't want to stumble.

"Here, let me help you with the—"

"I don't need your help." His words sounded angry as he managed to open the door. He headed across the foyer toward the stairway in a kind of stiff-legged walk. He was obviously limping. Savannah followed in his wake like a mother chasing after an unsteady one-year-old. Boy, he had really put on a bender tonight, hadn't he?

Maybe he was so sad about Uncle Harry's passing he'd tried to numb his grief with booze.

Or maybe he put on a bender most nights.

He took the first step and let out a groan. He stopped, bending over to massage his knee. He was listing to one side. In a minute, he was going to fall ass-over-teacart. Savannah snagged his shoulders and steadied him on his feet. "Whoa there, pardner," she said in a phony drawl, as the feel of bone, sinew, and soft cotton beneath her fingers triggered an unexpected and entirely unacceptable internal response.

She resisted the instinct to draw back as if she'd been scalded. If she did that, Dash would fall.

"Thank you, princess," he said under his breath. He steadied himself and took the first couple of steps up to the landing. "You know, I'm not nearly as drunk as you think I am."

"Oh, really?" she said, letting go of his shoulders. Releasing him didn't seem to help her spiky heart rhythm one bit, especially since her field of vision filled with a view of his Wranglered butt. He had a very nice butt. She hated herself for even noticing.

He stumbled again as he attempted the quarter turn on the landing. She darted up beside him, and he sagged against her, his arm snaking over her shoulder. She took a portion of his weight and became uncomfortably aware of Dash's muscular chest.

"What kinda perfume you got on?" he asked.

"I don't wear perfume, Dash. And I don't want to hear one crack about BO. I wash every day. I washed when I was ten, too. Now, here we go; one step at a time." They wobbled forward and up the stairs. He was limping on his right side.

He sniffed her hair. "You smell like the lilacs my granny used to grow." His voice took on a soft and far-away sound that she didn't want to hear. But her brain registered the longing in his words, and her heart reacted by doing a real Texas two-step right on her ribs.

Why the hell was she having this reaction to *Cousin* Dash? She had to distance herself, fast.

"You, dear cousin, smell like a brewery," she jibed.

"That's only because Roy dumped his beer on my head after he knocked me out. Damn, that hurts."

"What hurts?"

"My effing knee. Doc says I'll have to go get an MRI

if it's not better by tomorrow. And I had finally gotten to a pain-free place. I know now why I decided against playing football. Roy still has a few moves he hasn't used up." It certainly sounded like Dash was using booze to self-medicate. She tuned out his drunken ramblings and focused on helping him get to his bedroom on the second floor.

When they reached his bedroom door, he let go of her shoulder and steadied himself against the wall. He continued to press the slightly bloody ice pack to his mouth, but he looked down at her out of a pair of sharp blue eyes.

"Honey, I think it's best we be honest with each other, right off the bat," he said, after a very long and uncomfortable moment. "So I think it's important for you to know that—"

"Save it, cuz. We know each other too well. We're like oil and water. We always have been. I don't approve of you going off and getting drunk. Good night. I hope you're clearheaded in the morning. It's the least you could do for Aunt Miriam and Uncle Harry."

CHAPTER 2

Dash awoke to the sound of his brains being sucked from his head.

No, that couldn't be right. If his brains were being sucked out, he would be unconscious. Unconsciousness would be better than this. He lay on his back, and something roared at him from someplace.

Inside his head, perhaps?

Or maybe he'd been abducted by aliens who were about to probe him.

He cracked an eye and immediately closed it against the bright morning sunlight streaming through the dusty windows of his bedroom. His face was pounding. His lip was throbbing. And his knee...

Well, there weren't words to describe that pain.

He lay there panting and mentally cursing himself and Roy Burdett. Everyone was going to think the worst of him. Why had he gotten all riled up at Dot's? Why had he lost his temper?

What is *that sound?*

He rolled over and peeked at his bedside clock. Shoot, it was eight-thirty. The funeral was scheduled for ten. He needed to get himself some ibuprofen.

He pushed himself out of bed. Every muscle screamed. He was bruised in all kinds of places. Damn. Football was a vicious sport. He staggered across the floorboards and pulled open the door.

The roar got louder, and the sight that greeted him didn't make him feel any better.

Savannah, wearing a skirt, a pair of high heels, and a tight sweater that showed off her breasts, was pushing the old vacuum cleaner across the worn carpet in the hallway. She looked up from her domestic chores and greeted him with a regal smile as bright as the light shining from her blond ponytail.

A tight coil of unwanted reaction wormed its way through the haze of his pain. She was uppity all right, but boy howdy, was she ever built.

He drew in a breath and held it for a long moment as he reached for the robe hanging on the back of the door.

She stopped running the machine across the threadbare carpet. One proud eyebrow arched as her gaze narrowed. If he didn't know better, he'd swear she'd just gotten one hell of a good look at his morning erection.

But, being a princess, she kept calm and carried on. "Good morning. I thought you were never going to get up," she said.

"You're vacuuming." His voice sounded as rusty as nails left out in the rain. "Princesses don't vacuum."

She scowled at him. "I'm sorry I disturbed your beauty rest, but I'm vacuuming because this hallway was dusty, and we'll be having a house full of people this afternoon." She cocked her head, and her ponytail swished.

"'Scuse me. I need to hit the head." He staggered past her and into the bathroom, where he fumbled around until he found the ibuprofen and knocked back three. Cupping his hands under the water, he gulped down ten or twelve mouthfuls before raising his head and looking at himself in the mirror.

A sorrier sight he'd never seen. His lip was swollen out to there. The shiner was impressive, to say the least. He felt the back of his head. Yeah, the knot there was still tender to the touch.

Shoot, he looked like he'd been on a three-day bender.

How in the hell does a sober man end up looking like this on the day of his uncle's funeral?

He stared at himself, replaying every humiliating moment of the previous night. His heart bumped against his rib cage as he recalled Savannah helping him up the stairs. She'd thought the worst of him, hadn't she? And all the while, he was getting kind of turned on by the way her hair smelled, and the pressure of her warm, soft curves against his bruises.

Well, that was just the AA celibacy talking. Because having sexy thoughts about Savannah was ridiculous. All of Aunt Miriam's friends might think that Savannah was sweet. But Dash knew the truth. Behind that facade, she was meaner than a junkyard dog.

His first summer in Last Chance, she'd come waltzing into his world and immediately run her mouth about all his private business to all her friends. She'd tried her darndest to turn her friends Rocky and Tulane Rhodes against him. She'd made his life miserable. She'd made him feel small and insignificant and unworthy.

He let go of a deep breath. All that had happened a very long time ago, and he needed to grow up. He had choices now. Choices he could control. And right now he was choosing to shower off the beer that Roy had splashed all over him and to stay the hell away from Savannah Reynolds White.

"Damned woman," Dash muttered. "It's gonna be a long few days until she goes back where she came from."

Forty-five minutes later Dash stumbled into the kitchen, where he found Savannah brandishing a coffeepot like a Viking queen flaunting her sword. The field of battle was so spotless, the shine off the linoleum floor hurt his eyes. Did the woman stay up all night housecleaning?

"Coffee sounds good," he said.

"How do you take it?"

"Hot and naked, please."

Color rose right up Savannah's high cheekbones. Score one point for him in this lopsided battle. She was a sight to behold when she blushed like that.

"Naked?"

"That's right, princess, naked. That's the way I take my coffee and a lot of other stuff."

She turned and poured the steaming brew into a jade-ite mug and handed it to him. "You just sit yourself down, Dash. What can I make you for breakfast?"

She was talking too loud and smiling too perfectly. And then it occurred to him that she thought he was hung over. She probably expected him to turn green and run from the room. Ha! He was going to call her bluff. He was betting the princess had no idea how to cook.

"You make omelets?"

She blinked. "You want an omelet? Really?"

"Yeah. You know how to make a real western omelet? With onions and green pepper and ham and hot sauce."

"You want hot sauce?"

"Yes, princess, I don't eat naked omelets." He sat himself down at the kitchen table and grinned at her.

"I'll, uh, see if we have the ingredients." She headed toward the fridge. And she kind of bustled like she knew her way around a kitchen. Which surprised the heck out of him.

It had been a long time since anyone had bustled in this particular kitchen. And then he remembered that Savannah had spent a lot of time cooking with Aunt Sally. Which meant she probably *did* know how to make omelets. And if they were anything like Aunt Sally's, then Savannah might be a useful houseguest after all.

Just then Miriam shuffled into the kitchen. She didn't look good. Her hair was kind of all over the place, like she'd had problems getting it braided right.

"I heard y'all talking real loud," she said as she sat down. Savannah poured a cup of coffee for her. She took a sip. "My, but you make good coffee."

"I would hope so. I have a part-time job as a barista."

Miriam rested her cup on the table and squinted in Dash's direction. "Lord'a mercy, Dash, you look like you walked into a fan blade." She leaned in. "Do you have stitches in your lip?"

"I'm fine, Aunt Mim."

"Ha!" Savannah said over the sound of the cabinet doors she was slamming and banging. She'd apparently found eggs, onion, and ham.

Miriam turned her attention to the princess. "Sugar, if you slam the eggs, you're liable to break them."

"I'd like to break them over Cousin Dash's head."

"Oh, I wouldn't do that. He looks like he's already been hit by something. I'm dying to know what. Did you and one of those fancy horses of yours get into a fight?"

Savannah stopped slamming cabinets and kitchen utensils. Now she was beating the eggs with a whisk. Dash felt sorry for the eggs. "No, it wasn't a horse. It was Roy Burdett."

"Oh, for heaven's sake." Miriam shook her head. "Was he drunk again?"

"He was."

Savannah put the bowl down on the counter. Good thing it was made of plastic.

"I feel so sorry for Laura-Beth," Miriam said.

"I do, too," Dash replied. "The mention of Laura-Beth was kind of what set him off."

"Really? Did he think you and Laura-Beth were—"

"No. I got into trouble by pointing out that Laura-Beth would be happier if Roy stayed sober. I tried to give him the number of the Allenberg chapter of AA."

"Well, good for you."

"Right. That didn't go over too well. And also, he was mad because I unplugged the jukebox."

"Well, I can see that a thing like that might set him off."

"Yeah. I forgot that he used to be one hell of a good

football player. He decided I needed to get the same treatment he used to hand out to pass rushers from Central High."

"Oh, honey, are you in pain?"

"I'll be okay."

Savannah turned around. She cast her glance from Dash to Miriam and back again. "Aunt Miriam, you don't believe this crap, do you?"

"Crap?"

"He came in drunker than a skunk last night. He smelled like a brewery. He couldn't walk straight. He was slurring his words."

Miriam smiled up at her. "Oh, I don't think so. Dash goes down to Dot's Spot to watch his baseball games on account of the fact that we have only one television, and I like to watch my programs in the evenings. He doesn't drink anymore, sugar. But Roy Burdett—well, he *is* a drunken fool. And an ex-offensive-lineman."

Savannah turned back to her cooking, looking surprisingly competent, even if she didn't believe a word Miriam had just said. But then, what else was new? Savannah had always believed the worst about him.

Not much had changed, had it?

"Oh, my God, darlin', it's been years and years." The Baroness Woolham, otherwise known as Rocky Rhodes deBracy, enveloped Savannah in a ferocious hug and a cloud of expensive-smelling perfume. Rocky Rhodes used to be tangle-haired, grubby-kneed, and barefooted. How, in the name of all that was holy, had she grown up into this sophisticated woman? She was dressed to the nines in a pencil skirt and a black-and-white floral jacket.

And she'd arrived at Uncle Harry's wake on the arm of a man who could pass for Colin Firth.

Her husband was genuinely swoon-worthy. He even sounded like Colin Firth when he introduced himself. And then, like every other guy who had arrived for the wake, he quickly excused himself to go in search of a slice of Jenny Carpenter's pie.

Rocky stayed behind on Granddaddy's porch and kept Savannah company as she welcomed a steady stream of post-funeral mourners. Since Rocky knew everyone in town, her help was truly appreciated.

"So how long are you staying?" Rocky asked when the stream of visitors trickled down.

"Well, I…I…" Savannah stumbled over the words, then took a flying leap of faith. "To be honest, Rocky, I was thinking about staying permanently. I thought, maybe, I might try to renovate the theater and live in the apartment above it. Todd and I are used to small spaces."

Rocky blinked a couple of times. "Really?"

Rocky's surprise shouldn't have thrown Savannah for a loop, but it did. Of course Rocky thought her idea was stupid. Rocky had *finished* college and had worked for a senator at one time. She had gone on to marry an English baron and industrialist. Rocky probably saw right through Savannah's pitiful half-formed ideas for salvaging The Kismet.

"Have you told Dash about your plans?"

Resentment replaced self-doubt. "Why would I punish myself by discussing this with Dash?"

Rocky cocked her head. "Punish yourself?"

"He'll laugh at me. Dash is the last man on earth I would discuss my plans with."

"You know, he's grown up a little bit since the two of you were kids. And he's also rich as sin. He might be interested in investing in a theater renovation. He was pretty close to your grandfather, as I recall."

Savannah clamped her mouth shut. The idea of asking Dash for money was the absolute height of humiliation.

"Dash is Hugh's partner, you know. He's the only reason Hugh was able to locate his factory here in Last Chance," Rocky added.

That was a surprise. The idea of a classy guy like Hugh having a partnership with a drunk like Dash was kind of hard to figure. "I didn't know. In fact, I didn't even know Dash was living with Miriam and Harry until a couple of days ago."

Rocky rested her behind on the porch railing. "Really? He's been living here since he retired from baseball."

Well, *that* was a delicate way of putting it. Dash's "retirement" from baseball hadn't been voluntary. The sports pages had been full of the scandal, when Dash had gotten on a motorcycle after drinking one too many beers. Thank God he'd only messed up his leg and not killed anyone.

This was not the kind of man she wanted as a partner.

Just then the minister who had officiated at Harry's funeral came striding up the drive, saving Savannah from having to express her thoughts about Dash out loud.

Bill Ellis was long-legged, slim-hipped, and handsome. His dark hair curled over his forehead in a way that begged to have someone push it back into place. His eyes were sky blue and sober. His mouth was soft and expressive. All in all, he reminded Savannah of young James Stewart, the old-time actor in Frank Capra's Christmas movie, *It's a Wonderful Life*. Bill Ellis conveyed the feeling that he was one of those everyday small-town American heroes that Capra had featured in practically all of his classic films. The Episcopalians must be packing them in every Sunday.

The minister bounded up the porch steps and formally introduced himself. "I'm sorry we didn't get a chance to speak before the funeral. I'm very sorry for your loss, but I'm so glad you had the time to drive down from Baltimore. I think you being here means a lot to Miriam. I gather you are her last living relative. Aside from Dash, of course."

His hand was warm, and his smile was kind. "Dash and I are kissing cousins," Savannah found herself saying.

He cocked his head and gave her an earnest stare. "So I've heard." There was a hint of dimple in both cheeks.

"Miriam and Dash are inside. Dash is nursing his split lip," she added with a smile.

"Then I'll go pay my respects. Is there any of Jenny's pie left?"

"I think so."

"I better get going, then, because it usually doesn't last long." He continued into the house in search of Miriam, Dash, and a slice of pie.

"Who the heck is Jenny Carpenter and why is every man in love with her pie?" Savannah asked.

"She's a math teacher up at the high school. Her pies are legendary."

"So I gather."

"You know, it's just a shame one of the single men around here doesn't marry that woman. I think Reverend

Ellis might be inclined except she's a Methodist. Lillian Bray would have a heart attack if our minister married outside of the faith, so to speak."

"The minister's not married?" Savannah asked. She stomped on the thought forming in her head. The last thing she wanted was another romantic entanglement. She needed to stop leading with her heart all the time.

Rocky snorted a laugh. "No, he's not. And before you ask me how a man of God who looks that good could reach the age of thirty-five and not be married, let me make it clear that I do not believe he's gay. Although I think Lillian Bray is starting to worry about that. Lillian is the chair of the Ladies' Auxiliary, and she would not cotton to our having a gay minister. Which explains why she is on a mission to find Bill a wife. So you be careful now, you hear?"

"I'm not interested," Savannah said. But of course, what single woman in her early thirties wouldn't be interested in a guy like Reverend Ellis? He was handsome. He was gainfully employed. He looked like a movie star. Which, of course, was the problem. Next time, she was going to go for a guy with a face like a dog.

"Honey, I need to warn you. A single woman your age is like fair game in this town. The old ladies will be working overtime to match you up with someone, and Bill is the most eligible bachelor in town."

Savannah shook her head. "If Jesus Christ Himself walked up that path and got down on His knee and begged me to be His wife, I would turn Him down."

Rocky's smile turned wicked. "Honey, I don't think I'd want to marry Jesus either. That sounds kind of boring."

"I'm not looking for anything exciting. I just want to be on my own."

Rocky put her arm over Savannah's shoulder. "Now, *that* I understand. But not forever. You're just regrouping after a failed relationship."

"More than one. I'm a disaster at love. I was divorced at twenty-two. And over the last few years, I've gotten engaged and subsequently broken up with two more complete losers."

"Aw, honey, I'm sorry to hear that. But I have a prescription for your heartache."

"Please don't tell me it's Bill Ellis. He's cute but—"

"Oh, no. I was thinking that I need to take you to the Last Chance Book Club meeting tomorrow night and introduce you around. If you want to talk about failed relationships, the book club is the place for you."

"What is it, like a lonely hearts club or something?"

"No, not exactly. It's just that Nita Wills, our librarian, doesn't believe in happy endings. So every book we read has a sad relationship at its core. I swear, the girls are getting tired of it. Tomorrow's meeting might be the last straw. Nita told me just this morning when I ran into her at the post office that she was thinking about another Nicholas Sparks book for this month's read. And you know what that means."

"No, I don't."

"It means either the hero or the heroine will end up dead at the end of the book."

The lady with the dark hair and the flowers on her jacket told everyone that Mom was planning to move to this stupid town. Forever.

Todd couldn't believe it. The place was boring. There wasn't anyone here but old people. And there wasn't anything fun to do. Besides, Last Chance was way far away from Baltimore. And if Dad had to come this far, he might not come at all. Dad was really busy a lot of the time. He was a lawyer during the week, and almost every weekend he was playing in some kind of billiards championship. He was a really good pool player, which was why he sometimes didn't have time to see Todd.

Todd didn't like the way his stomach felt. Like maybe he'd had too many pieces of cherry pie. Or maybe he shouldn't have mixed the pie with the macaroni.

He headed across the crowded room. Mom was standing with the minister. Todd didn't like the way she was looking up at the guy, like she was thinking *OMG he's hardcore* or something. Whenever Mom looked at guys like that, it usually meant trouble. Mostly for Mom. He hated it when Mom cried. And guys always made her cry.

"That lady says we're not going back home," he said. He knew he'd interrupted the conversation, but who cared. This was important stuff.

Mom gave Todd the squint. She thought it made her look tough or something.

The minister dude looked down at him. "It's rude to interrupt."

"Is it true?" Todd asked, ignoring the minister.

"Todd, apologize to Reverend Ellis."

Todd gave the guy a quick look. "Sorry." He turned toward Mom. "Is it true?"

"We'll talk about it later."

"No, now. Because if we're not staying then you need

to tell that lady to shut up about it." He yelled this time and pointed to the woman in the flowered jacket.

Everyone in the room stopped talking. Everyone stared at him. Typical.

"Todd, go to your room."

"Is it true?" Cousin Dash said. Todd turned around. Dash was standing by the doorway with a plate of pie in his hand. He didn't sound like he was all that thrilled about what the lady had been saying either.

"Is *what* true?" Aunt Miriam asked.

"That the princess is staying, and she plans to revive The Kismet," Dash said.

Everyone looked at Mom. Mom looked kind of annoyed. "Well, I guess it is," she said.

The grown-ups started clapping. Mom looked super surprised. And in all that excitement, everyone forgot about Todd.

He turned away, his stomach feeling like crap. He got as far as the landing on the staircase before Cousin Dash chased him down.

"Cheer up, kid," he said as he leaned into the railing at the bottom of the stairs. "Your momma won't last long. Once she realizes that the old theater is falling down, she'll be heading back to Baltimore lickety-split."

"It's okay," Todd replied, "you don't have to worry that I'm gonna get all emo."

Dash frowned. "What does emo mean?"

"It means all depressed and stuff."

"Oh. Well, I wasn't worried that you were going to get depressed. Especially since y'all will be headed home in a week."

Todd assessed his older cousin. He was pretty tight for

a grown-up. And at least Todd and Dash were on the same side.

"I hope you're right," Todd said. But just to make sure of it, Todd planned to borrow Mom's iPhone and call Granny Katie. Granny Katie would tell Mom what was the right thing to do. She always did.

CHAPTER
3

The next morning, Savannah got up early to make cinnamon rolls. They were Todd's favorite, and she had hoped to get on his good side. But it didn't work. He'd barely said a word as he scarfed down two rolls and then beat feet out to the porch. He was still ensconced on the swing with his PSP and his earphones.

Dash wasn't much better. He took his cup of coffee and his bun out to the porch to eat.

It was a little disheartening to have her son and her bad-boy kissing cousin out there sulking. Together.

"You should go out and talk to both of them, sugar," Miriam said. Her aunt was still wearing her house robe, and her hair was a mess. But at least Miriam had thanked Savannah for the home-baked rolls and had kept her company while she drank her second cup of coffee.

"I sure wish Rocky had kept her mouth shut," Savannah said on a sigh. "That wasn't exactly the way I wanted Todd, much less you and Dash, to hear about my plans. The thing is, I've been thinking about doing this for a long time. And when Uncle Harry died, I just pulled the trigger. But now that I'm here, I'm, well . . ."

Miriam laughed. "I know it's a big step, but everyone in town would be overjoyed if you could revive the theater. Me especially. Earnest loved that place so much."

"Yeah, he did." Savannah drained her coffee cup, then took it to the sink to rinse.

When she was finished, she turned and leaned her backside into the counter. "I don't want you to think we just invited ourselves here. My plan is to move into the apartment above the theater. That way, you and Dash won't feel like we've descended on you without his permission."

Miriam frowned. "But you're family, and this house has more rooms than a dog has fleas."

"I know, but Dash—"

"Hush. You and Dash and that boy of yours are all the family I have left. I want you to stay here. Nothing would please me more. Now do me a favor and go on out to that porch and have an adult conversation with your cousin. I can understand why Todd is sulking—you're taking him away from his home—but Dash is a grown man and knows better."

Miriam stood up. "And if you don't mind, my arthritis is bothering me, so I'm just going to go have a little lay-down." The old woman shuffled out of the kitchen. It probably wasn't Miriam's arthritis that was bothering her. Now that the funeral was over, the reality of Harry's loss was starting to sink in. Miriam seemed a little depressed this morning.

All the more reason Savannah shouldn't be rocking any boats.

She squared her shoulders and headed out to the porch. "Dash, do you have a minute?"

Dash looked up without any expression on his face. His swollen lip looked a little better today, and the bruise under his eye had turned green.

"Sure thing, princess." He gestured toward an adjacent rocker.

"I was thinking maybe inside." She glanced at Todd.

Dash turned toward the boy. "Hey, kid."

Todd ignored him.

"Hey, you." He nudged the boy's foot, and Todd finally looked up from the screen of his PSP.

"You know how to work a lawn mower?"

Todd gazed at Dash as if he'd spoken in an alien language.

"Uh, no, he doesn't. We live in an apartment complex and—" Savannah tried to explain, but Dash interrupted.

"Well, shoot, I guess I'll have to show you. Because if you're staying here, you're not going to sit around on your lazy behind. Uncle Harry left a lot of chores."

Todd's eyes narrowed, but he didn't say anything. He simply stood up and stalked off into the living room.

Savannah didn't know whether to laugh or yell. Yelling won. "Look, I get it. You're still pissed off at me for some reason I don't understand. But I would appreciate it if you wouldn't take it out on Todd. I came out here to settle this thing between us once and for all."

"Princess, I wasn't taking anything out on Todd. I was just making the rules of the house clear to him. Folks living in this house have chores. You do remember that, don't you?"

For just an instant, he sounded like Granddaddy. All

the summers Savannah had spent here as a child, she'd always had chores. Which probably explained why she had gotten up so early yesterday and today. She'd done a lot of cleaning. A lot of dishwashing. And some cooking. And it felt right. Whenever she stayed here, she always got up early. There were always things that needed doing.

She glanced at the sagging porch step. "I can see how you're holding up your end of the chores."

"I'm going to fix that step. I was just waiting on Uncle Harry. He had a long list of things he wanted to fix around here, but if anyone tried to help him, he would get madder than a grease monkey with a bent dipstick. And getting that mad was bad for his heart. So I just let him go on believing the fiction that he was going to get well enough to do his chores, and I found other things to keep me busy. Now that he's gone, I can finally get around to making repairs. Speaking of chores, are you going to take over the cooking? Because those cinnamon rolls reminded me of when Aunt Sally was alive."

Savannah flushed with pride in spite of herself. Had Dash actually complimented her on something? That would be a first. "It's Granny's recipe, thanks. But about our staying—I just want you to know that Todd and I are not planning to live here with you and Miriam. We're going to live above the theater while I fix it up."

Dash stopped rocking and gave her one of his holier-than-thou looks. "Princess, I've been sitting out here try-ing to figure out how to explain to you that this plan of yours is not going to fly. Do you have the slightest notion of how much money it's going to cost to 'fix up' The Kismet?"

Heat crawled up Savannah's face. Of course Dash

would point out the holes in her plan. Dash always did that sort of thing. She squared her shoulders and looked him straight in his perpetually twinkling eyes. They were an odd shade of blue, like a bright October sky.

"No, Dash, I haven't figured that out yet. I'd have to go see the place first."

"Well, *that's* a good thing to do. Maybe you should have done that before you announced your plans to everyone."

"I didn't announce my plans to everyone. I just mentioned them to Rocky."

"It's the same thing. Once you go see the place, you'll realize that the only sensible thing to do with The Kismet is to take a wrecking ball to it. The place is falling down. And even if it weren't, you'd have to be certifiable to think about running a small movie theater in the middle of nowhere. Everyone wants 3-D and multiple screens with stadium seating. You won't be able to compete."

Dash had neatly summed up every excuse Savannah had ever made for why she'd be crazy to follow through with this dream. He wasn't being negative. He wasn't being mean. He was just pointing out the obvious.

The way he always did.

Which made her mad. Dash always did that, too. She squared her shoulders and decided that if Dash wanted a fight, he could have one. "But I have a distinct advantage since I own the building and the real estate free and clear. And I'm current on the taxes."

"Good points. You have any experience? What do you do for a living in Baltimore?"

"I'm an administrative assistant in an insurance agency. And on weekends, I work as a part-time barista."

"What in the Sam Hill is that?"

"I make fancy coffee drinks at the local coffee shop. And sometimes the owner buys my pastries for resale. I like to cook."

"Ohhhh," he said on a long, sarcastic breath.

"I know a lot about the movies, especially old ones."

Both of his eyebrows rose. "Do you have a business plan? Have you done any market research? Do you have a structural engineer? Because you're going to need one before you're finished."

She felt dizzy. "No, but I just got here."

Dash pushed up from the rocking chair. "Let's go take a tour of the old place. I'm sure one look at it will convince you that it's a lost cause."

The Kismet sat at the corner of Palmetto Avenue and Chancellor Street in Last Chance's business district. Built in 1929, the theater was a miniature version of the movie palaces of a bygone era. Its facade was heavily influenced by Moorish design. Inside, it had carved wooden columns and a high domed ceiling painted dark blue and speckled with small recessed lights that simulated twinkling stars. Once, when Savannah was very little, she had believed that Granddaddy made the real stars shine in the sky.

But that had been decades ago. Now Savannah stared up at the minaret above the marquee and couldn't miss the obvious signs of decay and neglect.

"What a dump," Todd said, looking up from his PSP.

"My thoughts exactly," Dash echoed.

Her heart stumbled. She refrained from telling Dash and Todd that they could shove their negative thinking up their collective behinds. They were right. The place looked bad.

She stepped up to the front door and slipped the old key into the lock. The doors creaked as she pulled them open. A rush of dusty, fetid air hit her square in the face. She fought the urge to cough.

"It stinks like butt," Todd said.

"You better watch your mouth, son," Dash said. "If Miz Lillian Bray ever heard you saying something like that, she'd be reaching for a bar of soap and asking questions later."

"Soap? What for?"

"To wash out your mouth. Take it from me, kid, soap tastes like total crap. You want to avoid that fate. It's actually worse than standing here breathing in bat dookey."

"Bat dookey?" Savannah said through the dust in her throat.

"Yeah, honey, you got bats in the belfry in more ways than one." He gave her a little crooked smile. He was really enjoying her humiliation, wasn't he? She wanted to take her fist and bloody his lip a second time.

She turned away and headed into the theater's lobby. Dash and Todd followed. "You're just exaggerating. You always exaggerate," she said over her shoulder.

"Princess, do you even know what bat droppings smell like?"

"Uh, no."

"Well, then take it from me. You've got a bat problem. And I'll be willing to bet you got mice and who knows what else. I wouldn't be surprised if you had snakes in here."

Savannah turned toward him in the gloom of the lobby. "You're just trying to scare me. So quit it."

"In these parts, we get snakes indoors all the time, especially if we got mice first."

"Do you get rattlers inside?" Todd didn't sound too happy about that.

"Well, we have timber rattlers in South Carolina but they're rare. It's the water moccasins and cottonmouths you have to watch out for down here, son. But black snakes are as common as the rain."

Todd squinted his eyes. "Why do you call me that? I'm not your kid."

Dash's crooked smile flashed again. "It's just a figure of speech. Everyone down here uses it. It used to really tick me off when I first came here, too. But you kind of get used to it after a while."

"Well, I'm not gonna—ever. So don't call me son and don't boss me around. You aren't my dad." Todd leaned against one of the mildewed walls and gave Dash his snotty-kid look. Dash smiled.

Savannah shook her head. "Okay, guys, can we all try to get along? And Dash, quit trying to scare us with your snake stories, okay? I'm tired of having that incident thrown in my face."

"You still don't know why I put that snake in your bed, do you?"

"Oh, really, Dash, can we please *not* talk about that. Whatever I did to you, I'm sorry."

"An apology doesn't mean a thing if you have no idea what you're apologizing for. And if you remember, you apologized back then, too."

Yes, she remembered apologizing. She remembered

Granddaddy blaming her for the entire snake episode and making her apologize. She still wasn't entirely sure why she caught the blame when it was Dash who put the snake in her bed. Even now, as a full-grown woman, she always checked under the covers before she crawled into bed. Shouldn't Dash apologize for that? Didn't he have some blame for leaving her terrified of snakes?

She turned her back on Todd and Dash and headed deeper into the lobby, past the dusty concession counters. The carpets were littered with dirty popcorn boxes, candy wrappers, and mouse droppings. The auditorium was no better. The mice had taken over. They'd chewed through the ornate carpets and nested in the seats. She would need to fumigate the entire place. Soap-and-elbow-grease wasn't going to cut it. Everything had to be replaced.

They headed upstairs and discovered that the apartment was uninhabitable, and the projection equipment had been attacked by the rodents.

Savannah's dream was never going to come true. It wasn't just the rodents, either. The roof was bad. There was water damage and mold. And bats had created nests in the rafters.

She surveyed the disaster, and her eyes began to itch. Not just from the dust, but with tears she refused to shed. She'd been through more than her share of heartbreak in the last few years, but for some reason this blow seemed harder than all the others. She'd dreamed about reviving the theater for years.

But it was impossible. You can't bring the dead back to life. And The Kismet was dead. The wonderful show palace of her younger years was gone. It would never light up Palmetto Avenue again.

"C'mon, I've seen enough. Let's get out of here," she managed to say. Her voice hardened with the strength it took to keep from crying.

She turned and headed toward the stairs that would take them back to the lobby. "C'mon, Todd, let's go."

"So, I reckon you're going home then," Dash said, no doubt gloating over his victory.

"Yeah. I guess so. You win, Dash, the theater is a lost cause."

Zeph Gibbs tucked the sleeping puppy into the folds of his old flannel shirt. The critter snuggled there, soft and warm. The pup was much healthier than he'd been a week ago. He was fully weaned now.

It was time to pass him on.

Zeph got out of his old truck and ambled up the street. He stopped for a moment at the intersection of Palmetto and Chancellor. His feet wanted to turn right, but his heart said no. It was Wednesday evening, and the ladies of the book club were meeting. There were too many people in the library.

And besides, someone needed this pup more than Miss Nita.

He walked on past Chancellor Street and into the main business district. The days were getting longer, but dusk had finally settled. That was good. During the day, he could see his reflection in the shop windows out of the corner of his eye. And Zeph's reflection was a little bit scary. It wasn't his overalls or the flannel shirt, or even his gray hair that was frightening. No, the scary thing followed him like a shadow.

So Zeph always looked down when he walked through

town. And he didn't have any mirrors in his house out on Bluff Road.

He turned left onto Baruch Street and walked a block until he ducked into the strip of pines that separated Miriam Randall's house from the sidewalk. He stood in the cool shade of the pine trees. Miz Miriam was sitting on the porch. She looked tired and sad. He'd been watching her at Mr. Harry's funeral yesterday. Her and her niece and nephew.

And the boy.

Zeph reached into his shirt, put the sleeping puppy down on a soft bed of pine needles, and took a few steps deeper into the woods. The wind rustled in the pines, and Zeph could almost hear the shadow speaking to him. He halfway recognized the voice.

But he didn't speak to it. He never spoke to it. He fought the shadow with all his strength, but he always ended up doing what the shadow wanted.

He hunkered down and waited for the puppy to wake. He wouldn't leave until he knew his mission was accomplished.

"I don't really read all that much," Savannah said as Rocky hauled her down Palmetto Avenue in the direction of the Allenberg County Public Library where the book club met the first and third Wednesdays of every month. "And besides, I haven't decided to stay."

"Oh, honey, don't worry about the reading. We let Nita pick the books. They're always kind of boring, so naturally we don't spend a lot of time talking about them. It's mostly a social club. And you can't go back to Baltimore. You have to stay and fix up the theater."

This was not the time to tell Rocky that she had abandoned her half-baked plans. So Savannah clamped her mouth shut and followed Rocky into the library. The place was relentlessly cheerful, with yellow-painted cinderblock walls festooned with lots of kid art. A number of other book club members had already arrived. They stood around the refreshment table eating red velvet cupcakes.

"Oooh, I forgot that Arlene was responsible for refreshments this time," Rocky said. "She always buys cupcakes at the bakery over in Allenberg."

Rocky pulled Savannah into the knot of women by the table and started making introductions. Someone handed Savannah a paper plate with a red velvet cupcake. She taste-tested it. The icing *was* excellent, but the cake was a skosh dry. Granny's cake recipe was better.

"Come meet Jenny," Rocky said as she dragged Savannah away from her thoughts.

Jenny wore one of those shapeless flowered dresses that came down below her knees. Her brown hair sat atop her head in a messy bun, and she wore a pair of big eyeglasses.

"Savannah was just telling me how much she enjoyed the pies you baked for Harry's wake, Jenny," Rocky said.

Jenny gave Savannah a shy smile. "I'm so sorry I couldn't make Mr. Randall's funeral. We had school that day."

"The pies were much appreciated," Savannah replied, stunned that this wallflower of a woman had captured the male population of Last Chance by their taste buds. Heaven help the female population if Jenny ever got a makeover. Because despite the specks, bun, and dress, she was attractive—with golden skin and amber eyes.

Savannah was about to ask Jenny about her piecrust recipe when Rocky grabbed her by the arm and pulled her away. "C'mon, you need to meet Molly Canaday, her momma runs the yarn shop and her daddy is the coach of the football team. She wasn't at the funeral either, because she's a mechanic at the Grease Pit."

"Really?"

"Yup. You shouldn't ever take your car any other place, because Molly and Bubba are the best mechanics in Allenberg County. And if you ever decide to take up knitting and need a teacher, go to Molly, not her mother. Molly has a gift with yarn and cars."

Molly had a beautiful mane of curly black hair that had to be the envy of everyone in that room. But her hair was her only concession to her gender. She wore no makeup, her jeans had holes in the knees, and her gray T-shirt said, "I love the smell of gasoline in the morning."

Jane Rhodes, Rocky's sister-in-law, was standing next to Molly. Savannah remembered the pregnant woman from the funeral. Jane worked at the Cut 'n Curl and was married to Rocky's older brother, Clay.

On the desk in front of them, Jane had spread out the ugliest, most misshapen sweater-in-progress Savannah had ever seen. The yarn was a pretty shade of pink, but the stitches were a mess.

"Well," Molly was saying to Jane as Savannah and Rocky approached, "you clearly lost count of the decreases for the raglan sleeves."

"I did?" Jane said.

"You'll have to frog it back to here." Molly pointed to a place in the knitting.

"I'm never going to figure this out. If the baby wasn't

due so soon, I would start something new." Jane looked up. "Oh hi, Rocky, Savannah."

Rocky snorted a laugh. "Jane, honey, how many unfinished sweaters do you have now?"

"A few," Jane said, and then turned toward Savannah. "I think what you're planning to do with the theater is really great."

Savannah gritted her teeth. How on earth was she going to tell everyone that she'd abandoned her plans for the theater? Her stomach felt queasy. There were too many new people here.

One of them came up carrying a Vera Bradley bag. She dropped it on the table and pulled out a knitting project. "Molly, honey, you have to help me. Where have I gone wrong?"

Molly sighed. "Cathy, why don't you take your knitting to Momma? She's the one who owns the shop."

"I do, but her instructions never make much sense to me. On the other hand, you are a natural-born teacher, not to mention that you're a yarn whisperer if I ever saw one. Now, how exactly do I do that three-needle bind-off you were telling me about?"

The newcomer was introduced as Cathy Niles, and within a few minutes Cathy and Molly were bent over the project in deep consultation. Rocky pulled Savannah away, and in the space of the next few minutes Savannah was introduced to half a dozen other women whose names went right out of her head.

Hettie Marshall was the last to arrive. She strolled in ten minutes late dressed in a royal blue knit ensemble that might have been Armani. She had all the élan of a movie star at the Oscars, and her arrival seemed to signal the beginning of the meeting. The book club members took seats around one of the tables. Almost half of them, not including Molly the yarn whisperer or Hettie the fashion plate, had brought knitting projects with them.

The meeting was called to order by Nita Wills, the librarian. "So, what did y'all think about our book this time?" she asked.

The silence was so deep that Savannah could hear the clicking of knitting needles. Nita didn't look pleased. "Did any of y'all read it?"

"I did," Jenny whispered, a blush rising to her face.

"And?"

"Well, I thought it was sad."

"All the books we read are sad," Cathy grumbled.

"But what about—"

"Cathy and Jenny are right, you know," Molly interrupted. "Every book you choose is a complete bummer. I read most of this one, and to be honest, I hated the hero. He was pathetic. I mean, how many times is he going to talk himself out of doing something about his situation? He could have had love and freedom and a good life. All he had to do was quit his job. The fact that he ultimately dies at the end is only what he deserved for being such a wimp."

"I never got all the way through it," Arlene said. "I kept falling asleep when the hero would start talking to himself."

"Didn't any of you get the theme?" Nita asked.

"You mean that losers always lose?" Molly asked.

Nita glowered. "No. The book is a statement on how big corporations grind the average man into a fine pulp."

Arlene cleared her throat. "Right, and that message is so uplifting."

"It's not supposed to uplift. It's supposed to be a warning. Just look at what corporations are doing to our culture. Have you watched any reality TV lately?" Nita said.

Arlene met Nita's stare without a blink. "Nita, honey, you need to get a life. Have you even watched *Real Housewives*? It's entertaining."

"No, I haven't watched that show," Nita said. "You realize it's not really reality. And this book we've just read is a social commentary on that."

"Right," Cathy said, "but could we, for once, read a book without any social commentary in it? Could we maybe read a romance. I'm a particular fan of June Moring."

"Oh, my God, yes," Arlene said. "Did you read *Destiny*? I swear that pirate made my heart sing. I just love her heroes."

"Ladies, this is a literary book club. We don't read romance here." Nita glared at the women around the table.

"But couldn't we just once?" Cathy asked in a small voice.

A muscle ticked along Nita's jaw, and Savannah worried that she might be about to stroke out. In fact, aside from the color of her skin, Nita looked exactly like Savannah's ex-mother-in-law when Claire was about to blow a fuse. And when Claire blew, you didn't want to be in the same room.

So Savannah stepped right into the breach. The way she always did when Claire looked like she was ready to explode. "Uh, I know I'm a guest here, but couldn't you read a literary romance? You know, like *Pride and Prejudice* or something?"

Everyone turned to look at her. And then they turned to look at Nita. It was sort of like being at a tennis match, only with knitting needles and no rackets or balls. Savannah's palms began to sweat, the same way they always did when she found the gumption to stand up to Claire. Only this wasn't Claire. Nita was the local librarian, and while she was clearly the leader of the book club, she seemed like a pretty reasonable person. Way more reasonable than Claire had ever been.

Nita smiled. "Thanks for that suggestion, Savannah, but I'm sure everyone has already read that book."

"I haven't," Savannah blurted. "Of course, I *have* seen every version of the movie. I think the BBC television series is the best one."

"Oh, I completely agree with you there," Rocky said. "Colin Firth is the best Darcy, bar none."

"You're only saying that because your husband looks and sounds like Colin Firth," Cathy commented.

"Am not. Hugh is nothing like Colin Firth."

"Much," Arlene said, batting her mascara-laden eyelashes.

Nita looked down her nose at Savannah. "You really haven't read *Pride and Prejudice*?"

"Well, don't get up on your high horse, Nita," Molly said, "I haven't read it either."

"Neither have I," Hettie said.

Everyone looked down the table at Hettie.

She smiled. "Don't y'all look at me that way. I haven't read it. And I haven't even seen the movie. Let's have a show of hands. How many of y'all have read the book?"

Only Rocky and Nita raised their hands, and Rocky punctuated the point by saying, "I've read it, but I wouldn't mind reading it again. It's a particular favorite of mine."

"Well then, that settles it, girls," Hettie said. "We're going to read *Pride and Prejudice* next."

"Now, Hettie, I'm sure that we can—"

Hettie cut Nita off. "Nita, honey, I know you love the idea of having a literary book club. But that doesn't mean light comedy or happy love stories can't ever get onto our reading list. To be honest, I'm tired of having my mind improved. I just want to read something fun. With a happy ending. And besides, I think reading *Pride and Prejudice* would be a wonderful way of welcoming Savannah to our group. That was a very good book suggestion, Savannah. I'm so glad you're here. I'm sure we're going to be great friends."

Savannah stared at Hettie. There was an avid look on Hettie's face that made a shiver of warning skip up Savannah's spine. Hettie wanted something from her.

CHAPTER 4

Dash sat in the rocking chair, trying not to worry about Aunt Mim. And the more he tried to push his worry aside, the more annoyed he got at the kid. Todd was sitting on the porch swing with his video game and his earphones.

The kid was not his problem. Miriam was. But every time he glanced Todd's way, something jolted through him. He recognized that kid. He knew him inside and out. And having to sit here and watch him was driving Dash right up a wall. He wanted to escape to Dottie's place, but she'd made it clear that he was no longer welcome there.

He ground his teeth together and glanced at the kid again. Jeez, he looked pasty white. He needed to get out in the sun. Too bad it wasn't quite warm enough to take him down to the river for a swim.

Maybe he could put the kid to work mucking out stalls. He smiled at the thought. Then he checked himself. What the hell did he know about kids anyway?

Dash closed his eyes, leaned his head back on the rocker, and listened to the crickets. If Uncle Earnest were still alive, he would put the kid to work at the theater. Dash's heart thumped against his ribs. Yeah, and Uncle Harry would have picked a fight. Harry and Dash had fought with each other from day one. The old man was still being feisty the day before he died. Dash and Harry were way too much alike. It was the Randall blood in their veins.

But Uncle Earnest never raised his voice. He just showed up with a pair of baseball gloves and a ball.

Of course. Why hadn't Dash thought of that before?

Dash stood up and headed into the house. He took the steps as quickly as his bum knee would let him. His gloves were tucked into a wooden trunk at the foot of his bed. He pulled out his gamer and a slightly smaller mitt that he still kept oiled, with a baseball tucked into the pocket so it wouldn't lose its shape. It was old now, but it had the patina of a glove well used. He remembered the day Uncle Earnest had brought it home.

He picked it up and headed downstairs. "Hey, kid," he said when he reached the porch again.

He didn't get much of a reaction. The kid was tuned out most of the time.

He leaned over and plucked the PSP from Todd's hands. The earbuds came out of the kid's ears.

"Hey, gimme that back."

Dash turned and hurled the game into the pine trees along the front of the yard. Hopefully the pine needles would provide a soft landing for the gadget; otherwise Dash was going to be out a few hundred to replace the thing.

Todd stood up, the expression on his face telegraphing pure belligerence. "Mom's right, you're crazy."

"Well, even a stopped clock is right twice a day," Dash said.

The kid frowned. "What's that supposed to mean? Move, I gotta go find my PSP."

"Nope. You're going to play catch with me."

Todd glared at the baseball gloves in Dash's hand. "I don't want to play catch. Baseball sucks."

"Watch your mouth, young man," Miriam said from her rocker, proving that the old woman was not dozing like Dash had thought.

"Are you afraid?" Dash asked.

"You're kidding, right? What would I be afraid of?" The kid's face got just a tiny bit pink, proving that he *was* scared.

"Oh, I don't know," Dash said, "dropping the ball, throwing like a girl, getting hit in the eye."

"No." Todd's reply was pure bravado.

"Well, you should know something about baseball. It's the only game where you fail two-thirds of the time. Dropping a ball is as common as the rain."

"Well, I don't want to play. And you can't make me. I'm going to get my PSP, and it better not be broken."

Todd sidestepped Dash. He marched himself down the porch steps and into the pine trees where Dash had tossed the game.

"Nice try," Miriam said, "but throwing the video game was a little over the top."

"Yeah, but it was direct. I've been watching Savannah, and she doesn't seem to be able to stop him by reasoning with him."

Miriam shrugged. "She's doing the best she can. It's not easy being a single mom. And you don't remember, but it took Earnest a few weeks before you gave in and played catch with him." She looked up at him with a smile that burned a hole in his chest. He loved Miriam with all his heart. He couldn't remember his mother, and his memories of his grandmother were so vague. But Miriam had always been there. Miriam and her brother Earnest. Not even blood relations, but they had changed Dash's life in countless ways. He had screwed things up, but he knew that he would probably never have made it this far were it not for Miriam and Earnest.

"I'm mighty proud of you for trying. Don't give up," Miriam said. "That boy needs help."

Dash didn't know whether to feel good about earning Aunt Mim's praise or just scared that he'd sort of blundered into a role that he had no idea how to play.

But before he could figure it out, Todd called from the shadow of the pines. "You won't believe what I just found."

Dash and Miriam turned just in time to see Todd come striding from the pines holding the ugliest damn puppy Dash had ever set eyes on. Its body was a nondescript brown with a white face and a head that was way too big for its skinny body. The puppy's hind end was wagging, and its pink tongue was giving Todd's face a going-over.

"Well, if that isn't an answer to my prayers," Miriam said. "Just look at the smile on that boy's face."

Hettie snubbed the cigarette out on the pavement just as Nita came out of the library and locked the front doors.

"You know," Nita said, "you aren't fooling anyone,

Hettie. We all know you smoke. And I, for one, know you have read *Pride and Prejudice*."

"And how do you know that?"

"Call it a librarian's intuition. What are you up to?"

"I'm trying to save the town."

Nita chuckled.

"You need a ride home?" Hettie asked.

"Is this a peace offering?"

"I reckon. I didn't mean to usurp your leadership, Nita. But the girls need a break, and I didn't want you to make Savannah feel unwelcome. You have heard that she owns The Kismet."

"Yes, I've heard. And I also know that it would take a ton of money to fix up that old place. Any fool can see that. Where is a person like Savannah going to get the money to do that?"

"She needs an angel."

"Oh, Lordy, are you going to start in on that now?"

"Get in the car, Nita. I'm sorry if I cut you off during the meeting today."

Nita slipped into the passenger's seat, and Hettie started the engine. Her little Audi purred.

"Well, I'm all right with reading *Pride and Prejudice*. I'm sure Cathy will enjoy herself, and maybe y'all will come ready to talk about the book instead of swapping recipes and asking Molly to fix your knitting projects."

"Oh, Nita, life is short. We love your book club because you always let us swap recipes, and talk about knitting and babies, and whatever else happens to be on everyone's mind at the moment. We love you, even if you *are* trying to improve our minds."

"And you could use some improvement. All of y'all."

"Don't sulk, now. We need to join ranks and make sure Savannah stays and fixes up the theater. And you are part of that, whether you like it or not. Rocky's on a mission to get Savannah all tied up in our social life. And my job is to find the angel."

"You might try talking to Bert Rhodes. He's got a whole golf course filled with angels."

"I am not talking about that kind of angel. I'm talking about an angel investor."

"Oh."

"You know, someone who puts money into a lost cause for the love of it instead of the return it's unlikely to give." Hettie turned her car on to Palmetto Avenue just in time to see Zeph Gibbs shuffling down the sidewalk, heading toward his old Ford truck.

"Poor old Zeph," Nita said.

"It's just disgraceful the way he camps out in the swamp," Hettie said. "He probably should be living in a VA hospital. Maybe we should do something about him."

"No. He's fine where he is. He loves the woods. And I don't think it was Vietnam that made him the way he is. He kind of withdrew after Luke Raintree died."

"You talk like you know him well."

Nita shrugged. "I knew him real well when I was a girl. We were in the same graduating class at Dubois High. The last one, in fact, before Dubois and Davis were integrated. He was always shy. But I do remember how he used to sing in the AME choir. He had a beautiful baritone. But he hasn't been to church recently. I hire him sometimes to do odd jobs around the house. There are a lot of us living south of Julia who do that. He's got a gift for carpentry."

"I didn't know. I always thought he was living on disability or VA benefits, or something."

"I don't think so. I think Zeph is just way off the grid." Nita let go of a mournful sigh as they passed Zeph and The Kismet's sagging marquee. "Hettie, where on earth are you going to find an angel like the one you've been talking about?"

"I believe he may be closer than we think."

Dash leaned on the fence and watched Lizzy Rhodes as she put Desperado through his paces. The teenager's riding abilities had become so impressive that she'd exceeded his skills as a teacher. Dash made a note to talk to Sheriff Rhodes about getting Lizzy a more experienced trainer. She was good enough to consider show riding.

Dash let go of a breath and looked away, over the gently rolling hills that surrounded the Painted Corner Stables. The place was his pride and joy. Unfortunately, his program for breeding American Paints had been less than a financial success. Not that he cared about money all that much. He had more than any man could possibly want.

The Astros had given him a forty-million-dollar, five-year contract to play for them. He'd busted up his knee during the last year of that agreement, right in the middle of a contract renegotiation that would have probably netted him more than one hundred million for an additional five years. Dash had been hitting .290 with thirty home runs when he had one too many beers and let a blond bimbo talk him into getting on a Harley.

And even though that mistake had cost him millions of dollars, he still didn't regret the lost money. He regretted his lost reputation far more.

He cast his gaze over the land surrounding the stables. He owned most of it. He'd bought it up cheap, and even considering the economic downturn, he'd done okay reselling some of it. Last Chance was booming because of deBracy Ltd.

He caught sight of the cloud of dust in the corner of his eye. He'd been expecting it.

Every afternoon, Hettie Marshall took her rescued Thoroughbred, A Wing and a Prayer, out for daily exercise. And every afternoon, Dash awaited her return like a faithful puppy. Of course, he pretended to be busy with stable business, but he was waiting for that moment when she'd come riding up the old clay road. He lived for the few minutes they would share together de-tacking her horse.

Lizzy finished putting Desperado through his paces just as Hettie arrived. The girl dismounted and started walking Desperado around the corral to cool him down. Wing trumpeted a greeting as he came up. Dash hung on the fence and watched Hettie dismount and gather up Wing's lead. She sure had a nice figure. Hettie joined the girl in the corral as they walked their horses.

When Lizzy's horse was cool enough, Dash took him into the stable and de-tacked him.

He was just finishing up when Hettie and Wing came down the aisle.

"You're just the man I want to see," Hettie said.

"I've been waiting decades to hear you say that to me."

Hettie gave him a long look that didn't bode well for his suit. He could practically feel the annoyance coming off her in waves. Hettie knew too many of Dash's secrets.

And he knew too many of hers.

That balance kept them in each other's orbit like gravity.

"So what have I done now?" Dash said, coming up to walk on Wing's right side.

"Rocky called me. She told me all about Mr. Brooks's granddaughter and her idea for reopening The Kismet. And I met Savannah last night at the book club meeting. She stood up to Nita Wills. I was pretty impressed by that."

"I really don't want to talk about Savannah. She annoys me. Last night, she came home from the book club and told her son that he had to get rid of the stray dog he'd found. Honestly, she completely missed the way the kid had bonded with the dog. She reminds me of her high-and-mighty mother, and I always hated Aunt Katie Lynne."

Hettie slipped the reins back over Wing's head and started taking off his bridle. "She didn't come across as high and mighty to me. What else do you know about her?"

He rested his hand on Wing's neck, his gaze zeroing in on Hettie. The horse nickered. "She's my cousin, sort of, but that doesn't mean I know all that much about her."

"Sort of?"

"She's related to Miriam. I'm related to Harry. Savannah and I aren't related at all. Except we seem to have family in common."

"Is she as smart as she seems?" Hettie stared at Dash over Wing's back. She slipped the horse's halter over his ears and snapped the left crosstie onto it.

"I don't know. I guess. Her momma, Aunt Kate, is a snob and a college professor. I don't like either of them. We were not close cousins."

"In addition to not really being cousins at all?"

"I guess."

"Is she well financed?"

He snorted as he snapped the right-hand crosstie to Wing's halter. "She has no money. She has no real idea. I mean, it would be crazy to try to reopen a theater here in the middle of nowhere."

Hettie stared at him, and Dash got that perennial sinking feeling right in the middle of his chest. Damn it, he'd disappointed her again. "What?" he asked.

They stood staring over the horse's back. And, boy howdy, did Dash get lost in those violet eyes of hers.

"Don't you look at me like that, Dash Randall."

"Like what?"

"Like a lovesick puppy. I'm not interested."

Dash decided it was time to be brave. "Hettie, is it just me you're not interested in, or is it men in general? I'd like to know so I can devise my plan of attack."

"Your plan of attack?"

"Yes, ma'am. I have decided to make a play for you."

She looked away. "Dash, please. I've always liked you. But I don't want to be tying myself down again to any man. For the first time in my life, I'm living the way I want to. And I'm thinking I could do some good things for this town. And that includes doing something about that old theater. So can you just focus on that? I need to know as much as I can about this sort-of cousin of yours."

And so Dash found himself once again talking about his least favorite subject—Cousin Savannah.

"There isn't anything to say about Savannah," he said. "She was a spoiled kid. Her granddaddy left her the theater. And up until yesterday, she believed she could revive it. I set her straight."

"You what?"

"I set her straight. We went over there. The roof is falling down, there are bats in the rafters, and the projection system is both antiquated and rat-chewed. It would take more money than Savannah could raise to bring it up to code. And even then, she couldn't make a living at it. There's no way a theater like that competes with the new multiplex up in Orangeburg. She's just pipe dreaming, Hettie. And folks like you and Rocky shouldn't be talking all over town about how this is going to happen. People miss The Kismet's lights, but the theater is dead."

Hettie started unbuckling the left-hand girth of Wing's saddle. "So," she said after a long moment, "you don't have any pipe dreams?"

Of course he did. Returning to the major leagues was one of them. Having Hettie Johnson Marshall fall head-over-heels for him was another. But he wasn't going to talk about his dreams. That would expose too many raw nerves. "What do my dreams have to do with The Kismet?" he asked instead.

"Nothing. I was just thinking that, after what you did for Lord Woolham, maybe you could help with this Kismet thing, too."

"Hettie, investing in Hugh's business was a good idea. He had a revolutionary, patented improvement to the industrial weaving process that was practically guaranteed to give me a return on the investment. But The Kismet is..." His voice faded out.

"What is it, Dash?"

He sighed. "Well, it's sort of like the Painted Corner

Stables. It's a nice idea but it's never going to make anyone rich."

"You don't need to become rich. You're already richer than anyone else in town."

"That's not the point."

"Isn't it?"

Dash didn't respond. He focused on unbuckling the right side of the saddle. He lifted it off Wing's back, then turned and lowered the saddle and pad to a rack sitting outside Wing's stall.

"Dash, if you really want to change the way folks around here see you, you'll think about this. Last Chance is in the middle of a mini revival. We've got more jobs here than we've ever had before. We've got new people moving in. Those people need a business district that they can be proud of. Not some ghost of ages past. You could do something for this town, too."

He stared at Hettie for a very long moment. If he did this for her, would she change her mind? And if he put himself out there, would she hurt him again?

"Savannah doesn't strike me as the kind of person who has the first idea of how to write a business plan," he said. He knew it was a lame excuse even as the words left his lips.

Hettie bent over, pulled up Wing's front left hoof, and attacked it with her hoof pick. "Well then, you can teach her."

"But—"

"No buts. If we let her leave town without giving her a helping hand, we might never be able to do anything about that eyesore right in the middle of town. This is our chance, Dash, and like it or not you, me, Rocky, and

Tulane Rhodes are the people who have to step up and become the town's economic boosters. Rocky is all for this thing. She's been introducing Savannah around town, and people like her. You should have seen the way she turned things around at the book club last night."

"Of course everyone likes her. That's how she lures people in before she strikes."

Hettie put the horse's leg down and straightened up. She gave Dash a smile that could still melt his heart. "Dash, you need to get over whatever happened between you and that woman when you were children. And besides, it would make me happy if you did this. So, won't you please do it? For me?"

God in Heaven, she looked like the debutante he'd fallen in love with when he was seventeen.

He should walk away. She had hurt him so many times before. Like everyone else he had loved. But Dottie Cox had been right on Monday night. If he didn't do something to make a change, then he would be alone for the rest of his life. And besides, he would do anything for Hettie. He loved her that much.

So he squared his shoulders and looked her right in the eye. "Okay, Hettie. I'll do it for you."

CHAPTER 5

Savannah pulled the biscuits out of the oven and began transferring them to a basket lined with a red-and-white-checked napkin. She loved cooking in this kitchen where she had learned at the elbow of her grandmother. It almost felt as if Granny were standing right beside her telling her how to roll the dough and cut each biscuit.

"Good gracious, that smells good," Miriam said as she shuffled into the room. She was leaning heavily on her cane today.

"Did you have a good nap?"

"I rested." Miriam sat down at the small kitchen table. "I declare, when I opened my eyes I thought, for just one minute, that Sally was still alive."

Savannah looked over her shoulder. "I was just thinking about how close I feel to Granny when I'm cooking in this kitchen. I wish I had a kitchen this big in Baltimore. Of course, a big kitchen would be wasted, since it's just me and Todd most nights. But still."

"Sugar, I thought we'd decided you were staying and reviving The Kismet."

"Bringing The Kismet back to life is more than I know how to do. It's a mess, and I have no money. I don't know what I was thinking. I guess I was just dreaming."

"And when you came here as a child making gravy and biscuits was more than you knew how to do. But you learned. My nose is saying that Sally taught you everything she knew about cooking and, she sure knew more than any other cook in Allenberg County."

"Learning how to cook and reviving The Kismet are different things. The Kismet is beyond my abilities and my means. Dash helped me to see that quite clearly."

"You call that help? So you're just going to give up?"

"What other choice do I have?"

"You could learn what you need to learn. You take it from me, when you stop learning stuff, that's when you get old."

"But I need more than knowledge. I need money."

"That's just your fear talking. Tomorrow I think we need to get Todd registered for school. And then you need to visit Miz Ruby. Once she's done with you, you'll start seeing things straight."

"Miz Ruby? Is she, like, the local banker or something?"

"No, of course not. She's Rocky's momma. You know, the beautician who owns the Cut 'n Curl. I go there every Friday for a manicure, but you need more than that, sugar. Rocky called me this morning, and we both agreed. Ruby will fix you right up. And believe me, when she's done, you'll have a spring in your step. And I'm sure you'll figure something out for The Kismet."

Savannah stifled a laugh. If only it were that easy. "I don't need a makeover."

"Don't you? You're sitting in this kitchen pining away because you don't have a crowd to cook for like your granny did. Sugar, the only way to get a crowd for dinner every night is to find a new husband and have more babies. And believe me, you aren't going to catch that hero you've been searching for if you don't take care of yourself first."

"What hero? What are you talking about?"

Savannah turned away from the pots on the stove and sat down facing her aunt, suddenly concerned. Miriam had a gleam in her eye that hadn't been there before. Savannah took Miriam's knobby hand in hers. The thin, cold feel of Miriam's skin was a little alarming. She was getting up there in years. Was she going senile now that Harry had passed?

"I'm fine. And I'm not senile," Miriam said as if reading Savannah's mind. "All I'm saying is that you need to be looking for a man with an appetite. Just like your grandmother did."

"But I've sworn off men altogether. Greg was a huge mistake. And my recent past is littered with men who were commitment-phobic workaholics, and not very interested in kids."

"Well, I'm sure none of those men was your soulmate. So don't give them any more thought than they deserve."

"Soulmate? Really?"

"Now, sugar, you listen. You want a man like your granddaddy was."

Savannah stroked Miriam's hand. "Men like Granddaddy are hard to find. I thought Greg was like him, but I was wrong." She let go of a frustrated breath. What she really wanted was a man like George Bailey, the protagonist in *It's a Wonderful Life*. And she knew that was impossible, because George Bailey wasn't a real person. Real people were not like the ones in those old black-and-white movies that Granddaddy had taught her to appreciate.

"Savannah, I know you've been hurt. But I also *know* that you're going to find the kind of man you've been searching for. I know it in my bones. It's just not going to be easy to find him. You're going to have to delve beneath the surface."

Savannah stood up and crossed back to the stove to check on the gravy. Miriam was too old to understand. Her great-aunt had been married to one man for more than forty years. Marriages like that were rare. Savannah's marriage had failed in its third year. And Savannah's mother had been unable to keep three different husbands. All in all, it seemed wiser to figure out a way to be independent.

Her cell phone rang. Savannah checked the caller ID. It was Mom. She had been expecting this call for at least a day. She had told everyone in Baltimore that she'd be home by now. So of course, Mom was checking in.

Savannah pushed the talk button and put the phone to her ear.

"Savannah Elizabeth Reynolds, are you insane?"

Uh-oh. When Mom used her full maiden name, it was always a tip-off that one of Mom's rants was headed Savannah's way.

"Hi, Mom, how are you?" Savannah said carefully.

"I'm not good. What's this nonsense about you staying in Last Chance and trying to renovate The Kismet?"

"Who told you this?"

"Todd called me earlier. He apparently borrowed your cell phone when you were in the shower. Savannah, what about Greg? He has a right to see his son, you know."

Great. Her son had tattled on her. It wouldn't be the first time.

She took a deep, calming breath. "Mom, you know and I know that Greg couldn't care less about visitation. It's been months since he's paid any attention to Todd. And then it was just to give him that infernal PSP that he plays all the time. Maybe coming to South Carolina will wake Greg up. I would be happy if that happened. Of course, we both know that Greg is sort of like Dad, and that is probably not going to happen."

"Okay," Mom said on a long sigh. "I'll concede that point. But you don't want to live in Last Chance, and you sure don't want to subject your son to that. I know, I grew up there, and aside from church and football games there wasn't much to do."

"There was the movie theater."

"Right, like that's the height of culture." Mom's voice rose in pitch. "I knew I should have put my foot down when Daddy started filling your head with all those silly ideas about reopening that place. That was *his* dream, not yours. How are you going to pay for a thing like that? And have you any idea about the quality of the schools in that little town? This is a huge mistake you're making. Don't be an idiot."

Savannah looked through the kitchen window at the Spanish-moss-laden oak in the side yard. She remembered the tree house Granddaddy had built for her. It was gone now, but the memory remained steadfast and true.

Why couldn't Todd have a father like that? Why couldn't she have had a father like that? Or a mother who encouraged her to follow her dreams instead of pointing out how hollow they were.

"You know, Mom," she said in a shaky voice, "it would be nice if just once you would support me in the things I want to do."

"I certainly *would* support you if you were opening a business you knew something about, in a city where you might get customers. My goodness, Savannah, you can't be successful in a place like Last Chance."

"When was the last time you came down here?"

"I don't know. Decades. I avoid the place. I don't want you bringing up Todd in that one-horse town."

Before Savannah could counter, Mom rolled on. "And Todd said Dash was there. He told me Dash destroyed his PSP. Really, I can't believe you're letting Todd have anything to do with that man. My God, Savannah, don't you remember the way he treated you as a girl? He's fully capable of abusing Todd. Or worse."

Mom was silent for a moment, obviously letting her arguments take their toll, before she continued, "And I don't think Greg will be wild about the situation after I explain it to him. And you should know that Claire is fit to be tied. How could you turn down her offer to pay Todd's tuition to the Gilman School?"

Something deep inside Savannah snapped. "I turned her down because she wants to turn Todd into a big snob, just like you've become. Just like Greg is. I'm sorry, Mom, but I'm going to stay in Last Chance. Miriam needs a cook. Todd needs the fresh air. And Dash is not a child molester. I may not have approved of his methods, but he did me a huge favor by breaking that idiotic game. Besides, this is *my* life, not yours or Claire's or Greg's. It's mine, and if I want to come live here with Aunt Miriam and Cousin Dash, well then, that's what I'm going to do."

She pulled the phone from her ear and pressed the disconnect button.

"Bravo."

She looked up to find Dash leaning in the kitchen doorway clapping his hands. His fitted cowboy shirt accentuated his broad shoulders and narrow hips. He looked tanned and healthy and incredibly male. The puppy Todd found stood beside him looking up with total adoration on his face.

"I take it that was Aunt Katie Lynne on the phone telling you how to run your life?"

Savannah nodded, suddenly unable to get a word out. How much had he heard of her rant?

"Thanks for telling her off on my account. I've been wanting to do that since I was thirteen, when she called me a bad seed."

Savannah's eyes began to itch. She'd heard her mother's opinion about Dash. In fact, she'd *repeated* her mother's opinion. Everywhere. To everyone. And now that she thought about it, repeating her mother's ugly words had set off the infamous snake incident.

Guilt slammed into her. She hadn't really understood when she was ten. But now, suddenly, it all came back in a rush. She'd been cruel and mean-spirited.

Sort of like Mom.

Savannah took a deep breath and turned back toward her gravy. She needed to get dinner on the table and not think about what had happened in the past or what might happen in the future. Either way it was bad.

She squeezed her eyes shut and prayed for courage—and maybe an investor with a really, really deep pocket.

"Princess, I've changed my mind about The Kismet," Dash said.

She looked over her shoulder. "What?"

"Last Chance needs a movie theater. So I reckon I'm going into business with you."

Dash took one look at the frown on Savannah's face and decided he didn't want to hang around long enough for her to refuse his help. He hadn't considered the complexity of what he'd promised Hettie. It was irksome, to say the least, that Cousin Savannah could stand in the way of his plan to win Hettie back.

He turned and stalked down the hall and out to the front porch, where he found the kid sitting on the front step looking pitiful. His annoyance at Savannah disappeared, replaced by deep empathy for the boy.

"Bad move, calling your grandmother and having her call your mother."

The kid looked up over his shoulder. "Who asked for your opinion?"

"No one. Just sayin'. Your momma got all riled up and told your granny that there was no way in hell she's going back to Baltimore. And I think Aunt Miriam plans to get you registered down at the school tomorrow. So it looks like you're here for a while."

"My father's going to come and get me, just as soon as he has a free weekend where he's not playing in a pool tournament."

Dash felt for the kid. How many times had Dash told himself the same thing? Dash's daddy had been a rodeo rider always promising to come home after the next rodeo on the circuit. It sounded like Todd's daddy loved pool more than his boy. Dash prayed the man wasn't some kind of hustler or gambler.

The puppy crawled into Todd's lap and started washing his face with a darting pink tongue. The kid's lips quivered. "I can't even keep him," he said, stroking the dog's floppy ears.

"Well now, that can be arranged," Dash said as he sat on the porch railing. "Aunt Mim has no objections to the puppy. I have no objections either. And your momma is a guest in this house until she can fix up the apartment above the theater. So she doesn't have much to say about it. I reckon the dog can stay. Which means we need to find him a name. I've been calling him Boulder Head. What do you think of that?"

The corner of the boy's mouth lifted just a little. "That's a stupid name."

"Yeah, but it describes him. It's like someone stuck a head as big as a boxer's on a frankfurter's body. That is one weird-looking dog you got there."

The kid sniffled and stared down at the dog's face for a long time. "He's not weird looking. We should call him Champ."

"Champ?"

"Yeah. He's got a head as big as a boxer's, right?"

"Yeah, I guess. Champ it is, then." Dash paused for a long moment. "And, uh, I went up to Orangeburg this afternoon, and I got you something."

The kid raised his head.

"It's in my car." Dash nodded toward the Cadillac in the drive. "Go on and get it."

The kid hopped down from the steps and ran to the car. He opened the passenger's side door and found the PSP Dash had bought that afternoon.

"You bought me a new one?" The kid looked really confused.

"Yeah I did. See, I probably shouldn't have destroyed your property like that. But I reckon it worked out because, if I hadn't, we might not have found Champ."

"Yeah, I guess."

"And there's another thing. If you're going to be living in this house, you're going to have to do some chores. I was twelve when I came to live in this house, and I was required to mow the lawn. And Uncle Earnest—that would be your great-grandfather—insisted that I work at the movie theater and that I go to church and a bunch of things that I wasn't all that wild about. But there were some good things. I got to help out at Mr. Nelson's stables, and I like horses. And I got to play baseball."

"I hate sports. I'm not any good."

"Have you ever played football?"

He shook his head. "My dad did in college. He was an offensive lineman. He's always talking about how he almost made it to the NFL."

Dash had to stifle a snort of laughter, because the boy was built like an offensive lineman. He might only be twelve, but he was one big child. Dash couldn't wait to introduce him to Red Canaday, the Davis High football coach and one of Allenberg's Pop Warner football commissioners. Dash made a mental note to run up to Orangeburg tomorrow and buy a football.

"Well, maybe you just haven't had much chance to play anything but that video game. So here's the deal. You can play that game in the evening after you finish your homework and walk the dog. I also need your help with some repairs around the house."

He didn't mention anything about tossing a football. He would try to ease into that one slowly, like Aunt Mim had suggested.

"You're kidding, right?"

"Nope. It's all that stuff in order for you to keep the dog and the game. Deal?"

Champ stood at Todd's feet wagging his tail and looking up at the boy like he hung the moon. The dog was more eloquent than Dash could ever be. Todd left the game on the front seat of Dash's car and got down on his knee and petted the dog. Champ responded by wagging his tail and giving the kid a bunch of sloppy puppy kisses.

Dash tried not to smile, but he couldn't help it. He said a quiet prayer of thanksgiving to the angels who looked out for lost kids and abandoned dogs.

Just then a tornado hit the front porch. It came down the hall with fists clenched and blond hair bouncing. "You know I've been standing in the kitchen stirring the gravy, trying to control my temper and figure you out. I give up. What do you mean, I'll have to go into business with you?" Savannah put her fists on her cute little jean-clad hips.

She'd lost the apron she'd been wearing in the kitchen, but her cheeks looked pink, and there was a little smidgen of flour on her navy T-shirt that kind of accentuated her assets, so to speak. Oh, boy, homemade biscuits for dinner. His mouth started watering.

"Well now," he said, leaning his backside into the porch railing and folding his arms over his chest, "I think the words are self-explanatory. You're going into business with me. Actually, I think it's more accurate to say that I'm going into business with you." He smiled.

She gave him her imperious-princess look. "I am *not* going into business with you."

Well, that was predictable. But he wasn't going to give up. Hettie had asked him for his help, and he regarded it as a test. Besides, if Hettie had asked him to swim the English Channel in his birthday suit, he'd have done it with a smile. "Princess, I hate to disagree, but you and I are about to become partners."

"Over my dead body." She turned and stalked back into the house.

"Mom really hates you, doesn't she?" Todd said in a snarky tone.

Yes, she did. And Dash had the feeling that once Savannah made up her mind about something, she wasn't ever going to change it.

CHAPTER
6

On Sunday, Savannah sat in a pew at Christ Church letting memories wash through her. How many times had she heard this hymn? Enough, at any rate, to know the words:

> *Father of all, to Thee*
> *We breathe unuttered fears,*
> *Deep hidden in our souls,*
> *That have no voice but tears;*
> *Take Thou our hand, and through the wild*
> *Lead gently each trustful child.*

The words seemed appropriate, seeing as she had taken the step of severing her ties to Baltimore. On Friday, she'd taken Todd down to the school and signed him up for the remainder of the term. On Saturday, she got herself a part-time job at the doughnut shop. The boxes of stuff she'd shipped before she left had arrived.

She was officially here in Last Chance, and she was staying.

When services ended, she followed Aunt Miriam, Dash, and Todd down the aisle toward the double doors where Reverend Ellis stood wearing his Episcopalian regalia. His sermon today had not been terribly original, but he sure was easy on the eye. That probably explained the big crowd at church this morning. Or maybe it was just being in the Bible Belt. People down here sure did take their religion seriously.

When it was her turn to greet the minister, he took her hand in his. "Welcome back to Christ Church."

His hand was big and warm. His eyes were sky blue. He was handsome. But she was not interested. "Thank you. It was a nice sermon." Actually it had been long and boring, but sometimes a white lie was necessary.

The preacher smiled. His dimples came out. "I guess you'll be wanting to sign Todd up for Sunday School. The kids are pretty busy this time of year, what with planning the Easter hunt as part of our Jubilee." He glanced down at Todd.

Todd looked up with a frown. He opened his mouth.

At that moment, everything went into slow motion. Todd was about to say something embarrassing, or heinous, or rude, or maybe all three. And there was no way to stop him. She could see him taking a deep breath, she could see the wheels turning in his sharp, snarky little brain, but it was too late to slap her hand across his mouth and muffle the words.

She braced herself.

And then Dash jumped right into the fray. He squeezed Todd's shoulder so hard that the kid squeaked instead of holding forth on his opinions about egg hunts and Easter and Last Chance. Dash didn't let go of her son's shoulder.

But he did smile at the minister and say, "Todd would love to attend Sunday School, Reverend. In fact, I think he'd make a great altar boy."

The minister turned his blue gaze on Dash, his soft lips pressing into a small grimace that spoke volumes about the minister's views on Dash Randall. "Dash," he said with a curt nod.

"Bill," Dash replied in a like manner, then looked up at the sky. "Looks like it's going to be another warm day for March, don't you think?"

Without waiting for a response from the minister, Dash pressed forward, still clutching Todd by the shoulder. Miriam and Savannah had no choice but to move on, letting the parishioners behind them have their post-service moment with the preacher.

Savannah didn't know whether to be grateful or furious. "Let him go," she hissed as they stepped down the church steps.

Dash ignored Savannah's request and kept his big hand on her son's shoulder. "Princess, you have no reason to be riled at me. I just saved Todd from screwing up his life." He looked down at the boy. "Son, you don't dis the minister in this town. Not if you're smart."

They reached the landing and headed down the path to the fellowship hall at the back of the church where coffee was being served. Dash finally let go of Todd's shoulder.

The boy stopped before they reached the door. His face was a study in resentment and anger. "Why'd you do that? I'm not going to help anyone put on some lame Easter egg hunt. I'm old enough to know that there is no

Easter bunny. And I'm sure as hell not going to Sunday School."

He said these words loud enough for just about everyone to hear.

Before Savannah could scold him for his poor and untimely choice of words, Dash was all over him.

"Son, you don't use language like that in a churchyard. And you don't say rude things to the minister. And you don't embarrass your mother, or me, or Aunt Mim. Not while you're living with us. Is that clear?"

"I don't want to live with you."

"I get that, but you *are* living with me and you will show some respect. And while you're living here, you will go to Sunday School, whether you like it or not, because that's what the children in Last Chance do. And becoming an altar boy would probably straighten you out some. Do I need to remind you of that little deal you and I worked out the other day?"

Todd's brown eyes widened with surprise, then narrowed with a look of pure disdain. "That had nothing to do with Sunday School. And besides, you are not the boss of me." He looked toward Savannah, expecting her to take his side.

Savannah had to hold her entire body in check as her momma lion instincts kicked in. A part of her wanted to spit right in Dash's eye for talking to Todd that way. But another part of her felt supremely guilty for not having sent Todd to Sunday School in the past. When she was a little girl, she had been required to attend vacation Bible school. Granddaddy had insisted upon it.

She counted to three, took a deep breath, and shot Dash an icy stare intended to put him back in his place.

The issue was not whether Todd needed discipline. She knew her boy was a brat. But she had come here to take charge of him, not to cede the territory to someone else.

She looked down at her son. "Todd, you're grounded. When we get back home, you have to stay in your room, without your PSP, and think about why it's not acceptable for you to use curse words in the middle of a churchyard."

"But, Mom, I don't—" His voice pitched up into a whine she knew very well.

"Not now. We'll talk about this after we get home. And just so you know, *I* went to Bible school when I was a child, and most of the children around here go, too. Now, why don't you help Aunt Miriam into the fellowship hall? Dash and I will be right in." She gave Todd one of her patented motherly scowls. He seemed to understand that further argument was futile.

"C'mon, sugar, I'll bet they have some cookies for a hungry boy like you," Miriam said. Savannah blessed the old woman as she and the boy headed back down the path toward the fellowship hall.

Savannah turned toward Dash, feeling another rush of adrenaline. "That was uncalled for," she hissed.

"No, it wasn't." Dash's intensely blue glaze was filled with irritation.

"Look, Dash, I'm Todd's mother, okay? I would appreciate it if you would respect that. If he needs discipline, I'm the one who should do it."

"Okay, I respect that. But, princess, you need to start acting like his mother. That boy is rude. If I hadn't stepped in, God knows what he would have said to Bill. And if he said something ugly, it would get around until Lillian Bray heard it. And that wouldn't be fun for him. Take it from me. I've been there."

Irritation flared into full-fledged fury. This was precisely the kind of thing she'd left Baltimore to escape. She might take criticism from her mother and mother-in-law because of family ties, but Dash was hardly family. She needed a big jock who got sloppy drunk at honky-tonks telling her how to be a model mother like she needed a root canal.

"Back off, cowboy," she hissed, trying to keep her face as neutral as possible while the parishioners paraded by on their way to fellowship. "Todd is my child. I will raise him as I see fit. You can keep your thoughts to yourself. And don't you ever make a decision for my child again without consulting me first."

His lips narrowed into a thin line, so unlike his usual half smile. "Okay, Savannah, I'll stay out of it. You and the boy just keep away from me, though. I swear, I hear that kid say one more rude thing about Miriam or Last Chance or anything, and I'm gonna take him right out to the woodshed. He's as spoiled as you used to be."

Stupid, stupid, stupid. Dash filled a Styrofoam cup with coffee and took a sip that scalded his tongue. It took a great deal of self-restraint not to let fly with a colorful expletive. But he managed—depriving the blue-haired Lillian Bray, who stood behind the refreshment table, from obtaining another reason to dislike him. Miz Lillian was the chairwoman of the Ladies' Auxiliary, a group that was synonymous with gossipers anonymous. Any right-minded male in Last Chance made sure he put on his best manners when addressing the old hen.

He could chalk one up for his side. Anytime he could thwart Lillian Bray counted as a moral victory for his gender.

He headed off to a vacant corner where he could brood in peace. What on earth had he been thinking, jumping in like that and telling the prissy Reverend Ellis that Todd would attend Sunday School? And where the heck did that last comment about taking Todd to the woodshed come from? Shoot, the boy needed discipline, but not a beating. Dash knew firsthand about the difference. He'd been walloped one too many times as a boy before he'd come to live in Last Chance. Guilt and dark emotions percolated in his gut.

He scanned the crowd of parishioners, and of course his gaze got stuck when it reached Savannah. That demure pink dress and those high heels made her look like Go to Church Barbie. Sex appeal oozed from every pore in her body while she still managed to exude a certain regal quality. After just a few days of living in the same house with her, Dash was having trouble ignoring the fact that she had a winning smile and way of putting most people at ease.

But not him. She did not put him at ease. Especially not at the bathroom door, where he always noticed her long legs and her soft, round curves.

Finding Savannah attractive was confusing and complicated, not to mention annoying as hell. He had a weakness for blondes. And it was showing up right on cue, eighteen months into his recovery. He needed to recognize this lust for what it was—just another old habit he needed to fight.

He watched his cousin as she helped herself to some coffee and then engaged the minister in a conversation. She was flirting with him, and Bill didn't seem to mind. Oh, boy, he could practically hear the gossip. Everyone knew Bill was looking for a wife who was good in the kitchen, and Savannah was some kind of cook.

"Hey, Dash." A sultry voice pulled him away from his speculation about Savannah and Bill. He looked to his left to find Hettie Marshall, dressed in a light purple dress that kind of matched her eyes. How the hell had she snuck up on him? Usually he spent his Sundays watching her every move.

Shame and confusion washed through him. How on earth had Savannah managed to make him forget about Hettie?

"So," Hettie said, "how are the plans coming for the theater?"

He sighed. "Hettie, I'm the last person on earth Savannah wants as a partner. The plans are nowhere. She got a part-time job pushing coffee at the doughnut shop. She's staying, but she's kind of given up on the theater."

"Well, you'll just have to work harder to convince her not to give up. I can't imagine why a woman would turn down an angel like you."

"A what?"

Hettie looked down her beautiful nose at him. "An angel investor. The proper definition is a person with deep pockets who takes on a project because he or she believes in it, not because it will necessarily lead to any significant income."

"But that's just it, Hettie, I *don't* believe in this project." He was tempted to tell Hettie that if she cared so much about The Kismet, *she* could be an angel. But Dash knew that Hettie's late husband had left her with a lot of financial issues.

The truth of it was that Dash wanted to help Hettie, not Savannah. But Hettie was too proud to take his help.

And so was Savannah.

Which put him smack dab in the middle of a conundrum.

"Come on Dash," Hettie wheedled. "I know you. You're a very generous person on the inside. And you love that old theater just like you used to love Mr. Brooks. Can't you see your way through to doing this? For your own self if not for the town?"

He finished the bitter brand of coffee in his cup and then crumpled the Styrofoam. "Hettie, you don't understand. My uncle used to call Savannah 'princess,' and she is just about as proud as one. She won't take my money or my help. She hates me. She always has."

"That's just silly, Dash. I'm sure you can charm her. You've charmed every other female in Allenberg County at one time or another, even me. I'm counting on you."

And with that, the love of Dash's life turned away from him and headed off toward Bill Ellis. She gave Bill a huge smile that practically lit up the room.

Why the hell didn't Hettie ever smile at *him* that way?

Dash knocked on Todd's door, but he didn't wait to be invited in. He opened it and found the kid reclined on his bed, staring off into space. The sight knocked the breath right out of Dash, like a wild pitch to the solar plexus.

"Can I come in?" he asked quietly, knocking on the door frame.

Todd shot him a sullen look. "Are you going to give me a lot of crap about Sunday School?"

The boy turned away, studying the live oak outside his window. He crossed his arms over his chest, and the muscle along his jaw bunched. Dash knew this body language like he knew what most power pitchers would throw on a three-one count.

"I came to apologize," Dash said.

He got no reaction. The boy continued to study the Spanish-moss-draped tree through the big, curved windows.

Dash didn't wait for an invitation. He entered the room and pulled the boy's desk chair over to the bed. He straddled it backward and leaned his elbows onto the seat back. "I really do want to apologize. Saving you from making a life-altering mistake isn't my place. If you want to go out and step in horse shit, son, I'm not going to stop you."

The profanity surprised the boy. Dash figured it would. That's why he'd used it.

"Well, it's too late. Mom told me I have to go to Sunday School, and I have to help with that lame Easter egg hunt. So the damage is done."

Dash worked to stifle his smile. He could almost hear himself in the kid's words. "Well, that's how it goes, sometimes. But hey, look on the bright side—you'll meet other kids there."

Todd wasn't buying his BS for one instant. "Like I care

about the kids here in South Nowhere. Like I would ever be friends with *them*. That is so not going to happen."

Dash took a big breath and wondered if he should ask if Todd had any friends up in Baltimore, but he reckoned the question and the answer might humiliate the kid.

So he headed down another alleyway. "Actually, I came up here because I need your help with something."

The boy's mouth quirked up at the corner. "Yeah, well, I've been grounded. I have to stay here until dinnertime."

"That can be fixed."

The boy frowned. "How?"

Dash smiled. "When your momma sees what you're helping me with, she will forgive you for leaving your room and everything else you've done today. That's how."

"You mean you want me to disobey my mother and leave my room without asking permission?"

Dash nodded. "Yup. That's about the size of it, 'cause if either one of us asked permission right now, we'd get our heads handed to us."

The boy snorted. "That's probably the truth. She's madder at you than she is at me."

"Did she say that?"

"Uh-huh."

"See, that's why I need your help. We're both in the doghouse, and we need to get out because there's nothing worse than having a woman put you in the doghouse. So hop up and put on your oldest jeans."

The boy looked doubtful. "What are we doing?"

"You gotta come with me to find out, but it involves a trip to Lovett's Hardware, some serious power tools, lots of noise, and a little bit of engineering. We can take the puppy, too."

The boy's serious eyes became a window into the workings of his mind. The wheels turned for a few seconds as Todd weighed duty to his mother against the prospects of a real adventure involving power tools. Dash was betting on the power tools winning out.

CHAPTER 7

Savannah rolled the dough for an apple strudel. Thank God for Sunday supper. Cooking kept her mind off her problems.

Miriam sat in one of the old vinyl chairs at the kitchen table keeping her company. "Dash knows his way around a kitchen all right for a man, but he doesn't do roast beef and homemade biscuits and gravy. Not to mention strudel the way Sally used to make it. I tell you, Sally's strudel was the most delicious thing I ever tasted. I can't wait."

Savannah chuckled. "I'm glad you like my cooking." And she hoped Miriam ate more than a few mouthfuls tonight. Earlier this morning, Savannah had had to help her braid her hair. The old woman was losing it, and Savannah was deeply worried.

"Oh, while it's on my mind, you'll need to set an extra place this evening," Miriam said.

Savannah paused the rolling pin as her stomach flip-flopped. She had this horrible premonition that Miriam might be planning on setting a place for Harry.

"Who's coming to dinner?" Savannah invested her voice with a casual air that any right-minded person would see through in a New York minute.

"Bill Ellis."

Savannah turned around to stare at her great-aunt. "Oh, my goodness. You invited the minister to dinner?"

The old woman smiled at her out of a pair of mischievous eyes that looked half a century younger than the woman's wrinkled face. "I most surely did. Sugar, were you even halfway conscious of the way that man looked at you this morning? I declare I had the feeling he addressed the entire sermon directly to you."

Savannah started moving the rolling pin again. "Uh-huh, and as I recall, the sermon was heavily laced with admonitions on the wages of sin. Oh, Heaven help me. The last thing I need right now is a preacher bent on saving my immortal soul. I already have a whole legion of folks with notions about how I should live my worldly life."

"Well, I don't believe that's precisely what he has in mind, although his sermon did wax poetic when it came to the sins of the flesh. I reckon the man's just lonesome for some female companionship."

"Aunt Miriam!" Savannah rolled her eyes in her aunt's direction. "I can't believe you just said that about the preacher."

"Well, he is a man, and he's looking for a wife, and I already know that you think he's cute. The best thing about him is that he has a good appetite. Once Bill tastes that strudel, he'll be back on a regular basis. The man has women all over Allenberg County cooking for him. But I reckon none of them, not even Jenny Carpenter, has Sally's strudel recipe."

Savannah let out a frustrated breath. "Aunt Miriam, we talked about this a few days ago. I'm not looking for a husband. For that matter, I'm not looking for a boyfriend. The last thing I want in my life is some man telling me what to think and what to do and how to be."

"Is that why you've refused Dash's help with the theater?"

Savannah leaned against the kitchen counter, staring down at the dough on Granny's marble rolling board. She didn't have any good answer for Miriam on that score. "I guess so."

"Well, that's just silly. Dash loved Earnest as much as you did. Besides, he has the money, and you can cook. It seems like a partnership that might be successful."

"What does cooking have to do with it?"

"Oh, I don't know. I was just thinking that maybe you could turn The Kismet into one of those dinner theaters where people come for a movie *and* dinner. That way you could cook to your heart's content, and maybe you'd have something that the big multiplex up in Orangeburg couldn't compete with. Because, honestly, your biscuits are amazing."

Savannah turned and stared at her aunt. "That's a brilliant idea."

Miriam smiled. "And as for marriage, honey, you need to get to know Bill. A finer, more God-fearing man I have never met. And I have a feeling about you, and when I get one of my feelings, well, it usually means wedding bells in the future."

"Aunt Miriam, you cannot seriously be trying to match—" The whine of a power saw coming from the general vicinity of the front porch interrupted her.

"Good God, what is that noise?" Aunt Miriam said.

"Stay here, Miriam," Savannah directed as she sprinted down the hallway. The scene on the other side of the front door both pleased and upset her. There stood Cousin Dash in the unseasonably hot March sunlight, leaning over a table saw. He looked like the God of DIY wearing a pair of faded jeans, a tool belt, and not much more. Sweat darkened the band of his ball cap and the waistband of his jeans. It ran in glistening rivulets down his craggy cheeks and across his shoulders. A more masculine sight Savannah had not seen in many years.

Then she got a good look at her equally naked son, whose pale, and somewhat flabby, white skin was beginning to turn lobster red. Todd was not in his room where he was supposed to be. He was down on his knees with a crowbar, prying up the worn-out porch step. His puppy was there with him. Prancing and wagging and being infernally adorable.

Savannah opened her mouth, but before she could fire the first salvo in the continuing battle over the proper way to discipline a preteen, the screen door squealed, and Miriam shuffled out onto the porch. She scowled at Dash and shook a finger at him. "George Dasher Randall, just what do you think you're doing to my porch? You know darn well that your Uncle Harry will have your hide for tearing up the step like that."

"But Aunt Miriam, Uncle Harry is—" Todd started.

"Out helping Bobby Pine with his watermelon harvest," Dash said before the boy could finish the sentence. Savannah watched the man's eyes roll around as he cast his mental net to find some expanded explanation for a watermelon harvest in March. "Um, and Uncle Harry told me he wanted me to fix this rotten step before he gets back."

"He did?" Miriam asked, her dark eyes growing wide. "Do you know what you're doing? Harry can be mighty particular about work done around the house, you know."

"Don't you worry, Aunt Mim. I got a list of instructions written out by Harry. You want to see it?" Dash started in the general direction of the pickup truck in the driveway. He sold his lie like a professional tale teller.

Miriam waved a gnarled hand. "Oh, no, that won't be necessary. But I declare, Dash, you nearly 'bout scared me out of my skin. You should have given me some warning before you started all that banging around. Now if y'all don't mind I'm going to lie down for a spell. Savannah, I told Reverend Ellis that dinner was at six-thirty. Would you call me around five-forty-five so I can get ready?"

Savannah nodded, and the old woman turned and headed back through the doorway.

"Jeez, Mom, she thinks Uncle Harry is still alive," Todd whispered once the door had closed behind the octogenarian.

The three of them stood there looking at each other, suddenly at a loss for words.

"Is that the first time she's done that?" Savannah finally asked.

Dash nodded. "Right after Harry died, she kind of checked out for a little while, but she's never forgotten something that important. She was fine before you got here."

"She's hardly okay. She hasn't been eating well," Savannah said.

"We need to get her to Doc Cooper's. She'll fight us all

the way, though." Dash pressed his lips together. "I think she worries about senility more than anything else, even falling."

"I'll see what I can do. She wants me to go to the Cut 'n Curl tomorrow. Maybe I can get the ladies there to put the idea in her head that it's time for a checkup."

He nodded.

"You should also know that she invited the minister for dinner. I think she's got some crazy idea about trying to match me up with him."

Dash's eyebrow arched. "She told you directly that you and the minister were a match? Really?"

"Well, kind of."

He snorted a laugh. "Oh, boy, the old gals at the Cut 'n Curl will be interested to hear that." He looked at Todd. "We'll have to be on our good behavior."

"Dash, why is Todd out here? He's supposed to be in his room."

"Well, see, I figured that it would be better for him to make himself useful than for him to be up there." He smiled.

Savannah wanted to be angry, but she couldn't pull the trigger when he smiled like that. What was it about his grin that made her own mouth want to curl up? And there was no denying that Todd was helping out for once. He was also getting sunburned, but that was beside the point.

"Todd, did you put on any sunscreen before you took off your shirt?"

She rolled her eyes in Dash's direction. "You know, he's pretty fair, so when you encourage him to take off his shirt, in the future you need to make sure he puts on some sunscreen."

She turned toward Todd. "There's some sunscreen in the bathroom cabinet," Savannah told him. "Go on inside and put some on your face and shoulders."

Todd headed inside, letting the screen door bang behind him with a sharp thwack.

"Okay, I'm braced. You can yell at me now, princess." Dash said.

"I'm not going to yell." She took a big breath. "Thanks for fixing the step. And thanks for including Todd in the effort."

"You're welcome."

He picked up his T-shirt and used it to wipe the sweat from his face. "I bought you a present. I guess you could call it a make-up present. I need to apologize for that stupid comment I made about the woodshed. Todd doesn't need the woodshed. No kid needs that. I figured helping fix the step was a better thing."

She found herself smiling. "Thank you. And your apology is accepted. But you didn't need to get me a present." She paused for a moment, then put her hands on her hips. "This present isn't like that time you gave me a spider in a box, is it?"

He laughed right out loud, the sound surprisingly sexy. "No, ma'am. I am sorry about that spider thing. That was mean. This is a present I picked up this afternoon at the Allenberg bookstore after I picked up the lumber for the step." Without waiting for her reaction, he turned on his heel and headed to the 1970s-vintage pickup in the driveway.

The old vehicle had once belonged to Uncle Harry, and the last time Savannah had seen it, it needed a paint job and some new floorboards. Apparently those needs had been seen to because, like Dash's vintage Eldorado convertible, it sparkled in the Carolina sun.

Dash opened the door and pulled out a plastic bag that bore the name of a bookstore. He jogged back across the lawn and hopped up onto the porch, immediately invading Savannah's space. He raised his right arm above his head and leaned on the porch column, presenting the bag to her with his left. The pose gave Savannah a bird's-eye view of the fine hair that grew in the space between his pectorals. She hauled in a big breath and told herself she needed to look someplace else before she embarrassed both of them.

But looking up into his craggy face had absolutely no impact on her suddenly erratic heartbeat or the butterflies that took flight in her stomach. Now, instead of finding his chest hair fascinating, her eyes fixed on the swirl of stubble that grew around the cleft in his chin. She had to curl her fingers into a fist to resist the temptation to reach out and touch his face.

"You gonna take this gift or leave me standing here feeling like a piece of beefcake?" he said.

His words jolted her back to reality just as she felt the blush run up her cheeks. She dropped her gaze and took his peace offering, grateful to have her hands and her vision occupied with something other than Dash. She reached in the bag and drew out a large-format paperback with a yellow cover. The words *Business Plans for Dummies* in big block letters filled the entire front cover.

Maybe she should be offended, but she *was* a dummy when it came to writing business plans. And besides, Dash was the first person to give her practical help in realizing her dream. A knot of thick emotion seized her by the throat. Oh, Heaven help her, he made her mad and weepy all at once.

She looked up into his face, now softened by that three-dollar crooked smile and those sparkling eyes. His lip was almost healed now. And the shiner was gone.

"Is this part of the town's campaign to turn us into partners?"

"I reckon so. Hettie can be mighty persuasive."

"She was all over me at church about how I should take your money."

"Folks around here refer to her as the Queen Bee, which means she outranks you, princess."

"And you were watching every move she made."

He shrugged. The little rise and fall of his shoulders spoke volumes.

"You have a thing for her, don't you?"

"A thing? Now, there's a word."

She dropped her gaze to the book in her hands. Its title seemed to mock her. "Miriam said the most amazing thing a few minutes ago."

"Really? What did she say?"

"She suggested that I turn The Kismet into a dinner theater. She said it would give me a chance to cook for a crowd. And I would love to cook for a crowd."

"Well, you are a good cook," he said. Then he touched her. Such a small touch—just the pad of his rough index finger under her chin, tilting her head up so she could meet him eye-to-eye. It shouldn't have unleashed such a tsunami of response. She wanted to fall right into his wide, sturdy chest. She wanted to taste the salt of his sweat and know the texture of his skin.

Instead she clutched the book to her chest like a barrier

and closed her eyes. She needed to get a grip. She always fell for good-looking jocks. And they had all disappointed her. Every last one.

"Look at me, Savannah, I have something important to say. And you need to listen."

She opened her eyes as he retreated a bit.

His smile faded as he spoke. "This morning it occurred to me that you and I have a whole lot in common. Neither one of us has exactly lived up to expectations.

"In my case, all the scouts predicted that I'd make it to the Baseball Hall of Fame. But instead I ended up in the Hall of Shame. And you were the golden girl who could do no wrong. You were expected to be anything that you set your heart to be."

"Dash, please. Stop."

He shook his head. "No. You listen. I arrived in Last Chance with a chip a mile high, and I guess I must have left here with the same chip, even though Uncle Earnest tried his best to knock it off some. See, he always expected me to grow up to be more than just a great ball player. He wanted me to be a good, strong, kind man. Uncle Earnest was a man like that. He was the only one in this town who expected anything from me, and I promised myself I would never let that man down. Unfortunately, I ended up doing just that. Many times. And I'm not like him in any way that matters."

She lost the battle against her emotions the minute Dash started talking about Granddaddy. Her eyes filled up with tears, and her throat felt so tight she didn't think she could breathe for the longing Dash raised in her. Oh, God in Heaven, she missed Granddaddy. His absence was like a hole in her life; and it seemed like Dash felt the same way.

She looked down at the book. "So this is about Grand-daddy, then."

"No, ma'am, it's about you." He took a deep breath and let it out softly. "Savannah, if it's your dream to run a dinner theater, then you should pursue it like nothing else in this world, no matter what I say, or your momma says, or what anyone else in the world says. That's what it means to believe in your dreams."

She looked up, losing the battle with her tears. "But it's beyond me. What if I fail—"

"Hush now." His finger brushed over her lips, sealing the doubts inside. "Babe Ruth used to say, 'Never let the fear of striking out get in your way.' I believe no truer words were ever said." He managed a soft smile, so much more intimate than the grin he usually gave her. His thumb rode back over her cheek again, knocking away teardrops. "I declare, Miz Savannah, you look like some kind of refugee from a flour factory. I guess that means there will be pie for dinner?"

Good Lord, what on earth was she doing? His comments about pie pulled her right back into the real world where she had more problems than just a business plan for The Kismet and her growing appreciation for her cousin Dash.

She had a mother who was on the warpath. Ex-in-laws who were unhappy with her. An aunt who was losing her grip on reality. A son who needed discipline and exercise. And if that wasn't enough to keep her busy, Reverend William Ellis—who seemed like the kind of sane and well-adjusted man any right-minded woman should adore—was coming to dinner in less than two hours.

She took a step back, putting much-needed distance

between herself and Dash, breaking the physical connection that had so clouded her senses. She sniffled and wiped the tears away with the palm of her hand. "Look at me. I'm a mess. And I promised myself years ago that I'd never let you make me cry again."

He leaned his shoulder into the porch column, his gaze narrowing. "I can see you're never going to forgive me. And I probably deserve your resentment. You and I are like oil and water. We'd make terrible partners. But that doesn't mean you shouldn't follow your dreams. There are lots of ways to raise money. You just need a business plan first."

And with that, he turned away from her and went back to his table saw. She headed toward the door, opening it and hollering up into the darkness at the head of the stairs. "Todd, where are you? Dash is down here waiting for you. We've got company coming, and the porch step needs to be fixed before dinner."

For some reason, Aunt Mim put Dash at the head of the table. It wasn't exactly a comfortable place for him.

Bill ended up sitting in Dash's regular seat. And then Savannah put the bouquet of bright pink flowers that Bill brought right in the middle of the table. Those bright blossoms mocked Dash the way a sixty-mile-an-hour curveball mocks a serious power hitter. Dash felt like the lesser man. Even if he *was* seated at the head of the table.

He tried to focus on the dinner Savannah had cooked. The food was unbelievably good. But it all turned to ashes in his mouth when Bill took one taste of Savannah's biscuits, closed his eyes as he chewed, and then pronounced: "This is the bread of angels."

Savannah blushed to her hairline, lapping up the compliments like a hungry cat laps milk.

Dash took up his knife and attacked his roast. Damn it. Savannah's biscuits *were* like manna from Heaven. And for some immature reason, Dash didn't want to share them with Bill.

Bill started talking about the building committee down at the church, and how Hettie was helping with their fund-raising efforts. The church was in desperate need of more Sunday School space, what with all the new folks moving into the area because of deBracy Ltd.

Bill was a relentless fund-raiser, and Dash had already contributed generously—because Hettie had asked him to. Dash begrudged the time Hettie spent with Bill. And if he were a smart or devious man, he would probably try to encourage this thing between Savannah and the preacher. Maybe if Bill was busy eating Savannah's sweet buns, Hettie would have more free time. Maybe Dash could screw up his courage and ask Hettie to go out riding with him one afternoon.

He rolled this idea around in his head and decided that it wasn't going to work. For one thing, he hated the idea of Bill and Savannah being together, even though they probably deserved each other. And for another, the idea of asking Hettie to go riding scared the bejesus out of him.

He chewed his roast and pushed these sour thoughts to the back of his mind. He looked up and turned his attention to Todd, who sat to his right. One glance at the kid told Dash that Todd wasn't paying any attention to his dinner or the minister. When that boy ignored his mother's pot roast with gravy and biscuits, it had to be a sign of trouble. The kid was looking down at something in his lap.

At first, Dash thought it might be the dog. But Champ had been left in the mudroom off the kitchen, seeing as the puppy was not quite housebroken.

It was probably the infernal PSP.

Dash speared a bite of potato. He ought to do something about Todd's behavior, but heck, Bill was so boring Dash understood why the kid had tuned him out.

Just then the biggest, most sustained, practically melodic fart erupted from the kid's general direction.

Everyone turned to look at Todd. The kid started giggling, tears in his eyes, his cheeks pink.

"What in the world?" Miriam said.

Another fart erupted. This one was high and tight enough to classify as a soprano fart.

"Todd Avery White, what do you have in your hands?" Savannah descended on her child like an avenging angel. She snatched away the iPhone the kid was playing with.

"Did you take this out of my purse?"

Todd shrugged.

She looked down at the phone, and her face got deliciously pink. It was kind of fetching. "What is this?"

"It's a fart app," the kid said, barely constraining his mirth.

Dash bit his cheek to keep from laughing out loud. He failed, and Savannah rounded on him. "You. You have a lot of nerve laughing at his bad behavior after what you said this morning. Honestly, this is just the kind of stupid and immature thing you used to do." She turned toward Bill. "I'm sorry, Reverend. The two of them are incorrigible."

"The rod and reproof give wisdom: but a child left to himself bringeth his mother to shame," the minister

intoned. It was truly irritating the way Bill could come up with Bible verses on command.

Savannah turned and glared at the minister. Boy howdy, she was some kind of protective mother.

"I don't agree with spanking," she said in a quiet voice. She had told Dash much the same thing this morning. And she'd shamed him with her disapproval. She'd made him think.

And Dash had come to the conclusion that Uncle Earnest's approach was way better than his grandfather's approach had ever been.

Right now, she was giving the minister the same evil eye she'd given him this morning. It evened up the score a little bit.

"Contrary to the prevailing opinions at this table, I *do* believe in discipline," she said in a strong, tough voice. She turned toward Todd. "You are excused from the table, young man. Go to your room and write a sincere apology to the minister. It had better be at least five hundred words."

Dash had to give the kid credit. He didn't argue with his momma. He didn't complain. He simply got up and sauntered from the room. There was an unmistakable bounce in the kid's stride. And he gave the minister the stink eye behind his back.

Good for Todd. Dash didn't much like Bill either.

Savannah watched Todd leave and then turned toward Dash with another royal glower. Dash had no doubt that she would have sent him to his room, too, if she could have gotten away with it. She sat down, offered Bill another biscuit, and asked him to continue his discussion of the church's expansion plans.

An hour later, Dash found himself sitting in his regular easy chair in the living room trying to read the Sunday sports page while Aunt Mim watched Miss Marple solve another murder on *Masterpiece Theater*.

Savannah and the preacher were sitting together out on the porch. Every once in a while, the preacher's high-pitched laughter made its way through the front windows. The preacher had the goofiest laugh Dash had ever heard in his life.

Dash struggled to pay attention to the article he was reading. But he was antsy. He couldn't shake this terrible feeling that Savannah's arrival was pushing him out of the only home he'd ever known. And that scared him. Because he loved Miriam. And losing her would hurt.

Todd came clumping down the stairs. He had a piece of paper in his hand. He sidled up to the chair and leaned on the back. "Any news about the Orioles?"

"Aren't you supposed to be grounded in your room?"

Todd waved the notebook paper in his hand. "I've written my apology."

Dash squashed down the urge to take the note from the boy and read it. "I hope it's sincere."

"I guess."

"You know if you rile up your momma any more, she's going to blame me."

"I noticed. In my apology, I made sure the minister knew that you had nothing to do with the fart app."

Somehow, the boy's words calmed Dash's sudden anxiety. What was it about the kid, anyway? Dash apparently had an ally. It was an odd feeling.

"I really appreciate that, Todd," he said. "And I gotta say, that whole fart app thing was brilliant, if you ask me.

I surely do wish they had had something like that when I was a kid. There were a couple of teachers at Davis High I would have loved to have interrupted."

This earned him a real smile. Something deep inside Dash's chest let go. He smiled back.

"I'll have to show it to you sometime," Todd said. "But for that, I'll need to borrow Mom's phone, and I'm pretty sure she's going to keep it locked up now."

Dash pulled out his own iPhone. "Here. Load that app up for me. I can think of a whole lot of uses for it."

Todd moved around the easy chair and sank down onto the ottoman. Four minutes later, the kid handed back the phone. The screen was lit up with the word "Fartmaster" across the top. There were a dozen colored buttons underneath.

"This one is really tight," Todd said pointing to the fifth button.

"Yeah?"

"It's bathtub bubbles."

Dash started to laugh. He put his newspaper aside. "C'mon." He nodded his head, and he and Todd headed off toward the kitchen. Once they got there, he tested out the aforementioned bathtub bubbles button. He laughed so hard the tears filled his eyes.

Before five minutes were out, they were both giggling like idiots and helping themselves to leftover strudel.

Twenty minutes later, Dash was teaching Todd how to create an armpit fart. And wouldn't you know it, just as the party was about to get truly rowdy, Bill came sauntering into the kitchen looking for his own second helping of strudel.

Unfortunately, there wasn't any left. And it was a little

disturbing to have the minister of Christ Church staring down his blade of a nose at Dash's unbuttoned shirt. Dash slowly but deliberately let go of one long, loud armpit fart.

The minister's mouth thinned.

And that's when Todd came to Dash's rescue. Boy, that kid put on the biggest suck-up routine Dash had ever witnessed. He had some mad skills in that department. And by the time Bill left the kitchen, Todd had convinced the preacher that he wanted nothing more in all the world than to help the Sunday School kids put on the egg hunt during the Easter Egg Jubilee.

And all Dash could think was that the parishioners might want to rethink the idea of letting Todd White hide Easter eggs. He was liable to put them down abandoned wells, just to see the little kids fall in.

Which, as it turned out, was exactly what Dash had done the year he'd helped hide eggs.

CHAPTER 8

Lillian Bray, chairwoman of the Christ Church Ladies' Auxiliary, beamed a smile at Aunt Miriam. Savannah and her aunt were spending Monday morning at the Cut 'n Curl, where Jane Rhodes was diligently working over Aunt Miriam's manicure, while Jane's mother-in-law, Ruby, was working on Savannah's haircut.

Lillian was having a body wave.

"I declare Bill is smitten," Lillian pronounced, "right down to the toes of his tasseled loafers. Miriam, I just don't know how you manage to match folks up year after year. I'd say we'll be hearing wedding bells before the end of the summer."

Savannah stared at Lillian's reflection in the mirror at Ruby's workstation. Lillian's hair was a mass of body-wave rollers. And even though she had a magazine in her hands, the woman had shown no interest in actually reading it. Planning the preacher's wedding seemed to be much higher on her list.

"So, my dear," Lillian continued as she met Savannah's gaze in the mirror, "we all want to know everything that transpired last night when Bill came to call. I declare that man was nervous as a kitten when he stopped by and asked if he could cut some of my camellias for you."

"We were sure they came from your garden, Lillian," Aunt Miriam said. "Weren't we, Savannah? They were such a pretty pink."

Savannah wasn't sure of any such thing. In fact, she didn't even know those flowers had been camellias. But she forced a fake smile to her lips and said, "Oh, yes, we certainly did think they came from your garden, Ms. Bray. They were stunning."

Savannah had already figured out that Lillian Bray was a person she didn't ever want to cross.

"So, what's it like being courted by such a wonderful specimen of southern manhood?" Lillian asked.

"Well, he has a very unique approach," Savannah said politely, thinking that she'd been more titillated watching paint dry on a wet afternoon. He'd actually put his arm around her at one point when they sat on the porch last night, and she'd felt not one iota of reaction. In contrast, Dash made her body parts pucker when they passed each other in the hallway. Her libido had definitely emerged from its cocoon. And right on schedule. Jeremy had dumped her about six months ago. And of course, her libido had a thing for jocks.

Or maybe it was just the way Dash exposed his chest on a regular basis. It was hard to ignore an athletic body like that. She really needed to take him aside and explain that a robe would be appreciated. But then, if she did something like that, he would know she'd noticed his naked chest and manly butt.

And that would be humiliating.

"I'm sure he is the perfect gentleman," Lillian said, and Savannah had to force herself to think about Bill and not her kissing cousin. Because Dash was not a gentleman. He was complicated and well built, but he wasn't nice. She thought about the way he'd laughed at Todd's dinner table stunt. She thought about how he'd looked yesterday all sweaty and naked. These thoughts sent blood rushing to her cheeks in an amalgam of irritation and lust.

"Savannah?" Miriam seemed determined to help her keep her mind on this conversation.

"Oh, yes, quite gentlemanly," she said a bit breathlessly.

"My goodness, look at the girl blush," Ruby said as she fussed with Savannah's hair.

"So, he's very romantic, is he?" Lillian asked on a sigh.

"Well, no, I'd say he was very serious."

"My goodness, did you hear that, girls? It's just so like Bill, isn't it? Such a spiritual man." Lillian tittered.

"I'll bet he quotes all the romantic parts of Song of Solomon," Ruby said, her eyes smiling at Savannah in the mirror. There was something wise in Ruby's eyes, like maybe the hairdresser knew Savannah was merely sucking up to Lillian.

"Well, he does know his Bible, but then you'd expect that," Savannah said. And, really, that quote from Proverbs about using the rod had been over the top. Surely Bill Ellis wasn't one of *those* ministers who exhorted his flock toward corporal punishment.

Aunt Miriam waded into the conversation. "He called Savannah's biscuits the bread of the angels. I think that's from one of the Psalms, isn't it?"

"Well, that's a very positive thing," Lillian said. "I mean the man appreciates good home cooking. Just look at the way he's been running after Jenny all these years."

"I wouldn't say he's running after her, Lillian," Ruby said. "I don't think Jenny would be that hard to catch if he was serious about her."

"Of course he isn't running after Jenny; she's a Methodist. And besides, he has supper regularly with half a dozen ladies in town, including Hettie, and Hettie couldn't cook her way out of a carryout bag. Jenny isn't Bill's soulmate," Miriam said.

Everything stopped. All the women—Ruby, Lillian, and Jane—turned to stare at Miriam. "You know something about the preacher's soulmate?" Jane asked.

"Well of course. Bill needs to be looking for a woman who is active and useful. Someone with a sense of humor and the ability to make his limited paycheck go a good, long way."

Everyone turned and looked expectantly at Savannah. A little uncomfortable giggle percolated from her middle right out of her mouth. "What?" she said on the laugh. "Just because I know how to put a good meal on the table without breaking the household budget doesn't mean I have any special qualities."

Lillian's mouth curved up before she said, "Oh, praise the Lord. At last. Thank you so much, Miriam."

Savannah must have let her confusion show. "Huh?"

"Honey, don't you know that your aunt has a gift?" Ruby said as she patted Savannah's shoulder. "What she joins together never comes apart. You take me and my Elbert. We weren't exactly a match anyone would have expected. But we've been so happy together. And you could say the same for dozens of folks here in town."

"Including me," Jane said, "and all of Ruby's children. Heck, she matched Stone up twice."

Savannah shifted her gaze from lady to lady and wondered if everyone in Last Chance was nuttier than Granny's fruitcake. But before she could say another word, Ruby asked, "So what did your aunt tell you to be looking for?"

"Uh—"

"A man with an appetite, among other things," Miriam supplied.

"Well, that settles it," Lillian said. "Bill fits that description to a T. Congratulations, honey. I'm sure you two will be happy together."

Thelma Polk delivered the gossip to Hettie before the noon hour was finished. Hettie sat at her late husband's desk at the Country Pride Chicken corporate office and tried, without much success, to regain her composure.

She told herself that she didn't personally care that Miriam Randall had finally made a forecast for Bill. She wasn't interested in Bill. She and Bill were just friends. They had been friends for a long time—since, well, before Jimmy was killed.

She wasn't jealous in the least. She had sworn off romance of all kinds.

She stared down at the well-thumbed copy of *Pride and Prejudice*. Well, maybe not all romance. The make-believe romances were fine. Real romances were simply disasters waiting to happen. In that one way, she and Nita

Wills agreed. The real world didn't have many happy endings.

Not that she was all that experienced in love. She'd had exactly one romance in her life—with Dash Randall—when she'd been sixteen. The affair had not turned out well. It had cost her virginity, not that losing it had been terribly traumatic. But she hadn't counted on falling *out* of love with Dash so quickly. She hadn't counted on Dash falling *in* love with her. Her dalliance with Dash was supposed to be an adventure. But it had turned into a millstone around her neck.

No, she wasn't at all concerned that Bill would soon be married to someone.

She just didn't want that person to be Savannah White. If Savannah married Bill, she would probably give up her quest to revive the theater. She was just the sort of wholesome, pretty, churchgoing woman who would give up everything for a man. Heck, Hettie had been exactly like that when she was twenty. And Mother had encouraged her right into that role.

She thought about that pretty pink dress Savannah had worn to church. She even looked like a minister's wife. It made Hettie downright queasy to learn that Savannah was also one heck of a good cook. And really, Bill lived for good food. Savannah would love cooking for him. He would want to keep her in the kitchen—probably barefoot and pregnant.

A frisson of emotion coursed through her. She wasn't even sure what she was feeling. She propped her hand on her chin. She needed to do something about this situation. Last Chance needed that theater more than Bill needed a pregnant wife. Hettie needed to head off this marriage, and get Dash off his backside.

This was an emergency.

It was time for the Queen Bee to actually do something. So she picked up the phone and called Lady Woolham.

"Rocky, we've got a big problem."

"We do?"

"Yes, we do. Savannah can't marry Bill."

"Why not? They're perfect together."

"Because if Savannah marries Bill, she'll give up on the theater."

"Oh. Well you do kind of have a point. I can't see Bill married to a person who owns a theater. But from what I've heard from Dash, the theater is in such bad shape it's almost not worth trying to fix up."

"Now, see, that's the problem right there. Dash is being difficult."

"He's always difficult," Rocky said. "It's one of his most charming traits. He's difficult with a crooked smile."

Hettie let go of a frustrated sigh. "I'm only saying that he has the money to fix that place up, but he seems to be less than enthusiastic about helping me out this time."

"Really? That would be a first. Maybe there's hope for him, bless his heart."

"Rocky, that was mean."

"I'm sorry. But you have to face it, Hettie. It would be good for him—and you—if he could move on."

Hettie swiveled in her chair and stared through her office window, her brain suddenly going into overdrive. "Rocky, that's it. That's the solution."

"What's the solution?"

"We need to get Dash and Savannah together."

Silence beat on the phone for a few seconds. "Hettie,

honey, that is never going to happen. Dash and Savannah hate each other."

Hettie turned and stared at the well-thumbed copy of *Pride and Prejudice* sitting on her desk. "So what? Elizabeth Bennet hated Mr. Darcy, and look where they ended up."

"Hettie, this is real life."

"Does she really hate him *that* much?"

"Oh, boy, does she ever. And I can't blame her. He put a snake in her bed when he was like thirteen."

"And she still holds that against him? Really? He's not the most mature guy in the world, but he's definitely older than thirteen."

"Yeah, and he's a recovering alcoholic who screwed up his baseball career. I love Dash like a brother, but I'm not entirely sure that he's great boyfriend material. And besides, I wouldn't do that to Savannah. She's an old friend. I think we should focus on the business at hand. There's another way to help her get The Kismet off the ground."

"Oh?"

"Sarah and Lark have cooked up an idea. They want to create a nonprofit development corporation to revive the downtown district. Sarah told me just last night that she and Tulane are interested in Savannah's project. Tulane's racing career has taken off. He's almost as rich as Dash."

"Well, hallelujah."

"And I'm really glad you called. Because Sarah and Lark are at the point of forming a board of directors, and they asked me to ask you if you were interested in being a member."

"Of course I am. I'm flattered. But I don't know that I can make much of a contribution." She stared at the spreadsheets on her desk. There was a lot of red ink on those financial statements.

"Hettie, don't sell yourself short. Maybe you can't give money right at the moment, but if we're going to form a group of young gals in this town, you have to be one of them." Rocky's voice sounded warm.

"Young gals?"

"No one wants to be part of an old-gals network, Hettie. We're all young. And we're going to be different from the Ladies' Auxiliary."

The Last Chance grapevine was notorious for circulating rumor, innuendo, and factually incorrect information. But this time, the rumor mill had been accurate.

Dash stood just inside the door of the Red Hot Pig Place, sucking in the aroma of Earl Williams's Carolina-style barbecue. He hadn't really expected to find his objective here. After all, the Pig Place wasn't the sort of restaurant where a corporate CEO, a Pulitzer Prize–winning photographer, a marketing wizard, and a baroness usually dined. Especially if they were all women.

But this was Last Chance, and strange things often happened in this town. Yep, the girls were definitely up to something. They huddled around one of the red-and-white-checked tablecloths, a pitcher of sweet tea sitting between them. Hettie had her back toward the door. Sarah Rhodes, the wife of NASCAR driver Tulane Rhodes, was punching something into a smartphone. Lark Rhodes, the wife of Allenberg's sheriff, was listening intently, while Rocky was doing most of the talking. As usual.

Dash sucked down a deep breath and told himself that facing these women was not nearly as intimidating as facing a ninety-seven-mile-an-hour fastball with lateral movement. Dash had been known to knock fastballs a long way.

These women couldn't throw worth a damn, but at least one of them sure knew how to play hardball. He had this horrible feeling he was about to strike out with the one woman he wanted more than anything.

But he was determined to see this through. So he squared his shoulders and marched across the room.

"Evenin', ladies," he said, tipping his Stetson. He'd worn the cowboy hat because it was black and looked a little more professional than one of his baseball caps. "Y'all mind if I join you?"

Four pairs of eyes looked up at him, displaying a range of emotions.

"Dash, what a surprise," Hettie said.

He didn't wait for a gold-plated invitation. He pulled a fifth chair from an adjoining table and sat down. "So I hear y'all are annoyed at me and have decided to take matters into your own hands."

"Where did you hear that?" Hettie asked. Danged if she didn't sound exactly like a Queen Bee.

Rocky's cheeks immediately turned pink. "I'm the guilty one," Rocky said. "I told Clay, and he told Jane, and Jane told Lizzy, and I'm guessing that Lizzy mentioned something to you, Dash?" Rocky's eyebrows arched.

"Yup, that pretty much sums it up. Did you plan it that way, darlin'?" he asked.

"Of course I did. Everyone knows Clay is incapable of keeping a secret."

"You could have called me directly, you know." He said this to Hettie.

Hettie didn't respond.

Instead, Rocky shrugged and said, "I know. But I promised Hettie that I wouldn't tell you about this meeting. So I used the tried-and-true Rhodes-family method of communicating important information to the community at large. That way I had plausible deniability."

Sarah shook her head. "Rocky, you spent way too much time working for a politician, you know that?"

Dash turned his gaze on Sarah. "So it's true, then, Tulane is interested in investing in the theater?"

Sarah picked up her smartphone and tapped it a few times. "Well, I don't know specifically. I'd have to see the numbers. But Tulane and I have been talking about creating a foundation that could invest in Last Chance. I've just sent you an e-mail with some ideas we've been roughing out for something he calls the Last Chance Development Corporation." She glanced at Rocky and then Hettie. "I know Tulane would love to have your support on this."

Dash reached into the breast pocket of the blue blazer he almost never wore anymore now that he didn't have to meet any kind of team dress code. It was kind of ridiculous to wear a sport coat to the Pig Place, but these ladies meant business, so he'd dressed for the part. He pulled out some papers and handed them around. "Well, since you've brought the topic up, I would like to be involved with this new organization."

"You would?" Hettie seemed surprised.

"Yes, but only at arm's length, darlin'. I don't think

I could stand being on a board of directors. Especially being the only dude on a board of directors." He smiled.

"What kind of support did you have in mind?" This from Lark, who was very much like her husband, the sheriff. She didn't say much; she just observed.

"The handout has an estimate of costs associated with the theater project. I've done a survey, and the structure has some serious problems. To bring it back, we'll have to replace the seating, the sound and projection systems, and the roof. It probably needs some additional work to bring the building up to fire and ADA standards. And we'll need to add a kitchen."

"A kitchen?" Lark asked.

He shrugged. "Savannah wants to turn it into a dinner theater. She needs the biggest damn kitchen we can squeeze into the place.

"I made a rough guesstimate of the amount we'd need to do all that, and an equally back-of-the-envelope analysis on the theater's likely profit and loss. For that, I did some research on other theaters that have been rescued by nonprofit organizations. Most of them lose money. You'll find all of that in my handout."

He gave Sarah a hard stare. "So if y'all are in this for a profit, you need to rethink. The Kismet is going to be the biggest money pit this side of the Mississippi. The good news is that Savannah owns the building free and clear. So she's got some collateral. You could minimize some risks by insisting that she take out a mortgage. But it would have to be pretty small, otherwise she'll have a long-term problem meeting the payments."

Hettie's violet gaze bored into him. "Did you come here to talk us out of this project? Because—"

"No, Hettie, I came here to talk sense. Dollars and cents. You were right last Sunday. I *would* like to see the old place lit up again, but we have to face the fact that it's never going to be a moneymaker. And Savannah may know how to make biscuits that are Heaven's bread, but she doesn't know crap about business."

"She can learn," Sarah said. "We can teach her."

"I'm sure she can learn. And I'm sure *you* can teach her. But Savannah isn't interested in learning anything from *me*. And she sure as shootin' isn't interested in taking *my* money. She's prejudiced against me, and for good reason."

"Dash, if that's the case, why did you come here tonight?" Hettie asked. "Because it sure does seem like you're spouting nothing but negativism."

Dash leaned forward a little bit. "I'm just speaking the cold, hard truth. And here's another truth—I'm prepared to put a couple of million dollars into this development corporation y'all are dreaming up, but please don't call it the Last Chance Development Corporation because that would be a stupid name."

"A couple of million?" Sarah's hazel eyes lit up.

"Yes, ma'am, but I have a requirement that the corporation, whatever you call it, gives Savannah at least five hundred thousand dollars for the theater renovation."

"Give her the money?" Sarah said.

"Yes, ma'am," Dash replied.

"She's going to know the money came from you," Rocky said.

"She won't if you keep your mouth shut about it. And that means not telling Clay a thing about it." He gave Rocky a meaningful look.

"Are you asking us to lie to her?" Hettie said.

"Hettie, do you want the theater renovated or not? Because if you want it renovated and you want me to pay for it, then it's got to be done on the QT. I'm only trying to do what you asked me to do, you realize that, don't you?"

Hettie's gaze didn't soften one iota. He'd come in here with all his flags flying, determined to be all she wanted in a man, and here she was arguing with him.

"Half a million dollars? You think she'll need that much?" Hettie asked.

Dash shrugged to hide the disappointment that almost overwhelmed him. What the hell did he have to do to please Hettie, anyway? "The structure needs work," he said through his clenched teeth. "I want Savannah to have enough money to hire an architect who could preserve the history of the building. I don't want to lowball this. I want her to have the means to do it right."

"That's really nice, Dash, doing this for your cousin, even though you don't get along," Sarah said.

"I'm not doing it for my cousin." He glanced at Hettie, whose expression remained utterly neutral.

He was a fool. He couldn't buy her love for any price. And he couldn't earn it either. Hettie was never going to love him the way he loved her.

The truth should have devastated him, but it didn't. It was just one more truth he had to soberly face as a part of his recovery.

He couldn't win her love, but he could make atonement, especially for his failure to live up to the expectations of Aunt Mim and Uncle Earnest. The kink in his gut eased, and a sense of purpose replaced it.

There were other, better reasons for him to help Savannah revive The Kismet.

"I cared a lot about Earnest Brooks," he said. "And I know he would appreciate it if I helped his granddaughter. I'm doing this for him. You could say this is sort of like one of my twelve steps."

CHAPTER 9

Four days later, Savannah and Todd sat at the kitchen table, doing their homework together. Todd was working on social studies. Savannah was working on her business plan.

Todd let go of a big sigh. "I don't know why I need to learn about South Carolina history. It's not like I'm going to live here for that long. Dad is going to come any day now, and Champ and I will be out of here."

Savannah didn't rise to the bait. Todd had made it abundantly clear that he hated almost everything about Last Chance, except for the dog. He hated his new teachers at the middle school. He hated having to do chores around the house. He whined incessantly about everything, especially the fact that Bill Ellis was coming to dinner every other night.

Savannah felt like whining about that, too. But Miriam kept inviting the preacher. And Bill kept coming even though Savannah had done everything in her power to discourage him. Maybe she should switch shifts at the doughnut shop so she wouldn't be available for supper.

Of course, then she wouldn't be able to cook for the family either. She didn't like that idea. Not one bit. She loved having a crowd to cook for.

Todd turned back to his textbook, and she continued to work on putting together an estimated profit and loss statement. As she punched numbers into her cell phone's calculator, she remembered why she had flunked math so many times.

She was just no good at this stuff.

Just then the phone buzzed to life. The caller ID screen flashed, and Todd saw it before Savannah could send the call to her voice mail.

"It's Grandmother." He squinted at her. His look was a dare that Savannah couldn't pass up. No way she was showing Todd how much his paternal grandmother scared her.

So she sucked it up and answered the call. "Hey."

"My God, you've been there for two weeks and already you sound like a hick." Claire White's clipped voice came over the line. Claire would never sound like a hick. She had proper diction. Claire had gone to the best finishing schools and then to Barnard College. She had married Daniel White, a Harvard grad and a high-powered attorney.

Savannah's defensiveness climbed like the mercury on the porch thermometer on a hot day. The Whites had always looked down on her. They had challenged her abilities as a wife, a mother, and a human being. She wiped her suddenly sweaty palms on her jeans. "Hello, Claire. What can I do for you today?"

"You can come back where you belong."

She cast her gaze over Granny's wonderful kitchen.

She felt more at home in this room than she had ever felt anywhere.

"I've decided to stay here to look after my aunt. She's getting up in years. You and Daniel are welcome to visit anytime." There, she had spoken in a cool and calm voice even though Todd was staring at her as if she were the worst mommy in the entire universe.

"Now, Savannah, you can't be serious. We're expecting you home next week. Remember, Todd has an interview with the Gilman School. You don't want to deprive your son of something like that, now, do you?"

Savannah gripped the phone a little tighter and counted to three. "Todd isn't going to the Gilman School next year."

"But it's the best school in Baltimore."

"Todd won't be living in Baltimore."

Todd slammed his book closed and stood up, knocking over the kitchen chair in the process. He gave Savannah one of those dramatic preteen looks and then marched out of the room. A moment later she heard the screen door slam.

"Now, Savannah, see here. Greg went to Gilman. Daniel went to Gilman. Your son is going to go to Gilman. There is no debate on this topic."

"Well, he can't go to Gilman if he's living in South Carolina."

"Greg is not going to be pleased about this."

Ha! Greg wouldn't give a rat's behind about any of this. Greg had hated every minute at Gilman and had rebelled when his father wanted him to go to Harvard. Greg had wanted to play football, and he'd eventually ended up at University of Maryland on a football scholarship, thereby depriving his parents of the ability to control him.

When Savannah had first met him, he'd been a barrel of fun. But that hadn't lasted, had it? He'd gotten sullen when he didn't make it all the way to the NFL. He'd eventually gone to law school, and now her ex was too busy screwing his twenty-two-year-old paralegal to care about anything his parents or his ex-wife wanted.

"Savannah, are you listening to me?" Claire said after several beats of silence. "You cannot be seriously thinking of enrolling Todd in public school."

"I've already done it."

"In rural South Carolina?"

"Well, that's the general idea, Claire. I'm going to settle here, and Todd is going to live with me and go to school. You tell Greg that, if he wants a relationship with Todd, I'm more than willing to speak with him. But Claire, your son has not even spoken to Todd in more than three months." Savannah's heart rate spiked, and every muscle tensed. She was suddenly very angry, and she hated the way it felt.

The silence stretched into what seemed like an eternity. "There is no need to be tart with me, young lady. Your mother and I are in total agreement. You can't deny Todd this opportunity. He's a bright boy. Just think of the connections he will make. Gilman is one of the best schools in the nation."

Savannah's stomach churned as the anger turned to anxiety. She looked down at the legal pad where she was struggling to put together a business plan. She had to be crazy. Maybe she was being selfish for no reason at all. Gilman was a great school. Todd would be accepted regardless of his grades because he had a family tree filled with alums. Maybe she should reconsider.

She stood up, righted the overturned chair, and then moved to the window. She pulled aside the curtain. What met her gaze changed everything in an instant.

Todd was in the back yard throwing a Frisbee for Champ to chase. He didn't look angry anymore. He was smiling. He was happy. And then to her surprise, the Frisbee came flying back at Todd. He had to jump up to catch it. His cheeks were red, but there was a spark in his eye that hadn't been there before.

A second later, Dash came into view. He was carrying a football under his arm.

"Aren't you going to say anything?" Claire said. It was amazing that the woman had remained so quiet for so many moments. No doubt Claire thought she'd scored a bunch of points.

"Yes, Claire, I do have something to say. There are more important things than getting my son into the best school in the mid-Atlantic. There are lessons he can learn here that are just as important." Her heart dropped back into its proper place, and a deep sense of rightness settled over her.

"Savannah, don't be stupid. You know good and well that you and Greg have a custody arrangement. He could demand that you bring Todd back."

Boy, that would be the day. Savannah refrained from saying that out loud. Instead she took a big breath and spoke in the calmest voice she could muster. "Claire, I have no desire to keep you away from your grandson. You're welcome to visit him here if you like. But I'm not coming back to Baltimore. If Greg wants time with Todd, he needs to call me and we can work something out."

"Well," came Claire's clipped voice on the other end of

the line, "we'll see about this. Savannah, you don't want to cross me."

"You can't scare me, Claire. I've made up my mind."

"You'll be sorry." The line clicked dead.

Claire wasn't finished making threats and stirring up trouble, but Savannah refused to worry about it.

Because right now Savannah's kissing cousin was doing something Todd's father had never, ever, done for him.

He was playing catch in the backyard.

Dash leaned back against the porch rocker and glanced at his watch. It was just after nine o'clock. Before Dottie had banished him, this was the time he usually headed down to The Spot to drown his sorrows. Of course, a man could hardly drown much in a glass of Coca-Cola, but hanging out at Dot's and listening to the Wild Horses on a Friday night seemed safer than hanging out here where he was likely to bump into Savannah and her long-stemmed legs.

He'd been noticing those legs a whole lot more these last few days, since his meeting with the girls on Monday at the Pig Place. He wasn't exactly sure why, but he'd burned a bridge that night. He'd even talked about it yesterday at the AA meeting. He'd sworn off Hettie like he'd sworn off booze. And he felt much better. Hettie had been an addiction, too.

This realization should have underscored the danger of feeling any kind of attraction for any woman. It should have made him comfortable with the advice they always gave newly recovered alcoholics—to stay away from romantic entanglements.

It was good advice because Dash was starting to feel as if he might have swapped one addiction for another.

The warning signs were clear. He had carefully timed Savannah's morning routine and rearranged his own to ensure that he'd meet her at the bathroom door every morning.

And then he would race through his shower and shave so he could have a few minutes alone with Savannah drinking the magic elixir she made in Aunt Mim's coffeemaker.

Boy howdy, she could make a good cup of coffee. Every morning, she filled up a thermos for him to take up to the stable.

Savannah wasn't supposed to be nice like that. She wasn't supposed to be thoughtful or take care of people. She was supposed to be a spoiled and self-centered brat of a princess.

The fact that she was genuinely sweet and could also cook like nobody's business explained why Bill Ellis showed up for supper on alternate weekdays. And that made Dash grumpy as hell. Especially since Aunt Mim insisted that Bill and Savannah were a match made in Heaven.

Dash rocked a little harder as the rumble of distant thunder rolled across the humid night. Aunt Mim was never wrong about who belonged with whom. Hettie was not for him. And Savannah wasn't for him either.

There was nothing worse than being addicted to something you couldn't have. But that was the theme of Dash's life.

He needed to fight this thing with all his might. He owed it to Aunt Mim and Uncle Earnest.

• • •

Savannah took a giant breath and told her heart to stop racing and her hands to quit sweating. Neither heart nor palms listened.

Is this fear of rejection, or something else?

Definitely something else. Like the jolt of female reaction she felt every morning when she bumped into Dash at the bathroom door. At least he had taken to wearing a robe in the mornings instead of parading around in his skivvies. Still, the robe only came down to his knees, and she found his calves and long toes utterly fascinating. Not to mention the dark shadow of beard on his cheeks, or his sleep-tousled hair, or the little V of chest the robe revealed.

She gripped her twenty-three-page business plan with its charts and estimate of costs and told herself that Dash was her annoying cousin. Not anything else, except a man with money who might help her realize her dream.

If she asked nicely.

She shoved that thought aside. She didn't want his money. She just wanted his advice. Then she would go get her own money.

She closed her eyes for a moment and prayed to the Lord that He would give her strength to see this through. Then she added a plea for a well-heeled angel, or maybe just a sympathetic mortgage broker.

Dash was pushing up from his rocker when she finally came through the door. Clouds obscured the moon, and the only illumination came from the yellow porch light that made his eyes look green.

"Hey," he said in that southern drawl that sounded like it came from deep within the earth.

"Hi. I, um...you got a minute?"

His mouth quirked; he didn't want to give her any time at all. He didn't like her, and she was willing to admit that she had given him ample reason for feeling that way.

"Sure, princess, what's up?"

She hated it when he called her that. It reminded her of the mean things she'd done when they were kids. And besides, she didn't want to be a princess. She wanted to be a businesswoman. That single word seemed to sum up all the barriers she faced. With him, and herself.

She forced her hands to stop shaking. If she wanted him to respect her, she needed to respect him. It was pretty simple.

"Well, first of all, I'd like to thank you for what you've been doing for Todd."

He chuckled. "Don't tell me you've changed your opinion of me. I could have sworn that, just a few days ago, you thought I was a terrible role model for the boy."

Touché. The man sure knew how to cut right to the heart. "I'm sorry, Dash. You're right. I wasn't so sure about you. But thank you for getting him the football. He can be so difficult about exercise and, well...thanks. If you let me know how much—"

"Shoot, Savannah, you don't have to pay me back for the football. The way I see it, I'm doing Davis High a favor. That kid has talent he doesn't even know about." He grinned.

She felt the corners of her own mouth turning up. What was it about his smile that was so infectious? She cleared her throat and started again. "Well, anyway, thanks, and thanks for playing catch with him and for goading him into doing his chores."

"Shoot, Savannah, that stuff isn't any different from what Uncle Earnest did for me when I first got here. I was twelve, too. And mighty unhappy."

Lightning flashed, and thunder rolled, as a knot of emotion seized Savannah by the throat. A princess-sized load of guilt spilled through her. She had resented his appearance in her special world. She had been jealous of every moment Granddaddy spent with him.

She looked up into his eyes, noticing the sadness in them. A rush of maternal feeling coursed through her. Would a hug be so bad? The man needed a big hug. He needed someone to fix the hurts that he still carried around with him.

She stopped herself just in the nick of time. Throwing herself at Dash would be a huge mistake. Physical contact of any kind—even an innocent and well-deserved hug between kissing cousins—was likely to lead to places neither one of them wanted to go.

"I…I'm sorry about what happened when we were kids," she said.

He shrugged. "Apology accepted." He pushed away from the railing. "Now, if you don't mind, I was on my way to Dottie's for a long, cool one." He looked up at the sky. "Looks like we're in for a spring storm."

He headed toward the porch steps and was halfway to the garage before she remembered her business plan. She followed after him, the wind whipping her ponytail as she left the protection of the porch.

"Hey, Dash," she yelled to his retreating back.

He stopped and turned around, the flare of lightning illuminating his craggy face. "Darlin', it looks like it's about to pour down buckets. Get on back to the porch."

She rushed up to him, a little breathless. "I, uh." She took a couple of deep breaths.

"What?"

She held out the bound papers. "I finished my plan," she announced, feeling a rush of joy that seemed out of proportion to the moment.

He smiled and took the document just as the skies opened up.

"Oh, crap," he said as he put the precious document over his head as a shield. They turned and ran back to the porch, but by the time they reached its shelter, the rain had soaked them both.

"I told you we were about to get a gully washer," Dash said as he ran his long fingers through his hair, "but you never did listen to me, princess." He turned away from his contemplation of the storm and backed into the post. The porch light sparked in his eyes as he looked down at the soaked business plan and then up at her. "I hope you had this on a computer," he said.

She nodded as he tossed the soggy document to the seat of a nearby rocker. "I'll print up another one and have it for you in the morning," she said. "I would appreciate your thoughts on what I did right and what I screwed up."

One of his dark brows arched just a little. It balanced out the little curl at the corner of his mouth. "Okay."

And suddenly there wasn't much else to say. They stood like frozen statues listening to the rain drumming on the tin roof above them, the rumble of thunder, and the hiss of lightning.

The self-conscious silence lengthened as Savannah's gaze journeyed from his eyes with their water-spiked lashes, to his tangled damp hair, to the small drop of water that poised on his earlobe. And then farther down, to the shirt that clung to his chest.

When her gaze returned to his face, the muscles along his jaw were bunching. His eyes darkened, but she told herself it was just a trick of the moonless night.

Her womanly core knew different. Quivery feelings like Saint Elmo's fire danced along her skin. Deep muscles tensed, and her heart rate quickened as it tried to push suddenly hot and thick blood through her system. Her head roared, but not from the sound of the tempest. Every atom of her body coiled and tensed.

Without thinking, she responded to these inner demands. She reached up and touched the cleft in his chin where the stubble grew in a little swirl. She never imagined that such a small touch could unleash such a cascade of sensations. His skin was warm and the whiskers sandpapery. One touch led to another as the rest of her fingers joined in, exploring their way up his cheeks and over his ears and up into the silky damp curls of his hair.

To her utter surprise and infinite delight, Dash stretched himself into her touch like a cat looking for a good scratch behind the ears. A little groan escaped him, and his eyes closed. The tension eased from his jawline.

She pulled his head down toward her. He came willingly, big hands settling on her shoulders as she pressed her mouth against his.

The last rational thought that crossed her mind was that this was not a friendly hug.

Desire flooded through her. Her tongue assaulted his lower lip, and he opened his mouth. She licked into the soft warmth of him, meeting tongue-to-tongue as her hands finished their journey over his scalp and came to rest at his nape. Excitement roared through her body like the storm around them.

Dash's passivity evaporated. He drove his tongue into her mouth, matching her thrust for thrust. His hands slid erotically down over the bumps in her spine, coming to rest on her hips where he pulled her against the hard contours of his thighs.

But when she tried to back him up against the railing and climb right up onto his hips, she hit a dark and forbidding wall. She found herself suddenly at arm's length, looking up into his craggy face with its kiss-swollen lips. He looked dangerous and aroused. But his gaze was utterly sober.

"This is crazy," he said. "We can't do this. We have to think about Miriam and Todd, not to mention Bill and everyone else. And I'm supposed to stay away from women. I mean, it's part of my recovery."

Heat flowed up her cheeks. What on earth had she been thinking? This was Cousin Dash. Bad boy. Recovering alcoholic. A major-league screwup, quite literally.

"Uh. I'm sorry," she muttered, then turned on her heel and ran like a raccoon with a hound on her tail.

CHAPTER 10

On Saturday morning, Savannah allowed Dash to take Todd with him up to Painted Corner Stables. She could hardly refuse, seeing as her son had expressed an interest in learning how to ride a horse.

It was the first time he'd ever expressed any interest in doing something physical. And hadn't she brought him here for the fresh air?

She found herself thanking Dash again in the morning, but barely able to look him in the eye this time. Their kiss kept playing in her mind like a movie.

A really hot movie.

With Dash and Todd out of the way, Savannah took Aunt Miriam to town for a girl's day out, with the notion of lulling her into complacency and then springing a trip to Doc Cooper's on her. The doctor was in on the plan. He was well aware that Miriam hated doctor visits.

They brunched at the Kountry Kitchen where Miriam announced, quite loudly, that Savannah's biscuits were

ten times better than T-bone Carter's. Thank goodness
T-bone had a sense of humor.

He stuck his head out of the kitchen and said, "That's
all right, Miz Miriam. I don't aim to marry no preacher."
He grinned and returned to his kitchen.

Everyone in the café turned and smiled at Savannah. A
blue-haired lady in the next booth, whose name Savannah
didn't know, took that moment to say, "You keep cooking,
honey. We're all mighty glad you came to town. It's not
good for a minister to be without a wife."

Heat ran up Savannah's neck and face. Some of the little old ladies in Last Chance sounded just like Mrs. Bennet in *Pride and Prejudice*, who was single-minded in her
attempts to match up her daughters with anyone wearing
pants.

Right at the moment, Savannah felt a great deal like
Lizzy Bennet, the book's heroine, when the odious Reverend Collins comes to call. Lizzy's mother was practically
apoplectic when the heroine of the book told Reverend
Collins where he could take his marriage proposal.

Savannah hoped against hope that Bill Ellis didn't get
any ideas about getting down on bended knee. She feared
the entire over-sixty female population of Last Chance
might just go into hysterics.

And then it occurred to her that if Bill Ellis was the
Mr. Collins in her life, then who was Dash? Wickham, the
villain? Or Darcy, the hero?

She flashed back to Dash's kiss on the porch last night,
and her temperature climbed into the stratosphere.

"Oh, honey, it's so sweet the way you blush," the lady
at the next table said.

Savannah gave her a phony smile and then popped the

last of her fried egg in her mouth. Boy, she didn't have a
whole lot of privacy in this town, did she?

"Can we stop by the yarn shop?" Miriam asked.

"Of course we can. I remember you used to knit all the
time."

Miriam sighed. "I'm afraid that was before my hands
got so bad. I miss it. I like going in there and fondling the
yarn, though."

Fondling? Yarn? It really *was* a good thing Savannah
was getting Miriam to the doctor's for a checkup today.

She looked down at Miriam's less-than-half-eaten
bowl of oatmeal. "Well, finish up, then," Savannah said,
"and we can go."

"Oh," Miriam said on a long sigh, "I'm not that
hungry."

She hadn't been very hungry for the last two weeks.
Savannah tamped down on her concern.

A few minutes later, they strolled into The Knit &
Stitch, a little shop located in an older brick building in
the heart of the Palmetto Avenue business district. It had
a bright red awning and door. Inside, blond wood shelv-
ing cubes crammed with yarn occupied all available wall
space. The yarn had been sorted by color and texture
so that stepping into The Knit & Stitch was almost like
walking into a rainbow.

In the corner, near the front window, stood a group of
comfy-looking easy chairs, with a scarred coffee table in
the middle. A couple of women whom Savannah recognized from the book club sat in the chairs knitting away.
One of them, a young mother with a sleeping infant in
the stroller beside her, was someone Savannah had yet to
meet.

The tall, gray-haired woman behind the checkout counter gave a big wave. "Hey," she whispered loudly, giving the slumbering baby a meaningful look. "How are you doing, Miz Miriam?"

Aunt Miriam's eyes lit up behind her trifocals. "Hey, Pat, I'd like you to meet my niece, Savannah White. Savannah, this is Pat Canaday, Molly's mother."

Pat smiled. "Well, hello. I've heard a lot about you. I'm so glad someone is going to do something about The Kismet." She glanced through her front window, which provided a bird's-eye view of the dilapidated theater. "That place is an eyesore. The other merchants on Palmetto will be ever so grateful when The Kismet is restored to its former glory."

Savannah smiled politely while simultaneously wishing that Rocky had kept her mouth shut. So many people seemed to be depending on her. She wasn't used to that.

"So, Pat, what's new?" Miriam asked.

"Well, I just got a shipment of possum yarn."

Possum yarn? It was a joke, right?

"Oh," Miriam said, "I heard about that stuff. It's supposed to be very soft."

Apparently it wasn't a joke.

"Oh, it is. Here, let me get you a skein of it. You have to touch it to believe it." Pat crossed the room and pulled down a hank of dark purple yarn. "Here, have a feel. Isn't that the yummiest thing ever? They call that color claret."

Miriam stroked the yarn as if it might be a real live possum. "Oh, that *is* soft. And I do love the color, too." Her voice sounded wistful.

Savannah watched her aunt and knew right then that she needed medical attention. If not for the arthritis then for her obvious dementia.

"Don't you look at me that way," Miriam said with a suddenly sharp stare. "I'm not crazy." She turned toward Pat. "Am I crazy?"

Pat snorted a laugh and turned a pair of gray eyes on Savannah. "Honey, you have obviously never knitted or crocheted. It's always about the yarn. Now, you take that yarn, for instance. It's as soft as cashmere. It's spun of forty percent possum, fifty percent washable merino, and ten percent silk. It comes from New Zealand where possums are an ecological threat to the kiwis. So it's even environmentally sound."

Miriam held out the skein of purple possum. "Touch it, honey. You'll see."

She took the yarn. And it almost took her breath away. It was the softest thing she had ever felt. "Wow."

"So, you want to take lessons?" Pat asked. "You could make your aunt a beautiful sweater."

"No!" Savannah said.

"Yes!" Miriam said at the same time.

"Miriam, I have no desire to knit." She handed the yarn back to her aunt, who stroked it against her cheek.

"Cooking is my thing," Savannah said.

"So we've heard." This came from the young mother sitting by the window. She smiled at Savannah. The sun coming through the shop window lit up her red hair. She had the classic looks of a carrot top, including the freckles. The baby in the stroller had red hair, too.

"I'm Kenzie Griffin. I'm also a member of the book club, but I missed you last time, because Junior had a bad cold. I heard all about how you stood up to Nita. Thank you. I really enjoyed reading *Pride and Prejudice*. I'm looking forward to discussing it on Wednesday."

"Uh, thanks."

"Amen to that," the African-American woman sitting beside Kenzie said. Savannah recognized this woman from the book club, but she didn't remember her name.

The woman gave her a big smile. "Honey, I'm Lola May Lindon. And for the record, I think what you're doing for the town is just wonderful."

"This town really needs a theater," Kenzie said. "I'm a newcomer here. My husband just got a job at deBracy, and we're not used to having to drive an hour to see a movie."

Savannah gave Kenzie and Lola May a smile but didn't say anything for fear of exposing herself as the fraud that she was.

This was horrifying. Everyone seemed to have the wrong idea about her. She wasn't some mover or shaker. She didn't have the first clue what she was doing. It scared her to death that people were looking up to her and expecting something grand.

She'd never done anything important in her life. She was so very ordinary.

"I do so wish you'd learn to knit," Miriam said on a long sigh. "I would surely love to have a purple possum sweater."

"I'll think about it, okay? Meantime we have a few more errands to run."

Miriam handed the yarn back to Pat. "We do?"

"Yes, we do."

And with that, she took Miriam's arm and led her from the store.

"Where are we going next?"

"We're going to see Dr. Cooper. I want him to check your arthritis."

Miriam stopped in her tracks. "I don't like going to the doctor." She frowned. "I especially don't like being tricked into it."

Savannah took in a deep breath and let it out. "Okay, look, I'll make a deal with you. You go quietly to the doc's. When we're finished, we can come back here and buy some purple possum fur, and I will learn how to knit you a sweater."

A cherubic smiled lit up Miriam's face. If Savannah didn't know better, she could have sworn that Miriam had played her like a fine violin.

"How is Miriam?" Rocky asked, "I heard she saw Doc Cooper on Saturday."

"Boy," Savannah said, "it's amazing how everyone knows what everyone else is doing in this town. Doc Cooper says she's probably just depressed, but I'm worried."

Rocky put her arm around Savannah as they walked up the path to the Last Chance Public Library. It was book club night. "Honey, don't you worry. Miriam is one tough old girl. She'll bounce back from Harry's death, I'm sure."

Rocky eyed Savannah's brand-new Vera Bradley knitting bag. "I see Pat Canaday has ensnared you."

"With a little help from Aunt Miriam. I swear, Rocky, I am no good at this, but I promised I would knit Aunt Miriam a purple possum sweater if she would go to the doctor."

"Possum, really? You bought some of that yarn? I heard it was as soft as cashmere."

Savannah rolled her eyes. "You knit, too?"

Rocky shrugged. "I have a lot more time on my hands since I gave up my job with Senator Warren. Pat ensnared me, too. Be careful. It's addicting. One small slip with possum yarn and *ffffpt*, you're hooked for life."

They entered the library. "I see Jenny has brought pies," Rocky said. "I think I'll go get a slice. I bet she used cherries from her daddy's orchard."

Savannah bypassed the pies and headed in Molly Canaday's direction.

"Hey," Molly said as Savannah approached, "I heard Momma suckered you in with a few skeins of possum and a Vera Bradley bag." Molly grinned as she eyed Savannah's blue-and-pink-paisley knitting bag.

"It's amazing how everyone in town knows I bought possum yarn on Saturday." Savannah pulled out her pitiful project and thrust it in Molly's direction. "What am I doing wrong?"

Molly took the knitting in her hands. "Wow, that's a really bright color. Is this for Miriam?" she asked as she ran her fingers over the fabric.

Savannah nodded.

"Well, you haven't made any mistakes. You're just trying to knit too tight. You need to loosen up. Knitting is supposed to be relaxing. It's Zen."

"Right. Zen. I'll keep that in mind."

"You might want to frog that and restart. Or maybe practice on some throwaway yarn before you tackle a sweater. I've got lots and lots of leftover yarn. Stop by Bill's Grease Pit tomorrow, and I'll give you a bag." Molly handed back the purple possum monstrosity.

Just then Jane Rhodes and several others showed up with projects in hand. But since Jane's baby sweater project was still messed up, and the baby was due in a month, Molly helped her first. Everyone else stood around and watched Molly do her thing. It was hugely educational.

"All right, y'all," Nita called a few minutes later, "let's stop with the knitting and gather 'round to talk about the book."

Everyone took their seats, but most of the knitters ignored Nita and kept right on stitching. Savannah left her possum in the bag. She didn't think she had mastered the art of talking and knitting at the same time.

"So," Nita said, "I have a number of questions I can pose, but before I do, does anyone have a particular topic related to the book that you might want to discuss?"

"I do," Jane said, looking up from her knitting. "I have to say I lost all respect for Charlotte when she decided to marry Mr. Collins even though she didn't love him. I mean, the man was a peanut-brained weasel, and she even knew it going in. I found myself cheering for Lizzy when she told the preacher to take a hike."

"I admired Charlotte for taking her life into her own hands," Molly said. "She had gumption."

"Well, that may be true," Jenny countered, "but she was also a cynic. Remember how she tells Elizabeth that once you get married you'll eventually end up hating your husband? Even if you start out loving him."

"Amen to that," Lola May Lindon said. "It didn't take more than six months before I knew Lyle had to go. He just got so resentful every time we went fishing and I caught more than he did."

"Oh, hush, you said the same thing about Michael and Charles," Cathy said. "A woman who's been married and divorced three times is no judge of what it takes to make a good marriage."

Lola May shrugged. "Well, all those husbands sure have weaned me off happy endings, I can tell you that.

I'm thinking we should stick with Nita's books next time. This one was dumb."

"I think Charlotte would have remained unmarried if she could have," Savannah said, stepping in to ease the conflict between Lola May and Cathy. "I mean she didn't have any means of supporting herself. It wasn't like she could go out and get a job."

"Or renovate a theater," Jenny said. The hostility in the comment took Savannah aback. She hardly knew Jenny, except for her pies. The mousy math teacher was staring at her from across the table, her cheeks going red. It sure looked like Jenny believed she had some prior claim on Bill Ellis. Savannah needed to find a moment to tell Jenny that she didn't have anything to worry about. If Bill was in love with anything, it was her biscuits. Of course, that might be enough to make Jenny jealous. After all, Bill was arguably in love with Jenny's pies.

"Well," Hettie said, "you've got a point, Jenny. Charlotte didn't have anything else to fall back on. But Savannah does. I mean, she's going to be a great success. In fact, ladies, I have an announcement to make."

"Now, Hettie, we're talking about the book, not making announcements." Nita glared at Hettie, and Hettie glared right back.

It was a standoff until Rocky said, "Y'all, Hettie, Sarah, Lark, and I have created this new development corporation. We—"

"It's called Angel Development," Hettie said with a grin. "And we're giving Savannah half a million dollars for the theater. So, honey, if you want to be like Lizzy and tell Bill Ellis not to darken your door, you can do it."

Savannah's mouth dropped open. "A half a million dollars? But how—"

"Dash gave me your business plan," Rocky said, "and I shared it with Lark and Sarah and Hettie. We were all impressed."

"He what? I've been waiting for him to give me his thoughts on it. I didn't think it was very good."

"Well, it's a moot point now, honey, because Angel Development is giving you everything you need to bring The Kismet back to life," Hettie said with a big grin.

Rocky laughed. "Don't look so surprised. You can do this, Savannah, and we think it could be the beginning of a real downtown renaissance."

Hettie beamed and nodded. "Yes, ma'am. So don't you do anything stupid like that Charlotte character, you hear? The old ladies of this town are just like that Mrs. Bennet, always trying to match folks up. But you have us. And we're your angel investors. We'll make sure you're okay."

Savannah stared at Hettie like she'd blown in from some other planet. "Half a million dollars?" she said again. "Is this a loan?"

"No, honey, it's a grant. We want that theater reopened."

They were angels. And they had answered her prayers.

"Well, darn," Dash said. "You beat me by four strokes. Son, have you ever played golf before?"

Todd shrugged. "My dad took me to play putt-putt once up in Atlantic City. But that place wasn't as weird as this one." The kid waved his hand to encompass the entirety of the newly refurbished miniature golf course located a few miles south of Last Chance.

"You might be careful using the word 'weird' around Aunt Miriam or any of the other members of the Ladies' Auxiliary. They held a whole lot of bake sales to raise money for the renovation of this place."

"Why?"

"Well, it's our main tourist attraction."

"It's still weird." Todd rolled his eyes as he looked up at the fiberglass statue of Jesus that presided over the eighteenth hole.

"Just remember that the church ladies in town have embraced this place. In fact, your momma will probably praise me for bringing you here."

"Why?"

"Because of all these Bible verses." He pointed to the verse on the eighteenth hole.

"Mom isn't all that into God."

Dash laid his hand on Todd's shoulder, and for once, the kid didn't shake it off. They'd had a pretty good evening out here at Golfing for God. And while putt-putt was no real test, Todd was showing some serious eye-hand coordination. Dash was determined to get Todd into the football program that Red Canaday, the Davis High football coach, ran every summer for younger boys. After playing catch and Ultimate Frisbee with him, Dash was starting to think the kid might make a heck of a running back. He had real good hands.

They turned in their putters and headed home. Dash was surprised to find Savannah waiting for them out on the porch, sitting with Miriam. Savannah must have gotten home from the book club a little early.

"Hey, Mom, have you ever played miniature golf at Golfing for God?"

Savannah smiled. "Many times."

"It's kind of weird, but fun."

"I always liked the plague of frogs best," she said.

"I liked it, too. Dash said that at the Easter Egg Jubilee they have a frog jump. He said he'd take me down to the river to get me a frog."

Savannah frowned. "A frog jump?"

"Oh, yes," Miriam said. "It's so much fun. You missed a lot coming only in the summers. Your granddaddy took Dash out to the river on a lot of frog hunts. You remember that frog you had that took second place that time?"

"Her name was Frogzilla. She was one big bullfrog."

"You guys aren't kidding, are you?" Savannah said.

"Nope. Last Chance is a homey kind of place. Mark Twain would have felt comfortable here," Miriam said. She turned toward Todd. "Have you ever read that Mark Twain story, the one about the jumping frog?"

He shook his head.

"Well, you should. I think it's in Harry's library. I'll get it for you. You should read the story before you enter the frog jump." Miriam gave Dash a big smile that he felt down in his middle.

But Savannah looked at him as if he'd lost his mind. She turned toward her son. "Have you finished your homework?"

Todd gave her an eye roll. "Mom, Dash made me do it before he took me to Golfing for God."

Savannah's expression softened just a little, and Dash felt a rush of warmth. Damn. Pleasing Savannah was kind of fun. But dangerous. He had to remember that. He was already halfway hooked on her smile.

"It's time for bed. You get ready, and I'll be up to tuck you in," she said.

"Jeez, I'm way too old for that." The kid turned and stomped into the house, slamming the door behind him.

Miriam chuckled. "What is it about boys and screen doors?" she mused.

"You got a minute?" Savannah asked Dash.

His warm fuzzy feelings evaporated. Savannah was ticked off about something. He could sense it. Her shoulders were all tense. "Sure." He started toward one of the rockers, but she stood up.

"Not here. Inside."

"Honey, you be careful with him, now, you hear?" Miriam said.

"Be careful with me how?"

Miriam smiled, her eyes twinkling in the porch light. His aunt was up to something.

He followed Savannah into the living room. She turned and put her fists on her hips.

"Who gave you permission to show my business plan to Rocky?"

"I didn't think it was a secret."

"Well, I wasn't totally finished with it. I gave it to you so you could give me advice on how to improve it. I didn't expect you to hand it off to Rocky or for her to hand it off to Hettie and Sarah and Lark. I don't even know who Lark is."

"She's the sheriff's wife. And the sheriff is Rocky's older brother, Stone. You remember Stone from your summers here, don't you?"

"Vaguely. Look, Dash, I gave you that plan in draft form so you could tell me all the things I did wrong."

"But you didn't do anything wrong."

"I didn't?" She seemed genuinely surprised.

"No. It was a really good plan."

"Oh. Why didn't you tell me that?"

"I didn't think you wanted my advice."

"Of course I did. Why would I have given you the plan in the first place?"

"Because I told you I would invest in the theater."

She squinted at him. "And I told you I didn't want your money."

"Exactly, which is why I gave your plan to Rocky and the gals. I figured they were planning a fund to reinvest in downtown Last Chance, and you had a plan for reviving The Kismet. I just played matchmaker. Sort of like Aunt Mim, only different."

She stood there frowning at him.

"What did they do, honey? Criticize your plan at the book club tonight?"

"No, they want to give me a grant of half a million dollars. I don't think I even need that much. What the heck am I going to do with half a million dollars?" Her voice rose into the stratosphere, and she turned around and strode across the room to the fireplace. She was really upset.

"Honey, getting half a million dollars to realize your dream is not something to get upset over."

She didn't say anything. She just stood there all stiff in the back.

He battled his feelings for a long moment. He should walk away. He should tell her the truth. There was a long list of things he should do.

But instead, he behaved exactly like the addict he

was. He walked up behind her and put his hands on her shoulders. Her bones were so tiny. Her skin so warm. He wanted to spin her around and plant a kiss on her like she'd planted one on him last Friday. He had to fight that urge with every sinew in his body.

"I'm so angry at you." Her voice was low and didn't sound angry at all. The sound of it burned a hole in his middle.

"I only did you a favor, princess. And besides, if I didn't think you'd done a good job on the business plan, I would never have shared it with Rocky."

She turned.

He jammed his hands into the pockets of his jeans. He could look, but touching was forbidden.

But looking proved disastrous. Because something had changed. When she'd first arrived for Harry's funeral, he'd thought she was only average in looks. She had good legs and pretty blond hair, of course, but he didn't think she was a beauty. But then he'd begun to notice the way her eyes lit up when she was with Todd, and the way she helped Aunt Mim around the house, and the way she sang old Alabama songs to herself when she was in the kitchen.

She had turned into a ravishing beauty. How had that happened? How had his perception of her altered so much?

It was a danger sign, pure and simple.

"Did you really think my plan was good?" she asked.

"I did. You must have spent hours on the phone talking to contractors. Those numbers were dead-on."

"How would you know?"

Ooops. Busted. He smiled. "Just experience," he said.

He couldn't tell her about the hours he'd put in getting ballpark estimates for the work needed.

"But I don't need half a million dollars."

He shrugged. "So don't use it all. But getting half a million dollars means you could consult an architect. You could register the site as an historic building and really do the right kind of restoration."

She stared at him like a deer caught in the headlights. She didn't say a word for a good thirty seconds. Looking at her was driving him crazy.

But he would beat this thing. It was kind of like going down to Dot's Spot and drinking Coca-Cola. He had conquered that demon, and he would conquer this one, too.

"Savannah, what is it? Are you scared?" he asked.

Her chin quivered but she remained silent.

He stifled the urge to pull her into his arms. "You're going to be fine. Just put your plan into action. You start by taking a look at other theater renovations. See which architects they used. In the meantime, you could work on cleaning the place up. And once you consult with an architect, you need to find a general contractor. You just take one step at a time."

It was almost as if he were talking to himself and repeating the mantra of one day at a time.

"But half a million dollars, free and clear? Why would Sarah Rhodes do that for me? Rocky and I were friends, but Tulane was almost as big a pest as you were."

"Honey, he was a piker compared to me." He smiled. "You know, I reckon Hettie is behind this. The Queen Bee has told me a dozen times that she wants that theater revived. And she can be mighty persuasive. So, I think you should just go with the flow. Don't stand here being mad at me. I have nothing to do with this except handing your plan off to people looking for a project."

He turned on his heel and headed up the stairs to his room. He prayed like hell that she wouldn't follow him and that she believed his lies.

Hettie lit the tall taper on the dining room table. Violet Easley, her longtime housekeeper, had outdone herself this time. The table was elegant without being showy, and Violet's fried chicken, warming in the oven, was to die for.

Probably literally, given the amount of fat it contained.

The doorbell rang, and Hettie rushed to answer it. Her pulse kicked up a notch as she opened the door to find the rector of Christ Church standing there with a bunch of Lillian's camellias in his hand. Bill was a startlingly handsome man, with dark hair that curled over his brow and serious, deep-set blue eyes. Hettie hated to admit it, but Bill had settled down in the back of her mind, and he wasn't budging. Every encounter with him was like a secret, guilty pleasure.

"Hey," she said like some lame high-schooler.

"Is that some of Violet's fried chicken I smell?"

"Are those some of Lillian's camellias?"

He stiffened ever so slightly.

"Oh, come on, Bill, I'm just teasing you. Smile."

That elicited a little quirk at the corners of his mouth. His dimple flashed and then disappeared. He stood on her threshold for the longest time staring down into her eyes. These moments of connection were truly embarrassing.

She took his flowers and led him to her table. They

ate Violet's fried chicken and then took coffee and lemon meringue pie into the living room. They sat side by side poring over the latest financial statements for the Christ Church building fund. Hettie had been its treasurer and chief fund-raiser for some time.

"Honestly, Hettie, I'm so impressed by what you've done. We're at least six months ahead of where we thought we'd be at this time. And you did this at the same time you were managing the Golfing for God restoration and dealing with Jimmy's death and the chicken plant. I had no idea you were such a wiz at finances."

"I was always good at math. Unfortunately, I wasn't ever encouraged to use it—at least not until—"

She swallowed the rest of the sentence. She knew good and well that Bill knew all the bad things Jimmy had done before he'd been killed. His mismanagement of Country Pride Chicken was unconscionable. The irony was that her husband had been cleaning up his act when he'd lost his life. In fact, Jimmy got himself shot for standing up for the truth and trying to be a good man. Hettie would always feel responsible for that.

She laced her fingers together and stared down at her hands.

"What is it, Hettie?" Bill asked. His voice was laced with concern. Bill could always sense when she was worried. And he always had a way of making her feel better.

"Things aren't good at the chicken plant, but we'll muddle through."

"If things are that bad, why are you spending your time on Angel Development? Don't get me wrong, now. I think it's a wonderful idea. And I'm amazed at the help you've offered Savannah. But sometimes, Hettie, I think you get all wrapped up in helping others and don't think about yourself."

"I take that as a compliment. I was raised up with the idea that I should care about others. And I would think that you, being a minister, would understand that."

He reached over and patted her hands. His palms were warm and masculinely rough. His touch ignited feelings she didn't want to have. Not just feelings for Bill. But feelings in general. She wanted her independence more than she wanted anything in the world.

"I do believe in charity. But I think sometimes that charity starts at home. You're in trouble. All you have to do is ask for help."

She smiled. "I do ask for help. Nightly. I pray. And I know the Lord will take care of me."

Bill patted her hand. "You inspire me at times, you know that?"

She wanted to grab his hand and hang on. But she didn't allow herself that luxury.

"I'm just curious, though," Bill said. "Y'all are giving Savannah a great deal of money. And she doesn't have any business experience. Where did this money come from? And it seems to me that if y'all wanted to invest in something, it ought to be Country Pride Chicken. It's still one of the largest employers in the county."

"Yes, but I sit on the board of Angel Development, so I can't ask them for money. Besides, I don't need help. I'll figure it out. Things are getting better, slowly."

"You didn't answer my question. Where did all that money come from?"

"We have investors. Tulane Rhodes is rich. Lark Rhodes has money she inherited from her father. Hugh deBracy's business is doing incredibly well. These people want Last Chance to become a model of a thriving small town."

"Well, it still seems like an awful lot of money."

"What's the matter? Don't you want to see The Kismet rise from the ashes?"

"I suppose."

"You suppose? Aren't you happy for Savannah? I thought you and she were close. If you listen to the talk in town, y'all are practically husband and wife."

"I wouldn't go that far. She's a wonderful woman. A good mother, a great cook, and last night she played piano for us. She's quite accomplished."

"I'm sure she is." Hettie tamped down on her jealousy. Hettie couldn't cook, had no musical talent, and didn't have anything even closely resembling Savannah's curvy figure. She just had a knack for putting together spreadsheets so that she could obsess over them.

She took a sip of coffee, feeling disgruntled. "How do you feel about marrying a woman with a day job?" she asked, even though she knew it was an ugly thing to ask.

"I am not opposed to working women."

Hettie laughed at his unfortunate choice of words. "You mean women who work outside the home, don't you? The term 'working women' is sometimes used to mean something else entirely."

Bill stared at her for a long moment before he got the joke. His face flushed bright red, but then he laughed. "Ah, yes, I'm sure that Lillian Bray would object to working women on the streets of Last Chance."

"She also has old-fashioned views about women working outside the home," Hettie said.

"Well, I don't. And I'm sure Savannah will be very successful."

"Will that make you happy?"

"Of course it will. I admire her greatly," Bill said.

"I'm happy for you then."

"Are you?" He raised an eyebrow.

Did he suspect the turmoil that was running through her at this moment? Hettie had no reason to feel jealous. She'd done everything she could for Savannah's project. And she even admired and liked Savannah. These feelings were confusing. She needed to ignore them. She was independent for the first time in her life. And she was enjoying every minute of it.

"Bill, I *am* very happy for you and Savannah. The Ladies' Auxiliary believes that every minister should be married. And she seems to suit you. And, as you have pointed out, she's destined to be a great success."

His bright blue eyes softened ever so slightly. "Yes, but Last Chance is full of accomplished women. It's hard for a man to choose. Take you, for instance. You've done so much for the people of this town. You resurrected the golf course. You're trying to save the chicken plant. You're part of this new downtown development thing. You've raised a lot of money for the church. I would say that you've begun to live up to that name everyone calls you."

"What? Queen Bee? I don't regard that as a very nice epithet."

"I do," he said.

That sent a warm flush coursing through her. He noticed and appreciated the work she was trying to do. And that made her feel strong and independent.

• • •

Zeph stood in the deep shadows cast by a magnolia tree. He watched the house as dusk turned to full dark. The kitten in his hand wanted to be turned loose. This particular critter was loaded with P and V. If he let him go, he'd be gone for good.

He'd had a problem kitten like this a couple of Christmases ago, and he'd stashed that one in the manger with baby Jesus over at Christ Church where Annie could find her.

But it was almost Easter time. There weren't any mangers around.

He stood in the dark for the longest time, watching the lights come on inside the houses on Maple Street. He couldn't bring himself to knock on the door.

He was about to turn away and go back to his truck when the front door opened. "I declare, Zeph Gibbs, is that you standing there still as a statue?"

Nita came out onto her porch. She was dressed in a real pretty yellow dress. She kind of looked like spring in that dress. Like the jonquils that were blooming out on Bluff Road. "Ma'am," he said. His voice sounded rusty, and behind him, he could almost hear the ghost laughing at him.

"What you got there?" she asked.

Zeph screwed up his courage and crossed the street. He stopped at the edge of Nita's lawn. "It's a kitten, ma'am."

"Oh, for heaven's sake, Zeph, you and I went to high school together. Don't call me ma'am."

"Yes, ma'am, I mean Miz Nita."

"Well, bring that kitten over here."

He stepped up onto the lawn, conscious of the ghost

waiting behind him. He sure hoped Nita couldn't see that haunt. She might get scared. He didn't want to scare Nita.

He got as far as the porch steps and held out the kitten. "It's a little calico stray. Someone dumped her in the swamp a few days ago."

Nita looked down at him from the porch, and he lost himself for a little while in her dark, kind eyes. She came down the porch steps and took the kitten from his outstretched hand. And just like that, the little critter quit trying to get away.

But then Zeph knew that would happen. He didn't exactly know how he knew, but he knew. This one was for Nita.

"Aw, he's adorable. Is it a he?"

"Yes, ma'am."

Nita frowned at him. "I told you I don't want to be called ma'am."

He nodded. "I thought you might like a cat."

"Is that why you were standing across the way like that?"

"You saw me?"

"I did. I was scared for a minute until I realized it was you. You looked like a ghost standing there so still. How have you been, Zeph?"

"I been fine, Miz Nita." He felt a little odd calling her by her first name. She was the finest lady in all of Last Chance.

"You still living out in the swamp?"

"No, ma'am. I don't live in the swamp. I built me a very nice house right off of Bluff Road. Near the Jonquil House. The flowers are in bloom. It's right pretty out there this time of year."

"I'm glad to hear you aren't camping out. What have you been doing lately?"

"Oh, I work for Mr. Dash up at the stables, when I'm not fishing or hunting."

"Oh. I didn't know that. I'm glad to hear you have a real job."

"You want to keep the cat?"

Nita looked down at the calico. "I've been thinking about getting a cat. Did you know that?"

Zeph smiled. "Yes, ma'am."

She frowned at him again.

"I mean Miz Nita," he added hastily.

"How did you know I was thinking about getting a cat?"

He shrugged. "I don't rightly know, but I saw that critter and I said to myself he was perfect for you." He needed to change the subject and fast. He didn't want anyone to know how the ghost was always telling him what to do with strays. It was kind of uncanny the way the strays always came to the ghost.

He took a step back. "So, how did the ladies like *Pride and Prejudice* this Wednesday? If you want to know the truth, I liked *Emma* a whole lot better."

Her frown deepened. "You've read those books?"

"Yes, Miz Nita. I read a lot of books. I get them down at the thrift shop, and when I finish them, I trade them in for more." He backed up a little bit more. The ghost behind him was getting restless.

"I need to go," he said.

"Zeph, if you like to read, you should come in to the library. Don't you have a library card?"

"No, Miz Nita."

"Well, you must get one. And if you like Jane Austen, why don't you join the book club?"

He shook his head as he backpedaled, "Oh, no, Miz Nita, I couldn't do a thing like that. No, ma'am. I have too much to do in the evening."

Like walking the streets and keeping the ghost in line.

CHAPTER
11

On Saturday, Savannah put on her oldest jeans, a flannel shirt that had once belonged to Greg, and a pair of heavy-duty rubber gloves.

She opened the door to The Kismet and hauled in a load of cleaning supplies from the bed of Uncle Harry's truck, which Dash had magnanimously loaned her for the day.

Angel Development was going to have a check ready for her to deposit by the middle of next week, and she was scheduled to meet with several architects and contractors on Thursday. But in the meantime, she was antsy. She would have to hire a professional cleaning crew, but her goals today were simple. First, she wanted to see if any of the woodwork in the lobby could be salvaged. It would be a shame if she lost all that intricate carving on the columns and the candy counter. And second, she wanted to assess the state of the small apartment above the theater. She needed to figure out a plan to revive that, too.

She stood in the middle of the lobby feeling over-whelmed. The place was falling down around her ears. It was ridiculous to think she could accomplish anything by herself.

She pushed that negative thought to the side. She was trying not to listen to that little party pooper who lived in her head.

She firmed her resolve and started by setting up a few humane mousetraps around the perimeter of the lobby, then she rolled up her shirtsleeves and headed to the jani-tor's closet. She had spoken with the water company on Friday, and to her delight, there was cold water available in the old slop sink. She filled a bucket and dumped in some Murphy Oil Soap.

She set to work wiping down the grime on the candy counter. She'd been at it for about twenty minutes when she became aware of a high-pitched squeaking sound.

She soon discovered that the noise was coming from one of her traps. She stood there looking down at the cut-est little gray mouse. He (or she?) had eaten the saltine cracker bait, and now the poor thing was caught in the green plastic box and wanted to get out.

Uh-oh. Her humane trap posed some pretty big issues that she hadn't considered before. If she released the mouse into a field outside town, would it find its way into some farmer's barn only to be killed by a cat, or a hawk, or an owl?

And what about the mouse? Did it have a mate? Little baby mice?

Then there was the much more practical issue—to save the mouse's life she would have to pick up that box—and do something with it. Eeeek.

She closed her eyes and prayed for guidance.

"Hey, princess." Dash's deep baritone pulled her right from her mouse-induced moral dilemma. She opened her eyes and turned toward him.

In addition to his ball cap, white T-shirt, work boots, and faded jeans, the man had a serious-looking tool belt strapped across his lean hips.

"Hey," she said out of a suddenly dry mouth. He was devastatingly sexy.

He sauntered over and looked down at the frantic mouse. "Honey, why'd you buy one of those traps? You'd be better with poison. Although with poison, the critters crawl off into the walls and die and start stinking to high heaven. My own preference is the old-fashioned mousetrap that kills them dead."

She stared at him. He was teasing her, wasn't he? Sometimes, with Dash, it was hard to tell. She decided not to rise to his bait this time. "I wanted to be humane."

His lopsided grin appeared. "Uh-huh. You know mouse droppings cause all kinds of disease."

"I'm just now realizing that humaneness is a complex issue."

He snorted a laugh as he picked up the box. He turned and strolled out of the theater. He returned two minutes later, without the box or the mouse.

"I have a feeling I don't want to know what you did with that mouse."

"You can rest assured that I took care of it." He looked at the other mousetraps she'd set out. "These have to go. With these traps, you'd just be fighting a losing war."

He scooped all of them up and dumped them in the big

plastic trash can that she'd brought for debris. "You need a cat," he pronounced.

"I already have a dog I don't want."

"That dog isn't yours. He's Todd's."

"Right, and when Todd forgets to take care of him, who is going to take him for walks?"

"Well, so far, it's been me. So I reckon Champ is closer to being my dog than yours. But we're not talking about Todd's dog, so don't change the subject. You need a serious mouser for this theater. You get a cat and your mouse and snake problem will disappear. I seem to recall that your granddaddy had a long succession of theater cats."

"I don't have a snake problem. You're just trying to scare me, and I've decided not to behave like I did when I was ten. I've grown up some since then."

He swept his gaze over her from the top of her head to the tips of her toes. She had seen that kind of look before, whenever she decided that her love life needed a boost and she went out to a bar with her girlfriends. That look was very close to an ogle. And for some reason, having Dash ogle her wasn't bad. It was kind of okay, actually.

"You sure *have* grown some," he drawled, his gaze glued to her bustline.

"That's right, I have. I know we don't have snakes in this theater."

He shrugged. "Have it your way, princess. You usually do. But in my opinion, you need a mouser."

He strolled over to the candy counter. "This old wood-work is real pretty, isn't it?" He was clearly changing the subject. Good. She could chalk this round up to her being mature and recognizing when Dash was teasing...or ogling.

"The wood's damaged in places," she said. "It needs to be refinished, and there are parts that need replacing. I have no idea where I'm going to find someone who can do it justice."

"Probably the same place as you'll find the cat."

She turned and frowned. "Will you stop with the cat, please?"

"Sorry, princess. I was just thinking that Zeph Gibbs might be the answer to your problems."

"Who is that?"

He smiled. "He's a little bit of a ghost."

"A ghost?"

"Not really. He's a little shy. He came back from Vietnam a changed man. I hired him as a hand at the stables and discovered that he's a master carpenter. He also has a thing for cats and has kept me supplied with excellent mousers. Because the last thing I want in my barns is a snake. I'll talk to him about your woodwork and your mouse problem. If he decides he wants to help, you'll save a lot of money, not to mention mouse aggravation."

"Thank you, but I'm sure I can find a real professional to do the work. What are you doing here?"

"I'm here to help."

She stared at him for the longest moment.

"What? You don't think I'm capable of helping?" he asked.

"I'm just surprised is all." Except she wasn't surprised. Dash had been amazingly helpful on so many fronts. And that tool belt looked good on him. It looked as if he knew how to use those tools, too.

"I thought I could mosey up to the apartment and see what it needs."

"Ah, I get it. You're looking forward to the day I move out."

He smiled. "Yes, ma'am, I am. I'm getting tired of having to wear a bathrobe every morning when I bump into you."

His eyes twinkled when he said that, and she realized that he was teasing her again. But before her addled brain could form a sexy comeback line, he turned and strode toward the grand staircase.

"You don't have to wear a robe," she said to his back.

He didn't react. He just kept walking away, giving her a great view of his Wrangler-clad butt. It was official, Dash Randall's backside was hot. Real hot. And she hoped he quit wearing his bathrobe so she could get an even better look at it.

She turned back to her sponge, but her equilibrium had been disturbed. It was shattered completely five minutes later when her scrubbing was interrupted by a loud crash. Followed by the sound of Dash cussing in two languages. No doubt he'd learned those Spanish words from his Latin teammates over the years.

"Dash, are you okay?" she yelled, her heart suddenly in her throat.

She dropped her sponge and stripped off the rubber gloves. She got as far as the landing when Dash came barreling down the stairs in the opposite direction. "Honey, there are rattlesnakes up in the projection room. I don't know how many. After I freaked out, I shut the door on 'em and called animal control, but we need to get out of here. I don't know how many more might be lurking around."

She blinked, her heart rate returning to normal. "Dash, come on. I'm not falling for this a second or a third time. So you can just quit. If you came here to play some kind of practical joke on me, I—"

She never finished her sentence because Dash picked her up and threw her over his shoulder like a sack of potatoes, thereby giving her the close-up-and-personal view of his Wrangler-clad backside that she had just been wishing for. Unfortunately she was so furious with him that she couldn't entirely enjoy the moment.

"Dash, put me down."

She got no response. Instead he marched down the stairs oblivious to her demands or even the fists she used to pummel his sexy derriere.

She was still hollering when he finally set her down on the sidewalk outside the theater.

"You overbearing, annoying, cowboy-hat-wearing, practical-joke-playing ass—" She took a big swing at his face, but he caught her fist before she got anywhere close to his jaw.

"You know, princess, you always did have one heck of a temper."

"There aren't any snakes up there. You just came here to make me feel—" She bit off the end of her words because right then a big van bearing the words "Allenberg County Animal Control" rolled to the curb.

About this time, Pat Canaday and two of her customers came piling out of The Knit & Stitch, across the street. "Hey Savannah, is Dash giving you a hard time, honey? Should I call Bill Ellis?" she hollered.

"Oh, brother," Dash muttered, turning away to greet the uniformed man in the van.

At the same moment, a police vehicle pulled up, and Damian Easley, the Last Chance chief of police, rolled down his window. "I got a call from dispatch. What's this about snakes in the theater?" he asked just as a big, red, shiny fire truck arrived on the scene, blocking one lane of traffic. At least half a dozen big guys in raincoats and fire hats and big rubber boots started jumping off the truck.

Within minutes, shop owners and Saturday shoppers started gathering on the sidewalks. And for the first time in Savannah's memories of Last Chance, there was a traffic jam on Palmetto Avenue.

"Hey, princess, you believe me now?" Dash asked.

She found herself looking up into his ball-cap-shaded eyes. "I'm sorry," she said in a tiny voice.

He cocked his head. "Say it louder."

"I'm sorry I didn't believe you."

He smiled. And that full-mouthed grin was devastating. "I accept your apology."

He didn't even offer to apologize for the way he carried her out of the building. But for some reason, she didn't mind. He probably considered it a rescue.

"Dash, honey, did I hear you say *snakes*. As in more than one?" Pat yelled from across the street.

"Yes, ma'am. And I'm curious about how they got there. I mean rattlers are kind of rare, and the last time I checked that room it was snake-free," Dash yelled back.

"You think someone put 'em up there?"

He shrugged. "It's mighty strange."

Pat and her customers began to speculate among themselves. Meanwhile a little farther up the block, Clay Rhodes set out a folding chair for Arlene Whitaker in front of Lovett's Hardware, and across the street it looked like Lessie Anderson was standing on the sidewalk outside the Cut 'n Curl with permanent rollers in her hair.

Pat sauntered across the street. "I declare this is fun. We haven't had such a ruckus since last summer when Rocky Rhodes told everyone off and then allowed Hugh deBracy to carry her off in his rented Mustang."

"Well, if y'all will excuse me, I'm a member of the volunteer fire department," Dash said. He turned and headed back into the building along with the other firemen, dog catcher, and chief of police. A moment later, Bubba Lockheart came huffing up the street carrying a lawn chair and a video camera.

He handed the chair to Savannah. "Clay Rhodes sent this up from the hardware store. You just sit tight, Miz Savannah, and we'll take care of everything." He held up his camera. "I'm going to tape this. I'm thinking we could get an eyewitness video on the news tonight. And that would be good for business." He hurried into the theater while Savannah sank down into the chair.

"It's a shame you didn't have a gator. I think gators are way more dramatic than snakes. I can't believe how much free publicity this is going to get you," Pat said.

"You mean negative publicity, right?"

Pat shrugged. "People love a good snake story. Just look at that movie about snakes on a plane. You know, you might think about showing that movie at your grand opening."

"Right. I hated that movie. I hate snakes."

Pat patted Savannah's shoulder. "Honey, you live here long enough and you get used to them."

Fifteen minutes later, the men marched back out of the

theater bearing a big wooden box that was making a very unsettling noise.

Damian Easley was grinning from ear to ear. "I declare, Savannah, your cousin is one hell of a snake wrangler. I knew he was good with horses and kids, but I swear, it was kind of amazing to watch him. I'm thinking we should put him on call with the animal control unit."

He tipped his Stetson and got back into his cruiser. The firemen got back on their truck and drove away. The crate of hissing and rattling snakes was loaded into the animal control van.

Dash and Bubba came out of the theater.

"Oh, boy," Bubba said, "wait until WLTX sees this footage. We're going to make the evening news, I'm sure. Especially since Dash did most of the work, and he's a former big-league baseball star." Bubba ran up the street, headed for Bill's Grease Pit.

"You're all clear," Dash said. "But, honey, you need a cat."

"Don't snakes eat cats? I wouldn't want to put a cat in danger," she replied. "I like furry animals better than scaly ones."

"I figured that when I saw those humane mousetraps. You will be happy to know that we didn't kill any snakes today, because rattlers are practically an endangered species in these parts. But, princess, snakes and cats both eat mice. And without a cat to eat the mice, you can get snakes. Usually just black snakes, which are harmless. But I'm telling you, you need a cat."

There was a mischievous gleam in his eyes. He'd had a lot of fun catching those snakes. She could tell. And that made her want to laugh for some reason. Despite the scary nature of this problem, she found herself looking up into his bright blue eyes and feeling lighter than air.

"Well, c'mon," he said, "we made a full sweep of the place. It's snake-free, but I can't say the same for the rodents. Let's get back to work. The excitement is over."

He offered her his hand, and she let him pull her up out of the lawn chair. That was a big mistake. His hand was huge, and warm, and obviously competent. Not only had he played baseball with those hands, but he also fixed broken porch steps, played Ultimate Frisbee, and wrangled snakes. Her libido woke up and made a number of urgent demands. This time the fluttery, hot feelings in her middle weren't entirely unwanted.

A girl could get used to a guy like this. He wasn't Superman. He couldn't fly, but he was doing a real impersonation of a hero.

Dash was wrestling with a bunch of vet bills in his office at the Painted Corner Stables on Monday morning when Stone Rhodes, the sheriff of Allenberg County, paid him a visit.

"I guess you're here to talk about Lizzy," Dash said.

"Uh, well, no, not exactly," the sheriff said.

"What's up?"

Stone sat down in the chair facing Dash's desk. "It's about those snakes you found in the theater."

"What about them?"

"They're western diamondbacks. According to the herpetologist up in Orangeburg, they aren't native to South Carolina.

Stone leaned back in his chair. "We're working on the

assumption that those snakes were put there on purpose. Do you have any idea of who might want to sabotage Savannah's theater renovation?"

Dash looked down at the bills on his desk. "Savannah's ex-mother-in-law isn't too wild about her moving down here. I gather that she wants the kid to go to some fancy prep school in Baltimore. But I don't think Savannah's mother-in-law would put snakes in The Kismet's projection room."

"Probably not. And that's my problem, Dash."

"You think it's someone local?"

Stone shook his head and let go of a big sigh. "Who else has keys to the place?"

"Savannah has keys. And I also have a set. I reckon that makes me a person of interest."

Stone didn't laugh. Dash went on alert. "Stone, I didn't put snakes in the theater."

"I'm inclined to believe you, but I have to investigate every lead. And right now, you are probably my main suspect."

"Why would I put snakes in the theater?"

"Well, because you don't like Savannah, and everyone knows that. And then there's the whole TV angle."

"TV?"

Stone's lips quivered slightly, but it wasn't a full-fledged smile. "Obviously you missed the local news. Bubba got footage of you snake wrangling, and WLTX ran it as an eyewitness report on the late local news last night. Lizzy says the video's gone viral on YouTube."

"Do you *really* think I would do something like that for publicity?"

"To be honest, Dash, I don't know what to think. All the

coverage has created a cascade of additional problems. You see, the environmentalists and conservationists, not to mention the anti-animal-cruelty people, have all mobilized and now Lurleen can't hardly keep up with the paperwork because the phone is ringing all the time."

Dash squared his shoulders and spoke as earnestly as he could. "I'm sorry, Stone. But I didn't put those snakes in the projection room. If I wanted to scare Savannah, I would have used a much less dangerous snake."

Stone nodded. "Well, for what it's worth, I believe you. But I have to investigate. And I have a much bigger problem, because if you didn't do this as a very nasty practical joke, then who did do it, and why?"

"Maybe it was kids or something."

"I don't think kids could get their hands on western diamondbacks all that easily." Stone stood up. "Well, if you get any ideas on who might be responsible, you know where to find me. I'm sorry about the bad publicity, but I have to do my job."

"Are you going to talk to Savannah about this?"

"You know I have to."

"Great. Just great. She's going to think the worst of me."

"I'm sorry, Dash, I truly am."

The sheriff left without having a conversation about Lizzy's need for a riding instructor. Dash propped his chin on his fist and stared out his office window for a long moment.

Well, he shouldn't be all that surprised. His own past actions had contributed to his reputation in this town. He couldn't blame the town for gossiping.

The man he used to be would probably act out in some

way, or take himself down to the local bar and drink himself into oblivion.

But he wasn't that man anymore. The man he wanted to be would behave in a totally different way. That man would do everything in his power to make certain that Savannah was safe from whoever had perpetrated this sick joke.

Someone had tried to hurt her, and Dash didn't like it. Not one iota.

He picked up his phone and called his attorney, who gave him the name of a private investigation firm, and Dash made a call.

Savannah closed the door behind the sheriff and leaned her head on the wood. She didn't want to believe that Dash had staged the snake episode. Even if all the evidence suggested that he had.

"You know he didn't do it, don't you?" Miriam said from her place in the living room where she had been watching her soap operas.

"You eavesdropped?"

Miriam shrugged. "Y'all were talking in the dining room. It's not like I'm deaf."

Savannah came into the living room. "Dash knows that I'm terrified of snakes."

"Everyone knows that."

"The sheriff says he has a key. I didn't know that."

"Of course he has a key. It's my key. Your granddaddy gave me that key a long time ago."

"There wasn't any sign of forced entry."

"It's an old lock. Someone who was determined could have picked it."

"Who would do that?"

Miriam shook her head. "I don't know. But I'm just saying that Dash didn't do it. If you think long and hard about the first snake episode, you'll realize that this one is all backward."

"Backward?"

"Yes, sugar. I'm talking cause and effect."

Savannah stared down at the Persian rug. The first snake episode had occurred when Dash was thirteen and Savannah was ten. It was that first summer when Dash had come to live in the big house with Uncle Harry and Aunt Miriam and Granny and Granddaddy.

Dash had taken one look at her and made up his mind that he hated her. And the feeling was completely mutual. Especially since they constantly battled for Granddaddy's attention. Dash was always getting into trouble: stealing things from the dime store, using bad language, staying out all hours. Savannah remembered how the grown-ups would talk about him in the parlor, sometimes, really late at night.

Savannah had overheard it all, standing on the stairs, eavesdropping like a little brat. They said his parents left him, and his grandfather and father were both drunks, and a lot of stuff like that. And Mom had called him a bad seed.

Savannah should never have repeated any of it, especially the ugly things Mom said. But Savannah *had* repeated Mom's words. To everyone.

Dash had retaliated by blowing up her Twirly Curls Barbie. And in her anger, Savannah had called him a bad seed right to his face and told him he was so bad that he didn't deserve to have parents.

The snake had arrived in her bed the next night.

Savannah let go of a long sigh. The night of the snake episode, after the screaming and the crying, Granddaddy had made it very clear that he was disappointed in her. She had resented it at the time. After all, Dash had almost scared her into peeing her pajama pants.

Worst of all, Granddaddy had made her apologize to Dash. And he'd never once asked Dash to apologize to Savannah. Looking at the incident now, from the perspective of motherhood, she finally understood.

"You're right," she whispered. "He only put that snake in my bed because I hurt him. I hurt him with words. I hurt his reputation."

"That's right, sugar."

"I was wrong."

"Yes, you were."

"Dash wouldn't have put those snakes up there in the projection room, not if it would lead to this kind of gossip about his reputation. He's been working on that, hasn't he? It's part of why he goes to his AA meetings every Thursday," Savannah said.

"That's right, sugar. Dash might tease you about snakes until the cows come home, but he wouldn't do something like that. Especially not now. He's been working to put aside that tough exterior he used to hide behind. And inside, he's got the gentlest heart. Have you ever seen him with his horses?"

Savannah shook her head.

"Well, I know you've seen the way he is with kids and dogs."

She nodded.

"He can't help that he was born with the genes that

make him and alcohol a deadly mix. But he's been sober for almost two years. And that fight at Dot's the day before Harry's funeral was all Roy Burdett's fault."

"I've misjudged him. I know that."

"I'm glad you know it. And there's one other thing, sugar. If Dash wanted to scare you with a snake, he'd go find a garden snake or something a whole lot less dangerous than a couple of western diamondbacks. Those snakes had to cost someone a lot of money, and it's funny because any fool could have gone out into the garden and found a harmless snake that would have scared you just as badly. Dash is a tease, but he's not vicious."

Aunt Miriam patted her knee and continued, "I'm glad you're here. And I'm glad that you brought Todd. And I'm glad to see that you and Dash have started to get over all that stuff from when you were kids. Don't let this set you back. You know in your heart that Dash is innocent."

She examined her heart, and much to her surprise she did know that Dash was innocent. She knew it because she'd seen his face right after he'd discovered those snakes. He'd been surprised. He couldn't have faked that.

And she knew he was innocent because of a bunch of other things that had nothing to do with the snakes. She knew it because of the way he paid attention to Todd. The way he made time for him, like he understood what Todd was going through. And he probably did.

Just then the front door opened, and Dash came striding in. He got as far as the archway. The look on his face spoke volumes. He expected her to blame him for the snakes.

Savannah stood up. "I just talked to Sheriff Rhodes, and I know what folks are saying about those snakes. And

I just want to let you know that I don't think you put them there. This situation is not at all like what happened when we were kids. It's backward," she said, borrowing her aunt's words. Thank goodness Miriam was lucid today.

His mouth twitched, and he stood frozen for a moment. "Uh, thank you."

She smiled. "You're welcome."

CHAPTER 12

As a child, Savannah had attended the Watermelon Festival, held every year in midsummer. But she was ignorant of the other important celebrations that marked life in Last Chance.

She had never attended the Annual Egg Toss and Frog Jump Jubilee that occurred every year on the Saturday before Easter. And she had most certainly never gone frog hunting before.

But here she stood, clutching a flashlight and wearing a pair of oversized rubber boots that had once belonged to Uncle Harry, trying to keep up with her cousin and her son. They were walking along the trail off Bluff Road that skirted the old derelict Jonquil House, heading toward the swamp.

At night.

And the only reason she was here was because Dash and Todd had dared her to come. And she, like the idiot she often was, had risen to the challenge.

When would she learn? She should be back at home,

cooking a casserole or something for the covered-dish Easter brunch that was held annually at the Baptist church after sunrise services. It was attended by every congregation in town. And, in addition to a bean casserole, Savannah wanted to bake an apple pie, just to prove the point that her crust was flakier than Jenny Carpenter's.

But no. She'd opened her mouth at dinner tonight, and here she was.

"All right, now, son," Dash said as they tramped along the path. "We'll need to be quiet and listen to hear a bullfrog."

"What does a bullfrog sound like?"

"Lord have mercy, boy, you really have been living in the city, haven't you?"

Todd made no comment.

"It's all right. I know what a bullfrog sounds like."

It was at that point that Savannah noticed another light up ahead. "Uh, we're not alone."

"Of course we're not alone. It's the Friday before the frog jump. Practically every boy in Allenberg County between the ages of five and fifteen is out here with his daddy frog hunting."

"I see. And you did this as a child?"

"Of course I did. Uncle Earnest brought me out here every year. He was a champion frog hunter. He even won the competition a couple of times, but he never entered any frogs in the national frog jump in Calaveras County. Which reminds me, Todd, you need to read the Mark Twain story."

"Sure."

They reached the edge of the swamp. On either side, flashlights were moving through the trees.

"All right now, son, the first thing you need to do is wet down your bag." Dash aimed a flashlight at the water, and Todd dunked the bag.

"All right. Let's listen for a minute."

They fell silent, and sure enough, not more than ten seconds went by before they heard the unmistakable sound of a bull frog serenading the night in search of a mate.

Dash touched Todd's shoulder and pointed. They circled the water's edge to the right. The sound got louder.

"All right," he whispered, "he's right over yonder. We'll need to wade into the water. You take the flashlight and kind of shine it along the edge of the water. When you see the frog, you have to be real quiet and move toward him, keeping the light on his eyes. I'll take care of the rest."

"I'm not going into the water," Savannah whispered.

Dash laughed. "Princess, I'm surprised you got this far. You stay here. We'll do the huntin'."

Dash and Todd slipped into the waist-high water, and all Savannah could think about was gators and water moccasins. She wondered if Dash was a gator wrangler, too.

Of course if a gator decided to eat her, Dash would be too busy frog hunting to notice. On the other hand, it was amazing what was happening to Todd. Everything she had wished for and hoped for was unfolding before her eyes.

And she would be an idiot not to realize that Dash was responsible. Todd was doing his chores, bringing home good marks in school, taking care of the dog, learning to ride a horse, and frog hunting. He was also getting taller and slimming down. He still played video games, but not all the time.

So maybe facing down her fear of snakes and gators was worth it, just to see her son fearlessly wade into dark waters intent on catching a frog for the big jump tomorrow.

The undergrowth rustled behind her, and her own fears sent a shiver right up her backbone. She turned to find a man-shaped shadow standing on the path behind her. Her skin went cold as scenes from *The Creature from the Black Lagoon* spooled through her mind.

She aimed her flashlight at it.

And it turned out to be only a man. Carrying a cat. Which seemed kind of strange here in the middle of what was turning into a community frog hunt.

"Ma'am," he said.

"Hello."

"I'm Zeph. I think Mr. Dash must have told you about me."

"Oh. Yes."

He took another step forward. "This here is Maverick." He held out a very large, black cat. "He's the best mouser I've got. He don't need much attention either."

Savannah didn't want the cat. But she could hardly say no, standing there alone in the middle of a swamp. So she took the cat into her arms. It was heavier than she expected. It started to purr.

Suddenly she was ten years old, hanging out in the small apartment above the theater playing with Bogey, the black cat who lived at The Kismet. She hadn't thought about that cat in years. Mom didn't allow pets at home, so Bogey was the first cat she'd ever known. She had loved that cat.

This one settled right into her arms as if he belonged there.

She looked up at Zeph. He stood in the darkness now. "Thank you," she said.

"I knew you and Maverick were going to be friends. He's been waiting a long time to find a home."

And with that, Zeph turned and walked into the darkness as if he knew the path so well he didn't need a flashlight.

And that raised an interesting question: How had he found her out here in the dark? The answers that came to her were a little bit creepy.

Dash stood at the edge of the City Hall Park. The egg hunt was in full swing. Little kids with Easter baskets ran all over the place looking for plastic eggs, while the members of the sixth-grade Sunday Schools for five different churches ran after them providing hints.

The older kids had hidden the eggs this morning at o-dark-thirty, which had been kind of a challenge since most of them had spent the previous night frog hunting. It had practically taken dynamite to get Todd out of bed this morning. The kid thought frog hunting was "tight," but Easter egg hunting not so much.

Dash and Todd had done okay last night. They'd caught three frogs, and a few hours of sleep, while Savannah had caught a big fat monster of a cat.

He smiled. Zeph was a piece of work.

He cast his gaze over the people in the park, searching for her. Savannah looked good enough to eat in her little blue dress. She stood behind a card table festooned with helium-filled balloons, handing out brownies and Rice Krispie squares. Her blond ponytail bounced as she talked.

She was cute. And built. And she believed in him, when everyone else seemed to be thinking he'd staged the whole snake rescue for some nefarious reason.

And that was a big breakthrough. Maybe what he was feeling for her was more than just an addiction. More than just lust.

And every time he allowed himself to think that way, it scared him silly. He could see that Savannah wasn't like the blond bimbos he'd hung around with when he was playing in the majors. Those women were trouble. They were looking to party, and he'd been the original party animal. He couldn't remember one of their names.

Savannah wasn't a party girl. She was wholesome. She was a terrific mother, a dedicated niece, and a member in good standing of the Last Chance Book Club.

She was exactly like Hettie. Hettie was the Queen Bee, and Savannah was the princess. Dash had a weakness for royalty, evidently. Because he was falling in love with Savannah.

And love was the worst kind of addiction a man could have. Especially when the woman in question was destined for someone else.

He needed to keep his distance. It was the right thing to do, even if it was harder than staying away from Dot's Spot.

He shifted his gaze, looking for the kid. As usual, Todd had disengaged. He stood by one of the big oaks at the back of the park. Watching.

Dash's phone rang as he headed across the park toward the kid. One look at the caller ID had him tumbling right into the past. Condy Dombrowski, his erstwhile agent, hadn't called in at least nine months.

He pressed the talk button. "Hey, Condy."

"Dash. I'm happy to see you're recovering."

"How would you know that? We haven't seen each other in more than a year."

"Since yesterday when Sal Rizzo sent me an e-mail with a link to a YouTube video of you charming snakes."

Oh, brother. "Yeah, well, I sure do wish Bubba Lockheart hadn't posted that video. Or sent it to the local TV station. I had reporters from Columbia all over me for a solid day, asking a lot of embarrassing questions about my so-called career. And there are people who think I put those snakes in that theater just so I could be the hero."

"I know. I saw the interviews. You've been sober for eighteen months, and your knee looks like it's okay."

"No, Condy, it's not."

"Oh." Dash could hear the disappointment in Condy's voice.

"What is it?" Dash asked, suddenly intrigued more than he wanted to be. His addictions took so many forms.

"Cincinnati might be looking for an experienced catcher for their single-A farm team."

Single-A? Dash had never played single-A ball. He'd been drafted right out of high school, and the Astros had put him directly into their triple-A ball club. He'd only spent a year in the minors. Being told that there might be a spot for him in single-A was almost an insult. Condy was like a drug dealer, trying to gauge Dash's desperation.

"I'm not biting, Condy, sorry."

"Listen, Dash, I know it's single-A, but Sal wants someone to bring the kid along."

"The kid?"

"Jeez, Dash, don't you read the sports pages? Dillon

Taylor needs someone to teach him the finer points of the game."

"Dillon Taylor has a ninety-nine-mile-an-hour fastball. He doesn't need much more."

"Yes, he does. Cincinnati wants an experienced catcher to work with him. It's a way back in, Dash. Rizzo thinks highly of you. He knows you can manage a young pitcher, and the organization thinks you could teach a couple of their young catchers, too."

"I see. Why don't they hire me as a coach?"

Silence greeted him. Dash knew the reasons why. He would need to prove himself first. And from what he'd read, Dillon Taylor was a hothead with a big ego. This was probably the worst job anyone in baseball could offer him.

And the sad thing was that he wanted it. He wanted it the way he wanted a drink sometimes. "I'm not interested," he said.

"Dash, come on, this is a great opportunity. You take on this kid, and you can prove to them that you've changed. This is a road map that might get you a coaching job. Sal told me he thought you could be a great teacher if you got your life together. He wants to give you a chance. He told me he's a great fan of yours."

Dash stopped and gazed at Todd. There was another kid who needed him. A kid who needed him more than some single-A ballplayer with a million-dollar arm. And even though Dash was trying hard to stay away from Todd's mother, he was still coming to feel like God had put Todd in his way for a reason. Dash had something important to give that boy. The truth hit him hard, and something cracked inside his chest.

"Sorry, Condy, I can't do it." He pulled the phone from his ear and hit the disconnect button. And in that moment, a weight lifted off his shoulders.

Savannah stood in one of the large party tents set up in the parking lot of the First Baptist Church. The Annual Allenberg County Frog Jump was in full swing. Contestants bearing Tupperware containers filled with bullfrogs large and small were gathering and getting their competitor numbers.

Todd was set to jump his frog in the next group—the twelve- to fifteen-year-olds. Dash was giving him last-minute pointers.

"All right now, son, there's a trick to handling a frog." He picked up the slimy green amphibian in his gigantic hand while Todd watched. "See, you hold him with your thumb and middle finger, and you put your trigger finger right between his eyes. That kind of hypnotizes him or something."

Sure enough, the frog hung there in Dash's hand without wiggling or squirming.

"Tight," Todd said, obviously impressed by Dash's frog-toting knowledge.

Dash turned the amphibian over and massaged its stomach. The frog closed its eyes. Todd looked up into Dash's craggy face with utter devotion.

Savannah didn't know how to feel about this turn of events. Her boy was falling in love with Dash. And she could understand why. Dash went out of his way to spend time with Todd—whether it was playing Frisbee, or catching frogs, or playing with an iPhone fart app. And Todd behaved, just to please him. More than that, Dash had made himself a model that Todd wanted to emulate. Where on earth had this man come from?

"Okay, lemme try." Todd reached into the Tupperware container and pulled out a great big, slimy frog. But he'd used perfect technique because the frog just hung there in his hand.

"That's the way," Dash said. "Now, when it's your turn to jockey the frog, you have to drop him on the little starting circle and then you slap the ground behind him to make him jump. If you keep your left hand over his eyes until you drop him on the starting circle, the extra light will startle him, and he's likely to jump further on his first hop."

Todd nodded as Dash spoke, as if the man were sending him out to do something truly important. And maybe he was.

She stood stock-still. In that moment, Dash reminded her of Granddaddy. The way he was teaching Todd was just the way Granddaddy used to go about things. And then the truth registered in her head. Granddaddy had tried to do his best for *two* fatherless children. It had probably broken his heart to see the way Savannah and Dash had squabbled.

"Dash." She said his name very softly.

He looked over his shoulder again. "What, princess?"

"I am truly, deeply, honestly sorry for the things I said back when I was ten. I was mean to you, and I think I'm going to regret it for the rest of my life."

He cocked his head. "Darlin', you've already apologized, a couple of times. And I believe I have accepted your apology. So why don't we just move on, okay?"

She nodded, only because her throat felt too thick

to speak. If she could have spoken, she would have told him that this time her apology came from deep inside her heart. In the place where true forgiveness lives.

But she couldn't quite say those words without breaking into tears. So she turned and walked away. Todd was in good hands. She'd go check on Miriam, who was hanging with her generation in the spectator tent.

She should have known that Bill would be hanging with a bunch of church ladies. He stood up from the lawn chair he'd been using when she reached the tent's shade.

"Savannah, I was wondering where you were," he said.

It was almost eighty degrees today, and Bill looked a little warm in his Roman-collared shirt and gray slacks. He presented a stark contrast to Pastor Mike of the Baptists, who had shown up to the frog jump wearing a green Kermit T-shirt and a pair of shorts. In fact, all the other ministers had shown up in shorts and golf shirts. Bill's was the only backward collar in sight.

And there was the problem, right there.

Bill had been hanging out with the old church ladies, while the real men had been coaching a bunch of kids on the right way to pick up a bullfrog.

"Bill, have you ever touched a frog?" she asked.

His eyes widened. "Uh, yes, in biology."

"I'm not talking about the dead, formaldehyde-soaked frogs we dissected when we were kids. I'm talking about a live frog. Have you ever participated in the frog jump?"

His cheeks were already kind of pink from the heat, so she couldn't tell if her question had caused his blush to deepen. "Um, I can't say as I have. Why?"

Savannah thought about the look on Todd's face as Dash explained things. She thought about the Ultimate

Frisbee games in the side yard. She thought about that fart app.

"I like you, Bill, but—"

"I like you, too, Savannah. In fact—" He reached into his pocket, and a moment later, he had a little black ring box in his hands.

"Uh, Bill," Savannah said as her pulse spiked. The man was not going to propose to her here in public, with Lillian Bray looking on. Was he? "Maybe this is not—"

He popped the top on the box. A diamond ring winked at her from the black velvet lining. "You can hardly doubt that I've been working myself up to this," he said. "You've truly captured my heart and my feelings."

The idea that he had any deep feelings at all was kind of laughable. He was proposing publicly at a frog jump?

"And," he continued, "as you can imagine, I've heard what your aunt has said, and I can see that you are truly the one that God has sent to me."

Okay, she couldn't let him go on any longer. As much as she loved Aunt Miriam, anyone in their right mind—especially the pastor of Christ Church—should realize that Miriam was suffering from some kind of dementia.

"Uh, Bill, you're going way too fast. I appreciate the offer, but I'm not ready to get married again."

Bill smiled, apparently undeterred. "I understand, perfectly. I know how it can be with someone who is divorced. But I am sure that eventually you will come around."

Oh, boy. He was denser than lead, wasn't he? "Bill, really, I'm absolutely sure that I'm not going to come around on this."

There was a collective in-drawing of breath from the

peanut gallery. Savannah suddenly felt like she was in one of those horrible dreams where you're standing completely naked on a stage and everyone you know is in the audience judging you. A dozen blue-haired church ladies in lawn chairs had their mouths hanging open. Aunt Miriam, however, seemed to be looking off in the distance with a frown on her face.

"Uh-oh," Miriam said.

The line of blue-haired ladies turned in Miriam's direction. "Uh-oh?" Lillian Bray said. "Your niece declines our minister's marriage proposal and all you can say is uh-oh?"

Miriam stood up. "Good Lord, Savannah, who let Champ out?"

At just that moment, screams came from the tent where the kids (mostly girls) who didn't want to jockey frogs were decorating Easter eggs. Everyone turned in time to see a smallish dog jump up on the table, upsetting various pots of paint and dye. He barked happily as children screamed and bolted.

The dog apparently thought this was a wonderful game. So he hopped down from the table, upsetting it in the process and splashing dye and eggs in all directions. He raced after one cute little girl with her hair all in corn-rows who led him right to the frog jump tent where her daddy was coaching her older brother.

Champ, it turned out, was going to grow up into a champion frog catcher. He made a beeline to the five-gallon buckets where the community frogs were staying cool. His tail wagged with joy as he nosed into each of the buckets. He barked happily and then upset three of them.

The suddenly freed frogs set about making a quick escape. They were real good jumpers.

The humans ran after them. They were not such good jumpers, and it has to be said that some of the adults in the crowd started cursing and swearing in a way that had the old ladies tittering like hens.

And Champion was having a heck of a time until Todd screamed at him and told him he was a big screwup. Suddenly aware that he'd misbehaved, Champ took off down Palmetto Avenue with his tail between his legs.

It looked like the excitement had exited along with the dog until one of the frog jockeys—a kid bigger than Todd—turned toward Savannah's darling son and asked in a bellicose tone, "Was that your no-account dog?"

"Yeah. You wanna make something of it?"

The big kid apparently did because he hauled off and socked Todd square in the face. But Savannah's boy didn't go down. Much to Savannah's surprise, Todd absorbed the blow, then tackled the larger kid and drove him right to the ground. Todd landed a pretty good punch to the kid's face, and his assailant cried uncle.

Todd didn't hang around after that. He stood up and took off down Palmetto Avenue in the same general direction as his dog. The bigger boy didn't give chase; he was too busy nursing a bloody nose and crying.

That left Dash to do the job. And despite his knee injury, the man could still run pretty good.

"Savannah, I think this episode confirms that your son needs discipline," Bill said.

Savannah's hands formed into fists, and she might have coldcocked the minister if it hadn't been for the sudden appearance of Claire White, dressed, as always, in a designer suit and a pair of pointy-toed pumps. She was accompanied by Mom, who wasn't dressed nearly so well, but that hardly mattered, given the look on Katie Lynne Brooks's face. Savannah's mother and ex-mother-in-law had apparently joined forces.

"The reverend is correct," Claire said in that imperious tone of hers. "Your son is out of control. And who's to blame for that?" Claire didn't stamp her foot. She didn't have to. The little temper tantrum in her voice was sufficient.

Mom would have done well to keep her mouth closed. But she didn't, as usual. "Good Lord, Savannah, didn't I tell you it was a mistake to let Todd spend time with *that man*?"

"What are you two doing here?" Savannah said.

"We've come to take you back to Baltimore," Claire said. "It's clear we've arrived just in the nick of time."

"I can't let you do that," Bill said, moving to Savannah's side as if he were her knight in shining armor, ready to do battle with out-of-line grandmothers at a moment's notice.

"I beg to differ," Claire said.

"She's going to be my wife, and I say she's not moving to Baltimore."

The church ladies erupted into applause with a few soulful "amens" supplied by the AME church matrons. Lillian said, "Atta boy, Bill. You tell her the way it's going to be."

Mom straightened her shoulders, her gaze shifting from Bill to Savannah and back again. "Is this true?"

There was no good answer to this question that wouldn't leave Savannah torn and bloody. So she did the only sensible thing she could think of.

She took off at a run, heading down Palmetto Avenue in the same direction as Champion, Todd, and Dash. She hoped like hell that Todd's grannies couldn't run very far in their high heels. Bill, she figured, she could handle.

Maybe.

CHAPTER 13

Todd had tears running down his cheeks, blood oozing out of his nose, and the beginnings of a shiner. By the time Dash caught up with him, the kid had made it to the corner of Palmetto and Baruch, and Dash's knee was throbbing to beat the band.

"Where'd you learn to tackle like that? Corey Simms is a guard on the Davis High freshman football team, and you took him down without even a running start. He probably outweighs you by thirty pounds. I'm truly impressed."

"Great. Mom's going to ground me." Todd wiped the blood from his nose. "And no one in town is ever going to be friends with me."

Dash understood. He'd been there and done that. He put his arm around the kid.

Todd let him. Hell, the kid kind of leaned into him. Dash remembered doing the same thing with Uncle Earnest. "Well, I doubt that everyone in town is going to hate you. After they catch the frogs and pick up the eggs, all anyone is going to remember is the way you tackled Corey."

"That's not true."

"Oh, yes it is. Do not underestimate the importance of football to this town." He gave the kid's shoulder a squeeze. "And besides, it was damn funny to see those bullfrogs making their escape. Folks will be laughing about this for many years to come. And not at your expense."

"Honest, Dash, I took Champ out for a walk, and I left him in the kitchen. I don't know how he got out."

"I do," Savannah said as she jogged up to them, her cute breasts bouncing and her ponytail swishing. She was a sight. A mighty good one.

"You do?" Todd asked, sounding pitiful.

"Oh, God, your nose is broken."

"Probably not," Dash said, "just bloodied. I'm not sure you could say the same for Corey."

"Don't encourage him." Savannah glared at Dash. It was the cutest glare ever. It made his insides go all hot and bothered.

"Mom, you said you knew how the dog got out?"

"I have a theory that your grandmother let him out. Not intentionally, but nevertheless."

Todd frowned. "Which grandmother?"

"Both of them are here, but Grandmother Katie Lynne probably has a key to the house."

"Aunt Katie Lynne is here?" Dash asked.

"Yes, and she's brought my former mother-in-law. They've come to take me back to Baltimore, but, don't worry, Bill Ellis has sworn not to let them do that."

"Is Dad here?" The expectation in the kid's voice slayed Dash.

"No, hon, he's not."

The boy's mouth trembled, and he turned and jogged away from them. "I'm going to look for Champ," he announced.

Savannah was about to say something when Dash interrupted her. "Let him go. He's okay. He's more okay than you think."

"I'm not so sure. I think—"

He pulled her back. "Give him space. One day he'll figure out that his daddy's not worth the tears he's shed over him. But he'll never figure that out if you make false promises. Sometimes a kid just has to work through the pain."

She stared at him. "I guess that's right."

His heart kicked. "Did your momma make false promises?" he asked.

She shook her head. "I guess she didn't. Did yours?"

"My momma left when I was nine months old. My granny used to make promises, but she died when I was six. Gramps was never sober enough to talk much."

Dash didn't know why he said these things. He never spoke about his past. But then Savannah already knew almost everything there was to know.

"I wanted more for Todd," she said.

"I'm sure you did. Sometimes life sucks, but things are looking up. We're going to sign your boy up for football, and before you know it, he'll feel a whole lot better."

"We won't do any such thing. Football is rough. Have you read the recent stuff about—"

"Honey, your boy is tougher than you think. And Davis High needs his talent."

"He's only twelve." She looked over her shoulder as if

she were checking to make sure no one had followed her from the Baptist church.

"What is it? Are the grannies following you?"

"I don't think so. But Bill might be."

"Oh."

She let go of a long breath. "Bill wants to marry me."

Dash's stomach double-clutched. He didn't know why he was so surprised; after all, he'd been bracing himself for this news for a couple of weeks now. "When did this happen?" he asked, proud of himself for keeping his emotion from sounding in his voice.

"Just now. He proposed in front of everyone in the spectators' tent. I told him no, of course. But he didn't exactly listen, and the church ladies were egging him on. You know, Dash, sometimes Bill can be awfully dense. Not to mention boring as sin."

"Honey, sin is not boring. Take it from me." Something heavy lifted from around Dash's heart. She'd told Bill no? In front of everyone in town?

Dash stopped walking and turned toward her, just as she turned toward him. And for an instant, he got the same rush that occurred every morning when they bumped into one another or when they sat at the kitchen table drinking the day's first cup of coffee. They didn't even have to say anything; the current of connection was right there, vibrating like a deep bass string, low and hardly loud enough to hear.

"I can help you out with your Bill problem," he found himself saying.

"You can?" Her voice was soft, almost a murmur.

"Yes, ma'am. You could come to the street dance with me tonight. I think, if we danced all night, everyone would get the message that you're not all that interested in Bill."

She stared at him, her lips parted, her sun-kissed cheeks turned a little pinker, and her eyes closed. She took the deepest breath and blew it out. "I can't do that."

"Why not?"

She opened her eyes. "Because dancing is dangerous."

He grinned. "You think?"

"I *know* dancing is dangerous," she said. "I met Greg at a Delta Chi dance. He swept me off my feet. And three years later, when I realized the mistake I'd made, I swore on a stack of Bibles that I was never, ever going to another dance again."

"Wow. That bad, huh?"

"You have no idea. And unfortunately, I didn't heed my own good advice. I've had two more serious relationships with guys who were jocks. And I met them both at dances. They both turned into a-holes within eighteen months. A girl can take only so much. So I have given up dancing... again."

"Well, that's a shame, because everyone goes to the Easter street dance. It's a barrel of wholesome family fun."

"Family fun?" she said.

"Yeah, Savannah, it's a community thing. I doubt that it's anything like a fraternity dance. Like, for instance, the booze will be limited, and we don't have a whole lot of frat boys in Last Chance. In fact, I don't think we have any. Good ol' boys, sure, but no frat boys."

"My weakness isn't frat boys. It's jocks."

His gut dropped like he'd just hit the first dip on a monster roller coaster. She had a weakness for jocks. And he had a weakness for royal blondes.

He should fight that but he was weak and tired. He wanted to give in.

So he gave her a smile. "Well, honey, it's up to you. But if you want to get rid of Bill, you'll need to go to the dance and make sure to dance with every eligible man in sight, *except* him."

"You think that would solve my Bill problem?"

"It might. Of course, if you danced every dance with me and then were seen riding off to the Peach Blossom Motor Court in my Caddy, that would probably do it too." The words escaped his mouth before he'd fully thought them through. Taking her to the Peach Blossom was a deep fantasy that he'd played out in his head a few times late at night. But it would be crazy to do something like that; the fallout would be toxic.

"C'mon, Dash, I can't do something like that. It would ruin my reputation."

"Aw, that breaks my heart, princess." He made a big show of putting his hand over his heart, but in truth, he was glad she had put an end to this fantasy talk about the no-tell motel. There was a real possibility that Savannah *could* break his heart if he let himself fall for her.

She laughed. "C'mon, Dash, I'm not ever going to break your heart. We hate one another."

"Do we?" His question was more earnest than he meant it to be.

"I'm sure we hate one another," she said, but she didn't sound very convincing.

The dog came into Zeph's arms. He'd been waiting on it down in the playground by the elementary school. The poor thing was confused.

"Hey there, boy, you got yourself into a heap of trouble today." He gave the pup a scratch behind the ears. Its hind end wagged.

"You don't belong to me no more. You know that, don't you?"

The dog smiled and wagged.

Zeph waited, sitting on a bench by the school yard. He saw the boy heading this direction. Todd was walking, head down, a picture of misery with a bloody nose and a swollen eye. The boy reminded him of Gabe when he was a little boy.

That was unsettling and painful, especially since the ghost behind him didn't like it whenever Zeph remembered Gabe. So Zeph tried hard to forget that boy. Of course, Zeph didn't know how to forget. Zeph didn't know much of nothing. Except how to work wood, and catch fish, and care for the strays that came the ghost's way.

The boy continued to walk toward Zeph in that slump-shouldered way that boys sometimes get when the world makes them weary.

"Hey, Todd, over here," he hollered.

The boy stopped and looked up. His face changed. He came running up to the bench and fell to his knees. He wrapped his arms around the dog in a big, old hug. "I'm sorry," he said over and over again. "I'll never yell at you again."

The dog licked his face and tried to clean his nose.

The boy rested his banged-up face on the dog's neck. "It wasn't your fault."

And then he started bawling, and Zeph let him cry. Sometimes that was just the best thing a body could do. The ghost was peaceful. The ghost knew all about crying.

When the boy was ready, Zeph gave him a smile. "Son, this dog is your responsibility now, you do know that?"

The boy nodded and sniffled. He ran his hand over the dog's back. "I'm sorry, Champ," he whispered. "It wasn't your fault. Grandmother must have let you out."

Zeph shook his head. "Well then, see, you don't have to take the blame for Champ. You've been doing a good job of caring for him. I like the name you gave him."

"Thanks. Cousin Dash wanted to call him Boulder Head."

"Good thing Champ is your dog and not Mr. Dash's. You know a dog lives for ten years or more. So it's important to remember that you can't just abandon Champ when he's naughty, or you're tired of him."

The boy looked into the pup's big brown eyes. "I won't ever abandon you, Champ. Ever." The boy's chin quivered. And with good reason. Zeph hadn't seen any daddy around. This boy knew what it felt like to be left behind.

So did the ghost.

"You love this dog, and he'll love you forever. Until the day he dies. He won't ever leave you. He won't ever disappoint you when it comes to the important things. Now, you have to remember that he's just a little puppy, and today he got himself into trouble. But it wasn't really his fault."

The boy nodded. "And it wasn't my fault either, was it?"

"No it wasn't. You go on home, and you just keep loving him the way you've been doing. He'll take care of you for life."

The boy wiped blood and snot from his nose. "Who are you?"

"I'm Zeph Gibbs. You tell your momma that I'll be by the theater sometime next week to take a look at the woodwork."

"You're the one who gave her the cat. That cat hates the dog."

Zeph smiled. "Don't I know it. That cat hates just about everything, boy, except your momma and catching mice."

Zeph stood up. "Well, I gotta be going now."

He turned and strolled through the ball fields where Luke and Gabe had once played. The ghost was restless. He wanted to return to the swamp and the woods.

The grannies drove Aunt Miriam home. And since they drove, they beat Dash and Savannah back to the house on Baruch Street. Savannah walked through the front door to find Mom pacing across the Persian rug in the front parlor like a caged lion, while Claire sat regally in the side chair looking disgusted.

Mom stopped pacing and put her hands on her hips. As always, Mom had turned herself out to the nines in a tan linen pantsuit with an unconstructed jacket over a chocolate brown silk tee. Mom always dressed in professorial beige, and her ash blond hair, cut in a chin-length pageboy, never frizzed or moved or changed in any way. If she were to take a ride in Dash's convertible, every strand would stay perfectly in place.

Mom was a control freak. Which explained why Savannah's father had departed the scene early in Savannah's life. Dad was an archaeologist who loved clutter. He spent half the year in London and the other in Cairo these days with his second wife. Derrick Reynolds had made it clear over the years that his liaison with Katie Lynne Brooks had been the worst mistake of his life. The fact that he had fathered a child with Mom seemed not to matter much to him, one way or the other. Savannah had seen her father exactly four times since she was three years old.

"Where's Todd?" Mom asked.

Before Savannah could answer, Dash cleared his throat and stepped forward with an extended hand. "Aunt Katie Lynne, it's mighty nice to see you. You may not remember me, but I'm your distant nephew, Dash. We last met at your mother's funeral when I was seventeen."

Mom looked down at his hand and up at his face. "I know who you are." She didn't touch his hand, then she turned back toward Savannah. "Where is Todd?"

"He's looking for his dog."

"His *dog*?" Claire said. "You mean that vicious animal that lunged at us when we opened the back door?"

"Yes, ma'am. Champ is the most vicious puppy I've ever had the pleasure of knowing," Dash said.

"Good grief, Savannah, Todd has allergies. Why on earth does he have a dog of any kind, much less one like that?"

"Todd has allergies?" Dash asked, his mouth quirking a little bit.

Claire glared at Dash. "You—be quiet." Claire had the audacity to wag her finger in his direction.

Dash launched one of his disarming smiles at Claire, then he leaned into the archway between the parlor and the foyer. "Yes, ma'am," he drawled. He hooked his thumbs in his belt loops and assumed his cowboy pose.

Claire turned back toward Savannah. "Go find your son. Our plane leaves at five-thirty this afternoon. I don't want to miss it."

"Oh, I'm sorry. I didn't realize this was a drive-by visit. I thought you would be staying for Easter supper. You know, you all are welcome anytime, but an advance phone call would be nice, in the future." Savannah spoke in a truly saccharine voice as she struggled to control herself. It might have been the first time she'd tried sarcasm on Claire.

"Don't get smart, young lady. I am exasperated with you," Mom said.

"Why are you exasperated? I'm merely saying that it would have been nice to know you were coming. I'm not sure I bought a big enough ham for everyone. But, then, if you're leaving tonight I guess there isn't any food emergency."

"Savannah, stop," Claire said, "Todd is going to be on that airplane with us, whether you come or not."

"Uh, excuse me," Dash drawled, "but I don't see where a couple of misguided grannies get off taking a kid away from his momma."

"Who is this man?" Claire asked.

"He's my nephew," Aunt Miriam said, as she shuffled into the room bearing a tray with a pitcher of sweet tea. "And he has a talent for speaking his mind."

Savannah rushed to help her, but Aunt Miriam said sharply, "I'm all right, sugar. I'm not dead yet." She put the tray down on the coffee table. "Can I interest anyone in some refreshments?" Miriam's dark eyes were bright behind her trifocals.

"All right, that's it," Claire said, "I'm calling the local authorities."

"Uh, ma'am, I wouldn't do that if I were you," Dash said.

"And why not?"

"Because I already called them. They're keeping an eye on Todd. He's looking for his dog."

"But you don't know where he is?"

"Well, I have a general idea where he is. And I'm betting that Zeph will find him and the dog pretty quick and bring them both home. But just in case the dog doesn't go where I expect him to, I've got Damian keeping an eye on Todd. He's fine."

"Who is Damian?"

"The chief of police."

"Honestly, Savannah, have you lost your mind? If something happens to Todd, you're going to be in such a world of hurt," Mom said. "You could be charged with child endangerment."

"Nothing is going to happen to him." Dash's voice sounded sharp.

"Greg is not going to like this," Claire stated. "Not one bit. And if you let that boy come to harm, you'll lose him, Savannah. Wouldn't it be better if you just gave it up and came home where you and Todd belong?"

Savannah lost her temper. "Look, we're not going back to Baltimore. That's final. You both need to adjust. If Greg wants to own up to his responsibilities and have a conversation with me about Todd, I'm happy to talk with him and work out arrangements. He's the only one I'm going to talk to about this. Besides, I've got investors for my theater renovation project, my son is starting to blossom, and people here like and respect me. Why would I want to leave?"

"You've got investors?" Mom asked. The surprise in her voice only served to fuel Savannah's growing annoyance.

"Yes, I do."

"Who would be stupid enough to invest in that theater?"

Before Savannah could respond, the doorbell rang, and Dash said, "Well since I'm obviously not invited to this party, I'll go see who that is."

Dash opened the door and Lillian Bray came waddling in, her face beet red. "Dash Randall, what have you done?" she demanded.

"Me? I don't think I've done anything."

"Well you should have done something." She rolled into the living room and turned on Savannah. "Honey, you can't say no to Bill. I mean you and he are a foregone conclusion. It's written in the stars. Made in Heaven. Y'all belong together. Now, honey, he's on his way over, and you need to tell him that you've changed your mind."

"Who is Bill?" Claire asked in a tone very much like Dame Judi Dench playing Queen Elizabeth in *Shakespeare in Love*.

"Oh, he's the one who told you Savannah couldn't leave because she's getting married," Miriam said as she poured another tumbler of sweet tea.

"The minister?"

"Yes, ma'am," Dash supplied.

"Oh, my goodness," Lillian said suddenly, "is that you, Katie Lynne. Why you've gotten so . . . old."

Mom's jawline tensed. "So have you, Miz Lillian." Mom turned toward Savannah. "You have funding for the theater, and you're marrying a minister? And all this happened in a month?"

Savannah shrugged. "Well, I guess things happen fast in Last Chance."

Mom rolled her eyes. "My experience is that life moves at a snail's pace here. And knowing your history with men, I'm thinking this development is a very dangerous sign. Hon, you're always falling in love at the drop of a hat. And you're always disappointed in the end. And I know how that goes. God, I know. I've been married three times. You can't marry this man, not if you've only known him for a few weeks."

"Oh, yes she can," Lillian countered. "Miriam has blessed the match between Bill and Savannah. And what Miriam brings together stays together."

Mom stared at Lillian and then at Aunt Miriam and then back. "You all are crazy," she muttered. "Savannah, these people are crazy. You can't live here."

Just then Bill Ellis strolled through the open front door. "Hello, is anyone home?"

"C'mon in, Bill, your timing is impeccable, as usual," Dash said. "We're having a family get-together, and I have this feeling we may need spiritual guidance before it's over." Dash had resumed his place, leaning against the archway.

Bill strolled into the room bearing an Easter lily that he might actually have bought instead of picking from Lillian's garden.

"Meet Savannah's mother, Katie Lynne Brooks, and Savannah's ex-mother-in-law, Claire White. Ladies, meet Reverend William Ellis, our minister at Christ Church." Dash did the introductions in a voice that sounded low and brittle.

Bill didn't smile. "I'm here for you, Savannah. What can I do?"

"Leave," Claire said.

Lillian glared at Claire, and Claire dished it right back. It was a standoff as to who had the scarier evil eye.

"*Let every person be quick to hear, slow to speak, slow to anger; for the anger of man does not produce the righteousness of God,*" Bill intoned.

Lillian turned. "That's from Proverbs?" she asked.

"No, it's from James, Lillian, and you'd be well to remember the sentiment."

The church lady nodded and actually seemed to deflate. "You're right, Bill, we should keep calm and try to sort this out."

Savannah's patience snapped.

"Look," she said in a firm voice, staring right at Claire. "Bill is right, you need to stop talking and start listening. I don't want to live in Baltimore. My life is no longer there. I will do whatever I can to make sure you both have a chance to spend time with Todd. I know you love him and want the best for him. But Todd is living with me. If you'd like to stay, that's fine. You can join us for Easter dinner. But I won't have any more demands, from any of you."

She cast her gaze from Mom, to Claire, to Bill, and back again.

"And Mom, there is one last thing. I'm sick and tired of you always bringing me down. I have financing for the theater. There are people in this town who want to see it revived, and they've given me a grant. So don't look down your nose at me. Don't belittle my achievements. I'm not living your life. I'm living mine."

"They *gave* you the money?" Mom asked. "Don't you think that's a little strange? I mean, usually people *invest* in a project."

Before Savannah could address these questions, the

door burst open again to admit the prodigal son and his canine.

"I found him," Todd said. His announcement was completely unnecessary because Champ scampered into the parlor, his tail wagging, his nose sniffing. He went directly toward Claire and put his paws on her beautiful designer outfit.

And Claire flinched. She was obviously scared to death of that little puppy. "Get down," Claire ordered, but the pooch seemed oblivious until Claire started sneezing.

"Ah," Dash intoned, "allergies."

Todd came to a halt. "Oh, hey," he said, his gaze shifting from one grandmother to the other.

"Oh, my God, your face," Claire said as she pulled a tissue out of her Hermès bag. She glared at Dash. "You were there when it happened. Why on earth did you put him in a situation where he could get beaten up by a bully like that? And why didn't you stop it?"

Dash glared back, but said nothing.

"It wasn't Dash's fault. It was yours and Granny's," Todd said in a surprisingly adult tone.

"What?" Mom and Claire said in unison. Their expressions suggested that World War III was about to break out at any moment, probably with the force of a nuclear explosion.

Todd stood straight and tall in front of his grandmothers. He didn't flinch. "Well, I'm sorry, but it's only the truth. You all let the dog out. And he got into a lot of trouble. And then Corey Simms started a fight over it."

"That's right, son, but you're the one who finished it," Dash said, giving the boy a big smile.

"Who is this man?" Claire asked again, giving Dash

the stink eye. But Dash was impervious, so she turned back toward Todd. "Young man, I will not take insolence from you. Is that clear? Now go upstairs and pack your things."

Todd looked at Savannah. "Are we going somewhere?"

"We're going home," Claire said. "And you're going to interview for the Gilman School. Your interview is next week, and I only hope the black eye has faded by then. I'm sure the board of admissions takes a dim view of boys who get into fights."

"Now, Claire—" Savannah started.

"I don't want to go to the Gilman School," Todd said.

"Of course you do. Everybody in your family has gone there," Claire said.

"I didn't." Dash smiled. Todd smiled back.

"Really, Cousin Dash, you are not related to us in any way." Mom sounded like she was about to burst a blood vessel.

"You know, Aunt Katie Lynne, when you're not so angry, you'll realize that what you just said was kind of funny."

Champ decided that it was time to make friends with Mom. He jumped up on her beige ensemble and started licking her face. Her reaction was decidedly unfriendly. "Get off me, you mangy mutt."

She pushed the dog off her lap. He landed hard with a yelp.

"Hey, that was mean." Todd got down on the floor and gave the puppy a big hug.

"He's undisciplined," Mom said.

"Sort of like the boy," Bill muttered.

Dash snorted. "You know, people have been throwing

that word around a lot lately." He smiled in Savannah's direction and then glared at Bill. Bill glared right back.

Savannah felt the corners of her mouth lifting. It was kind of strange having Dash at her back.

"Stop playing with that disgusting dog and go pack," Claire said.

Todd turned toward Savannah. "Can I bring Champ with me?"

Before Savannah could open her mouth to tell her son that they weren't going anywhere, Claire and Mom said "no" in unison.

Big mistake.

The boy stood up, the dog at his feet. "I'm not going then."

"Of course you're going." Claire was almost as dense as Bill, who was still standing there clutching the Easter lily.

"No. I promised that I was going to look after Champ for the rest of his life. I'm not going to leave him here if I have to go back to Baltimore," Todd said.

He looked up at Savannah, and her heart broke. If she could find a way to make Greg love this child, she would do it in a New York minute. But she'd tried and failed. Greg was a spoiled brat and a louse. And she had a good idea why her ex had ended up that way. His mother was a piece of work.

"I'm proud of you," Savannah said to her little boy. "And we're not going anywhere."

The uncertainty in Todd's eyes fled. "That's good."

"Now, why don't you and Champ go upstairs? You need to wash your face and change out of those bloody clothes."

He turned and headed up the stairs.

Savannah turned toward Dash. "Can you make sure his nose is really okay?"

Dash nodded and followed Todd up the stairs. It was kind of strange. A month ago, she didn't trust Dash with her son. Now she couldn't imagine anyone better to check on him. In fact, Dash would probably give Todd a few words of wisdom while he was examining Todd's many hurts. Dash and Todd had a lot in common.

Savannah turned toward Miriam, who was sitting on the sofa drinking sweet tea and looking like nothing particularly ugly had been going on. "Aunt Miriam, are you okay?"

"Oh, I'm fine, sugar. Couldn't be better." She gave Savannah a slightly goofy smile.

"So," Savannah said to the assembled crowd in the parlor, "the excitement's over."

She turned toward the minister. "Bill, I appreciate your offer, but I'm not ready to be married to anyone."

"You'll change your mind." He thrust the lily at her. She took it, and he turned on his heel and strode from the room.

Lillian shook her head and turned, too. She hurried after the minister. "Bill, honey, don't be discouraged. It will all work out," she cried as she left the room.

"Mom, Claire, you're welcome to stay for the dance and Easter services."

Claire stood. "I wouldn't think of it. You listen, young woman, you don't know what you're playing with. Daniel is one of the most powerful attorneys in Baltimore. You will rue the day that you took my grandson away from me." She turned toward Mom. "Come, Kate, we'll have to rethink."

For a moment, Savannah hoped Mom would tell Claire where she could take her high-powered attorney husband and shove him. But of course, Mom didn't.

"You're a fool, Savannah," she said. "No one gets free money for a project like The Kismet. You've obviously gotten yourself entangled in something you don't understand. It's only a matter of time before you fail and come crying back to us."

And with that, Mom followed Claire out of the house.

"It's truly amazing," Miriam said, once the grannies had departed, "that Sally and Earnest managed to give birth to a person like Katie Lynne. I'm so sorry that your mother is the way she is."

Aunt Miriam's words provided no comfort. Suddenly all of Savannah's doubts and fears redoubled, followed by the sudden retreat of the adrenaline that had powered her defiance.

Tears filled her eyes, and she started to shake. She took the stairs at a dead run. When she made it to her bedroom, she threw herself on the bed and let the mother of all crying jags have its way with her. She always ended up crying when she got angry.

CHAPTER 14

Hettie surveyed City Hall Park. Everything was perfect. The members of her dance committee had outdone themselves. The paper lanterns hanging between the trees looked festive. Thanks to Jenny, the Methodists had loaned a collection of folding tables and chairs. There were votives on each table.

The Wild Horses were all set up on the bandstand that blocked Palmetto Avenue for the evening. People had already started turning up with lawn chairs, coolers, and thermoses filled with coffee and probably other beverages.

It was going to be a nice night. A little chilly perhaps, but not cold. Hettie loved the annual street dance. When Jimmy had been alive, they had danced away the nights here. She liked her husband best of all when they were dancing. Unfortunately, they hadn't danced nearly enough.

It looked as if she would be sitting with the matrons this evening. It made her feel old.

"Well, that's it, Ms. Marshall," Rachel Lockheart said.

Hettie's administrative assistant at Country Pride Chicken was the most organized person Hettie had ever met. Hettie had inherited Rachel with the business when Jimmy died, and Rachel was probably worth more than any other asset her husband had left her.

"Those lanterns and votives are a real nice touch, Rachel."

"Thanks." Rachel blushed.

Just then her Ladyship, Baroness Woolham, came striding across the grass. Rocky didn't look much like a baroness. She was wearing jeans, a pink sweatshirt, and a pair of slip-on sneakers that she would undoubtedly ditch before the night was over. "Hey, y'all, did you hear what I heard?"

"You mean the news about Bill Ellis?" Rachel asked.

Hettie forced a neutral expression onto her face. It wouldn't do for anyone to know how this news had affected her when she'd first heard it earlier in the day. She was shocked that Bill had asked for Savannah's hand and far too relieved that Savannah had rejected him.

"I can't believe he asked her to marry him after just a month of knowing her," Rocky said.

"Me neither," Hettie said.

"I can't believe Savannah told him no, and in front of Lillian Bray," Rachel said. "Lillian is in a perfectly foul mood. She snapped at me five times while I was setting up card tables. Honestly, I don't think it's such a big deal that the tables came from the Methodists." Rachel let go of a big sigh.

"She's just in a tizzy because there's a risk that Bill might settle for Jenny," Rocky said.

Hettie's stomach flip-flopped. She didn't like Bill

settling for Jenny any more than she liked the idea of Bill and Savannah.

Molly Canaday, wearing an absolutely gorgeous sea green hand-knit sweater over one of her ratty T-shirts, strolled over. "Hey, y'all. So what's the over-under on Bill and Savannah ending up hitched?"

"Honestly." Hettie shook her head. "Could we talk about something else, please?"

Rocky, Rachel, and Molly stared at Hettie, and then Molly said, "You know, it's way more fun betting on Bill's marital misadventures than speculating on how many runaway bullfrogs will end up as roadkill before tomorrow morning." She grinned.

"Honestly." Hettie rolled her eyes.

"Quit making fun, Molly. This could be serious," Rachel said.

"Serious how?"

"Well, what happens if Miriam says that Bill and Savannah are made for each other, but Savannah refuses to believe it?" Rachel asked. "You don't want to mess around with one of Miriam's marital forecasts."

"I'm sure the world will not come to an end," Rocky said. "Miriam's forecasts are always open to interpretation. Didn't everyone in town think I was going to end up with Dash, when in fact it was Hugh all along?"

"That's right," Molly said. She scanned the gathering crowd with slightly squinted eyes.

"What are you doing?" Rachel asked.

"I'm just thinking. If Savannah isn't supposed to be with Bill, then who else might fit the bill, so to speak?"

"Oh, please," Hettie groaned, "can we leave the puns out of it. And the matchmaking, too."

Molly gazed at Hettie. "You're right. We should pretend we don't care."

"But we do," Rachel and Rocky said in near unison. Which wasn't all that surprising since they had been friends forever.

"Hush up, y'all, he's coming this way," Molly said.

Hettie turned just in time to see Bill strolling across the street and heading right toward them. As usual, he was dressed in his black clerical shirt and a pair of gray slacks. He looked pale. And his appearance at the street dance was a huge surprise.

Usually the town's ministers chose to turn in early on Easter Eve so they could get up at o-dark-thirty for sunrise services.

"Bill, what a surprise," Hettie said, forcing a smile to her face.

He nodded, seemingly unaware that the members of the dance committee, book club, garden club, and Ladies' Auxiliary were watching his every move and speculating on what was going to happen next. Suddenly Hettie was ashamed of all of them. They should leave Bill alone.

He walked right up to her. "Hettie, do you have a moment?" he asked.

"Of course I do." She took him by the arm and guided him to one of the tables set back into the trees. Bill reached out to touch Hettie's hand once they took their seats. Warmth spread up her arm.

"I suppose you heard all about Savannah," he said.

"I did. I'm sorry. And I'm so sorry the entire town is talking about it. Savannah should have—"

"No, it wasn't really her fault. I should have known

better than to ask her in public like that. That was foolhardy."

"Is your heart broken?"

He straightened his shoulders, and a frown folded into his forehead. "I don't know. I'm embarrassed."

For some reason, this response made Hettie feel lighter. "Bill, if you were heartbroken, I think you'd know it. Maybe Savannah did you a favor."

"A favor?"

She tightened her grip on his hand, suddenly aware of the bones beneath his skin, the warmth in his palm, the slightly rough male texture of his fingertips. "Love is supposed to knock you on your butt. If you don't feel knocked, then it probably isn't love."

"Did Jimmy knock you on your butt?" His eyes were very sharp.

"No. He didn't. I married Jimmy to please my parents."

"Have you ever been knocked on your butt?"

She giggled. "Hearing you say the word 'butt' tickles me, you know."

He smiled. It was a warm, wonderful, beautiful thing. Watching it unfold on his face was like watching a big magnolia open up its petals. "You know, Hettie, you are always making me laugh, too."

"Thank you."

"So, have you?" he pressed.

"Have I what?"

"Ever been knocked on your butt."

She looked down at their conjoined hands. For an instant, she wasn't sure where her fingers left off and his started. It was a very odd kind of feeling that made her heart bounce around in her chest.

"I fell in lust once."

"Really?"

"I was sixteen."

"Sixteen? I take it you weren't listening to my predecessor on the need for abstinence."

"I'm sorry. I was weak."

"And he knocked you on your butt."

"Almost. Not quite. I think *I* may have knocked *him* on his butt, though. And you know, that's a real problem."

"What is?"

"When someone thinks they are in love with you, but you don't feel the same thing back."

"I guess I get that."

"It's no fun, to be honest. I'm always feeling guilty about it."

"I take it we're talking about Dash Randall."

She looked away, just in time to see Dash sauntering up to the bandstand to talk with Clay Rhodes.

Bill followed her gaze. "He's a good-looking man. He's rich. His money would solve all your problems."

"Yeah, it would. And if I were a different woman, I might give up my principles. But I can't. I don't love him. I did lust after him when I was very young, but I got over that mighty quick."

They sat there holding hands for the longest time, each of them gazing across the park to where Dash stood by the bandstand.

Finally Bill let go of a long breath. "I don't want to be like Dash," he said. "I don't want to go carrying a torch for someone who doesn't want me."

"Good for you. Dash is stuck, and you're already moving on."

"But I want a wife, Hettie. To be honest, I'm kind of lonely, and I'd really like a family. And Savannah comes with one, ready-made."

Just then Jenny Carpenter came hurrying up with a pie in her hand. "Oh, there you are, you poor thing," she said sitting down at the third chair at the table. Bill and Hettie quickly disengaged their hands. "I baked you a pie, and I took it to the rectory, but you weren't there. I'm glad to see you out and about."

Bill smiled at Jenny, his blue eyes lighting up. "Pie, oh my. I definitely could drown my sorrows in pie, Jenny. Thanks."

Hettie stifled the urge to punch Jenny's pretty little face. Damn it all to hell. She should have had Violet make some of her cookies for him. But it was too late now.

Hettie pushed up from the table. "Well, Bill, I think your problems are just a slice away," she said.

She started to stroll away, but he called her back. "Hettie."

She turned. "What?"

"Would you save a dance for me?"

Savannah arrived at the street dance and scanned the crowd. Bill was at a table under the paper lanterns talking with Jenny Carpenter. The book club, minus Jenny, had staked a claim to a portion of the sidewalk not too close to the bandstand. Nita, Cathy, and Lola May had brought refreshments.

Dash was standing by the bandstand, looking… perfect.

He wore a new pair of Wranglers, a pair of old cow-boy boots, a plaid shirt, and a cowboy hat. He and Clay

Rhodes were the only guys in hats. But Dash was the only guy wearing cowboy boots. Once a Texan, always a Texan. She remembered giving him all kinds of grief over the battered straw cowboy hat he'd worn that first summer when he was almost thirteen and she was a bratty ten-year-old. She'd told him he looked stupid in that hat.

Boy, things had changed.

Speaking of twelve-year-olds, Todd had found a few friends who had made him their champion for taking out Corey Simms, who apparently was a notorious bully.

Todd seemed to be having a lot of fun, despite his slightly swollen eye. In fact, that black eye was almost like a badge of courage. She watched him laughing with the other kids. He'd grown some. His shirt and jeans looked too short in the arms and legs. They seemed baggy around his middle.

"Hey, Savannah," Rocky called, "you've got to taste Cathy's banana bread. It's to die for."

Savannah squared her shoulders and headed toward the book club members. She unfolded her lawn chair as it occurred to her that Todd wasn't the only one with new friends. She had reconnected with Rocky and made some new friends, too.

Somehow, in a very short period of time, she'd come to feel as if she belonged here. It was an amazing feeling, given the ugly fight she'd had with Mom earlier in the day. For the first time in her memory, Savannah actually felt sorry for her mother.

Someone passed her a paper plate with a slice of banana bread and a cup filled with sweet tea.

"Where's your husband?" Savannah asked Rocky.

"Oh, he's over yonder somewhere, talking to Stone.

When they start playing waltzes he'll come over here and bow stiffly and ask for a dance. We can all pretend that we're at the Netherfield ball."

Molly snorted a laugh. "Hey, Savannah, if this were the Netherfield ball and you were Eliza Bennet, you'd have to dance with Bill Ellis first."

A chorus of laughter followed. Savannah looked down at her plate as it occurred to her that, if anyone had played out a scene from *Pride and Prejudice*, it had been her—when she'd told the minister where to take his proposal and shove it.

She looked up. Everyone in the book club was grinning at her. Savannah felt her lips tugging upward. "Well," she said, "he's a little bit like Mr. Collins. He quotes Bible verses incessantly."

Everyone started giggling except Hettie, who never giggled, ever.

Savannah looked up at the star-spangled sky. "I know that my aunt may have encouraged everyone to think about me and Bill in the same sentence, but maybe everyone needs to think again. Maybe my aunt is like Mrs. Bennet."

"Exactly the point I made earlier, before you got here," Molly said. "I mean, look at him. He's over there with Jenny sucking up pie. He doesn't look very heartbroken."

"Kind of makes him even more like Mr. Collins, if you ask me," Cathy said. "I mean, after Lizzy told Mr. Collins where he could go, didn't he just up and marry Charlotte? And I'll bet Jenny is a better cook than Charlotte Lucas ever was."

"And besides," Molly said, "didn't Miriam say that Bill needed someone who was good with numbers? Well, there you go, Jenny is a math teacher. It's just like last year at the barbecue dance. Everyone thought Rocky and Dash were the perfect fit."

Savannah turned toward Rocky. "You and Dash? Really?"

Rocky shrugged. "He's all right when you get him on the dance floor. And underneath that cool, calm, cowboy exterior beats a real living heart. He's got several soft spots."

Rocky paused for a long moment. "Hey, wait," she said. "We've got it all wrong. If this were the Netherfield ball, *you'd* have to dance with your *cousin* first." She laughed even harder. "That will be the day—to see you and Dash Randall dancing together."

Savannah's chest tightened. She wanted to dance with Dash. Earlier today he'd as much as suggested that she should dance every dance with him tonight.

But she refused to fall for Cousin Dash. That would mess up everything. Especially since Dash seemed to be so good for Todd, and Savannah was so very bad at relationships.

And just then Dash came striding across the lawn like Mr. Darcy, only with cowboy boots. He didn't look at all like Colin Firth. He had much shorter hair and no sideburns, thank goodness. No, he looked more like, well, no one in particular except his own gorgeously handsome self.

"Princess, get your butt out of that chair and dance with me." He delivered this line in a most Darcy-like snarl. As if he were asking against his own better judgment.

A definite tingle arose in Savannah's core, and her heart started to pound. The chill bumps climbing up her arms reminded her of just how dangerous it was to dance with a man she found attractive.

"Oh, go on," Rocky said. "Lizzy didn't enjoy her dance but she endured."

Dash blinked at Rocky. "What are you talking about?"

"Never mind," Savannah said, getting out of her chair. She shouldn't dance with him, but she was going to, and she had a feeling she would enjoy this dance a whole lot. "Let's go."

She took two steps and realized that the dancers were doing a country line dance that she didn't know.

"Uh, what is that dance, the Achy Breaky?"

"No, honey, it's the Boot Scoot Boogie, but have no fear, the next one is a waltz."

"How do you know that?"

"Because he requested one." Dash jerked his head in the direction of Lord Woolham, who managed a much better impression of Mr. Darcy as he strolled up and asked his wife to dance.

Dash snagged Savannah by the hand and pulled her out toward the street. She was overwhelmed by the heat of his touch, the rough texture of his skin, the bath-soap smell of him, and the fact that practically everyone at the dance was watching them.

The band struck up "Can I Have This Dance for the Rest of My Life," and Dash pulled her close. She placed her hand on his shoulder, immediately struck dumb by the hard muscle beneath her palm. He started moving, and Savannah was amazed to discover that he was light on his feet and knew exactly how to lead. They danced for quite a long time without speaking a single word, and the silence became charged.

She needed to break it. "This is quite a production, isn't it?"

"Yup," he said as he suddenly changed direction and put her through a number of steps that had her moving forward and then backward and then forward again.

The silence swelled between them.

"You know," she said, "people usually talk while they dance. Of course, I guess you and I don't have much to say."

He glanced down at her with a tiny quirk of his lips. "I reckon."

He moved her through another pattern of intricate steps.

"But maybe we *should* have more to say," she said.

"You think?"

"Yes. I do. It would be kind of weird for us to just dance here for fifteen minutes and say nothing."

"I don't know. I've danced with plenty of women who talk up a blue streak and manage not to say anything important. So if you're talking to be sociable, you can quit. I like dancing just for dancing's sake."

"You know, Dash, you and I are more alike than either of us would like to admit."

"How's that?"

"We're fatherless, to start with. And pigheaded. And kind of willful. And bratty."

He laughed. "Yep, princess, that describes you to a T. Probably describes me, too."

Just then Hugh and Rocky danced a little closer, and Rocky said, "See, I told you Dash was a great dancer. And y'all look so good together. I have to admit that I didn't know how to waltz until Hugh taught me. And the band was playing this song. But you seem to have it down pat."

Hugh twirled his wife away in a swooping turn. Hugh's dancing style looked like it might have been in vogue back when Johann Strauss was burning up the charts in Vienna.

Dash's technique was way more western, and infinitely more intimate. He glanced down at her. "What were we talking about, darlin'? I seem to remember it was a scintillating subject."

"Not hardly," she muttered.

"Okay, so maybe we should talk about books. Y'all have gotten pretty cozy with the ladies of the book club."

"Do you read books?"

"Mostly automobile repair manuals. I reckon that's not a good subject then."

The band moved from "Can I Have This Dance" right into "You Were Always on My Mind," and Dash pulled her close enough so that his rock-hard thighs grazed hers. He dropped his gigantic hands and spanned her waist. She had to move her own hands up over his shoulders. Only a couple of layers of denim separated them. That fabric was simultaneously not enough and way too much.

"Did Hugh bribe the band so they would play this song?" she asked.

The Stetson shaded his eyes, but the lopsided smile on his face told her all she needed to know. "You did?"

"Honey, you should know by now that actions speak louder than words. And we're sending messages here. Did Rocky ever tell you about the barbecue dance last summer?"

"No, but the book club was talking about it."

"Well, see, Rocky and I took one of Aunt Mim's marital pronouncements and used it to match up Rachel and Bubba. So, see, I figure you and me are doing Bill and Jenny a big favor right now."

Savannah cast her gaze in the minister's direction. He was definitely enjoying Jenny's pie, but Savannah didn't get the feeling he was really enjoying Jenny all that much.

She watched him for a long moment and realized that he was looking off into the distance, and he wasn't looking at her. He was looking at Hettie.

And Hettie, who was sitting with the book club, was looking at him, only she was trying not to be obvious about it. Goose bumps crawled up Savannah's skin, and she got this odd feeling, halfway between an itch and a buzz.

Hettie and Bill?

Of course. Why didn't anyone else see it?

Just then Dash pulled her so close that she was practically in the shade of his hat. And she momentarily forgot about everything else but him.

This was not the way cousins danced. Especially when he tucked her head under his chin, and she lost herself in the sturdy feel of him, the rhythm of the music, and the heat he kindled in every cell of her body.

Dash buried his nose in Savannah's hair and took a deep breath. She smelled flowery. He closed his eyes and swayed to the music.

It was sort of surprising the way the princess fit in his arms. She seemed to know which way he was planning to swirl her before he even seemed to know it himself. He'd never danced with anyone who actually knew how to let him lead before.

Boy howdy, he was hooked on this woman. And he didn't know what to do about it. If he told her how he felt, she was liable to slap his face or tell him exactly what she thought of him. And then what would happen to Todd and Miriam? He didn't want to cause a family rift.

Besides, he knew how dangerous it was to fall for Savannah. He'd just gotten over Hettie. He should have time alone to work out his problems and his feelings.

"This is dangerous," she murmured against his chest, giving voice to every single one of his fears. Her breath left a little warm spot at the neck of his shirt and sent a shiver up his backbone.

"Honey, you're already the talk of the town, so I doubt that dancing with a reprobate like me is going to get you in any more hot water."

She looked up, her dark eyes worried. "That's not what I meant. And you're not a reprobate."

Her eyes had darkened, and her cheeks were a little pink, and she looked as if she might move in on him like she'd done that night on the porch. Good grief, did she actually *want* that no-tell motel fantasy he'd talked about earlier in the day?

Hettie had wanted that fantasy, a long time ago. And he'd given it to her. And like an inexperienced idiot, he'd fallen in love with her. But she hadn't fallen back. She'd just used him to get her bad-boy experience out of the way.

It hadn't taken very long after that to realize that most women wanted a bad-boy experience. And the blondes who hung around professional baseball teams were all about that. In fact, the blond bimbo who had convinced him to ride that Harley after drinking a few beers had been looking for some low-down dirty fun, too.

And he'd been happy to oblige.

He'd been such a fool. But he was changing his ways.

"It's okay, Savannah, I get it," he said aloud. "Every woman is curious about us bad boys."

She shook her head. "No, Dash, that's not what I meant. I only meant that I fell in love with Greg because he could dance. It was the worst mistake I ever made."

"Well, I'm sorry to hear that. But you falling in love with me is pretty absurd." He said the words and realized how much he wanted her to fall.

She closed her eyes and put her head on his shoulder. "I guess I'm glad that falling in love with you is impossible. I guess that makes it safe to dance with you," she said.

No, it wasn't safe. It was suddenly terrifying.

The band finished the song and struck up "Save a Horse, Ride a Cowboy." Almost immediately the street filled with line dancers.

Some part of him wanted Savannah to stay there with him, but another part was relieved when she let him go.

"I should sit down now." She glanced at Bill. "Look, he's fine. He's with Jenny and her pies. We've accomplished our mission."

He stood there like an idiot agreeing with her, because his emotions were suddenly in turmoil. He turned away from her and put one boot in front of the other like a coward running from a fight. An instant later he found himself standing in front of Hettie.

"C'mon, dance with me."

She shook her head, but he could see the longing in her eyes.

"Honey, Jimmy's dead. I know the two of you loved this dance. And I know that you never sat for any of it. C'mon, my knee is better. Let's go boot scoot."

She sighed. "No, Dash, I can't. Because if I dance with you, you'll get the wrong idea."

He ground his teeth together. He'd asked her to dance because he knew how much Hettie loved dancing. And sitting on the sidelines had to be hard for her. She was probably missing Jimmy tonight. But once again, Hettie had thrown his kindness back in his face. So he marched right up to Jenny Carpenter, where she sat consoling the not-very-devastated minister.

That woman practically busted a gut when he asked her to dance. She got all red in the face and even stammered. And it was almost pitiful the look she gave Bill when the minister suggested that she ought to take Dash up on his offer.

And that's how Dash ended up dancing with Jenny. And how Hettie ended up dancing with Bill. And how Savannah ended up not dancing at all, which was a damn shame because she could outdance all of them put together.

CHAPTER
15

Savannah arrived at The Kismet at half past seven on the Monday after Easter. She was grumpy for reasons that she didn't wish to examine too carefully. For some reason, Dash had changed his schedule, and she didn't bump into him at the bathroom. And he didn't come down to share a morning cup of coffee with her.

In fact, from the moment she walked away from him at the street dance, Dash had been avoiding her. Conspicuously.

Which was probably just as well. After all, their two dances, coupled with her refusal of Bill's proposal, had unleashed a firestorm of gossip. The old church ladies, led by Lillian Bray, were saying that she was wayward and stubborn, just like she'd been as a little girl. They pointed to her slow dance with Dash as proof positive.

None of them was ready to admit that she wasn't Bill's soulmate. They just thought she was playing hard to get, and using Dash to do it. Apparently they believed this

because of the shenanigans that Dash and Rocky had perpetrated on them last summer.

Oh, if they only knew the way she'd tossed and turned
trying to find sleep on Saturday and Sunday nights. Those
dances with Dash haunted her.

And it was kind of strange how the church ladies were
missing the most obvious thing—that Bill and Hettie had
looked like they were having way more fun than anyone
else, even though Bill was a miserable dancer. Why was
everyone so blind?

She went to unlock the theater's doors, only to find
that they were already unlocked. She could hear voices
inside.

She pulled open the door to find Dash and Zeph standing in the lobby discussing the candy counter's woodwork.

Her reaction to this scene was complicated. She was
happy to see Zeph there. From what she'd heard, he was
the finest carpenter in all of Allenberg County.

But she was suddenly annoyed at Dash, while at the
same time being more happy to see him than she wanted
to be.

"What are you doing here?" she demanded.

"Talking to Zeph."

"Howdy, ma'am." Zeph nodded and gave her a big
smile filled with incredibly white teeth.

"You know, Dash, I'm perfectly capable of talking to
Zeph about the woodwork."

"Ma'am, don't you be blaming Dash, now. He drove by
this morning heading to the stables, and he saw me waiting on you. I got here real early. And he offered to open
the door for me."

Just then Maverick sauntered down the stairs meowing

loudly. He picked his way over the dirty floor and proceeded to wrap himself around Savannah's legs.

Zeph laughed. "Yessir, that cat sure does belong to you."

Savannah picked up the cat and stroked him, memories of Granddaddy's cat suddenly washing through her mind. Maverick settled into her arms, his motor running loudly.

It was suddenly hard to stay angry. "All right, so tell me what you've decided about the woodwork. I'll need to tell the contractor when he arrives."

"Contractor?" Dash asked.

"Yes, I've hired a contractor. You didn't expect me to rebuild the place with my own hammer and nails."

"I thought you were going to hire an architect."

"I talked to several, but their fees were astronomical. I thought the grant was a lot of money until I started talking to those people. Honestly, they all wanted six-figure consulting fees. I can't afford it. So I talked to some contractors instead."

He frowned. "Who did you hire? I didn't know you were interviewing contractors."

"Well, I'm so sorry. I didn't think I needed to check in with you. I hired JBR Construction." She checked her watch. "Mr. Rodgers should be here in a few minutes."

The look on both Dash and Zeph's faces gave her no comfort.

"What?"

Zeph smiled and nodded. "Well, ma'am, I need to be getting along. There are some chores I need to do for Mr. Dash." And with that Zeph turned and strolled out of the theater.

"Bad move, princess."

"They were the lowest bidder."

"Of course they were, but did you need to take the lowest bid? You should have plenty of money."

"Well, I do, but things cost so much more than I thought they would. I just wanted to keep a little cushion for contingencies, you know?"

"Yeah, I guess, but sometimes you can be penny-wise and pound-foolish."

"Can I ask you a question?"

"Sure."

"Don't you think it's kind of strange that Angel Development is giving me all that money with no strings attached?"

Dash smiled. "Honey, your book club friends are the folks behind Angel Development. Some of those women have more money than sense. So, no, I don't think it's strange. But you aren't going to make them happy by using John Rodgers as your contractor."

"They don't like him?"

"I suspect they never heard of him. But I have. And Hugh has. Hettie might have had some dealings with him. He's not straight, you know what I mean? He'll come in low and then he'll nickel-and-dime you. And he won't do things right."

"Well, it's too late. I signed the contract."

"Maybe I should talk to Eugene and see if you can unsign it."

She put her fists on her hips, anger suddenly flashing through her. "Dash, I didn't ask your opinion. And I deeply resent you coming in here without my permission and throwing your weight around like this was your project. It's not. I didn't take your money, precisely because I was afraid of this.

"I want to do this on my own. You heard what my mother said about me on Saturday. Can't you see why this is so important to me?"

"Honey, you're making a mistake."

"Yeah, maybe I am. But if someone always catches me before I make a mistake, how on earth am I ever going to learn how to walk, much less run? I need to do this on my own."

"All right. But you watch that man, you hear? And if he starts doing things you don't appreciate, then you tell me about it."

"Okay. I will."

He shook his head. "It's a damn shame about the woodwork."

"About that," she said. "Can you talk to Zeph? Everyone says he's the only one I should have touching the candy counter and the columns here in the lobby. If I promise him that the general contractor won't touch his work or give him any grief, do you think you could convince him to come back?"

"I'll try. But Zeph is funny about things."

"So I gathered."

"I'll see what I can do." And with that Dash pushed his back off the counter and sauntered from the lobby, just in time to meet John Rodgers on his way in. Dash stopped briefly, his face grim as he said, "Howdy, John. I can't say as I'm entirely happy that my cousin chose you for this job. But you should know that I'm watching every move you make, so don't you try to cheat her, you hear?"

And with that he was out the door, leaving her to deal with a suddenly annoyed and red-faced contractor.

Aunt Miriam's sweater was a big purple mess. Savannah had managed to learn how to knit and purl so that the stitches looked even, but decreasing to form armholes and yarning over to make button holes were quite beyond her.

Which explained why she was sitting here at The Knit & Stitch on a Monday night at the shop's bi-weekly knitting class. Pat Canaday was no fool. She knew the book club met on the first and third Wednesdays. So her knitting class was held on the second and fourth Mondays. That way, every Last Chance knitter was always within days of getting project help. Or having a gathering of women with whom they could share their strange addiction to yarn and their not-so-strange addiction to gossip.

Pat took one look at Savannah's purple pile of spun possum fur and shook her head. "Honey, that is the sorriest armhole I have ever seen. The problem is that you forgot to use an SSK for the right sleeve decreases and a knit-two-together for the left."

"Momma, that was completely confusing," Molly said. "C'mon, Savannah, just sit down here with me, and I'll show you the difference between an SSK and a knit-two-together, but I think you're going to have to frog that back to right below the armhole."

"I was afraid you'd say that," Savannah said.

"It's all right, sugar. It took me ages to learn how to knit," Aunt Miriam said. The old lady was sitting in one of the big easy chairs in the front of the shop leafing through knitting magazines. Aunt Miriam had suggested this trip to Pat's knitting class, mostly, Savannah thought, as an excuse to get out of the house.

Things had been kind of tense these days in the house on Baruch Street, and all because of the Kismet renovation. Dash had managed to sweet-talk Zeph Gibbs into working on the historic woodwork in the Kismet's lobby, and Zeph was doing an amazing job. But JBR Contractors were not, and that resulted in almost constant bickering between Savannah and her kissing cousin. The disagreements over the theater renovation masked the real truth. Savannah had developed a first-class crush on Dash. It was probably inevitable, given the fact that he was such a good dancer. But still, having a crush on Dash was stupid and dumb. He didn't love her back. He had a thing for Hettie. And everyone in town knew it.

So she went out of her way to avoid him. And when she couldn't avoid him she picked fights with him that he seemed to enjoy.

The truth was that Savannah kind of enjoyed the fights, too. At least when they were fighting, they weren't trying to ignore each other.

Molly gave her a short lesson that she finally understood, and then Savannah started ripping out stitches while the knitters around her gossiped.

"So, anyway," Kenzie was saying, "I saw Bill's car parked in Hettie's driveway again. Last night."

"Uh-huh, Violet Easley was saying at church just yesterday that she's cooking more now than she ever did when Mr. Marshall was alive," Lola May said. "Violet says Reverend Bill is particularly fond of her key lime pie. I swear that man has a serious sweet tooth."

Savannah was sorry she'd tuned back in to the conversation. Meanwhile her sweater unraveled, row-by-row.

"Violet is too old for Bill," Pat said.

"Not to mention the fact that she's a member of the AME church and black," Molly added.

"I don't think Bill would turn down a soulmate based on the color of her skin," Lola May said, "but Violet must be pushing sixty. I think the minister wants a family."

Savannah's sweater continued to shrink as she wound the yarn into a ball. She wondered why the women never considered the possibility that Bill was over at Hettie's house because of Hettie.

Once again, she got that odd-twitchy feeling deep in her gut—half tingle, half itch.

She looked up, right into the eyes of her great aunt. Miriam was smiling at her. Her big brown eyes, the very same big brown eyes that Savannah had inherited, were twinkling behind her trifocals.

Miriam leaned over and put one of her gnarled hands on Savannah's knee. "It's kind of uncomfortable, isn't it?" she whispered. "When that feeling comes over you, it's like an itch that you can't scratch. And then you just know."

Savannah looked around at the other women in the knitting circle. She leaned in toward her aunt. "Why don't they see it?"

Miriam shrugged. "Sometimes folks don't see the most obvious things." She grinned at this. Miriam didn't look very senile or demented, even if she did look kind of old and frail.

"What did you tell Hettie?" Savannah whispered as Kenzie and Lola May continued to speculate about the various cooks of Allenberg County and their suitability as potential mates for the unmarried minister.

"I never told Hettie anything worth saying," Miriam said. "I gave her my standard advice to be looking for a man with good values and a strong desire for family." She grinned.

"But what about Bill?"

"You think it through, Savannah, and you'll figure it out. It's never a good idea to just come right out with it, you know. People will rebel, and they'll make mistakes. You have to lead them to the decision."

A sudden flash of heat flamed through Savannah. "You never meant Bill for me, did you? Hettie is good with bookkeeping. It's always been about the bookkeeping and money management, not the cooking."

Miriam nodded ever so slightly.

"But you invited him to dinner every other day."

She shrugged. "A matchmaker has to use all of her wiles sometimes. Especially when the people involved are hardheaded, confused, and just a little bit willful. I figured Hettie would see you as a threat."

"But what if I'd said yes to Bill's proposal?"

Miriam snorted. "I don't think so."

"Oh, my God, you knew he would propose, and you knew I would..."

Aunt Miriam turned back to her magazine. She flipped a few pages then looked up. "Maybe. There is so much I've got to teach you before it's my time to go, sugar."

"Teach me? About what?"

"About the thing God put you here to do."

Savannah stared down at her knitting. "Obviously it's not to knit you a sweater."

"Obviously," Miriam said. "But there's something to matching people up that's almost like knitting a community together. You know?"

"No, I don't, but I have this feeling I'm going to learn."

"So what do you think, Miriam, will Bill ever realize that he and Jenny Carpenter are a match made in Heaven?" Pat asked.

Miriam pressed her hand onto Savannah's knee before she spoke. "Well, I don't know," the old woman said. "You know I only get the vaguest notions of what a person should be looking for. But then again, I think that's good. It doesn't limit his possibilities. There are so many good cooks in Allenberg."

Savannah stared at her aunt. Miriam was lying through her teeth and no one realized it. Miriam knew exactly who was the right person for Bill, and she'd been pulling that string for a long time.

"All I know is that Jenny isn't happy about Bill's car being parked in Hettie's driveway three nights a week," Kenzie said.

"Well," Lola May replied, "I wouldn't put too much in that. After all, she's the treasurer of the Christ Church building fund, and he's the pastor over there. And I'm sure he's just there because of Violet's cooking."

"Yeah, but three nights a week?" Kenzie asked, as she furiously worked on the Fair Isle sweater vest she'd told everyone she was making for her sister in Milwaukee. Kenzie didn't need knitting lessons. She was knitting with two colors, holding yarn in both hands, and her needles were flying as she talked. "It makes him seem like a food moocher or something. He ought to be allowing the good single cooks of Allenberg County to cook for him. Not putting so much extra work on Violet's shoulders."

"Of course, Hettie could always learn to cook," Savannah said as she laboriously picked up stitches in her much-reduced project.

"Ha, that's a laugh," Pat said. "Miriam, you remember that time Hettie brought Toll House cookies she baked herself to the Christmas Bazaar? I swear that woman put salt in those cookies instead of sugar. It was pitiful."

"Oh, my God, look at the theater." Kenzie stood up. "Oh my God. Oh my God, Pat call the fire department."

Savannah dropped her knitting, stood up, and looked through the windows.

Across Palmetto Avenue, a big, black cloud of smoke billowed up into the dark April sky from the back of the theater. She stood transfixed for the longest moment before she remembered Maverick.

The poor cat was trapped. She grabbed her keys from her purse and rushed from the yarn store, heedless of the women trying to stop her.

She tore across the street just as the sirens for the volunteer fire department sounded. She reached the door, only to find that it was unlocked.

The contractors left it unlocked?

She pulled open the doors and dashed inside calling Maverick's name. Flames and heat came from the auditorium, but the smoke was so thick and the night so dark that she was blinded almost immediately. And the damn cat was as black as the smoke.

She screamed Maverick's name, over and over again, but the cat was nowhere. And the fire was consuming what was left of Granddaddy's theater.

Everything she wanted, everything she had ever dreamed of, all of her most precious memories, and her cat, were going up in smoke.

Dash sat in the bleachers of the Davis High gymnasium watching Red Canaday put Todd through a battery of fitness tests.

The boy had done surprisingly well, considering his general lack of fitness. He'd scored high on eye-hand coordination. He had quickness side-to-side, even if he wasn't the fastest runner alive. He had great hands. Dash could see the gleam in Red's eyes. With a good fitness program, Todd could develop into an excellent athlete.

And no one knew better than Dash how important athletics could be to a kid who needed to blow off steam. Uncle Earnest had understood that. And Dash would be forever thankful that his uncle by marriage had signed him up for Little League all those years ago.

Dash was just climbing down from his perch when the volunteer fire department siren sounded. At the same time, both Red's and Dash's cell phones started to beep. Dash pulled his iPhone from his pocket. He read the message as a dose of adrenaline hit his system.

"C'mon, Todd, we gotta go."

"What is it?"

"The Kismet. It's on fire."

The next five minutes were a blur. Davis High wasn't all that far from downtown Last Chance, but it was too far to run. So all three of them piled into Dash's Caddy. They made it to the scene just about the same time as the Last Chance fire truck, the Last Chance police chief, and the

Allenberg sheriff, who had probably been home with his wife and kids when the siren sounded.

Red's wife, Pat, and her knitting class, including Aunt Mim, stood on the sidewalk across the street from the theater. Dash swept his gaze over them as he dragged Todd in their direction.

"Where's Savannah?"

"She went into the theater to save Maverick."

Todd made a funny strangled noise that might have broken Dash's heart if his heart hadn't suddenly started ricocheting around his rib cage.

"Don't you worry. She's going to be okay." He ran toward the theater, heedless of the shouts from the fire chief or anyone else who was organizing the effort to fight the fire.

His only goal was to find that idiotic woman who thought—

Zeph Gibbs emerged from the building, smoke billowing around him. He had Savannah and that damned cat in his arms.

Savannah's face was black but her eyes were open. She was hugging that stupid cat like it meant the world to her.

Zeph stopped in front of him. "Here you go, Mr. Dash. Safe and sound." He handed Savannah off.

She felt right in his arms. His little sooty princess. She wasn't too light or too heavy. She was conscious. She was alive. His heart could slow down now. But for some reason, his pulse continued to race.

"I'm okay," she said in a smoke-roughened voice. "You can put me down."

He ignored her and called over his shoulder to the Allenberg County sheriff. "Stone, I need EMTs, now!"

The sheriff replied, "Already called. They'll be here in a minute."

"I don't need—" The rest of Savannah's words were lost in a coughing fit. The cat seemed unusually subdued.

"I think we need the vet, too," he yelled.

"I'm on it," Sheriff Rhodes said, and Dash had every reason to believe it.

A moment later, a couple of EMTs from the Allenberg County Fire Department, which had also arrived on the scene, came running over with an oxygen tank.

"We'll take her," one of them said, but Dash wasn't about to let her go.

"No, I've got her. Just strap on the oxygen."

"Dash, we need to figure out if she needs to go to the hospital."

"I'm okay," she said, her voice sounding ragged. She had turned to look at The Kismet. The fire had engulfed most of the auditorium.

The EMT strapped on an oxygen mask just as big fat crocodile tears filled her eyes and spilled down her sooty cheeks. The tears left white tracks across her face. It broke his heart to watch her as she watched The Kismet burn.

A moment later Charlene Polk, one of the docs at the Last Chance veterinary clinic, showed up. She took Maverick.

"We'll just take him down to the clinic for observation. Smoke is dangerous for cats, too."

Savannah reluctantly let go of the cat. And Maverick let forth a howl when they were separated. But it was all for the best. At least that's what the EMTs said when they forced Dash to put Savannah down on the back step of their van while they checked her over.

Todd and Aunt Mim came over.

"I'm okay," she said again, her voice shaky as she reached out for Todd.

The boy came into her arms. "Mom, I was so scared when they said you were inside."

"I'm okay," she said again, as if she were trying to convince herself of it. Dash turned away.

The combined fire departments of Last Chance and Allenberg County already had the blaze under control. The Kismet's magnificent auditorium, with its painted-sky ceiling, was a total loss. But the front part of the theater, the minaret, and the marquee might be salvageable.

One thing was certain, though: The price tag for this project had just gone right through the roof, quite literally.

Still, a building could always be replaced. People couldn't.

He turned back toward Savannah. "Don't you ever do anything stupid like that again, do you hear me?" His voice came out louder than he meant it to.

"Dash, calm—"

"You hear me," he said again, as a wellspring of emotion bubbled right out of him. He didn't even know where it came from, just that it seized him by the throat and wouldn't let go. It hurt so bad. It was like all the bad things that had ever happened in his life all at once, starting with his mother leaving, and his grandma dying, and his daddy never being around, and Gramps being hard on him, and Uncle Earnest...

He got that far and lost it. Tears filled his eyes, and he couldn't breathe. It was like the smoke got into his head and he couldn't think.

He blinked away the water. "Don't you ever do

anything like that again. I couldn't bear it if something happened to you. You hear me?"

She stared up at him utterly surprised. And he realized right then that he'd made a stupid, stupid, stupid mistake that he might never recover from. He'd just told her how he felt about her. And now she was going to leave him.

And he could take just about anything but Savannah pulling up stakes and leaving town.

He couldn't stand here with everyone looking at him. So he turned and ran through the crowd to his Caddy. He fired it up and took off down the road.

There were bars up in Orangeburg. He could go up there where no one knew him.

He needed a drink. Bad.

CHAPTER 16

Savannah ripped the oxygen mask off her face and shook off the hands of the EMTs. "I'm fine."

She stood up and gave Todd a big hug. "I gotta go get Dash before he does something even stupider than I did."

Her son looked wide-eyed and scared. He nodded.

"Don't worry. I'll bring him back. He just got upset because of the theater."

"Here, honey, you take my car." Molly dangled a set of keys in her direction. "It's way faster than your POS Honda." She grinned. "Oh, and Momma sent you these." She handed over a small package of Handi Wipes. "Your face is all black."

"Any idea of where he went?"

"He headed off toward Route 70. You'll have to drive like the wind to catch him, though."

Molly pressed Savannah's purse into her hands. "If you're lucky, the cops will pull him over for speeding." She dragged Savannah off to the parking lot behind The Knit & Stitch.

Molly's car turned out to be a canary yellow 1970s-vintage Dodge Charger.

"Holy cow, this is yours?"

"You like it? I restored it myself. I restored Dash's car, too. So I know how fast it will go." She smiled. "Now get going, and don't drive like a girl."

It was a good thing the roads in South Carolina were more or less straight and usually deserted this time of evening. It allowed Savannah to peg the speedometer at ninety without having to worry about curves or traffic.

Please, God, I need someone to pull Dash over.

And to her utter astonishment, she topped a rise in the road, and there was an Allenberg County sheriff's deputy on the side of the road, his cruiser lights flashing. He was leaning up against Dash's cherry red Eldorado.

Savannah hit the brakes and pulled over.

The cop went immediately on alert when she pulled up in front of Dash's Caddy, sending up a pretty big cloud of dust. He put his hand on his weapon as he strolled up along the driver's side of Molly's car. Savannah lowered her window and gave him a smile.

He blinked a couple of times. "You're not Molly."

"No, I'm not. I'm one of her friends."

"Ma'am, are you all right? I mean your face..."

"Oh, I just came from the big fire in Last Chance. I'm sure you heard about it on your radio."

"Oh, yeah, I heard The Kismet burned down."

Savannah's heart lurched. "Well, not quite."

"You look like you were *in* The Kismet when it burned."

"I was rescuing Maverick."

"You mean someone was in that old theater when it burned down?"

"Maverick is a cat."

"Oh. I see. Ma'am, why are you here?"

"Well, you see, Mr. Randall's uncle used to own the theater."

"Uh-huh."

"And I guess when he saw the place going up in flames—see, he's a member of the volunteer fire department?"

"Uh-huh."

"Well, it must have just done something to him. He just got mad or upset or something. And he tore off, and I came after him to make sure he didn't do something stupid."

"You mean stupid like what he did that time on the motorcycle?"

"You know about that?"

The cop leaned on Molly's car. "Ma'am, everyone knows about that. Dash Randall was our hero, you know. He kind of disappointed us."

"I see."

"I remember watching him play in the those state championship games back in the early nineties."

"I'm sorry I missed that."

"He was amazing. In his senior year, back in 1996, he went five for five with ten RBIs."

Savannah understood this comment about as well as she'd understood Pat's advice for decreasing stitches around an armhole. She assumed it was something good.

"So, anyway," she said, "I was wondering if you could just give him a break on the ticket you were about to write him. That fire made something snap inside him. You know?"

The cop smiled. "I guess I do. It's a shame that old place went up in flames. I heard some woman was renovating it. I would have liked to see that."

"Yes, some woman was," she said with a long sigh.

"You?"

"Me."

"I'm so sorry, ma'am."

"Thanks. So, you won't give him a ticket, will you?"

"No, ma'am. You just see that he gets back home in one piece. He's still a local hero, you know. We wouldn't have deBracy Limited hiring all those folks without him. Not to mention the help he's given Molly Canaday. She wants to open a place to restore old classics like this one."

He rubbed his hand along the paint of Molly's Charger. "Man, that girl sure knows how to paint a car. That finish is smooth as a baby's butt."

He tipped his Stetson. "You take care, now."

He turned and walked back to his cruiser, stopping to say a couple of words to Dash, who was sitting in his car with his head back on the headrest.

Savannah pulled out a couple of wipes from the pack Molly had pressed into her hands. She ran them over her face. She was kind of surprised when they came back black. But then she smelled like a chimney sweep. The smoke smell and soot were everywhere. On her hands, under her nails, in her hair. She was a mess.

But at least she'd caught up with Dash before he did something idiotic.

He sat up the minute she climbed out of Molly's yellow

car. "What in the hell are you doing driving that car? I hope to God you didn't steal it."

"Dash, I'm not the kind of person who steals cars for joyrides. Molly loaned it to me. She said my POS Honda would never catch you."

She strolled up to the passenger's side of the Eldorado. She gave the white upholstery a glance before she climbed in.

"How did you talk Henry out of throwing the book at me?" he asked, apparently not concerned about her sooty clothes or his pristine upholstery.

"I batted my eyes."

The corner of his mouth twitched.

"You think I can't bat my eyes when I want to?"

"Oh, I know you are a champion eye-batter, princess. It's just that you batting your eyes with that dirty face is kind of amusing is all."

She wiped her hands over her cheeks. "Henry said he saw you play high-school baseball."

"Yeah, he did. It's annoying how many former high-school acquaintances still live here. Like most of them, Henry is annoyed at me because of my last idiocy with a motor vehicle."

"So I gather. I told him to give you a break."

"You should be with the EMTs," he said, changing the subject.

"I'm fine. I'm filthy but I'm fine. You want to explain what just happened back there at the theater?"

He leaned his head on the seat back and looked up at the sky. She followed his gaze, suddenly thinking about the painted ceiling at The Kismet. She had once thought Granddaddy hung the stars. But she'd been wrong. The real stars were more magnificent. And out here in the country, the stars were so much brighter than they were in Baltimore.

It surprised her that she wasn't nearly as devastated by the fire as Dash had been.

"It's just a building," she said.

He didn't say a word. She let him be silent, almost the way they had danced in silence, only this was way more uncomfortable.

They must have sat there for four minutes before he said "I want you."

Her insides went a little crazy because the feeling was mutual. When Zeph had handed her off to Dash, she'd felt safe. She'd rested her head on his shoulder, and it had felt so right. Why was it that Dash made her feel safer than she'd ever felt before? It made no sense.

"Dash, I—" she started.

"I don't want to want you, princess. I don't want to want anyone." His voice was gruff with emotion.

She understood why he didn't want anyone. She'd been there, too. "Well," she said as her heart rate spiked, "for what it's worth, I want you back. And I don't want to want you. I want to be independent. But apparently my libido doesn't want me living like a nun. It always gets me into trouble. Whenever I dance with a good-looking jock it goes into overdrive."

He laughed out loud, but it wasn't a happy laugh. "So, you want hot, dirty sex, is that it?"

"Yes," she whispered.

He sighed. "Of course you do. Everyone wants hot, dirty sex with me. And darlin', I'd be happy to oblige you, but not tonight. I have a headache." The corner of his mouth curled up and stayed there.

The joke didn't bring a laugh. Instead it turned her core molten. "Be serious, Dash. How can we do that?"

"Pretty easy. We just keep on driving on this road until we reach the outskirts of Orangeburg, and we find a no-tell motel. It's pretty standard practice if you want to be discreet. And in Last Chance, when it comes to people having hot, dirty sex, discretion is probably the better part of valor."

Silence stretched out between them while she contemplated this scenario and suddenly found absolutely nothing wrong with it. Her pulse raced, and the excitement of sneaking away and having the one thing that was utterly forbidden seized her. Two months of bumping into him, or trying not to bump into him, had made her completely crazy.

It had made him crazy, too, as evidenced by his behavior earlier in the evening.

"I must be insane," she muttered.

"Why?"

"Because I'm having this discussion with you like we're trying to decide where we should have dinner."

"Sometimes it's a good thing to talk these things out. There are huge downsides, of course. If we were smart we'd just continue to take lots of cold showers. Or swim in the Edisto." He sighed and ran his fingers through his hair. "I've been swimming in the Edisto a lot lately. It's freezing this time of year."

"Really? Since we're being utterly honest, I've been having hot and wicked dreams about you."

He let go of a deep breath. "Going to a no-tell motel

with you would be the second stupidest thing I've ever
done in my life."

"What's the first, putting a snake in my bed?"

He scowled at her. "When I tore out of town, all I
wanted was to find a place where I could get a drink. Sitting here thinking about taking you somewhere to have
sex with you is just the same damn thing. My addictions
are showing up, right on time."

"And why did they show up tonight?"

He pressed his lips together. "I reckon I cared about
the theater."

"And why is that?"

He shrugged. He wasn't going to open up to her. But
she had a pretty good idea of what was going on in his
head. Hell, she empathized with his pain on a very deep
level. And that surprised the heck out of her.

"Dash," she said softly, "I'm here. I didn't burn up. I'm
not going anywhere. I'm not going to leave. I know how
bad it sucks when people leave. Maybe that's why I was so
ugly to you when I was ten—because I knew exactly how
to hurt you. When I said that you were so naughty that you
didn't deserve a mother and father, I was halfway talking
about myself. My dad abandoned me when I was three."
Her voice began to waver.

She took a deep breath. "Sometimes I think I want to
fix up The Kismet because I've got this stupid idea that if
I do that, Granddaddy will rise up from his grave and live
again. He was the only one who ever had any faith in me.
He was the only real father I ever knew."

Dash stared at Savannah's dirty face. She had a big
splotch of soot on her nose and over one eye. The gold

in her hair was muted by ashes, and she smelled like a fireplace.

She was still beautiful. And alive, thank God. She was here, just for him. But like every other woman in the universe, she only wanted to have hot, dirty sex with him.

"We should go back," he said. "Check in with the fire department. I can't imagine what would have caused that fire."

"The door was open."

"What?"

She shrugged. "The door was open to the theater. The contractor must not have locked up."

"Great. I told you—"

"Don't. I don't want to talk about the theater right now. I want to talk about you and me and that motel."

"We're not going there."

She cocked her head. "No?"

Heat flowed through him. It was his addiction singing to him like a siren from the shore.

That was probably why he sat there like some fat, dumb, and happy idiot when she slid across the bench and pulled his hands away from the steering wheel.

He didn't fight too hard when she placed his hands on her rib cage and then moved in, slanting her mouth over his. She invaded him like the Union marching on Atlanta.

She tasted like barbecued heaven, all warm and soft and smoky. The breath caught in her throat right before the round, soft contours of her breasts pressed up against his chest. She threw herself into that kiss like she'd thrown herself into everything she'd done in the two months she'd been in Last Chance.

Fingers roamed up over his scalp, sending hot tingles down his spine; her tongue teased his and then danced away right before she thrust it back. Blood pounded in his ears and other places.

Damn, she was as hot as T-bone's chili special.

A man with his weaknesses could never stand up against something like this. Savannah was all over him, and he wasn't about to sit there like a lump.

Or push her away.

Not when she unleashed this torrent of longing and lust that he'd been battling for so long.

But she needed a bath. Which of course sent his mind racing in all sorts of directions that involved her naked in lots of water. With soap.

For low-down dirty sex, his fantasy was surprisingly clean.

"Okay," he murmured against her sooty cheek. "Okay, let's go."

She backed away. "Let's go? To a no-tell motel for discreet, but hot and dirty sex?" There was an impish grin on her face, and those dark eyes of hers were lit up with starlight. She wanted her bad-boy fix. And he wanted his Savannah fix.

"Aren't you even sorry about the fire?" he asked, his voice cracking like a teenager's.

Her face fell. And he hated himself for bringing up the topic. Although maybe, he'd just managed to get himself out of a really dangerous situation.

"I am." She rested her head against his shoulder. "I'm heartbroken. And I'm also kind of pissed off, to tell you the truth."

"Pissed off?"

"Yeah, at myself." She pulled back and looked right up in his eyes. He couldn't look away. "I should have taken your advice. I should have listened to you. But I had to do everything myself. And I don't know squat about anything, except maybe cooking strudel."

Her lip quivered. Why the hell had he brought up the fire anyway?

"Uh, there are other things you're good at."

"There are?"

"Yeah. You're a great dancer. And you sure can kiss, princess. And you're a pretty terrific screamer when it comes to snakes."

"Right. That's not very impressive."

"I'm not finished. You can cook more than strudel, you're kind to Aunt Mim, everyone in town loves you. And you used to make your grandfather's eyes light up. I used to be so jealous of that."

She blinked up at him. "I loved him. You loved him. But you know something? Bringing The Kismet back to life isn't ever going to bring him back." She rested her forehead on his chest.

And his heart swelled up and lodged in his throat. "Shit."

"What?" Her breath heated his chest through the fabric of his shirt.

"I want you."

"Yeah, we've established that. Can we do something about it or are we just going to sit here arguing with one another about who loved Granddaddy more?"

"You think he would approve of this?"

She raised her head and stared at him, the connection between them stronger than ever.

"I know he wanted us to be friends."

"This is a lot more than that. This is dangerous, princess. You don't even know how dangerous it is."

She wasn't listening to him, as usual, because she leaned forward and kissed him again. This kiss was demanding and wicked and not at all the kind of kiss a princess would unleash on anyone. Good Lord, that woman had a talent for dirty, sexy kissing. And then she dropped her sweet little hand to his thigh and started walking her fingers up to his crotch.

Well, of course he had to retaliate. So he cupped her breast. It was just the right size, and her nipples were straining against her T-shirt. He ran his thumb over one of them, and she growled. A flush of lust came at him like a big, fat, floating curveball right over the plate.

A man like him had no defense for something like that. None. Whatsoever. He had to take a swing at it. Didn't he?

The Orangeburg Motor Lodge looked like any motel you might find by the side of an interstate. In this case, the two-story stucco building stood right at the intersection of I-26 and Route 301, about twenty-five miles northeast of Last Chance and smack-dab in the middle of the route between Columbia and Charleston. Yessir, this jumping-off place in the middle of nowhere couldn't have been more anonymous if it tried.

Maybe that's why the proprietors had erected a giant sign for passing motorists that proclaimed a room rate of only fifty dollars a night. And for that you got a small swimming pool, cable television, and a continental breakfast in the bargain.

Dash procured the room key, no doubt paying cash for it, and he drove his Cadillac around to the back of the building, away from the access road.

He killed the engine and set the brake. He turned his hip into the seat, and for the first time in the last forty-five minutes, he looked her right in the eye. "Honey, are you sure about this?"

Was she sure? No way. Confusion, insecurity, and fear ruled her emotions at this moment. But all of that was nothing compared with the lust, which made her feel alive.

She needed to get back into his arms.

She looked out the passenger's window at the blue motel door bearing the brass numbers above its peephole. She needed to remember this, but the door couldn't have been less extraordinary. It looked like every motel door she had ever seen.

She could imagine the room beyond. A single picture window with a view of the parking lot and heavy drapes that hid the air-conditioning unit. A chair, a lamp, a couple of forgettable prints on the wall, a counter bolted to the wall in a dark, walnut Formica. Two double beds with rough sheets and ugly bedspreads, separated by another built-in containing a cubbyhole where you'd find Gideon's Bible.

She focused on the door number for a moment. Forty-seven. Nothing came to mind to connect this number with anything else in her life.

Maybe that was a good thing.

She pulled the car door handle and got out of the car. She wasn't going to look at Dash, and she wasn't going to talk to him either. She didn't quite trust him right at this moment. He might work himself back to the point of being noble and chucking the whole plan or he might actually talk her out of it.

He got out of the car, too. They walked to the room door in silence and he opened it. A blast of air-conditioning, heavy with that impersonal motel scent, hit them like a slap across the face.

A moment later, they stood in the room with the glare of highway traffic streaming through the large window. Dash drew the heavy curtains closed. Savannah switched on the lamp between the two beds.

He looked at her from across the room. Studied her, in fact, while she studied him, trying hard to memorize the contours of his face—the lines at the corners of his cheeks, the little fold of skin that appeared at the bridge of his nose when he raised his eyebrows, the dent in his chin, his lop-sided half grin. There wasn't anything not to like in his face.

"So now what?" she asked.

He crossed the distance between them and stood there looking down at her, without touching her at all. Time hung suspended, the venture suddenly teetering on a ful-crum. Which way would they fall?

She couldn't risk that he might change his mind. With a trembling finger, she reached out to touch the dimple in his chin.

He took a deep breath in through his nose and closed his eyes. "You need a shower," he said.

He hauled her over his shoulder and carried her into the tiny bathroom at the back of the room.

He set her on her feet in front of the mirror.

"Oh, my God," she said, "I look like a refugee from a coal mine."

She turned toward him. "And you let me kiss you looking like this?"

He shrugged. "Honey, you taste a little like Earl Williams's barbecue."

"I do not."

His mouth tilted. "Uh, well, there's a solution to that problem. And I gotta tell you, princess, I've been having a lot of shower fantasies recently."

"Me too."

"Well, what are we waiting for, then?"

That must have been some kind of rhetorical question because, in the very next instant, he pushed her back against the bathroom door, his big body invading her space. His mouth closed hot and heavy on hers, and his tongue assaulted her mouth. He undid her ponytail, and her hair tumbled over her shoulders. He ran his fingers through it, cocking her head back so that he had access to her neck. He had her imprisoned between his hard thighs, his massive chest, and his warm lips.

She couldn't breathe even when he backed off a fraction, letting his tongue travel lightly over her bottom lip, nipping at her, dipping back into her mouth, and then finally traveling over her cheek to the hollow of her neck.

While all this transpired, her hands developed a mind of their own. They crept around his waist and tugged at his shirttail until it came free of its moorings. She finally insinuated her hands under the fabric and came up against the warm skin of his back. The unexpected silkiness of his skin sent another rush right through her.

Her fingers climbed up his back as tension corkscrewed inside her belly. She wanted to climb right inside his skin, but instead of getting closer, he backed away.

"Okay, it's shower time." He pulled off his shirt. The T-shirt left his hair all spiked around his head, but she wasn't paying much attention. God, he had an incredible chest, sculpted by hours in the gym and sprinkled with just a little hair right over his nipples. He snaked his arms around her waist and pulled her a little closer, his hands sliding down to her backside. She resisted his pull because she wanted to study his chest, imprint the look of it in her mind. She ran her hands over him, zeroing in on his hard brown nipples, brushing them with the backs of her fingers. He tensed beneath her touch, his fingers clamping a little harder onto her butt. Then he chuckled.

"Honey, we're gonna run out of hot water if we don't hurry."

She ignored him and sank her head onto his chest, his unique male scent filling her head. If she couldn't crawl into his skin then maybe she could just eat him up. Oh, God, he tasted sweet and salty all at once as she let her mouth roam over the expanse of muscle and sinew until she found a particularly delicious spot on his neck. She nibbled at the warm skin there for a few moments until Dash captured her head and tilted it up to look at him.

"Darlin', there are a couple of rules about illicit sex in rural South Carolina that you need to learn, and the first one is—no hickeys above the clavicle. Love bites on the neck can be mighty hard to explain. And Lillian Bray has a way of noticing things like that. And if Miz Lillian sees a hickey on my neck, she's going to make some assumptions about Hettie Marshall that are liable to get the gossips in an uproar." He smiled at her like a cherub. "However, you may proceed to bite me anywhere else, if you are so inclined." He let go of her head and maintained his position against the door awaiting her next move.

She sank against his chest. "I can't believe you just said that."

"Sorry, did that break your concentration?" He didn't wait for her reply. Instead, he pivoted, and Savannah found the tables turned again, with her up against the door.

He ran his fingers down her jawline and over her collarbones. "He who hesitates is lost," he said softly. His gaze roamed briefly over her face then sank down to the vee in her cotton tee where her cleavage showed.

Dash pulled his gaze back up to her face, capturing her eyes. He licked her bottom lip, he pressed kisses along her jaw, he laved the lobe of her ear until she thought she would die from the pleasure that once again coiled down inside her.

Suddenly she needed more. "You're right, the water is hot. I can see steam or fog or something. I . . . I think I want to get naked."

His hands moved under the hem of her top and before she even knew what happened, Dash had unhooked her bra and pulled her T-shirt over her head. The garments hit the bathroom floor.

He pushed her back against the door again. His mouth traced a line of pure fire down her throat, while his hands roamed over her rib cage and then brushed the undersides of her breasts. His mouth and his fingers circled and circled, building up the tension in her until she thought she would scream. Just when she couldn't bear it a moment longer, his mouth finally closed over her nipple.

He drew it tenderly into his mouth. He suckled, and he licked, and he finally bit. She went a little crazy.

His hands, so incredibly warm, inserted themselves between her and her blue jeans. He unsnapped them and peeled back the fabric, all while his mouth was doing incredible things to her.

Her pants and panties dropped to her ankles. She braced herself on his shoulders and kicked them and her sandals away.

Without shoes, she came only up to his shoulders, and she suddenly felt tiny in his arms as he ran his hands down along the skin of her bottom and then up over the bumps in her spine. The caress was ever so gentle, and for the first time, she became truly aware of Dash's own state of arousal. He was breathing hard and his heart was racing against the fingers she had splayed against his chest.

He stepped away from her and undid his belt and then attacked the zipper on his pants. He seemed a little less graceful kicking off his boots and getting himself out of his old, faded jeans. His pants and underwear managed to tangle themselves around his ankles, and he had to hop on one foot and then the other to extract himself. Savannah stood there naked, not feeling remotely embarrassed as she watched his little floor show with undisguised interest.

"Oh, my," she said on a soft puff of air as he finally managed to get off his last sock.

He straightened up. "You like it?" he asked with an unabashed grin on his face.

"It's very...impressive."

His eyes traveled down to her ankles and back up to her chest. "So are you. Impressively dirty."

He pulled her into the tiny shower. And the next thing she knew, he had a washcloth and a bar of soap, and he was getting her all squeaky clean, and incredibly high.

And when the soot had been washed away, he pulled her close, all soapy, and he kissed her again. And he started touching her in all the right spots. Spots that sent up sparks in every direction.

"Oh, God," she ground out between her teeth.

"Does that feel good?" he asked in a hoarse voice.

"Oh, God, yes."

He chuckled against her breast. "Didn't your granddaddy ever tell you it was a sin to take the name of the Lord in vain?"

"Shut up. I can't think right now."

"That's good, darlin'. Neither of us should try that right at this moment."

She reached for him then, part out of pique and part out of sheer curiosity. Her hand glided down across the ridges of his belly and closed in a tight fist around him. He let the fondling go on for a long time until he finally said, "That's it, darlin'. I'm a strong man, but you have to stop doing that, *now.*"

"Now?" she said, her fingers running up and down him, ignoring his command.

"Yeah, now," he said, swatting her hand away. He pushed the shower curtain out of the way and reached for the jeans he'd left on the bathroom floor. Several choice curse words escaped his lips as he rummaged through the pockets until he came up with a small foil packet.

He tore it open, sheathed himself, then took her right to the stars.

Dash had serious talent when it came to sex. Unfortunately, Savannah's bad-boy cousin also had a finely tuned sense of guilt.

Once their *big moment* in the shower had ended, the guilt arrived right on cue.

"Our goose is cooked," he muttered as he turned off the water, which was starting to get cold. "We need to dry off, go get Molly's car, and get on back home before Miriam and Todd bust a gut."

So much for romance.

But he was absolutely right. Miriam and Todd could get seriously hurt by what they'd just done in the shower.

She dried off, using the tiny motel-rough towel. It took about five minutes to sort out their discarded clothing.

All in all, they spent a grand total of about forty minutes in that forgettable hotel room before they were back in the Cadillac heading home to Last Chance.

"You okay?" he asked after about ten minutes on the road.

She nodded. She didn't feel like talking.

He glanced at her. "You sure?"

She gazed at his handsome profile, lit up by the dashboard lights. She didn't know where to start a conversation. Should she thank him for giving her a sexual fantasy that she would never, ever forget? That seemed kind of silly. Two people sneaking around to have low-down dirty sex shouldn't have to talk, should they?

It seemed like a very dangerous moment to start talking. She was liable to blurt out all kinds of things. Like how she wanted to hear him laugh more, like he'd done in the shower. Or how she wanted to take care of him when he was sick or discouraged. She wanted to cook him a three-course dinner. She wanted, God forbid, to knit him a sweater.

Most of all, she wanted to sleep with him. But how could she do that? All the guys she'd ever slept with had turned into big mistakes. So maybe she should promise herself never to sleep with him or knit him anything. Cooking his dinner was already a done deal.

"I'm good," she said in answer to his question. "I had fun. How about you?"

What does a man say to the most incredible lover he's ever known? Does he tell her he thinks he loves her? Only he's not sure what love is because in his whole life none of his lovers have ever loved him back. Does he admit that he's kind of afraid of being loved back?

Or maybe he just says he's confused, which would be nothing but the unadulterated truth.

"I had fun, too," he said. It was an understatement of monumental proportions.

She gave him a sweet smile. Her chocolate-drop eyes sparked with the light from the dashboard. His body ached from wanting her. Again. Someone should have told him that sex was much better sober. It might have helped with his recovery.

They didn't speak again until he pulled the Eldorado off the side of the road where they had left Molly's Charger.

"So, you want me to follow you to Molly's?" he asked.

She shook her head. "Molly has my car. You go on home. I'll be fine." She hesitated before she got out of the car. "Uh, Dash?" she said.

"Uh-huh."

"Do you think we could sneak off again sometime?"

He had to struggle to keep a smile from his lips; now that he'd tasted this forbidden fruit, he was completely hooked. He wanted her more than ever. "Maybe we could find a better hotel next time."

"Okay, if you want. But, um, well . . . it was also kind of exciting to do it in a seedy motel like that. And I've never had shower sex before."

Great. She just wanted the low-down dirty part of it. Not all the rest. That was the story of his life, wasn't it? "Yeah, sneaking around lends a certain element of excitement to it," he said. He didn't think she wanted to hear him say that next time he wanted to sleep with her all night and wake up next to her in the morning.

"So, when do you think we could do it again?" she asked.

He was addicted. "How about tomorrow? Maybe we could sneak out to the river house when Todd's in school." He said the words, and a wave of lust washed through him.

"Tomorrow sounds good," she murmured. Then she opened the Caddy's door and got out.

Savannah stood in the ruins of The Kismet's auditorium staring up at what was left of the roof. The bright blue of another beautiful spring day shone through the burn holes.

The insurance adjuster and the Allenberg County fire chief had just left the premises after imparting the shocking news that he believed the fire had been purposefully set.

The Allenberg Fire Department had determined that the blaze started in a corner of the auditorium, far from any ignition sources. Their inspection of the scene suggested accelerants or some kind of flammable liquid had been used. The episode was still under investigation, and the determination wouldn't be final until the lab up in Orangeburg finished their analysis of samples taken from the scene.

Of course, the insurance company wasn't about to hand out any checks if this was a case of arson. And the two men had not been very impressed by the fact that she had been in the yarn shop when the blaze started.

"Ma'am, you could have hired anyone to start that fire. Heck, Zeph Gibbs has been in and out of here for two weeks, and everyone knows he's crazy. You should think twice about having that man around, if you ask me." The chief of the ACFD had been more than blunt.

Savannah didn't think, for one minute, that Zeph had started the fire. Not when he'd risked his life to rescue Maverick and herself.

She was processing all of this disastrous news when

John Rodgers strolled into what remained of The Kismet. He seemed more than chipper this morning as he started inspecting the damage and making notations in a hard-backed notebook. He had the audacity to whistle while he worked. No doubt he was totaling up the increase in his fees.

Savannah was just trying to decide whether to plead with him or kick him out on his backside when Dash arrived.

Her heart flipped over in her chest. She hadn't seen him since she'd left him by the roadside last night. She'd purposefully gotten up early so as to miss him at the bathroom door. She wasn't sure what she was feeling about him. Lust, certainly. But it was so much more than that.

And yet, all the angry tension disappeared the minute he strolled into the auditorium, replaced with something else altogether. Dash was here. She was safe. Even if someone *had* tried to burn down her theater.

"They think it was arson," she said, her voice shaky. "The insurance company is balking."

John Rodgers stopped whistling.

Dash frowned. "Who would want to burn down The Kismet? It was falling down anyway."

Savannah turned on Rodgers. "It might never have happened if your crew hadn't left the door unlocked. It was probably some kid pulling a prank."

"I didn't leave the door open." Rodgers turned and headed toward the front door. Dash and Savannah trailed after him.

"Well, shoot," Rodgers said, "there isn't any sign of a forced entry."

"Because your workers left it open," Dash said.

Rodgers put his fists on his hips. "Or maybe you did, Dash. Maybe you set the fire just like you put the snakes up in the projection room. Maybe you've just been trying to make everyone think you're still the hometown hero."

"I was never the hometown hero," Dash said. "And that's the reason folks think I put diamondbacks in the projection room."

"Well then, it was probably that old crazy man, Zeph," Rodgers said.

Savannah had to step in before the two men came to blows. "Zeph isn't the kind of man who would burn a place like this down. You've seen the way he is about the woodwork. And Dash wouldn't put diamondbacks in the projection room. If he wanted to scare me, all he'd have to do is find a little garden snake. So I have to conclude that your workers were not careful about locking up."

"Look, honey, you don't know squat about this. Why don't you just let me and Dash figure it out?" Rodgers said.

"You're fired," Savannah replied.

Rodgers straightened. "We have a contract."

"Too bad. You didn't lock the door and look what happened. That's grounds for dismissal," Dash said, folding his arms across his chest.

"Fine. Have it your way. I'll expect you to honor the termination clause in the contract. And you sure aren't going to get your deposit back. You won't be able to afford to fix the place up if the insurance doesn't come through either." The contractor turned and strolled out of the building.

"He didn't seem too upset about being fired, did he?" Dash said.

"Are you suggesting that he left the door open on purpose? That's crazy. Why would he do that?"

Dash turned and walked back into the auditorium. "Well, whoever tried to burn this place down did a pretty bad job of it. The ceiling may be gone, but the lobby's intact. We can salvage this."

"I don't have the money. If I don't pay Rodgers a cancellation fee, he'll take me to court, and I can't afford that either. And the project has gotten way more expensive. I don't think I could get a loan, and I have a feeling that Angel Development is going to want—"

"I have the money. We're going to renovate this place, if it's the last thing I do. And if it's true that someone tried to burn this place down, then I'm going to find out who the bastard is and I'm going to let him know just exactly how ticked off I am about it."

Savannah opened her mouth to argue and then stopped. "Okay," she said.

He turned, a surprised look on his face. "You aren't going to argue?"

She shook her head. "No. You loved Granddaddy as much as I did. I think he would be happy if you and I teamed up on this. And God knows, if someone tried to burn this place down on purpose, I won't stand in the way of your beating the crap out of them, when you find them. And also, I need the money."

He smiled. With both sides of his mouth. And that grin made her heart swell. God, she was falling for him in a big way.

"I'm ready to listen to your advice, too," she added.

"Apparently so. You just fired your contractor."

"I did. You've been telling me to do that for a while. I

should have listened. We need to change the locks on the door."

"And put up a locked construction fence. Seems like overkill in Last Chance, but I don't want the arsonist to come back to finish the job. And then we need to talk to those architects."

"Who would do this?" she asked, feeling suddenly vulnerable. She hugged herself.

"Someone who wanted to stop you."

"Who?"

He shrugged. "Your ex-mother-in-law comes immediately to mind."

Savannah shook her head. "Claire is a difficult person, but she wouldn't break the law. She'd be more likely to turn the law on me because her husband is a high-powered attorney. As a grandparent, though, she doesn't have many rights. I double-checked before I decided to move Todd out of state. On the other hand, if Greg ever got the wild notion that he wanted to actually visit with his son, then I'd have to accommodate him. Greg and I have a custody agreement that we entered into in the state of Maryland."

"You just outlined why Claire might be desperate enough to bribe a contractor into setting a *small* fire. One that might not cause all that much damage, just enough to discourage you. And then there is the mystery of the diamondbacks. Someone put those snakes in the projection room."

"That's crazy. She wouldn't do something like that."

"She's the only person I can think of who wants you to fail. Everyone else is rooting for you."

"My mother wants me to fail."

"She wouldn't set a fire in the theater or put venomous snakes where you were likely to get bitten. She's your mother, and she loves you."

"You think?"

"I know she loves you. She's misguided, but she thinks she's doing the best she can for you and Todd. She wouldn't burn down her father's theater."

"No, I don't think she would. It would never occur to her because she's convinced I'm going to fail regardless." Savannah's voice betrayed her emotions.

Dash closed the distance between them and gave her a big, warm hug. "You're not going to fail."

She shamelessly clung to him. Maybe it was okay to let him hold her up for a few minutes. Maybe she didn't need to accomplish everything all by herself just to prove a point. She wanted to bring the theater back to life. Did it matter if she needed Dash's help to make it happen?

CHAPTER
18

A week after the fire at The Kismet, Mrs. Andrews came into Todd's third-period history class and announced to everyone that Todd needed to go to the principal's office.

Everyone started to laugh. Todd collected his books and followed Mrs. Andrews. He was trying to think of what he might have done wrong. His hands got all sweaty, and his heart was pumping hard, like the night of the fire, when he thought Mom might get burned up.

He was still a little shaky over the fire. Everyone in school was talking about it. But he didn't want to. He worried that Mom might decide to go back to Baltimore.

And he'd have to leave Champ.

Even worse, he wouldn't get a chance to go to Coach Canaday's football camp. He'd decided that maybe if he got really good at football, Dad would pay attention to him.

He followed Mrs. Andrews into Mr. Middleton's office. The principal was sitting at his desk, and there was an African-American lady with him.

"Todd, I'd like you to meet Ms. Darrett," Mr. Middleton said.

"Hello, Todd," she said in a deep, husky voice.

The principal gestured to the empty chair in front of his desk. "Sit down, Todd. Ms. Darrett is here to ask you a few questions."

"About what? I haven't done anything wrong."

"Of course you haven't. We're just concerned that maybe there are things you want to talk about," Mr. Middleton said.

"What things?"

Ms. Darrett gave him a smile that Todd could see right through. She was a big, fat poser.

"Why don't you sit down?"

"I don't want to sit. I want to go back to history class."

"Sit down, Todd," Mr. Middleton said.

He sat.

"Now, I just want to ask you a few questions about the man you're living with," Ms. Darrett said.

"What are you talking about?"

"You know, the man you're living with. Mr. Randall."

"What about him?"

"Has he ever done anything that made you uncomfortable?"

Hettie pulled her Audi TT into the gravel drive next to her river house. The house had once belonged to her father and it wasn't anything grand. Just a five-room bungalow with a tin roof. She'd spent her summers in this little house, with its porch overlooking the flowing waters of the Edisto River.

The house sat in a long line of small bungalows owned

by other local citizens. Altogether there were about twenty homes here, and the homeowners made up the board of the Edisto Country Club.

It was an unusual country club because there wasn't a tennis court or golf course to be found. Just a big party pavilion where Allenberg hosted the annual Watermelon Festival barbecue. And the river, of course.

It was the last day of April—time to get the house ready for the summer. In past years, Violet would come out here and do the work. But this year, Hettie had come herself. And she'd almost enjoyed the sweeping and the dusting and the mopping. She was tired when she finally sat on the porch with a glass of sweet tea.

Now that Jimmy was gone, she was thinking about closing up the big house in June, July, and August and spending her summer here. She was thinking about letting Violet take a paid vacation. She was thinking about cooking and cleaning for herself.

She sat on the old porch glider and rocked back and forth, thinking about the mistakes she'd made in her life.

Her reverie was broken a few moments later when a big red Cadillac Eldorado came up the drive. She tensed, expecting Dash to pull into her driveway. He was about the last person on earth she wanted to talk to. He was one of the mistakes she'd made.

But instead of stopping to visit, he drove right past and pulled his big car into the driveway of Miriam's house. He seemed to have a little spring in his step as he walked from the car to the porch. He entered the bungalow, and a moment later the air conditioner kicked in.

Five minutes later, Savannah's little Honda came rolling up the drive. She pulled her car in behind Dash's and headed toward the porch steps.

Dash and Savannah were probably just getting the place ready for the summer. Hettie put it out of her mind until about an hour later, when they both emerged. Before they headed to their respective automobiles, they stopped and embraced.

Hettie felt like a voyeur, but she couldn't tear her gaze away. That kiss was not exactly what a couple of cousins usually shared. It was practically scorching. And you'd have to be a total idiot not to realize that they didn't really want to leave each other.

Hettie checked her watch. It was almost three-thirty. The middle school let out in about ten minutes, and Savannah probably had to go pick up Todd.

Hettie's first inclination was to pick up the phone and call Rocky. This was hot stuff. But her second inclination was something altogether different.

The loneliness that she'd been valiantly battling for years settled over her like a heavy blanket. It was one thing to be lonely when you knew a man like Dash was just waiting there in the wings. And even if she didn't love Dash and had never intended to be with him, seeing him with someone else made her envious.

And not because she wanted him. She just wanted what Dash and Savannah seemed to have found. She wanted to kiss someone like Savannah kissed Dash. Like she wanted to devour him.

Hettie squeezed her eyes shut and told herself that she was being silly. She reminded herself that her independence was more important than hot, sultry kisses.

But wait. Savannah was one of the most independent

women Hettie had ever met. And there she was kissing on Dash Randall like he hung the moon. And, of course, Dash had given her a ton of money for the theater, but she didn't even know it. Dash was doing everything he could to support that independence.

Damn.

She had misjudged him. Badly. He'd changed. He'd grown up. He was a better man than Jimmy ever could have been.

Of course, she didn't love him. She never would. But mixed in with her own self-pity was a little glimmer of happiness. For Dash. Because Savannah was a wonderful woman.

And now, of course, it all made sense. No wonder Savannah had refused Bill's proposal.

Hettie smiled. Maybe Rocky wasn't the first person she needed to tell about this new, interesting development. Maybe Bill needed to know. She had a feeling that Bill might be relieved to find out that it wasn't him Savannah had rejected. It was just a matter of chemistry.

And then she wondered if Bill knew anything about chemistry.

Todd seemed kind of subdued when Savannah picked him up from school.

"Did you have a good day?"

"It was okay."

"What did you do?"

"Nothing."

Sometimes trying to talk to a twelve-year-old was impossible.

When Savannah got home, a blue Chevy sedan blocked

her parking spot in the drive. She parked in Dash's normal spot and got out of the Honda.

A woman in a navy blue suit greeted her from the porch where she had obviously been waiting. "Savannah White?" the woman said, getting up out of one of the rockers.

"That's me. What can I do for you?" Savannah headed for the porch. Todd hung back.

"Your aunt said I could wait for you here," the woman said.

"And you are?"

"I'm Shawna Darrett with the Allenberg County office of the Department of Social Services." She thrust out her hand. Savannah shook it with as firm a grip as she could muster.

"What can I do for you Ms. Darrett?"

The woman gazed at Todd, who was still standing by the car. "Honey, why don't you go on inside while I speak with your mother."

Todd strode forward, up the steps. "Are you going to ask her a bunch of dumb questions, too?"

Savannah turned on Todd. "What questions?"

"Mr. Middleton pulled me out of South Carolina history so I could talk with her. She asked me all kinds of questions about how I got the black eye."

"How you got the black—honey, everyone knows how you got that black eye."

"Yeah, but she wanted to make sure it wasn't because Dash hit me or something."

"What?"

He shrugged and then glared at Ms. Darrett. "Dash didn't hit me, okay? And I don't think his taking me out into the swamp to hunt for frogs was a big deal, either. Or taking me to meet Coach Canaday. Or playing football and Ultimate Frisbee with me."

"Now, Todd, sometimes when an older man—"

"Zip it, lady. I'm going to walk Champ." Todd turned and stomped into the house and slammed the door.

"What's this about?" Savannah asked.

"Is your son always so rude?"

"Sometimes, when a complete stranger arrives and tells him that the only man who has ever shown any interest in him is being accused of abusing him. If you want to see abuse and neglect, try talking to Todd's father."

Ms. Darrett smiled. "Now, I know this is difficult. But we're required to investigate every allegation of abuse and neglect. And someone made a report to our office that Todd was being abused, or was at risk of being abused. That he was living in a household with a man who is a substance abuser and who has a history of violence."

"Who did this?"

"I'm not at liberty to say. It could have been an anonymous report. We get them all the time. Now, why don't we sit down and talk about this, shall we?"

Savannah sat in one of the rockers as her fury mounted. This was exactly the sort of thing Claire would pull. It was ten times more effective than arson. And, of course, Claire had the best legal minds at her disposal. While Savannah was here on her own.

"I have a few questions about Dash Randall. I see that he was a professional baseball player. I looked up his history. Did you know that major-league baseball sent him to rehab on three separate occasions?"

"No."

"You should have, especially since your son is living in the same house with him."

"He's family."

"Most abusers are."

"He didn't abuse anyone. And he's sober now. He goes to AA meetings every Thursday evening."

"I know that. But he has a history of addiction and that's not good. Now, during your time here, has Mr. Randall been involved in any violence? Any fighting or anything like that?"

Savannah's stomach dropped. She had to be honest with this woman. "Uh, well, he got into a fight at Dot's Spot a couple of months ago."

"Dot's Spot?"

She closed her eyes. "It's a bar in town."

"Was he drinking?"

"I don't know. You'd have to ask Dot Cox, who owns the place. But he did get into a fight with Roy Burdett. And I can guarantee you that Roy was drinking. But aside from that one time I haven't—"

"So he goes to bars on a regular basis."

"No. Just that one time."

"I see."

"And he's been showing a lot of attention to your son?"

"Yes."

"Don't you think that's odd?"

"No. I think it's wonderful. Todd needs a man around, since his father has been absent most of his life."

Shawna Darrett interlaced her fingers. She had very long nails painted an electric pink, and there were at least five rings distributed among her ten fingers. She might be wearing a blue suit, but behind that institutional exterior was a real human person.

After a long moment, the caseworker spoke. "Mrs. White, I know this is hard. And I know that Mr. Randall is well off and somewhat famous. But think about what happened up in Pennsylvania with that college coach. Sometimes predators look like the guy next door. They are the kind of men that kids gravitate toward. And I gather that Mr. Randall teaches a whole bunch of children up at that stable of his."

Savannah could not believe the way this woman was twisting reality. "I'm sorry. Dash teaches kids to ride horses, and from what I've seen, he's pretty good at it. And the kids he teaches seem to really like him. He also helps out the Little League, I've discovered. Not to mention Pop Warner football. And I'm not talking about just giving money. I'm talking about helping out with his time."

"Exactly. That's what predators do."

"Are you out of your mind?"

"And then there's the allegation of arson and something to do with snakes. I spoke with the Allenberg sheriff, and while he seems to believe that Mr. Randall isn't guilty of anything, it's also a fact that the only people who have a key to the theater are you, Dash Randall, and the contractor."

"The contractor left the door open. Dash did not burn down the theater."

"But what about the snakes? I gather he put the snakes in the theater and then had someone videotape him catching them."

"He did no such thing. I can't believe the sheriff told you that."

"Well, not exactly. But the sheriff did admit that Mr. Randall is still a person of interest in the case. As are you, I might add. Which is problematic."

Emotions welled up in Savannah's throat making it hard to respond to Ms. Darrett's indictment. "You think I burned the theater? You think I'm a criminal?" she managed to say, despite the knot in her throat.

"No, ma'am. I'm just investigating the facts to make sure that Todd is taken care of." Shawna leaned forward and put a hand on her knee. "I know this is hard. Mr. Randall is your cousin. But that's the way these cases usually go. The bad actor is someone everyone trusts."

"No. You're crazy. Dash is not abusing Todd. He's not a drug addict, or, God forbid, some kind of pedophile. And neither he nor I is an arsonist. Please, this is ridiculous."

"According to my research, Mr. Randall came from an abusive home. You know that a very large percentage of abusers were abused themselves."

"No. Stop. I'm not listening." Savannah stood up, tears forming in her eyes.

"Ma'am, please, calm down. We're just trying to do the best thing for your child. I have to tell you that, if you don't cooperate in our investigation, we'll have to take steps to put your child in a safer environment."

She turned. "Safer environment? You mean foster care?"

"Well, it's not perfect, but it—"

"You think foster care is better than living with his mother and his great-aunt and a guy who pays some attention to him?"

"Ma'am, if that guy is hurting him, and you're letting him do it, then yes."

"Oh, my God. This is crazy. This is my ex-mother-in-law trying to make my life a living hell. That's all this is."

"Well, that may be, but I would advise you to sit down and answer my questions in a calm manner. Otherwise things might not go so well for you."

Savannah buttoned her lip and sniffled back her angry tears. She was not going to let Claire White defeat her. She was not going to let that woman smear Dash either.

She sat down. "What do you want to know?"

Dash strolled from his car to the house, a goofy smile on his face. He'd been sneaking around with Savannah for a week. And he'd stopped being scared and started feeling happy.

Happiness, he discovered, was addictive.

He was hooked on Savannah. Bad. But it didn't feel bad. It didn't feel destructive. It was just... good.

Because he had a feeling she was also hooked on him. And that was new and different and wonderful.

He wanted to come out, so to speak. There was no way they could continue to skulk around having dirty sex every afternoon without someone finding out. And he didn't want to keep it a secret anymore.

He was in love. In a sober way. Which was kind of weird because being with Savannah was an incredible high. Why hadn't he ever figured this out before?

He opened the front door and heard Savannah's voice even before he reached the kitchen. Something was wrong. He quickened his pace. He'd learned how to recognize her moods.

"Claire, I can't believe you would stoop so low." She

was angry. Boy howdy, he didn't think he'd ever heard her voice sound so harsh.

"Well, if you didn't do this horrible thing, then who did? I would really appreciate it if you would back off and tell Greg that he needs to call me so we can discuss this like adults."

Dash entered the kitchen to find Savannah standing at the sink, looking out the window with her back to him. Her body was tense—practically rigid through the shoulders. The wicked witch of Baltimore was obviously on the other end of the line.

Savannah pulled the phone from her ear and stared at it. "Bitch," she growled.

"Did she hang up on you?" Dash asked.

She turned. Holy moly, her face was a mess.

"Darlin' what is it?"

"Nothing," she said, her lips tight. She pulled a paper towel from the dispenser and blew her nose.

"You've been crying. It has to be something."

"No, it doesn't." She dabbed her eyes. "I've got to get supper started. It's book club night." She didn't meet his gaze.

"Darlin', what's the wicked witch up to now?"

"It's nothing. She's being difficult is all, and she makes me so angry. I don't like feeling angry. So please, just leave me alone. I need to cook."

She started moving around the kitchen like a whirlwind. It occurred to him that Savannah's love for cooking was emotionally rooted. She and Aunt Sally had been thick as thieves. She might remember her grandfather better, but in some ways she was a whole lot like Aunt Sally. Aunt Sally almost never got angry, but when she did, she would cry. And the tears coming out of Savannah's eyes were a dead giveaway.

He ought to leave her alone. But he couldn't. All he could think about was the way Uncle Earnest used to handle Aunt Sally. So he sauntered up behind her, put his hands on her tense shoulders, and turned her around.

He didn't try to kiss her, or talk to her, or anything. He just gave her the biggest hug he could muster. She kind of melted into his chest, and that warmed him up from the inside out. It wasn't even a sexual warmth, it was just... good. To hold her like this was just the best thing in the world. Especially when she leaned on him. No one had done that before. Ever.

He held her for a solid two minutes before she pushed away. She wouldn't meet his gaze. She was still upset about something, but she wasn't going to talk about it.

He wanted her to share her burden with him. But he couldn't force that kind of trust. He needed to give her time. And the strange thing was that he knew he had all the time in the world.

She wasn't going anywhere. She was here to stay.

"I gotta cook dinner," she said.

"Okay. I'll get out of your hair. Where's Todd?"

"He's at Oliver's house. He's having dinner over there."

"We were going to go to Golfing for God for putt-putt tonight."

She shrugged. "I guess he forgot. I'm glad he has friends his own age."

Something wasn't right. But he didn't want to push it. "Okay." He headed down the hall and out to the porch. Aunt Miriam was sitting in her rocker. She looked like she was sleeping.

The skin along her jawline looked waxy. She had gotten so frail these last few months. His heart squeezed in his chest. Aunt Mim would be eighty-five in September. He had to accept that her days on this earth were numbered. In fact, lately, since Uncle Harry died, she seemed to be less interested in things. Like she wanted to go be with Harry instead of being here. With him.

He didn't like thinking about that. And he didn't like thinking about the way Savannah wouldn't meet his eyes, just now.

What in the world would he do if Miriam died and Savannah left? The question rocked him to his soul.

Savannah sniffled back her tears and finished layering the noodles and cheese for her lasagna.

She needed to stop crying. How the hell was she supposed to tell Dash what Claire had gotten up to? It would destroy him to know that people thought he was a danger to kids. If she fought this thing, they would drag Dash's reputation through the mud and back. She didn't want to think about the gossip. She didn't want to think about the hurt or the damage fighting this would cause.

She popped the lasagna into the oven and started pulling together a salad. Dash wasn't the only one who would be hurt.

Savannah had spoken with Doc Cooper several times over the last few weeks. They were both concerned that Miriam was losing weight, even though Savannah was pushing food at her. Doc was beginning to think that Miriam might be experiencing transient ischemic attacks—or mini strokes. But the only way to test that was to take her up to Orangeburg for an MRI. She didn't want to go.

Miriam was in frail health. She was old. This investigation might kill her.

More tears flooded her eyes.

If she went back to Baltimore, she could stop this attack on Dash and Miriam. But it would leave Todd brokenhearted. He'd have to leave Champ behind. He'd have to leave Dash behind. He'd have to leave the friends he'd been making. How could she do that to him?

How could she do this to herself? Because she had fallen in love with Dash. She didn't want to leave him. But she couldn't stay.

She wiped the tears from her cheeks. This was an impossible situation. No matter what she did, someone was going to get hurt.

CHAPTER 19

I'm trying to decide whether this book is about history or something else," Molly said. "I mean, the hero was kind of an eyewitness to his own life, wasn't he?"

"Well, that's because it's told through his journal," Jenny said. "Of course he's an eyewitness."

"Yes, but he doesn't seem to be really taking charge of his life. It's more like he's been swept along by historical events so the author can tell us all about Trotsky and the Red Scare."

"Yes, but he takes charge of his life at the end when he dives into that hole and never reappears," Jenny said.

"That's if you think he cheated death. Otherwise the guy just ended his life, which I think is pretty cowardly," Kenzie said. "All in all I liked *Pride and Prejudice* better. Maybe next time we could read *Mansfield Park* or something. I just hate these books where the protagonist dies at the end."

"How about one of—" Cathy started to say before Nita interrupted her.

"No, Cathy, we are not going to read one of June Moring's books, is that clear?"

Cathy let go of a deep sigh, and Jenny took up the discussion of Barbara Kingsolver's *The Lacuna* again. "Harrison Shepherd didn't die. He escaped from his life."

Savannah kept her eyes trained on the purple possum fur disaster in her hands. She wanted to escape from her life, but she wasn't about to do it the way the protagonist in *The Lacuna* had done it. Besides, she didn't exactly have an escape hole that she could swim through at low tide.

She probably should have stayed home tonight. But if she had, everyone would be calling her up to find out if she was okay. That was the way things worked in Last Chance. You couldn't weasel out of a commitment without having a really good, and verifiable, excuse. This was definitely one of the downsides of living in a small town.

The argument droned on between Molly and Jenny, while Savannah concentrated on purling across her row. She wasn't very good at purling either.

Rocky, who was sitting next to her, leaned in and whispered. "Honey, what have you been crying about?"

Savannah looked up into the concerned green eyes of one of her oldest friends. "I can't talk about it."

"Of course you can." Rocky patted her knee, then turned to the rest of the book club. "All right, y'all, that's enough of talking about this book. This book was depressing but educational, I suppose. I think we need to figure out a way to cheer up Savannah."

Savannah looked up. Everyone was staring at her.

"Honey, you're looking like the last pea at pea-time. What's the matter? Is it Miriam?" asked Lola May.

"Uh, well, I'm worried about her."

"Of course you are," Hettie said. "She didn't look good at church last Sunday. And I heard from Annie Jasper that Doc thinks she may have had a stroke."

Tears flooded Savannah's eyes.

"Aw, honey." Rocky turned and gave Savannah the biggest hug she'd had since Dash had hugged her in the kitchen earlier.

Rocky's hug was pretty nice, but it didn't hold a candle to that moment in Dash's arms. And somehow thinking about that and what her in-laws were trying to do to Dash made the tears come faster.

"Someone get her a slice of chocolate cake, quick," Hettie said.

Savannah pulled away from Rocky and sniffled back her tears. "I'm sorry."

"It's all right. We all love Miriam."

"It's not just Miriam," she said, and then immediately regretted her candor.

"What else?"

She shrugged. "Just trouble with my ex."

"What kind of trouble?"

"He and his mother are putting some serious pressure on me to go back to Baltimore."

"Oh, goodness, you can't do that, not after all the money Dash poured into the Kismet," Hettie said, and then a nanosecond later she followed with, "Uh-oh, I wasn't supposed to tell you that."

Savannah turned toward Hettie. "What do you mean? What money? I haven't taken any money from Dash. He's offered money but I've told him no. Until, well, recently. Since the fire."

Hettie let go of a big sigh. "Honey, don't be mad at Dash, his motives were entirely pure. He gave Angel Development a boatload of money on the condition that we give you the grant for the theater. I guess he knew that you'd never take his money after the way y'all squabbled as kids, and he wanted you to have it. He wanted the theater to be revived as much as everyone else."

Rocky rolled her eyes. "Okay, Hettie's putting a nice spin on it. He's helping you because Hettie wants him to."

"What?"

Hettie glared at Rocky, and Rocky glared back. "Now, ladies, this is a book club, not a—" Nita started to say but Hettie interrupted.

"Rocky, that's not exactly right. I asked him—"

"No, it's exactly right, Hettie. Everyone in town knows that Dash is carrying a torch for you. He's been carrying it for decades. And over the last couple of years, he's done every damn thing you wanted him to, and you don't ever thank him for it. You just... I don't know, Hettie, but you're a fool. Dash loves you, and he's a wonderful man, and you treat him like crap."

"Dash gave you money to give me?" Savannah asked in a tiny voice.

"Yeah, honey," Rocky said. "He made a big donation to Angel Development with the understanding that a big chunk would go to the theater."

"And he did that because you asked him to?" Savannah turned toward Hettie.

"I did. But that was—"

"Yes, she did," Rocky said. "Just like he gave Hugh the land for the factory—because Hettie needed for that to happen."

Hettie's face grew red as a beet. "No, not really, he—"

"No, really. Hettie, I don't want to start a fight, but any fool can see that Dash would walk through fire for you. He's ten times the man Jimmy ever was. When are you going to see the obvious?"

Savannah's emotions tumbled. "But he's not," she said.

Rocky laughed. "Savannah, honey, you didn't know Jimmy. He was a rich man's son and had all the swagger, but Dash has always been the better man, in my opinion."

"No, that's not what I meant. I just meant—" Savannah stopped herself. If she told the book club, and Hettie Marshall, that she thought Hettie and Bill were a match made in Heaven, they would laugh at her. More important, they would figure out exactly what she and Dash had been doing recently.

And she didn't want to expose herself. Not now. Not knowing that Dash didn't really care about her the way she'd come to care about him.

"What *did* you mean?" Hettie asked. She looked very regal at the moment. The kind of strong woman Savannah was never going to be. The kind of woman people didn't laugh at or challenge or doubt. Of course Dash loved her. Who wouldn't want a woman like Hettie? "Dash isn't what, Savannah?"

"Nothing," she murmured, letting Hettie stare her down the way Claire always did. She had to get out of here before she made an idiot of herself in front of people she was beginning to consider good friends. She stuffed her knitting into her Vera Bradley bag.

"I have to go," she said, and escaped.

But of course, Hettie came right after her. "Wait," she called.

Savannah got to the corner before Hettie caught up. "Honey, stop. What were you about to say?"

"Nothing."

Hettie gently grabbed her by the shoulder. "Listen, Savannah, I know what's going on between you and Dash. He doesn't love me. Rocky's wrong."

"He does." She knew it was true. Hell, Dash had even told her a couple of times that he had a "thing" for Hettie. And besides, she and Dash had just been having fun. There wasn't anything serious going on. No one had used the word "love." They'd been sneaking around having dirty, meaningless sex.

"He's loved you a long time," Savannah said. The words almost stuck in her throat.

Hettie sighed. "Okay, he *has* loved me for a long time. But I was married. I was not attainable, so it made me easy to love. The truth is, we had a fling when I was very young but I fell out of love with him a long time ago. He's just not ever been able to move on. But I think maybe he's getting ready to."

Savannah shook her head. "No. It's impossible. It can't be." Her insides kind of collapsed. She knew just how impossible it was. The Department of Social Services caseworker had made it quite clear what would happen if she even dared to go down that road. And the minute she did, Dash's reputation would be dragged through the mud. She couldn't do that to him again.

Besides, what was the point of hanging on so tight, knowing down deep that Dash was in love with someone else? Savannah couldn't compete with Hettie. She was the kind of woman who knew that a gift of five hundred thousand dollars was suspicious. If Hettie had been in charge of the theater renovation, she never would have hired John

LAST CHANCE BOOK CLUB   299

Rodgers. Hettie probably could have gotten financing on the merits of her business plan, instead of the kind of charity Dash had given out.

Savannah had been so stupid and naive about the theater. Mom was right. She was at her best when she stayed in the kitchen.

"Honey, it's going to be okay. Don't be mad at him," Hettie said.

"I'm not." She wiped the tears from her cheeks and straightened her shoulders.

Then she turned toward Hettie. "You know, you should quit screwing around and make a play for Bill. Y'all belong together."

Hettie's eyes widened. "What? I can't cook."

Savannah shrugged. "He doesn't need a cook. He needs someone to keep him pointed in the right direction. And you could do that with your eyes closed. I wish I was like that. I really do."

Hettie hurried up the walk to the front door of the Christ Church rectory house. The brick rambler, set back under a canopy of Carolina pines, was more suited to a family than the bachelor Reverend Ellis. Pine needles and cones made a soft russet carpet on the front lawn and perfumed the night air.

She pushed the bell, knowing it was far too late to be visiting. Coming here, after the scene at the book club, was insane, in fact.

And yet it wasn't. Something had snapped inside Hettie the minute Savannah had told her to make a play for Bill. A strange sense of peace came over her. As if all the puzzle pieces suddenly fit together.

The discussion of the book this evening pointed in this direction. She had been an observer of her own life for a long, long time.

Even when Jimmy had been alive, she'd felt disconnected from herself. But something had started to change a couple of years ago, when Sarah Rhodes made her remember what it felt like to be a girl, when her faith in the simple things hadn't become so jaded and eroded.

She'd changed. And the more she stopped hanging back in her life, the better her life got. And now there was just one thing she'd been procrastinating over. The one thing she'd kept telling herself that she didn't want.

But which she wanted more than anything.

She wanted what Savannah and Dash had. Savannah might be angry right now about the truth, but Hettie was glad she'd spilled it. Savannah and Dash needed to figure out that they had something really great going on.

So great, in fact, that Savannah was finally going to help Dash move on. And it was time for Hettie to move on, too.

Bill opened the door, and Hettie's pulse rate kicked up a notch. His hair was curled over his forehead, his serious, deep-set blue eyes full of concern. He was wearing a T-shirt and a pair of jeans, and without all that clerical garb he looked like a man.

A very handsome man.

The man who made her heart sing whenever he turned his gaze on her.

"Hettie?" Bill said. "What's the matter?" A frown wrinkled his brow.

"Do you remember that time last spring when we were

cleaning up Golfing for God and you told me that we were
friends?"

His lips twitched. "Of course I do."

"Well," she said on a puff of air as her mouth got
cottony.

"Well, what?"

"I don't want to be your friend," she whispered.

He blinked. "What?"

"I don't want to be your friend. I know I can't cook
worth a lick, but I would like to be..." She couldn't say
the word. It was absurd. She wanted to be his lover. But
he was an Episcopalian priest. Priests did not take lovers.

She stared down at his naked toes. He must have
noticed the direction of her stare because he wiggled them.

She looked up. He had a half smile on his face, and
the lines at the corner of his eyes softened his gaze. She'd
seen him look at her like that a million times. And it
always made her heart race. It had done that even before
Jimmy had been murdered.

"I...I..." Darn it, what was she supposed to say now?

Bill stepped out onto the landing. He caressed her
cheek. His hand warm and tender. "Yes?" he said, his
eyebrow arching.

"Oh, yes," she whispered as she placed her hand on
his. She closed her eyes.

And the next thing she knew, Bill had drawn her up
into an embrace. She drank him in like a sacrament. "I
know it's wrong, but I don't want to be friends anymore."

"What's wrong about that?" he murmured against
her ear.

She pulled back just enough so she could look him in
the eye. "Because what I want is not nice."

"No?" His mouth was curling at the corners. "I think it must be very nice. Would you like to come in? I could read you the Song of Solomon."

"Uh, that would be nice, but I want more than that. Am I'm crazy to want it, Bill? Just tell me that I'm crazy, and I'll go."

"Well, if you want it that bad, Hettie, we could always run off to Georgia together."

She straightened as if she'd been hit by a Taser. "Uh, did you just suggest that we should run off to Georgia to get *married*?"

"Yeah, I did. You can get married there without a waiting period. If you want to get married in South Carolina, we'll have to wait three days. I don't know about you, but I've been waiting on you for a long time."

"You've been what?"

He shrugged. "Well, I knew I couldn't just walk through the front door of your big house and get down on one knee. You weren't ready for that. I had to wait until you were ready."

"Then why did you have dinner with every single cook in Allenberg County?"

"Because I knew it would bother you?"

"But you proposed to Savannah."

"Yes, in public, where I knew she would turn me down."

"You knew she would turn you down?"

"Of course I did. I had Miriam Randall as my co-conspirator. She guaranteed it. She even gave me pointers on how to annoy Savannah. It was pretty simple, actually. I just turned into a grumpy old minister whenever her son was around."

Hettie's mouth dropped open. "No, you didn't. Miriam didn't."

"Yes, she did. She told me that Savannah belonged to someone else."

Hettie started to laugh.

"What's so funny?"

"Savannah and Dash are having one hell of an affair. I saw them at the country club kissing one another. Do you think you having dinner over there made Dash jealous?"

Bill smiled. And then he swooped in with a kiss that was way too sexy to belong to a man of God.

Not to mention the fact that his hands got busy touching her in a way that was truly sinful. And they were standing right on his front stoop in front of any neighbor, including Lillian Bray, who might have a mind to look in this direction.

Which was kind of exciting, actually. The notion of getting caught kissing Bill Ellis was a definite turn-on.

A while later (who was counting minutes?), Bill disengaged. "Hettie, I think we should go to Georgia." His voice sounded a little gruff.

"Uh, don't you think that would be—"

He pressed his fingers on her lips. "Yes, it would raise all kinds of gossip, but I don't care. I'm tired of waiting. Let's go."

"But—"

One of his eyebrows arched. "You have doubts?"

Hettie looked up at him, her heart pounding, her body singing. "No. I don't." And saying the words removed the silly barrier she'd erected around herself for years.

"I've always done the proper thing. I've always done what everybody expected me to do."

"Me too."

"But I don't want to be like that anymore. I don't want to be an observer in my own life. I want to jump into it with both feet."

"Me too."

She smiled. "Let's run away to Georgia."

Savannah's Thursday morning was almost as nightmarish as Wednesday evening. She got up way early to avoid Dash at the bathroom door. She drove Todd to school on the early side. Then she headed to the Kountry Kitchen for a cup of coffee.

T-Bone Carter and his waitress, Ricki Wilson, made a good cup of coffee. Maybe not as good as the coffee she made at home, but it would do. She was hiding out here, in plain sight.

She didn't dare go home and face Dash again. She was angry and guilty and devastated. She didn't even know where her heart lay anymore. She didn't want to leave Last Chance, but she couldn't stay. She sat there, toting up pros and cons on the back of a napkin. And the checkmarks in the columns didn't help her any.

If she stayed, she would have to take more money from Dash, at the same time that her ex-in-laws were smearing his reputation. It was impossible. Even if her heart wasn't mixed up in it.

"Oh, my God, Savannah, I've been trying to call you all morning." Rocky came bustling into the café and slid into the facing seat. "You won't believe what's happened."

Living in Last Chance, Savannah was ready to believe anything. What other town had a putt-putt on the outskirts of town called Golfing for God? "What?"

"Hettie and Bill have run off together."

A full-body adrenaline rush pushed through her. She got hot and then cold from her scalp to her toes. But she wasn't surprised, she was pleased. In a deeply spiritual way that she couldn't quite explain.

"Yeah, I know, I'm flabbergasted. Hettie. And Bill? I mean, your aunt said he should be looking for a cook, right?"

"No. That's not what she said. She said he should be looking for a woman who knew how to live on a minister's salary. To tell you the truth, the advice she gave Bill sounded a whole lot like the advice that Lady Catherine gives to Mr. Collins in *Pride and Prejudice*. Which I gather Aunt Miriam has read so many times that she's practically memorized it, which is odd because her memory is definitely slipping."

"You aren't even surprised, are you?"

"No, I'm not."

Rocky frowned. "What's the matter? You look like you cried yourself to sleep. Don't tell me you're sorry that you let Bill go."

Savannah shook her head. "No, it's not that."

Rocky straightened in her chair. "Oh, crap, I didn't think about what this means to you until right this minute. I'm so sorry. I guess Dash isn't all that enthused about helping you now that Hettie has run off with Bill." Rocky reached out and patted Savannah's hand. "Look, there are other sources of money. Forget about Dash."

Oh, if only it were that easy.

Just then the door opened, and Savannah's terrible day went right to hell.

"There you are. I've been looking all over town

for you," Greg said as he headed toward Savannah's booth. Boy, her ex had put on weight since the last time she'd seen him. He looked pale and puffy. When she was nineteen, he'd been twenty, and at his trim football-playing weight. He'd been a big man on campus, a terrific dancer, pretty good in the sack, and the son of wealthy parents.

He had been the perfect bait for a girl like her. When they'd hooked up, being with him made her feel important, smart, special.

And all that lasted about three years.

He was sweating hard as he stood by the booth glaring at Rocky.

"Lady Woolham, this is my ex-husband Greg White, Greg, meet Lady Woolham."

"Lady Woolham?" He cast his gaze over Rocky's new pink Angel Development, Inc., T-shirt and her obviously worn blue jeans. Her Ladyship was slumming today.

"Well," Rocky said, "I reckon I'll be getting along. Don't you worry, now, Savannah, things will look better tomorrow." It was amazing the way Rocky, and every other female in Last Chance, had a way of channeling Scarlett O'Hara when things fell apart.

Greg slipped into the facing seat. He pulled a couple of napkins out of the dispenser and blotted the sweat from his red face. He looked like a heart attack waiting to happen, which was pitiful seeing as he was only thirty-two.

"You have to come back to Baltimore," Greg said without preamble.

She glanced down at the columns and checkmarks on her napkin. "I have to?" she asked, suddenly angry.

He cocked his head. "We have a visitation agreement.

I get to see Todd every other weekend. Are you going to send him on a plane every week?"

Oh, wow, he was bringing out the artillery. "Do you want to see him every week? Because I seem to recall months of you calling up and canceling visitation week after week, and then you stopped calling at all. And then you stopped paying child support. I never told your mother that, you know."

"You have to come back."

"Yeah, or your mother is going to smear Dash Randall from one side of the state to the other. And I'll bet she has enough money to undertake a public relations campaign that would put him on CNN every night."

Greg smiled. It made her stomach crawl. "That's right. And you don't want that. To be honest, babe, neither do I. And think about what that would do to Todd. So coming back to Baltimore is the smart thing all the way around."

She let go of a big sigh. She'd been coming up with this conclusion all on her own. Even if it would break Todd's heart to leave Champ behind, she couldn't stand in the way of Todd having a chance to be with his father. She knew how it felt to have an absent father. She would have given anything to spend time with Dad. Even now. Even knowing he was a jerk who didn't really care.

She leaned forward. "Greg, I will come back if you give me your solemn promise that you will see Todd every other weekend."

He reached out with one of his ham hands and covered her fist. "I promise you. I know I've been a crappy father, but you really shook me up when you moved down here."

His voice sounded shaky, and the look in his big brown eyes was deep and sincere. "I know I've screwed things up. I know I'm the reason the marriage didn't work. And I'm sorry. I really am. You're a wonderful woman. A great mother. An amazing cook. I miss your strudel. I miss Todd."

She closed her eyes and sucked in a breath. It had been such a joy to cook for him. For three years, she'd been happy, until she'd discovered him in his office one day, with his pants down, bent over his assistant.

She couldn't deny her son this relationship. Besides if Greg wanted to, he could haul her into court up in Maryland and insist that she make Todd available every other weekend. She had known that the day she left Baltimore for Uncle Harry's funeral. In fact, one of the reasons she'd run away was in the hope that Greg would come to his senses and realize what he was about to lose.

She nodded her head and opened her eyes. "I'll come back," she said. "You want to go get Todd out of school and tell him the news?"

"Uh, well," he said reaching into the inside pocket of his suit jacket. "I've got a plane to catch and not much time to spare." He waved the ticket so she'd know he wasn't lying.

"I'm working on a big case, and I don't have time to drive back with you. But Mom says she's happy to have you guys stay with her until you find a new apartment."

Of course. Savannah might have argued with him right then, but she looked down at her marked-up napkin. There was no point in arguing. She was beaten. And maybe, just maybe, she could salvage something out of this disaster for Todd. If she could do that, then it would be okay. Because more than anything else, she wanted Todd to have a relationship with his dad.

"Okay," she whispered. "We'll drive up on Saturday. That gives me a few days to pack up and settle things here."

"Great." He slid out of the seat.

"But there's one thing you have to do for me."

"What?" He tensed.

"I need you to get your mother to call off the South Carolina Social Services Department. I don't want one word spoken about Dash Randall. Do you hear me?"

He relaxed and nodded, confirming her suspicion that Claire had trumped up that threat. "No problem. I'll take care of it. It's not an issue if you're coming home."

He turned and headed out of the café. She squeezed her eyes shut and thought about his parting words.

Baltimore wasn't home anymore.

CHAPTER 20

Dash knew Savannah was avoiding him. She'd been up and out of the house before him. And she hadn't even made coffee or a thermos. Now he was sitting in his office at Painted Corner Stables, trying to figure out what he should do next.

Because yesterday, when he'd held her in the kitchen, it had felt right. And he wanted to be the guy she leaned on like that. Not the guy she avoided. Or the guy she was having low-down, dirty sex with.

He loved her with all his heart. He just hadn't told her yet. He needed to say the words. But he didn't want her to react the way Hettie had all those years ago. He couldn't stand that.

He was mulling over his options when Rocky deBracy strolled into his office. She wore a serious look on her face that didn't exactly match her bright pink Angel Development T-shirt. "Dash, honey, I've got some bad news for you," she said, sitting down in his single office chair.

His gut tightened. "Is Aunt Mim okay?"

She cocked her head. "Relax, it's not Miriam, although I understand she's not doing too well."

"She's doing right poorly. But if it's not Miriam, then what? Another snafu at The Kismet?" He tensed. He wasn't in the mood for bad news today.

"I'm going to say it quick, sort of like pulling off a Band-Aid."

"Get on with it, honey."

"Hettie and Bill have eloped. They went to Georgia last night, and I gather they spent their wedding night at a hotel in Augusta. Lillian Bray doesn't know whether to be overjoyed or scandalized. I personally think this is going to shift the power balance in Last Chance. As the chair of the Ladies' Auxiliary, Lillian is going to have to deal with Hettie on a daily basis. I mean, Hettie is now the minister's *wife*."

Dash tried very hard not to smile.

"You don't look devastated."

He shrugged.

"C'mon, Dash, don't be a tough guy. I know this has to hurt."

"I guess I'm a little surprised at Bill choosing Hettie. I mean, Hettie can't cook."

"Yeah, I know. But Savannah says that the cooking part wasn't the important part of Miriam's marital advice. In fact, I just saw Savannah, and she wasn't even surprised. Man, I'm striking out this morning with my gossip. I thought both of y'all would be really shaken up by this news."

"Sorry to disappoint you. Would it make you feel better if I wept into my coffee? To be honest, this is inferior coffee. I had to make it myself this morning, and I'm not very happy about that."

"I don't want you to be unhappy. But I did think that you'd be shocked at the very least. I mean I was under the impression that you were still trying to impress Hettie. I thought, well, you know, with the money you gave to the theater that you were—"

"Trying to buy her love?" he said into the silence.

"Well, yeah."

He shrugged. "I guess maybe it started out that way. I mean, I just wanted to make her happy, but things change."

"Oh, my God." Her eyes widened. "I came up here as a friend to offer you comfort and compassion. To make sure that you didn't fall apart and go down to Dot's and screw up a good thing. But now I'm thinking you don't need me."

He shrugged. "I appreciate your concern, Rocky, but I'm fine."

She frowned, and he could practically see the wheels turning in her mind. And Rocky had one of those very active minds that was liable to put two and two together and come up with more than just the correct answer.

She gave him the stink eye for a minute, and then suddenly a smile blossomed on her face. "Oh, my God. You stinker. You and Savannah. Oh, God, I should have seen it coming. It's like…It's like…well, to be honest, it's just like *Pride and Prejudice.*"

"What?"

"It's like the book where the hero and the heroine hate one another until they don't." She smiled, and then she frowned.

"Oh, no, Dash, this is a disaster. You need to get down to the Kountry Kitchen in a hurry because Savannah's ex just arrived in town. And he looked like a guy who means business. And I don't mean the honest kind."

"What?"

"Dash, that man looked like he was ready to drag her back to Baltimore. And she looked like she was having the worst day of her life."

Well, *that* sure did light a fire under Dash's backside. He got up and ran to his Eldorado with Rocky on his tail, giving him advice.

"Now, remember that Savannah isn't going to be impressed if you knock her ex-husband's head off."

"I'm not about to do anything stupid like that," he promised as he climbed into his Caddy. He gave Rocky a little smile as he pulled out of his parking space. "I've grown up some."

"So has she," she yelled after him.

By the time he got to the Kountry Kitchen, Rocky and her ex were gone.

He looked for her at the theater. But she wasn't there. The work crew was making good progress on the structural reinforcements needed in the auditorium. Zeph was doing amazing work repairing and restoring the woodwork in the lobby. The old place was going to rise from the ashes, quite literally, and he was happy about that.

Earnest Brooks would be proud of him.

He headed home, relieved when he found Savannah's Honda in the driveway and no sign of the ex-husband. The time had come to confess his feelings. Hell, he was sort of inspired by Bill and Hettie. Maybe he should run off with Savannah, too. That would put the ex at bay.

Of course, if they did that, they'd have to bring Todd along, because it would be dirty pool to run off with

Todd's momma without making sure the kid didn't have any deep-seated objections.

So, okay, they couldn't run off. But they would figure something out. He was feeling almost optimistic as he took the porch steps two at a time.

He didn't find Savannah in the kitchen. Miriam was in the parlor, watching a soap opera, and didn't exactly know where Savannah was. Hell, Aunt Mim didn't sometimes know where her own self was these days. His optimism slipped a little.

He climbed the stairs and found Savannah in her bedroom. She was standing by the bay window staring out at the big live oak in the front. Her gaze was a little unfocused. She looked tired and sad.

His heart twisted in his chest. No one had to tell him he was a day late and a dollar short. While he'd been thinking things through, everything had changed.

She turned from the window with an expression on her face that might have been a smile. But it wasn't happy. Her gaze lingered on him for a moment, and then moved to the doorway he'd come through, and then down to the carpet.

He braced himself. She said nothing. But he could read the words on her face. She was going to say goodbye. Like every damn person in his life, she was going to leave.

But it was costing her. At least he could see that in her face. She hesitated as if she didn't want to say the words. As if she wanted to spare him the pain.

And then a big tear escaped her eye and rolled down her cheek, and he had to stop himself from crossing the room and holding her tight and speaking of love.

He couldn't do that. Not now. It was hard enough without laying himself open. God help him, he wanted to lock the door and keep her inside.

But he couldn't. He had never been able to keep the people he loved from saying good-bye. He wasn't good enough, or strong enough, or important enough to hold them.

"You're going." It wasn't a question. He didn't need to ask.

She brushed the tear away from her cheek. "I have to."

He didn't ask why. He didn't need to know why. It didn't matter anyway. People always left. There was always a good reason why someone couldn't stay. And the only way to survive a thing like this was to pretend it didn't matter.

He shrugged. "Well, the highway runs right through town, princess, and you know the way. It's probably just as well. Hell, that theater project was a big money pit."

She snuffled back her tears. "You told me that at the beginning, but I wouldn't listen. And now I know that all the money came from you. And it was all about Hettie."

"Honey, Hettie has—"

"I know about Hettie and Bill. But that's beside the point. I can't take your money."

"Is that the reason you're going? Because of the money? If that's the reason, then you're being dumb." His heart knew a moment's reprieve.

"That's not the reason I'm going."

"Oh."

"I have to go. Greg wants to spend time with Todd. He's promised. And I have a visitation agreement with him that gives him the right to see Todd every other weekend. He says that if I stay here, I'll have to fly Todd to

Maryland. Even if I wanted to fight him on that, the law is on his side. But I don't want to fight him. I can't keep Todd from his father, if his father is finally willing to make the effort. How can I do that?"

Oh, man. Her words were like missiles aimed right at his most vulnerable places.

"You can't."

"When I ran away in March, I knew this might happen. I knew that if Greg wanted to see Todd on a regular basis, I would have to rethink. Of course, Greg has surprised me, but I still have to do the right thing for Todd."

"Good for you."

"I knew you'd understand. We both lost out on time with our fathers. I can't do that to Todd."

He nodded. "You need help packing?"

She shook her head. "Most of my stuff is in storage up in Baltimore. We'll be going on Saturday."

He nodded again and then turned on his heel and walked out of the room.

This is why AA told guys like him to stay out of relationships.

Damn. He needed a drink.

Savannah didn't know what, exactly, she had expected of Dash. A little, stupid part of her wanted him to bar the door and tell her that she'd be a fool to leave.

A little part of her wanted him to get down on his knees and beg her to stay.

A little part of her wanted him to make some grandiose proclamation of undying love.

Yeah, the spoiled little girl she'd once been wanted that.

The grown woman knew the folly of those fantasies. First of all, she wasn't sure she could admire a man who begged. And second of all, Dash wasn't the kind of guy who begged. And third, just because they'd been sneaking off for hot monkey sex didn't mean it was love.

Right. Her head could say this over and over and over again but her heart wasn't buying it. She loved him.

But he didn't love her. He'd made it clear that it was just dirty, meaningless sex. And he'd given her money because of Hettie.

And his reaction to this news had been so...Well, he'd told her the highway ran right through town, and she knew the way out.

He'd not done one single thing to stop her.

So it only made sense that she go back to Baltimore, especially since Greg had bestirred himself to come here and promise that he'd do a better job with Todd.

Of course, he'd skipped town before even seeing Todd. Which was annoying. And typical. And confusing. But he'd come, and that was a major breakthrough.

She sat at the kitchen table and drank another cup of coffee. She'd had so many she was almost jittery, so it wasn't any surprise that she practically jumped out of her skin when Champ roused himself from his nap at her feet and started barking.

A moment later, the door slammed, and Todd's heavy footsteps sounded down the hall. "Hi, Mom, are there any cookies?"

The dog skipped around the boy, wagging his tail and smiling. Todd gave him a couple of pats on the head. "Just a minute, boy. I need cookies, and then I'll take you for a walk."

Todd made a beeline to the cookie jar, which Savannah kept stocked with his favorite peanut-butter-and-raisin cookies.

He grabbed three and reached for Champ's leash.

"Todd, before you go."

He turned with a question in his face. Boy, his face had slimmed down these last couple of months. And so had the attitude. He wasn't perfect, but Last Chance had been good for him. Dash had been good for him.

But biology trumped all that. "Honey, I heard from your dad today."

He stopped moving. The dog kept prancing and wagging its tail. "You did?"

"Yes. He wants us to go back to Baltimore."

Todd blinked. "Back to our old apartment?"

"Well, no. We would go back to live at Grandmother's for a while until I found another place."

"Grandmother's?" He looked down at the dog.

"I know. You'd have to leave Champ here, but I'm sure Dash would take care of him all right. The thing is, your dad has promised to be better about visitation. Don't you want to spend every other weekend with your dad?"

She saw that look in her son's face. That heartbreaking look. And she knew how he felt. "Yeah," he said.

"So, I think it's probably better if we go back. I mean, Grandmother wants to send you to Gilman, so…"

"Yeah. Maybe I can try out for football."

"I'm sure your dad would be proud of you. He played football."

"Yeah, I know. Dash and I looked up his college stats. He was a pretty good linebacker for Maryland," Todd said.

"He was. I saw him play," Savannah said.

"He could probably teach me stuff."

She doubted that Greg would spend the time, but she said, "Yeah." She had to say that because maybe, just maybe, there was a chance. If she thought otherwise, she wouldn't be taking this step. "We'll need to start packing our stuff. We're leaving Saturday morning bright and early. I have a bunch of errands to do tomorrow. I guess I'll have to shut down the theater renovation."

He looked down at the dog. His mouth quivered. He was learning how to be a man. He didn't cry. He didn't whine. He sighed. And then he snapped the lead onto the dog's collar. "I gotta take Champ for his walk."

Dash left the Eldorado in the driveway. Getting drunk was one thing, but getting drunk and killing someone was a whole different kettle of fish. He'd mixed booze and motor vehicles one too many times.

He hurried down the drive and onto the sidewalk. He kept walking, head down, counting the seams in the concrete. Counting was a good thing. It kept his emotions from exploding. It kept his heart from falling into pieces.

He could count and remember to breathe. Two cracks...breathe in. Two cracks...breathe out.

He made it all the way to Palmetto Avenue. He turned right toward Dot's, and he stopped.

The Kismet stood between him and the bar. He looked up at the marquee. Half an hour ago, he'd known without a doubt that Uncle Earnest was proud of him.

But now what? What would happened to The Kismet when Savannah left town? He made his way through the new security gate and into the theater. Zeph was hard at work installing a section of new fluting in one of the damaged columns. The new wood lacked the patina of the old, but the carvings lined up perfectly.

The old black man touched the wood with a reverence that captivated Dash. The smell of charred wood had diminished over the last week. Now there were other smells. Sawdust, and varnish, and plaster.

Something important was rising up out of the dust and dirt and ashes. And on Saturday, all of this would stop. Savannah would go.

He closed his eyes.

"I heard the news about Miz Hettie," Zeph said.

Dash almost laughed. If he went off to Dot's, everyone in town would misunderstand.

"I brought some Nehi," Zeph nodded to a battered plastic cooler that looked like it had been with Zeph through the Vietnam War. The old guy finished turning the handle on a wood clamp and turned around. Sawdust and wood shavings clung to his baggy blue jeans. The collar and cuffs of his old plaid shirt were frayed. But his smile was big and wide as he opened the cooler and brought up two glass bottles of Nehi orange soda pop.

He handed one to Dash and twisted off the top of the other. "There's nothing like a cold Nehi to fix what ails you." He raised the bottle in salute.

Dash hadn't tasted Nehi soda in years. He opened the bottle, took a gulp, and lost himself in reverie. Damn, he used to drink Nehi all the time. Uncle Earnest had a cooler of it behind the candy counter.

"Earnest always drank Nehi. He used to say that sweeping up was thirsty work," Dash said.

"Yeah," Zeph replied. "I remember old Mr. Brooks. Of course, when I was a child, I had to sit upstairs."

"I'm sorry about that. It wasn't that way when I was here."

Zeph shrugged. "Wasn't your fault. Mr. Brooks was a fair man living in unfair times. People wouldn't have come at all in the sixties if he hadn't put the blacks upstairs."

"He *was* a fair man. I miss him." Dash's voice wobbled in an embarrassing way. When Earnest died, Dash had been playing baseball. Earnest wasn't a member of his immediate family so, naturally, Dash wasn't allowed time off. Instead he drank himself into a stupor and got himself into trouble.

"You know there's a trick to living alone," Zeph said, looking Dash right in the eye, as if he knew what scared Dash most of all.

Dash took another gulp of soda, pushing away the memories, focusing on Zeph. Until this moment, he'd never really considered the kind of life Zeph had been leading. Zeph was probably the loneliest person in Last Chance.

"So what's the trick?"

"Read."

"Read? That's a surprise. I could have sworn you were going to tell me to get a dog."

Zeph smiled. "Oh, no, Mr. Dash, you don't need a dog. You already kind of have one. And you've got several good cats and all those horses. Not to mention all the kids who come to your riding and roping school. And the kids on the baseball teams and the football team. No, a good book is a whole lot easier to take care of than a dog. And when you read, you can go anywhere."

"I never was much of a reader."

"I didn't start out that way either. But a man does what he has to."

Dash wanted to ask Zeph why he was so alone. Why he lived out in the woods. Why he moved around Last Chance like a shadow. But he couldn't ask those questions. Zeph would never have answered him. The old man had demons, and Dash knew all about those.

Dash turned away, casting his gaze over the work in progress. God help him, he didn't want to give up on this project. He wanted it to go on. But he didn't want it to go on without Savannah in his life. "You think watching movies would be as good as reading?" he asked.

"Maybe. But a good book lasts a lot longer than a movie. And you can get books for free from the consignment shop. Or, if you had a mind to, you could get a library card. And when you go to the library, you could visit with Miss Nita, and that's always nice."

"Good point."

Dash finished his soda and handed the bottle back to Zeph. "You're doing a great job, Zeph. I don't think anyone else could have rescued that woodwork."

"It's my pleasure, Mr. Dash. I love giving new life to old things."

Dash turned around and headed toward the door. When he reached the sidewalk, his desire for a drink had eased. It was almost as if Uncle Earnest's ghost was there behind him. The taste of orange soda in his mouth was a reminder that a sober life was a much better life.

And Zeph had just reminded him that he wasn't alone. Not really. He had the horses, and the kids, and Miriam. Not to mention the gals of Angel Development, Inc.

He stared up at The Kismet's marquee. Uncle Earnest would never have stood between a boy and his father. Never in a million years. Never for selfish reasons. Never.

He was going to be like Uncle Earnest.

Dash would ask Savannah's permission to finish this project. It made no sense from a money point of view. But that didn't matter. If he built it, people would come. And he'd have the kids in the theater to go along with the kids in the horse program and the kids in Little League and the kids in the football program.

Heck, it was damned hard to feel lonely in a place like Last Chance.

Dash ran into Todd and Champ on his way back to the house. The boy was crying.

"Hey," Dash said, his voice sounding dry and rusty in his own ears. "What's the matter?"

The kid rubbed his eyes and gave a shrug. "Did Mom tell you? We're going back to Baltimore."

"Yeah, I heard."

"My dad said he wanted to see me on weekends."

"That's a good thing."

Todd nodded, his mouth quivering. "Yeah. I'd like that. But we have to live with Grandmother for a while." He gave Champ a little pat. And then it was almost as if the kid collapsed. He plopped down on the sidewalk and buried his face in the dog's flank. And Champ smiled and licked his face with the adoration only a dog could give.

Dash's chest got so tight he could hardly breathe.

He'd hung on to a dog like that once. On the morning, decades ago, when they'd come to take him away from the ranch where he'd spent the first eleven years of his life.

His life had been hell on that ranch, but he didn't want to leave it. Not if it meant leaving that old dog; Murphy was his name.

He'd cried himself out that day. That good-bye had been the hardest one of all. He never did know what happened to that dog. The social service people probably sent Murphy to the pound.

"I'll take care of Champ for you," he said. "You don't need to worry about him." Dash hunkered down and squeezed Todd's shoulder. "I've been where you are now. I know exactly how it feels. Like someone is taking away your best friend in all the world. But having a chance to spend time with your dad is more important. You don't have to worry about Champ. He'll never want for anything. Ever."

"But I promised Zeph."

"What did you promise, son?"

"I promised I would always be there for him."

"I'll take that on for you."

"I don't want you to."

Oh, God, this kid was going to grow into a good man. Even if his no-account father didn't come through, Todd had his mother. And Savannah was like a momma lion when it came to her boy. She would do the right thing by this child.

"I'm glad you're taking that responsibility so seriously, son. I'm proud to know you," Dash said, his voice growing embarrassingly gruff.

Todd raised his head. "Are you crying?"

Dash forced a laugh then. "No, I don't do that sort of thing."

The kid studied him. "You *are* crying, aren't you?"

"Well, I'm trying not to. I'm going to miss you." And the words got stuck in Dash's throat. Until he uttered them, he didn't even know how true they were.

A big fat tear rolled down the kid's cheek. "Me too. I wish my dad was like you."

A fountainhead opened up in Dash's heart, and a spring of something clean and heady bubbled right through him. The spring became a creek, became a brook, became a river that grew and grew until its current washed away the self-pity he'd been feeling and smashed down the walls that had taken a lifetime to build.

And he didn't fight the current. He expected it to smash him and batter him, but it didn't do that. It carried him along to a peaceful place.

In that humbling moment, he had a name for the emotion that clogged up his throat and watered up in his eyes. He loved the kid. And the miracle wasn't that he could love, but that the kid loved him back. But having Todd love him carried all kinds of responsibility with it.

He vowed, in that moment, that as long as he drew breath Todd would never want for anything. He would take care of this child, and he'd do everything within his power never, ever to let him down. And right now, doing right by this child meant letting him go.

"C'mon. I know you want to spend time with your dad, don't you?"

Todd nodded. "But why can't I have both?" He looked up at Dash. "Why can't I be your friend?"

"You can. I'll always be here. You can call me anytime."

Todd wiped the snot from his nose with the back of his hand. "I don't think so. They say you're a bad man."

"Who says?"

Todd shrugged. "Some lady who came to the school and asked me a bunch of questions."

"What kind of questions?"

"Like whether I ever saw you drunk. Or whether you ever got into fights. Or whether you..." The kid looked away and pressed his lips together.

"Whether I what?" Dash's temper made a sudden and unmistakable reappearance. His hands closed into fists, and the adrenaline surged through his system.

"You know."

"No, I don't know."

"Touch me."

Dash had to work very hard not to speak the long string of profanity that ran through his brain.

The kid looked up at him. "I told them you were okay. I told them that just because you liked to play catch you weren't some weirdo. The woman who came and asked the questions didn't believe me. She kept asking the same questions over and over again. I finally told her she was a bitch and that got me into all kinds of trouble with Mr. Middleton. But to tell you the truth, that woman *was* a bitch."

Dash stood up. "It was probably a mistake to use that word."

"Yeah, whatever. I've heard my father use it plenty of times."

Dash squeezed his eyes closed. The fury he felt was like a white-hot poker to his insides. But he held himself together. "I'm grateful you told the truth." It was amazing how calm he sounded.

The kid turned away. "Yeah, it didn't get me very far,

though. I mean, now I have to go to the Gilman School and live with Grandmother, and I can't take the dog, and I can't go to football camp." He sighed. "And Zeph was going to take me fishing."

"Zeph?"

He shrugged. "Yeah, I see him around town. He knows all the good fishing spots. There's no place to fish in Baltimore."

"Son, there are always places to fish. You need to get your daddy to take you."

The kid looked up at him. "Right, like that's going to happen. Dad is more likely to take me to some pool hall and make me sit in the car. But hey, he buys me video games."

The boy wiped the tears from his cheeks. "I'm going to walk the dog down to the theater. We're leaving on Saturday. So I need to say good-bye to Zeph."

Todd turned and headed in the direction Dash had just come from.

Dash headed back to the house.

He was furious.

CHAPTER 21

Savannah stood in the kitchen working on supper and trying to think of a good way to tell Miriam that she and Todd were leaving on Saturday.

She was wrist deep in biscuit dough when Dash came slamming into the house. His boots struck the hardwood floor like hammer blows as he stalked right into the kitchen.

"Why the hell didn't you tell me?"

"Tell you what?"

"About Todd being interrogated at school by the Department of Social Services."

Oh, good Lord. Todd must have spilled the beans. She closed her eyes and prayed for strength. "Because I knew it would hurt you. I didn't want you to be hurt."

"Don't you think I'm hurting right now? Don't you think this crazy decision of yours hurts me?"

He was breathing hard. His hands were folded into fists. His eyes were brighter than bright, which was saying something because no one had blue eyes like Dash's.

"Dash?" Miriam's frail voice came from the hallway. "Are y'all fighting again?"

"Yes."

"No."

They glared at one another as Miriam came shuffling into the kitchen leaning heavily on her cane and looking a little wild-eyed without her glasses. Her crown braids were a mess today. Guilt assailed Savannah.

She'd been so consumed by her own problems that she'd neglected Miriam. Lately the old lady needed help getting her hair done in the morning. Who would take care of Aunt Miriam when she left?

Dash would do his best, but he had no idea how to braid her hair. He couldn't cook for her either.

"What is it now?" Aunt Miriam asked.

"It's nothing," Savannah said, glaring at Dash.

"Oh, you think it's nothing? I want to know why some person at Todd's school is asking nasty questions about me."

"What kind of questions?" Miriam said.

Savannah let go of a deep sigh. "Look, this is just Claire White using every means possible to get me to see things her way."

"So that's why you're leaving?"

"You're leaving?" Miriam asked in a quavery voice.

Savannah wanted to punch Dash in the mouth. "Thanks, Dash. This is exactly the way I wanted to tell Miriam about my change of plans."

"You're leaving?" Miriam said again. "Oh, dear, I didn't count on that." The old lady immediately started messing with her hair. It sure did look as if she was taking it down so she could rebraid it, right there in the kitchen.

"Yes, Aunt Mim, she's leaving. She's running away from a fight."

"No, I'm not doing any such thing. And for the record, Dash, the last thing I want is for Claire White to smear your reputation in this town the way I did when I was ten. And furthermore, if I fight this thing, social services could swoop in and put Todd in a foster home. Is that what you want?"

He seemed to back down a little. "You don't have to go."

"Yes, I do. I told you before. Greg was here today, and he made it clear that if I don't go back, then I'm going to have to fly Todd up to Baltimore every other weekend."

"It could be done. Or you could work something out with him so Todd spends his summers up in Baltimore. You don't have to go."

"If I did that, Claire would smear your name from one end of this county to the other. And where would you be? No one would trust you. Your business would be gone. Little League and Pop Warner would shun you. Dash, I have to go. I won't do that to you. I care about you. Don't you realize that?"

He stood there breathing hard. She wanted to run to him. She wanted to tell him how much she wanted to stay. But she couldn't be that selfish.

"Will you let me finish the theater?" he asked.

She opened her mouth to ask him why, but then she thought better of it. Maybe he needed the theater, too.

"I'll give you the theater," she said.

"You'll give it to me?"

She shrugged. "I'll be living in Baltimore. I can't exactly take it with me, and I haven't been a great owner these last ten years. I let it fall down before I found the courage to do something about it. And even then, I couldn't have started the project without your help. So I'll talk to Eugene Hanks and see about having the deed transferred. It's the least I can do, given all the money you've poured into it."

"The money's not important."

"Yes, Dash, it is. It's important to me."

He took a deep breath. Then he turned and walked out of the house. It was an ominous sign when he didn't slam the door.

The theater was his. Dash had signed the papers on Friday afternoon in Eugene Hanks's office. And then he'd come here and collapsed onto this hard folding chair in the lobby. Champ's muzzle rested on his boot top. The puppy was asleep for the moment.

The workers had gone an hour ago. The theater was mostly dark, except for the utility lights strung up on the ceiling. The old, ornate carpets had been pulled up, leaving a bare concrete floor. The woodwork was beginning to come alive under Zeph's care.

Maverick sprawled on the top of the candy counter, purring like a fiend. The cat was not all that friendly to Dash or Champ, or anyone for that matter, except Savannah.

The cat had a serious thing for Savannah. Whenever she came into the theater, he would wrap himself around her legs and meow until she picked him up. Dash had never seen a half-wild mouser behave so shamelessly. The cat even let Savannah carry him around like a babe-in-arms.

"You and me, Mav," he said to the cat. "Just a couple of old toms in love with the wrong woman. And that, cat, is the story of my life."

He picked up his Nehi orange and took a long swig. "I wonder what Uncle Earnest would do in a situation like this?"

"*Meow.*"

"Thanks. That was very helpful advice. I reckon Uncle Earnest never would have gotten himself into a situation like this."

Dash let go of a long breath. "She'll be gone tomorrow, and all I have is the theater and a dog and a cat. I guess it could be worse. Although I'm having a hard time figuring out how."

He wanted to fight for her, but it was a lost cause. He couldn't keep Todd from his father. And he sure couldn't risk the fight that might ensue if Savannah stayed. He'd checked with Eugene earlier, and what the lawyer had told him made his blood run cold. A fight over Todd could be expensive. And since Dash already had a reputation, the fight would get ugly.

Dash didn't want Todd to have to endure something like that. He'd promised himself that he would do the best thing possible for Todd, and that was pretty clear.

It meant giving up Savannah. It meant letting her go. It meant letting the boy go. And it hurt. Bad.

He closed his eyes and thought about the twelve steps that he'd been working on as part of his recovery. The first step was to admit that he was powerless, and the second was to admit that only a power greater than himself could restore him to sanity. And the third step was to decide to give his life over to God as he understood Him.

He'd known from the start that Savannah was like an addiction. And even if it hadn't felt like a destructive addiction, he still wanted her with his body and his soul. He didn't think he could live without her. A part of him just wanted to find a bottle of bourbon in order to numb the pain.

But he also wanted to be the kind of man she saw in her dreams. He wanted to be her hero. He wanted to be a man like Uncle Earnest, who had been married to the same woman for fifty years. He didn't want to let her go. He didn't want to let her down. He wanted to be Todd's father. And this situation was tearing him apart.

"Please, God, please help me."

And he lost it. The tears flowed in a way that had never happened before. Not since he was old enough to know that crying only made Gramps beat him harder. He wept. All alone in Uncle Earnest's theater.

Champ woke up and put his front paws up on his knee. Dash sank down onto the bare concrete and hugged that dog the way he'd hugged Murphy all those years ago.

When he'd cried himself out, he just sat there holding the dog. Letting the pup lick his face. He'd have to take up reading. Maybe he could learn to be alone like Zeph. Maybe. But it was going to take everything he had to do it.

And then his cell phone vibrated. He didn't answer it. Five minutes later, it vibrated again, and this time he pulled it out of his pocket as he wiped the tears from his cheeks.

It wasn't a number he recognized.

He checked his missed calls. There were more than a dozen from this same number.

He pressed the talk button. "Dash Randall." His voice

sounded gruff. His throat was still thick with emotions he was working overtime to keep contained.

"Finally," a male voice said.

"Who's speaking?"

"This is Andrew Prior of Prior, Jacobson, and Howard."

The investigation company Dash had hired weeks ago. He'd almost forgotten.

"Oh, I'm sorry I didn't pick up before." He pressed the heel of his right hand into his right eye.

"Mr. Randall, we've just discovered something that you need to know."

"What's that?"

"It's about Gregory White, the man you asked us to investigate."

"Yes."

"Well, he's a deadbeat, but that's hardly very interesting. He's behind on all his bills, and he spends a lot of time at Pimlico. He's also at least a year in arrears on his child support payments, which makes him a scumbag. But that's not the most important thing."

Dash straightened, the knot in his throat easing. "What else?"

"We didn't figure it out until today. Back on April thirteenth, he had lunch with someone at McCormick and Schmick's in Baltimore. We didn't know who the guy was. We have photos, though."

"Yeah. Tell me it was a Mafia don."

"Sorry. It wasn't anything that dramatic. But we finally figured out that the guy in the photo is John Rodgers, the principal of JBR Construction of Allenberg County. White's been in South Carolina for the last few days, and he stopped by the offices of JBR. And then we realized that JBR was the contractor on the job when the fire was started. We haven't been able to find any link between White and the snake incident, but since that happened before we were retained, I'm not that surprised."

"April thirteenth, you said?"

"Yes, that's a week before the arson at the theater. And near as we can tell, John Rodgers doesn't have any reason to be in Baltimore. He's never traveled there before or since."

"You have a photo?"

"I do. Would you like me to e-mail it?"

"Yeah, right away."

They ended the conversation.

He stood up and started pacing the lobby. It seemed to take forever for that photo to arrive. The minute it hit his inbox, he forwarded it to Stone Rhodes, the Allenberg sheriff.

Stone called him before Dash could finish dialing the number. "Did you get the photo I just sent?" Dash asked.

"No, I didn't. I was calling to let you know that we've got a lead in the snake mystery. We think those snakes were purchased at Jungle Jim's Reptile World on Long Island. It turns out there aren't a whole lot of places where someone could buy a diamondback rattlesnake, so we were able to track down most of the dealers and review the purchases made in the weeks prior to the incident. It's very unusual for someone to buy two diamondbacks, but we found someone who did. He used a credit card, and he has a rap sheet a mile long."

"Who bought them?"

"His name is Nathan Martel, but he prefers to be called 'New York Nate.' He's a pool hustler. We haven't figured out a connection between this guy and Savannah, though."

"I think I can help you. Savannah's ex-husband regularly participates in pool tournaments. So Greg would probably know a few hustlers. And what's more, I just sent you a photo of John Rodgers having lunch with Savannah's ex. It was taken in Baltimore about a week before the fire. I'll bet you Greg White paid Rodgers to set that fire, and he probably got this New York Nate person to arrange for the snakes."

"So you think this is just some kind of domestic dispute between Savannah and her ex?" Stone asked.

"I don't know, to tell you the truth. I have a theory, though. I think Greg White is a gambler. I've heard Todd talk about how he plays pool a lot. And according to my private investigator, Greg is behind on all his bills as well as his child support, even though he's a partner in a fancy law firm."

"So Savannah was playing hardball with him and he got mad at her?" Stone asked.

"No, that's not what I'm thinking. I'll bet Greg's well-heeled mother has been bailing him out on his gambling debts. But this time, she told him he needed to get Savannah to bring Todd back to Baltimore as a condition for any further financial help. Claire White would use any means to get her mitts on Todd. She's even got the South Carolina Department of Social Services on my case."

"What?"

It took a lot for Dash to say the next words, but he forced them out. "They want to call me a pedophile."

"That's ridiculous."

"Thanks for the vote of confidence."

"Dash, everyone in town knows you're not some kind of predator. Jeez, these people are evil. I'm glad Savannah and Todd escaped."

Dash's shoulders relaxed a fraction, and he realized that he was going to be okay. The local law was on his side, and probably always had been.

"I'm looking at the picture you sent right now," Stone said. "I guess I need to go down to JBR tomorrow and have a little chat with John Rodgers. And I think I need to call the Baltimore police, too. Thanks, Dash, and... I'm sorry about what happened. You know I have to chase down every lead."

"It's okay, Stone. I know. And everyone in town is happy that we finally have a sheriff who knows what he's doing."

Dash disconnected and headed for the janitor's closet, where he washed his face.

He looked down at Champ, who stood at his feet with a smiling face and a happy tail.

He laughed. "I guess I *do* know what Uncle Earnest would have done," he said to the dog.

How many times had Uncle Earnest told him to believe in the goodness of people? How many times had he also said that when the road seemed impassable you just had to trust in God and pray?

"Thank you," he whispered as he turned off the lights and locked the door. And in that moment it almost seemed like Uncle Earnest was right there with him. Like a guardian angel or something.

Savannah folded her last sweater and zipped up the suitcase. Tomorrow at this time, she would be unpacking in Claire's big house in the Roland Park section of Baltimore.

It depressed her to think about it. Claire had a cook who didn't like Savannah messing around in her kitchen. And even after Savannah found an apartment, there wouldn't be a crowd to cook for.

There wouldn't be frog jumps, Easter dances, or Watermelon Festivals. She wouldn't have friends at the book club or The Knit & Stitch. She wouldn't be able to go to the theater every day and see it rising from the ruins. She wouldn't wake up and feel like she was doing something important.

And there wouldn't be any moments at the bathroom door. Or in the kitchen when she poured Dash a cup of coffee and handed him a thermos and a sandwich. There wouldn't be any stolen moments at the river house.

But she had to give these things up. The alternative was unthinkable.

She put the suitcase by the door and turned off the light. It was early yet. But she didn't want to sit on the porch and visit with Miriam. Her guilt ran so deep when it came to Miriam that she didn't even know how to plumb its depths.

This situation was breaking her heart into a million pieces. She threw herself on her bed, but she didn't cry. She'd cried herself out last night. She didn't have any more tears. She had only the determination to do the best thing she could for her son. And for Dash.

She lay there listening to the quiet in the house until Dash came home. His big car's tires crunched on the gravel driveway. His boots sounded on the porch and the landing. At the top of the stairs, he turned left instead of right. Damn him. Didn't he know that she didn't want to see him?

He knocked on her door.

"Go away."

"No." He opened the door. She should have locked it. The light in the hallway silhouetted him. He was wearing jeans and a western shirt. She couldn't see his face, but his presence made her heart sing.

"What do you want?"

"Savannah." He took a step into the room. "Honey, I've been doing a lot of thinking. And you know, there are some people on this earth who are so toxic that you have to accept that they have no part in your life. My father and grandfather were people like that. It's taken me a lifetime and I don't know how many AA meetings, not to mention a bucket of tears, to come to the conclusion that I was better off without my father and my grandfather."

She sat up in the bed and squinted against the sudden light. "Please. This situation is more complicated. And besides, Todd deserves time with his—"

"Hush, let me finish."

She shut her mouth. She listened. What else could she do?

"I know you want Todd to have a relationship with his father. And I know why. I even understand it. But you can't send him back there."

"Dash, I have to. I—"

"But he's a gambler and a jerk. He doesn't have any intention of spending quality time with Todd. You need to rethink."

"Well, thank you for that. I think I'm capable of figuring out what is the right thing to do." Of course she wasn't really, but she wasn't about to let Dash tell her what to do.

"Honey, listen, your ex is—"

"What in *the world* is going on up here?" Miriam's voice came down the hall. She walked into the bedroom and turned on the light. "Are y'all arguing again?"

Her hair looked perfectly braided, and her gaze was sharp and lucid behind her trifocals.

"Aunt Mim, I'm trying to have a serious conversation with your niece."

"Well, son, you're doing a terrible job at telling her what she needs to know. And all she needs to know right now is that you can't live without her."

The exasperation in Miriam's voice was clear as she turned her gaze on Savannah. "And as for you. Well, honey, I'm getting really old, and I'm tired of playing the poor, senile, old lady in order to guilt you into staying here. And I'm tired of you dancing around Dash making him crazy. And then there is the fact that I'm ready to retire as Last Chance's matchmaker. You have to stay so I can turn it all over to you."

Dash and Savannah stared at Miriam. She stared back at them. She raised one of her white eyebrows in an attempt to give them both her evil eye. "What?"

"You're ready to turn over matchmaking to Savannah?" Dash asked.

"Of course. She's got the sight."

"I do?" Savannah said.

"Of course you do. You knew Hettie and Bill were a match before anyone else did. I don't blame you for not figuring out Dash, though. He's always been a little hard to figure. Inside that tough hide of his beats a golden heart. You have figured this out by now, haven't you?"

Miriam turned toward Dash. "And you've figured out that not only can she cook, but she's got a kind heart. Not at all what you thought when you were young, but see what she's ready to do now, just to spare your reputation?"

The tears Savannah thought she'd cried out suddenly sprang to her eyes. She stood up and walked toward Dash. "There's no way I can stay."

"But there is." Dash took her hand and pressed it against his chest, right above his beating heart. "You can't go. Because I have a home for you right here. In my heart. I don't care what anyone says about me. I want to be with you. And I swear I will be there for you, Savannah, no matter what happens. You can come to me with all your problems. I'll be the guy cheering you on. I'll be here to pick you up when you fall. Savannah, I love you. I love Todd. I would endure anything in the world if I could have you in my life. If you leave me, it will break my heart." He pressed his hand on hers. "I've been left so many times in my life..." His voice faltered.

She didn't let him falter for long. She rushed into his arms.

"I don't want to go." She sagged against him. His arms came around her. "I only decided to go because I didn't want to hurt you, and I thought—"

"Hush, now. No one is going to hurt me. And no one is ever going to hurt Todd, as long as I live."

"I don't want to live in Baltimore. I love you."

His mouth came down over hers in a kiss that made her toes curl. She almost lost herself in that kiss before her common sense returned. She pushed away.

"We can't do this."

"Of course we can. We're not really cousins."

"No, I mean, Claire is going to ruin you if I stay, and I—"

He put his fingers over her mouth. "Honey, that's not going to happen. First of all, I realized tonight that everyone in Last Chance with the possible exception of Lillian Bray is going to give me the benefit of the doubt. People in the rest of the world might not, but I don't really care about the rest of the world. And second, it's not going to happen."

She pulled his fingers away from her mouth. "But it is."

"Nope. Not after Stone Rhodes is finished with your ex."

"What?"

"Well, I think Greg is going to go to jail for arson."

"No."

"I'm afraid so. John Rodgers met with Greg in Baltimore a few days before the fire. And Stone's got a lead on the snakes, too, that points in the direction of a pool hustler named New York Nate, of all things. So I think I'm off the hook.

"But all this is still going to hurt Todd. It's never easy to be the son of someone who is an addict. And I'm thinking Greg is addicted to gambling. So you and I are going to have to be there for Todd. I'm going to do my best to help your son get over this disaster in his life. Just like Uncle Earnest was there for me. That's my solemn promise, whether you marry me or not."

"Marry you?"

"Finally," Miriam said on an exasperated breath.

"Will you?" he asked.

She blinked up into his craggy face. "I want to."

"Then say yes."

"Yes."

Dash's mouth came back down on hers in the sweetest,

most tender kiss ever. She wrapped her arms around him. She wasn't ever going to let him go.

"What's happening?" Todd came wandering into the bedroom with Champ dancing around his feet.

"Your mother and Cousin Dash are having a moment," Miriam said.

"A moment?" Todd said. "It looks like they're playing tonsil hockey."

Miriam sniffed. "Boy, where did you hear that term?"

"From Oliver. He wants to play tonsil hockey with Sherrie Ann."

"Oh, my, she's all wrong for him," Miriam said. "You tell Oliver not to kiss that girl."

"Yes, Aunt Mim, I will."

The old woman and the boy stood there for a moment observing the kiss that went on and on. "I told you your mother and Dash loved each other, didn't I?" Miriam finally said.

"Yeah, you did. I'm sorry I didn't believe you. But hey, this is tight."

"Yes, very tight, indeed."

Todd gave Champ's big head a little pat. "C'mon, boy, Aunt Miriam was right after all. Looks like Mom and me are staying. C'mon and help me unpack."

READING GROUP GUIDE

Discussion Questions for
Last Chance Book Club

1. The romance in *Last Chance Book Club* is similar in some ways to the romance portrayed in *Pride and Prejudice*. Discuss some of the ways that Dash and Savannah are similar to Darcy and Elizabeth. In the contemporary story, who is the Darcy character? Who better embodies Elizabeth?

2. Matchmaking occupies a central part of both *Pride and Prejudice* and *Last Chance Book Club*. Compare and contrast the matchmaking efforts of Mrs. Bennet and Miz Miriam Randall. Which matchmaker would you prefer to consult if you were looking for marital advice? Why?

3. Savannah ends up tackling a pretty big undertaking even though the theater project overwhelms and frightens her. What strategies did she use to face her

fear and lack of confidence? Was the community a help or a hindrance? Have you ever undertaken a big project where people were depending on you? Did it make you confident or scare you to death?

4. Discuss the ways Dash Randall becomes the man he has always wanted to be. Do you think Dash's transformation would have been possible without Todd?

5. Scattered throughout the novel are several scenes that mirror *Pride and Prejudice*. Can you find them? Email your answers to hope@hoperamsay.com to be entered to win prizes and swag.

6. The loss of reputation is an important theme in *Last Chance Book Club* and *Pride and Prejudice*. Discuss how the threat of a lost reputation provides a barrier between the lovers in both books.

7. How is Reverend Ellis similar to Mr. Collins in *Pride and Prejudice*? How is he different? Is Hettie like Charlotte Lucas?

8. Discuss how Dash works through his various addictions and implements parts of the twelve-step program. In particular, how does Dash make amends for his past actions? How does he make a "searching and fearless inventory" of himself? How does Dash admit his shortcomings to Savannah and others? How does he turn his life over to a higher power's care?

9. Uncle Earnest was an important parental figure for both Dash and Savannah. Other than your parents, who was a major positive influence while you were growing up? Uncle Earnest instills many good values. What values do you think are most important for children? Do children need a religious education to learn these values?

10. Miz Miriam knows when a man and woman are right for each other, even when the couple can't see it for themselves. Do you think outside advice can be helpful when choosing a mate? Were you surprised when the townspeople wanted Savannah to get together with Reverend Ellis? Were you surprised when Dash ended up with Savannah, rather than Hettie? Or when Hettie ended up with Bill? Were you surprised when Elizabeth ended up with Darcy?

Molly Canaday is a tomboy with a passion for cars—and little time for romance.

But Simon Wolfe is about to race in and change her priorities.

Please turn this page for a preview of

Last Chance Knit & Stitch.

Simon Wolfe drove his rental car south on Route 321 toward the small town of Last Chance, South Carolina. He gripped the wheel and tried to quell the emotions tumbling through him.

He didn't want to be on this road. Eighteen years ago, after a particularly hostile Thanksgiving spent with his parents, Simon had vowed never to come home again.

But Aunt Millie had called yesterday, and when she said, "Your daddy's dead," something had snapped inside his chest.

Those three little words had sent him tumbling back in time, to his early years running interference between his mother and father. He loved them, but he couldn't stand to be with them both together for more than five minutes at a time.

He called on holidays. Daddy had come for a visit ten years ago. But Simon had not seen his mother for almost two decades. She had not forgiven him for abandoning her.

And so he had come home for the funeral. Mother

would expect it. Mother would expect other things, too. He halfway dreaded them.

He let go of the breath he'd been unconsciously holding, his filial obligations pinching acutely. He could not let his father's death suck him back into his mother's world. He had to return to his little house in Paradise, California, and his studio tucked among the redwoods.

He had a big commission he had to finish.

He topped a rise in the road, and the rented Hyundai hesitated. Then the radio and the AC kicked out. He floored the gas, but the car stalled completely.

He coasted to the side of the road.

Damn. He was going to be late to his father's wake.

Molly Canaday pulled the tow truck in front of the silver Hyundai Sonata. She killed the engine and used her side-view mirror to assess the stranded motorist.

He was not from around these parts.

For one thing, he was driving a rental car.

And for another, he was standing in the bright May sunshine wearing a black crew-necked shirt, dark dress pants, and a tweed sport jacket. The sun lit up threads of gray in his dark chin-length hair. He hadn't shaved today, but somehow the stubble looked carefully groomed.

This guy was seriously lost.

She straightened her ball cap and hopped from the truck's cab. "Howdy," she said, putting out her hand for him to shake. "I'm Molly Canaday from Bill's Grease Pit. We're located in Last Chance, just down the road a ways. The rental agency sent your distress call to us. What seems to be the problem?"

Mr. I'm-so-cool-and-sexy did not shake Molly's hand.

Instead, his gaze took in her battered Atlanta Braves hat, favorite Big and Rich T-shirt, and baggy but comfy painter's pants. And the jerk smiled, sort of. His mouth curled at the corners like a couple of ornate apostrophes. The smile was elegant and sexy. Molly might have been impressed if the expression on the guy's face hadn't also been just a tiny bit smirk-like.

She was tempted to tell him that he had a lot of nerve smirking when he was standing in the May sunshine and wearing dark clothes. But she held her tongue. LeRoy, her boss at Bill's Grease Pit, was always telling her that she needed to close her mouth and keep her opinions to herself.

She forced a customer-service smile to her face, even as she dropped her hand. Obviously the guy was above shaking hands with a mechanic like her.

He finally spoke in an accent that sounded like it came from nowhere. "Canaday, huh? Does Red Canaday still coach the Rebels' football team?"

Whoa, this guy didn't look like your average football fan. Much less like anyone who would know anything about Davis High's football program. "Uh, yeah, he's my daddy." She studied his face, trying to place him. He had nice brown eyes and a masculine nose, and he didn't look a lick like anyone Molly knew.

Mr. Cool continued to give her a deeply unsettling stare from underneath a pair of masculine eyebrows. His eyes weren't as cool as the rest of him. There was kindness there, even though he hadn't shaken her hand. She got the feeling, maybe, that he was just a little shy. "Nothing ever changes here, does it?" he asked.

"Uh, do I know you?" There was no way this guy had ever set foot in Last Chance before.

He shrugged. "You might remember me. I mean, I knew your father. But that was a long time ago, and you were little."

"Are you saying you're from around here?" No way.

"I'm Simon Wolfe. Carrie Jean and Ira's boy. I was the kicker on the team."

Oh. Wow. Talk about prodigal sons. She didn't really remember Simon exactly. She'd been like ten when he left Last Chance, but she'd also sort of been the Rebel's good luck charm back in 1990, when Stone Rhodes had taken the Rebels to the state championship.

But even if he had been a member of *her* team, she still didn't like him much. Anyone who would run away from his folks and never come back was a no-account useless person as far as Molly was concerned. Family was everything, and this idiot had thrown his family away.

And now his daddy was dead. Two days ago, Ira Wolfe had keeled over right in the middle of his Ford dealership's showroom. He wasn't a very old man either.

"I'm sorry for your loss," Molly said. Although Simon didn't look all that brokenhearted. In fact, the idiot shrugged as if he really didn't give a darn.

Then he changed the subject. "So Red Canaday's little girl grew up to become a mechanic. I guess that was totally predictable."

She clamped her back teeth together. If she kept her mouth shut, she wouldn't tell him where he could take his rental car and shove it. Instead she took a deep breath just like she'd learned in her yoga class. It only helped a little. "What seems to be the problem?" she asked in her sweetest voice, which admittedly was not very sweet. She tried to be sweet, but she was a miserable failure at it.

"I have no clue what's wrong with it. It stopped running," he said.

Boy, he might have been born in the South and even played football, once. But let's face it, he'd been the kicker on the team, and not a very good kicker either. Over the years, he'd clearly lost his southern accent and attitude somewhere. Any local man worth his salt would have already popped the hood and taken a look. Local men would also have dozens of theories about what had gone wrong.

Not this guy. This guy spoke in short sentences, dressed like a GQ model, and didn't want to get dirty.

"Did it make any funny noises before it died?"

"Nope. The AC and the radio went out right before the engine quit." He looked at his watch.

"I'm sorry, you have a wake to get to, don't you?" She didn't mention that she, also, had to get to Ira Wolfe's wake. She owed that man a great deal.

Simon shrugged again and turned his back. He put his hands on his hips and frowned at the cotton fields that spread on either side of Route 321. "God, this place is like being nowhere at all," he muttered.

"Yeah, well, some of us like living here," she snarled as she popped the hood and started poking around. "So, are you planning on staying a while?" she asked a moment later as she aimed her flashlight down into the engine to check the fan belt.

"No, I have to get back to Paradise."

"Paradise? Really?" The fan belt looked okay.

"It's a place in California."

"Ah, yeah, of course." He would live in a place called Paradise. She had a feeling he was about to discover that there could be hard times in Paradise, but far be it from her to be the bearer of bad news.

Instead, she inspected the battery terminals and connections, but didn't see anything obvious. There was probably a problem with the generator, or maybe the voltage regulator.

She pulled her head out of the engine compartment. "I'm going to have to tow it."

He checked his damn watch again. Boy this guy was wound up tighter than a spring. "Don't worry, I'll get you to the church on time. Or the funeral home, as the case might be. You know, being late to a funeral is not the worst thing in the world."

Simon stifled his laugh. It didn't seem right to find Molly amusing on the day of his father's wake.

She helped him transfer his luggage from the Hyundai's trunk to the back of her truck. Then he stood back and watched while Coach Canaday's only daughter hooked the Sonata up to a heavy chain and then winched it up onto the truck's flat bed. The woman sure had a way with machinery.

Which didn't surprise him, actually.

The last time Simon had seen Molly Canaday, she'd been a little kid in overalls, standing on the sidelines with Coach. She never missed a game. She could talk intelligently about football even as a five-year-old.

Simon never attempted a field goal without first patting Molly's head. Her hair had been short and curly, and he could almost remember how soft it felt under his hands. Her hair was longer now, but it was still almost inky black, and barely contained by the ball cap on her head. He had the sudden desire to paint a portrait of her, with all that glorious hair undone and falling like a curly black waterfall to her shoulders.

"It's going to be tomorrow before we can figure out what's going on with the car. So I'll drop you by the funeral home. I'm sure Rob or Ryan Polk or one of their kids can give you a lift home from there." Molly's words pulled him back from his artistic flight of fancy.

He climbed into the passenger seat and checked his watch.

"So, I guess you're just counting the hours until you can leave again? Paradise is calling, huh?"

He kept his gaze fastened to the cotton fields that whizzed past as she pulled the truck onto the road and headed into town. He saw no point in responding to her question. She had summed up the truth. He needed to get back home and back to work, especially since the work had not been going very well lately.

The fields eventually gave way to houses with big yards. Then the Last Chance water tower, painted to resemble a tiger-striped watermelon, came into view on the horizon.

It was a familiar view, frozen in his memory. And yet, nothing was quite the same as he remembered it. A large commercial building with a big parking lot occupied what had once been cotton fields just north of town. A big sign at the gates of the facility said deBracy Ltd. Not too far away, another parcel of land was being developed into new single-family homes.

Last Chance didn't look gray and used up, as he'd remembered it. There were bright awnings over some of the shops. Pedestrians hurried about their business on the sidewalks. The Kismet, the old movie theater, was covered in a scaffold where workers were repainting it. The place looked alive.

He wasn't prepared for the emotion that gripped him. It wasn't nostalgia. He'd buried a piece of himself here when he'd run away from home and the promise he'd made to his mother. He'd never planned on coming back and unearthing it. But here it was, stuck in his throat.

For all the pain he'd suffered here, Last Chance would always be home.

THE DISH

Where authors give you the inside scoop!

♥ ♥ ♥ ♥ ♥ ♥ ♥ ♥ ♥ ♥ ♥ ♥ ♥ ♥

From the desk of Hope Ramsay

Dear Reader,

I have three brothers and no sisters. So when I was young, I read a lot of "boy" books—mostly having to do with space travel. When I reached the ripe age of thirteen, my aunt decided I needed to have my horizons broadened. She put three "girly" books in my hand: *Pride and Prejudice*, *Jane Eyre*, and *Little Women*. Need I say more?

I was hooked the moment I read the immortal line: "It is a truth universally acknowledged, that a single man in possession of a good fortune must be in want of a wife."

Holy moly, I had no idea what I was missing!

So it's not surprising that I turned to these favorite books when I decided to write a series featuring members of the Last Chance Book Club.

In the first book in this series, LAST CHANCE BOOK CLUB, the ladies of the club decide to read *Pride and Prejudice*. And before long some of them are finding some interesting similarities between the book and their lives.

In the beginning of my story, the hero and heroine dislike each other intensely. Like Darcy, Savannah White has come to Last Chance from the big city. She's there to renovate the old run-down theater. Dash Randall, like Lizzy Bennett, isn't at all pleased with this new arrival in town. Dash thinks Savannah is a stuck-up snob. And she thinks he's a no-account good ol' boy. My hero is the one with the snarky sense of humor, and my heroine the one with the preconceived notions that will have to soften. Even though my plot and setting are wildly different from Austen's, the underlying theme of pride and prejudice is what makes the love story of Dash and Savannah so much fun. I've also included a few other Austen-inspired complications, like a minister who is looking for a wife, a whole passel of matchmaking matrons, and a street dance that's surprisingly like the Netherfield Ball.

I had such a fun time writing this story. It allowed me to connect in a much deeper way with one of my old favorites. I'm sure Jane Austen fans will enjoy searching for the Easter eggs I've sprinkled through the book. But even if you aren't an Austen fan, you're still going to love this story about a couple who discover the hidden depths of character in each other as they grow from enemies to friends to lovers.

Hope Ramsay

♥   ♥

From the desk of Debra Webb

Dear Reader,

I am so thrilled to be sharing the Faces of Evil adventure with you! This series has lived for several years in my heart. I can't tell you how pleased I am to be working with the fabulous folks at Forever to bring these stories to you.

I grew up in Alabama with deep roots in Birmingham. While my husband served in the army, we traveled far and wide, but Alabama was still home and we were most happy to return. Many years would pass before I realized that Alabama was not only home for me but also a place with a rich past and a vibrant present perfect for the setting of suspense stories. I zeroed in on Birmingham, where much of Alabama's most volatile and notorious history has taken place. Being no stranger to the city, it was easy to settle in and have my characters experiencing all sorts of dilemmas in the Magic City.

Birmingham also holds a special place in my heart for its renowned Children's Hospital and incredible doctors. When my first child was born she was in serious trouble and in need of immediate surgery—a surgery that was her only hope for survival and at the same time a procedure she was unlikely to survive. The quick thinking of my small-town doctor, Dr. Louis Letson, got her straightaway to Birmingham in the hands of a revered pediatric surgeon. Dr. Letson's decisive action and the unparalleled skill of the folks at Birmingham's Children's Hospital saved my daughter's life. Eight weeks later the tiny girl who changed our lives proved to one and all that she had come into this world to live. And thirty-six years later she is still living life with immense passion. As you can see, Birmingham really is the Magic City!

Please watch for all twelve installments of the Faces of Evil series featuring Jess Harris and Dan Burnett and their journey through a maze of evils to find the love and happiness they both deserve.

Best,

Debra Webb

Find out more about Forever Romance!

Visit us at
www.hachettebookgroup.com/publishing_forever.aspx

Find us on Facebook
http://www.facebook.com/ForeverRomance

Follow us on Twitter
http://twitter.com/ForeverRomance

NEW AND UPCOMING TITLES

Each month we feature our new titles
and reader favorites.

CONTESTS AND GIVEAWAYS

We give away galleys, autographed copies,
and all kinds of exclusive items.

AUTHOR INFO

You'll find bios, articles, and links to personal websites
for all your favorite authors—and so much more.

GET SOCIAL

Connect with your favorite authors, editors, and
other Forever fans, and share what's important to you.

THE BUZZ

Sign up for our monthly romance newsletter,
and be the first to read all about it.

VISIT US ONLINE AT

WWW.HACHETTEBOOKGROUP.COM

FEATURES:

**OPENBOOK BROWSE AND
SEARCH EXCERPTS**

•

AUDIOBOOK EXCERPTS AND PODCASTS

•

AUTHOR ARTICLES AND INTERVIEWS

•

**BESTSELLER AND PUBLISHING
GROUP NEWS**

•

SIGN UP FOR E-NEWSLETTERS

•

**AUTHOR APPEARANCES AND TOUR
INFORMATION**

•

SOCIAL MEDIA FEEDS AND WIDGETS

•

DOWNLOAD FREE APPS